THE CRYSTAL PROPHECY
Janice Tarantino

Winner Of The Romance Writers of America's Golden Heart Award

CRYSTAL DESIRE

"Jared?"

He looked up, a sad smile touched his mouth. "All finished?"

Susan shook her head. "No, I'd planned on bathing, but I couldn't get the dress off. This clasp seems to be stuck."

Jared grinned then, a genuine smile of amusement. "No, you wouldn't be able to get it off. The clasp needs the application of my ring."

"You're right. Give me the ring." She held out her hand.

If anything, his grin grew broader. "That's not quite the way it happens, Susan. I've given you as much time as we can afford to spare, Susan." He gestured back at the crystal strand that lay on the table. "The next part of the ritual must be completed before the crystals stop glittering. Already their brightness has begun to fade."

Susan felt suddenly awkward.

"I'll not hurt you," he murmured, bending his head down and touching his lips to her neck. "This is something we've both wanted from the moment of our first meeting in our dreams. And although we've both had to subdue our response to each other up until now, you're still my witch woman. The Woman of Fire whose touch rouses me with desire. For you

D1413217

Futuristic Romance

Love in another time, another place.

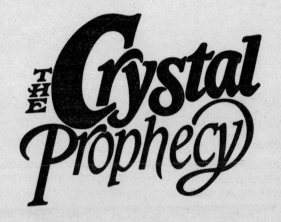

THE Crystal Prophecy

JANICE TARANTINO

LOVE SPELL   ◆   NEW YORK CITY

LOVE SPELL®

April 1995

Published by

Dorchester Publishing Co., Inc.
276 Fifth Avenue
New York, NY 10001

If you purchased this book without a cover you should be aware that this book is stolen property. It was reported as "unsold and destroyed" to the publisher and neither the author nor the publisher has received any payment for this "stripped book."

Copyright © 1995 by Janice Tarantino

All rights reserved. No part of this book may be reproduced or transmitted in any form or by any electronic or mechanical means, including photocopying, recording or by any information storage and retrieval system, without the written permission of the Publisher, except where permitted by law.

The name "Love Spell" and its logo are trademarks of Dorchester Publishing Co., Inc.

Printed in the United States of America.

For Vinnie, my real-life hero,
and for Nicole and Melissa with love.

Prologue

Anguished cries and moans of grief shattered the arid night air as the Clan Lords knelt by the bodies of their gem-starred women and children. Moonlight bathed the desert's edge with a soft, gentle radiance, making a mockery of the unexpected death lying on the coarse black sand.

Jared si'Dakbar crouched beside the death-stilled body of Evie. Outwardly there was little sign that his mind screamed in torment at the loss of the woman who had been his wife. He struggled to retain a grip on his sanity and to cope with the agony searing through him.

He clasped Evie's lifeless hand to his chest, his head bowed. Tears, as scalding as acid, wound their tortuous way down his face to drop one by one on the bright yellow silk of her gown. Gently, he traced his forefinger down the side of her face, innocent and childlike in the peace of death.

9

The white brilliance of death-dealing pain had come with no warning, flashing through the minds of the crystal women and children. None of them had been strong enough to survive the psychic blast—only the Widows had been protected because the pathways of the mind links had already been scarred by the deaths of their Clan Lords. Although the Clan Lords in the Council Chamber had experienced only a fraction of the discharge through the mental links with their crystal women, some of them had already gone mad from the pain and grief. Death for them would follow soon.

As he struggled to cope with the void in his mind resulting from the loss of the mind link with Evie, Jared's immersion into the death-grief affecting all the Clan Lords was deep. When a hand fell on his shoulder and broke his tenuous concentration, he lashed out in protective anguish, striking the hand from his shoulder. He was barely able to suppress the instinctive reaction to attack whoever it was who dared to demand his attention at such a time. Raising his golden eyes, the immutable sign of a Clan Lord, he saw his friend, Connor.

Connor knelt on the sand beside him, sympathy and helplessness evident in his pale blue eyes but not overshadowed by his determination. "Jared, you must come with me to the Council Chamber."

"Leave me," Jared growled, his deep voice raw. "I have no time for Techs—not even for you. I cannot leave her."

"None of the Clan Lords are capable of thinking rationally—"

"You're not one of us. You know nothing of what we suffer," Jared snarled. He turned back to the body of his wife, and his voice softened. "Her crystal is gone," he said as his callused fingertips gently caressed Evie's forehead. His fingers should be

10

touching the hard slickness of Evie's crystal surrounded by warm, living flesh, not the soft blank coldness of her skin. Who could have taken it? It was of no conceivable use to anyone but him.

"You must come with me," Connor said doggedly.

"I did not come to her soon enough. I was. . . ." Jared frowned, frustrated by how to explain what had happened to Connor who could not possibly understand. He recalled the frozen stillness of all the Clan Lords in the Council Chamber following that searing explosion of pain. He remembered the endless seconds it had taken before the Clan Lords had realized the truth—that tragedy had struck. There had been those who, even as they felt the ripping away of the mind link, had not believed in the reality of what the resulting emptiness meant.

Jared had been one of the few—one of those who had remained still and quiet against the agony, denying the sudden emptiness amidst the screams of anguish of the other Lords. It was not until Jared had knelt beside Evie's body that he had recognized the truth and had accepted it.

Evie was dead. All the crystal women were dead.

Connor grasped his arm, his firm grip demanding Jared's attention.

"A Tech is incapable of comprehending a Clan Lord's death-grief," Jared said, the muscles of his arm tensing resentfully under Connor's hand even as he explained so that Connor might understand. "It empties the mind and eventually the body. Madness waits on the fringes of our brains to fill the void and imprison us."

The screams and cries of the Clan Lords around him seized his attention. He watched his Clan brethren as they clasped their wives and female

11

children to them and cried their pain to the star-filled night. "We all surrender eventually," he murmured.

Trusted Clan members stood at a respectful distance from their Clan Lords, and yet close enough to ward off danger to their Lords as they suffered the debilitating death-grief. Jared's own people stood near him, their eyes sharp as they watched the night sky for predators.

Jared bent his head and closed his eyes, shutting out the overwhelming sorrow that surrounded him. They all suffered. All.

He felt Connor's hands on his shoulders as his friend of 22 years once again sought his attention. Jared knew that Connor was unaware how close to death he was at Jared's hands. Jared averted his eyes, trying to keep that knowledge from his friend, fighting the instinct that demanded he be left alone with the body of his wife.

"Go," Jared growled, clenching his fists on his thighs as he jerked away from Connor's grasp. "The longer you linger here, the greater your danger from us—from me. You don't understand, and you must not interfere."

"You must hear me," Connor demanded, not heeding Jared's warning. "Your brother has declared himself heir to your father's position as Kamen of the Council. None of the other Clan Lords are in any condition to oppose him."

Jared steeled himself against the instinctive compulsion to rid himself of Connor. He consciously reminded himself that Connor was a Tech—an off-worlder. Connor didn't know what happened to a Clan Lord when his crystal woman died. Connor didn't know that interference with the death-grief of a Clan Lord frequently ended in violent death.

As he frowned in an effort to regain control, Jared's words came slowly and with great difficulty. "Without a crystal woman he cannot hold leadership of the Council. Clan law prohibits it." He closed his eyes as he forced himself to see beyond this night. The effects of tonight's tragedy would be far-reaching. The lives and traditions of the Clans revolved around the existence of their crystal women. Now that the crystal women were dead there would be no Kamen, no Council. There would be nothing. The future no longer existed.

"Your brother's crystal woman lives," Connor said, his voice strong and forceful as he attempted to gain Jared's attention.

Jared's head jerked up in disbelief. He stared at Connor, his eyes flaring with violent anger. "You lie," he said viciously. His gaze swung in a wide arc, encompassing the bodies strewn across the sand. "They are all dead. All."

"Collis stands at Ruhl's side in the Council Chamber," the Tech replied quietly.

"It's impossible." But even as Jared spoke, deep in his mind a child's memory stirred—a memory that frightened.

Connor shrugged. "Impossible, perhaps, but true nevertheless."

Jared gathered his strength, then rose unsteadily to his feet, grasping Connor's shoulder for support.

"Take me there," Jared said, battling the part of his mind that screamed at him to stay with the body of his wife.

Connor supported him along the heavily traveled, tree-lined path that led to the white stone building of the Council, its high dome gleaming like polished bone in the radiant moonlight. Jared felt some of his strength return as the distance from Evie's body increased.

"What are you going to do, Jared?" Connor asked, his voice pitched low, as if he were afraid of being overheard.

"If Collis lives . . ." Jared's breath caught harshly in his throat at the idea that his brother should be so fortunate. "If Collis lives, then it is Ruhl's right and duty to claim leadership of the Clans." Jared dropped his hand from Connor's shoulder and stood taller, no longer needing Connor's support. "The Kamen must have a crystal woman as wife."

"Why is Ruhl's crystal woman the only one to survive?" Connor asked in a whisper. "Of all of them, why Ruhl's?"

"Be careful what you say, Connor," Jared said with a grim glance at his friend. "You're a Tech. As an off-worlder you'll be forgiven most things. But you'll not be forgiven questioning the leadership of the Clans. The Tech Wars may be five hundred years in our past, but the Clans will never forget."

"I am here to understand and to record. I don't understand this death-grief you suffer—but my heart cries for you. And for your people. I question only because I am your friend."

Jared grunted in response, blinking away the moisture that persisted in dimming his sight. "My grief makes me unreasonable, Connor. Perhaps you should ask your questions, but not now—not until after . . ." He sighed, thinking of what the dawn would bring.

In his mind he could already see the grief-stricken Clans bearing the bodies of their crystal women and children out past the desert's edge, the lengthy funeral rites, the consigning of the beloved ones to unmarked graves, returning them to the earth so that it might flourish.

Jared stepped forward, signaling his friend to stay behind. He entered the Council building, his footsteps echoing eerily throughout the stark white interior, his feeling of unease growing steadily. As he approached the entrance to the inner Council chamber, he felt an alien touch of something evil brush his wounded mind. He hesitated for a moment, thrown off balance by the intensity of the contact. When he stepped over the threshold into the Council room beyond, his perception of malignant corruption intensified. The hair on the nape of his neck rose as the dark miasmic horror struck him with full force.

"So, it's true," Jared said at the sight that met him. "Collis lives."

Ruhl, firstborn of the Clan of Dakbar, spread his arms wide. His golden hair gleamed in the soft blue-white radiance of the witch light that bobbed gently above him. "She lives, and I claim my right to be Kamen of the Council of Clans."

"No one disputes your right. I came only to see if what I was told was true." As he spoke, the questions Connor had asked but a few minutes ago echoed in his mind.

Ruhl's golden eyes narrowed as he looked up to where Jared stood among the gradually rising Council seats. "But you would like to dispute my right, wouldn't you, my brother?"

"No," Jared denied, his brows pulling together as he felt the strength he'd gathered begin to dissipate under the influence of the creeping evil. "Why was your wife the only one spared?"

As he templed his hand under his chin, Ruhl's golden eyes gleamed with what Jared recognized as malice. "Fate, perhaps?"

"A hundred women and children lie dead on the desert sand and you speak of fate?" Jared's voice rose in outrage at the inadequacy of Ruhl's response. Connor's questions clawed relentlessly at his mind.

"I am Kamen now." Ruhl seated himself in the Kamen's chair.

"Why did Collis alone survive?" Jared roared the question, suddenly knowing the truth even before he saw the smile that curved his brother's lips. Horror flooded through him. "It was you! You are the one responsible for the deaths! How was Collis shielded?"

Rage rose up in him; rage that propelled him a few steps toward the dais, his intention to deal death. But Jared fell to his knees, gasping for breath as a curling tendril of unseen evil twisted around his throat and tightened. His hands rose to his neck but found only air. He couldn't combat what he couldn't see.

"Do you mean to issue the Challenge? If so, a crystal woman must be at your side. Evie is dead, and you cannot challenge me now," Ruhl shouted up to where Jared knelt, struggling to breathe. His voice dropped as he sat back in his chair, smiling. "Do you wish to join her? Is that why you kneel before me? In supplication?"

Jared choked, gasping for air, and suddenly the tightness in his throat eased and slipped away. He struggled to rise. "What have you done, Ruhl?" he asked, his voice a rasp in his throat.

"If there is to be a Challenge against me, Jared, then you are the one to issue it." Ruhl narrowed his golden eyes and his voice dropped to a sibilant hiss. "The Prophecy foretold it. Evie's death—all of their deaths were necessary to prevent that from happening."

Jared felt a shiver pass over his flesh as Ruhl put into words the vague child's memory. "The Prophecy!" He cursed. "Because of an old women's tale you murdered a hundred women and children? Why?"

"Twins," Ruhl said, reaching up and stroking the hand of his crystal woman where it rested on his shoulder. "You and I were the first twins born to a Kamen and a crystal woman in more than five hundred years. The Prophecy foretold our birth even as it foretold our enmity."

Jared passed a shaking hand through his hair. "An enmity that has grown into black hatred this night, Ruhl."

"Return to your puling brothers as they weep over their dead," Ruhl cried, rising to his feet. "But heed my warning—if you issue the Challenge, I shall destroy you."

"There will be no Challenge," Jared said bitterly. "Not from me. As you've remembered from the Prophecy, a crystal woman is needed for the Challenge, and you have murdered all save yours. You have nothing to fear—for the moment."

"I fear nothing and no one," Ruhl shouted, jumping to his feet.

"Then you are a fool. A wise man fears much. Especially an assassin's knife in the darkness of the night. Beware, for your evil will be avenged." Jared turned and walked out of the Council Chamber, his fists clenched as he tried to control his rage.

"He is mad—only with less reason than the rest of us," Jared grated from between clenched teeth as he joined Connor. The evil he had felt within the Council building did not follow him.

Jared frowned, wondering how Ruhl had managed to cut off his breath, almost as if Ruhl had closed his hands around his neck rather than sitting across a room apparently at his ease. Had it been Ruhl, or had it been Collis?

Collis was highly skilled in the arts of a crystal woman, and she was known to dabble in the darker arts, those shunned by most crystal women. Collis was Evie's sister and she was a magic-user. Jared remembered well the fear that had widened Evie's soft brown eyes when he had once asked about Collis's magic. Evie had put her fingers to his lips, sealing them without words, her dark gaze pleading with him not to ask any more questions about her sister.

"What of the Widows?" Connor asked. "Do they not guide you when asked?"

"And sometimes when not," Jared said, frowning. The Widows were a bunch of meddlesome old women, inflated with their own self-importance. About to express that opinion to Connor, he hesitated. The Widows would know why Collis lived when the rest were dead. They would know about the Prophecy.

Jared turned and stared across the compound at the Widows' tent, black like the silk of the veils and robes they wore after the deaths of their Clan Lords, black like the sparkling crystals embedded in their foreheads. The Widows would know.

Chapter One

It had been three months since the dream had begun, and still it came again. Susan Richards murmured in distress, willing it away, but the dream would not go.

The 12 women gathered, materializing out of the darkness of Susan's bedroom, their black gowns fluttering behind them. They approached the bed where Susan lay and formed a half circle around it. They bowed their heads, their black veils falling forward in soft folds.

"Fear us not," one of the women murmured, and as she spoke, she pushed the veil back from her face, revealing the small black crystal centered on her forehead. "We come once again to prepare you for the task that will be required of you."

Susan knew it was a dream. She'd had this dream every night for three months. The dream had become so familiar that the black crystals on the foreheads of the women no longer seemed strange to her.

One of the women spoke. "Are you sure she is the one? We are so close to the end. We must be sure."

The oldest of the women tightened her lips. "Her mind resonance is the closest to matching his. Closer even than Evie's was. She is the one."

The crystals on their foreheads began to shimmer and sparkle, projecting a dark light that coalesced over her bed. Susan held her breath. She knew what the sparkle of black light portended.

"Behold!" the woman murmured, lifting her hand and pointing to the swirling light that formed directly above Susan into a three-dimensional picture of the desert at night.

A black stallion galloped across the desert, its drumming hooves striking the hard-packed sand ridged by the wind. The figure bent over the neck of the stallion appeared to be one with the animal as it thundered swiftly through the night. Over the pounding sound, Susan heard the murmur of the man's voice as he crooned to the animal beneath him.

Although she didn't know his name, she knew who rode the stallion. Night after night she saw this man in the dreams brought to her by the women in black.

Susan stared at him, and the familiar yearning that unfailingly assailed her during these dreams swept up and over her. Her heart beat faster and tiny beads of perspiration sprang to the surface of her skin in response to the magnetic attraction she felt toward the man.

Oh, how she wished she were riding the desert sands with him! She could almost feel herself behind him on the horse, her hands clasped tightly around his waist, her breasts tingling from the friction created by leaning against his muscled back.

He bent low over the horse's neck, grasping the mane in his fists, his eyes squinting against the wind. There was no saddle, no bridle, no reins, no bit. Control of the horse was dependent upon the strength of his powerful thighs and the soft lament of his urging. Without any discernible coercion, the horse's gait slowed from a gallop to a canter and then to a trot, finally halting. The horse stood still, its flanks heaving, its black coat flecked with foamy sweat. The man stroked the horse's neck as he sat straight and scanned the night sky.

He was a big man, requiring a strong horse. He wore dark, close-fitting trousers that faithfully outlined his muscled thighs and tucked into calf-high boots. A loose tunic, caught in at the waist by a leather belt, emphasized his broad shoulders. His ebon-dark hair gleamed silver where the moonlight touched it, the night breeze ruffling the strands that fell forward onto his forehead. His features were strong—his nose a straight blade, his jaw carved from granite.

He turned his head toward her. With a sudden wondering catch of breath, Susan felt the same dry desert breeze that ruffled his hair touch her perspiring skin. For a heart-stopping moment she was sure he saw her. His eyes locked with hers for a breathless second, and then he frowned. He leaned forward as if to see better, and his eyes glowed in the moonlight with a light all their own.

Night after night she saw his eyes, and each time her breath caught in her throat. In the deep Florentine gold of his gaze Susan saw torment and despair; she longed to be the one to assuage his suffering.

Then, as it always did, the dream dissolved abruptly.

Susan sat bolt upright in the double bed, shaking, her hands clutching her stomach as pain from her ulcer knifed through her. Her eyes were wide as she looked around the bedroom, searching out each dark corner in case some remnant of the dream remained behind to haunt her.

She was alone.

The muscles in her neck and shoulders relaxed. She sat motionless, sinking her head into her hands, waiting for the tremors that shook her to stop. When would these dreams cease tormenting her?

"Damn ulcer," she muttered, pressing her stomach. She had a successful job as a stockbroker, but she paid for her success with the agony she suffered when her ulcer acted up—as it had done quite frequently of late.

Milk, she thought, as she walked down the short hallway to the small U-shaped kitchen. She opened the refrigerator and poured herself a glass from the half gallon she'd bought yesterday. The creamy liquid would soothe her stomach for a while. She didn't want to resort to her prescription medicine unless she was forced to. She sipped at the milk as she wandered out to the dining area, where she stood at the sliding glass doors that led to the deck. She stared out into the night that was about to blossom into morning.

She'd told her brother Drew about the dreams when they'd first begun. Drew had laughed in typical male fashion, telling her she needed a man and a relationship. But when the dreams had continued, Drew had sent his sister to a doctor friend of his, Marcy Lanier. Marcy had proceeded to treat both Susan's ulcer and her dreams. To Susan's chagrin, Marcy had also agreed with Drew's assessment that Susan needed interests outside of her work.

Marcy had helped Susan see that her work

consumed her. Her cleaning lady did most of her household chores, the local dry cleaner took care of most of her laundry, and the take-out places near her Manhattan apartment provided her with well-prepared, if not particularly well-balanced, food. Which meant she had more time to work.

But after a couple of months had passed and the dreams had shown no sign of abating, Marcy had insisted that Susan take a vacation. Drew had offered her the use of his most precious possession—his chalet in the Poconos. Before leaving New York Susan had been convinced that a change of scenery and a release of the tension from work would dispel the strange dreams.

Now, Susan began to wonder if perhaps Drew and Marcy were right. Maybe she did need a relationship.

Susan closed her eyes and mentally formed a picture of the man from her dreams. Now, if she were to have a relationship with anyone, he was the kind of man she'd choose, even though she suspected his personality would prove too dominant for her taste. The flare of arrogance in the tilt of his head and in the set of his jaw held no hope at all that he would be able to coexist harmoniously with her redheaded temper. They would clash at every turn.

Her eyes still closed, she imagined for a moment the caress of his hands on her breasts and the softness of his murmurs in her ear as he whispered the erotic words of passion. Making love with him would be an indescribable experience. He looked like a man who would—

Her eyes flew open and pressed her hand to her chest, feeling the tight fullness of her breasts as they pushed against the silkiness of her pajama

top. What was she doing to herself? She was beginning to regard this dream man as if he were real,
as if she really had the option of choosing him over
some other man.

Maybe she really was going crazy. Maybe the
solitude of the mountains had been enough to
drive her over the edge. Drew's chalet was lovely,
but it was secluded. Susan suddenly wondered if
maybe she didn't need the bright lights and bustle
of New York to retain her grasp on reality. Here in
the mountains it seemed as if the whole world had
retreated and left her stranded and alone.

She wrinkled her nose at her reflection in the
sliding glass doors. This was the first vacation she'd
taken in four years. Maybe it would have been a
better idea to have gone on a cruise, surrounding
herself with people, music, and food.

There was a padding sound behind her. Still on
edge, Susan spun around, her heart in her mouth
until she saw the calico cat that was her only full-
time companion. Putting the empty glass on the
kitchen counter, she swept down and scooped up
the cat, nuzzling her nose into the soft fur.

"Pris, you scared the heck out of me," she murmured. "How was the hunting tonight?" Priscilla
purred in response and Susan laughed. "Good,
huh? Just don't bring me any more treasures, okay,
darling?" She shuddered a little at the thought of the
presents Pris had brought her in the last few days.

She put the cat down, aware of a sense of sadness and an empty loneliness. There had to be
more to her life than she'd experienced so far—
didn't there? Somehow she found it difficult to
imagine there would never be someone special in
her life.

A home. A family. Those were the things she was
beginning to understand she wanted. Home and

family, those were the things that counted—not the endless, pressuring telephone calls, the endless, phony business smiles and conversations, the endless, meaningless parade of posturing people who cared nothing about her except what her expertise and her uncanny sense of the stock market could gain for them.

When she finished eating breakfast, Susan forced herself to pick up the telephone to make the long overdue call to her doctor.

"Marcy? This is Susan Richards," she said, feeling slightly nervous and not sure why. "And before you ask me, let me tell you that my social life has taken a nosedive since I've been marooned up here in the boondocks."

Marcy laughed, her voice warm even over the long distance telephone line. "Susan, you don't have a social life. That's part of your problem. I thought you were going to call me days ago. I was beginning to worry."

Susan hesitated.

"Susan?"

"It's not working," she admitted with a sigh.

"You're still having them?"

Susan nodded. "Yeah, I'm still having them. And it's so godforsaken lonely up here." She skipped on quickly. "Priscilla, now, she's in seventh heaven. There are more mice up here than bees and that's saying a lot."

Her doctor chuckled. "Don't change the subject, Susan. Are the dreams the same?"

"Pretty much. Except for the scenes with the man in them. They're always different." Susan paced the length of the living room, whipping the long telephone cord behind her as she walked. "How's Drew? I didn't want to call him. I figured he'd worry."

"Drew's fine. He didn't want to call you because

he didn't want you to think he was acting the big brother." Marcy's voice was warm and comforting. "Other than those scenes with the man in them, are the dreams different in any respect? Even the slightest change could mean something."

Susan snapped the telephone cord, suddenly irritated and tense. "You know what the dreams are about, Marcy." She paced over to where she could see out the sliding glass doors. "Do you get your thrills listening to me talk about this man?"

"Susan," Marcy said dryly, "I'm dating a wonderful, sexy man who just happens to be your brother. Believe me, I don't need any more thrills than I'm already getting."

"For three months you told me I needed a vacation. Well, I'm on vacation, and I'm still having the same crazy dreams. What am I going to do now? You're the doctor. You tell me." Susan, about to pace back to the other side of the room, froze. She stared through the sliding glass doors at the woman who had just mounted the steps to the deck.

The woman looked like one of the women in her dreams. She wore a long black dress and filmy head veil that fluttered in the breeze.

"Susan, don't be difficult. I can't help you if you don't talk to me. I'm sure everything is connected to the stress you're experiencing at work—"

"Marcy, I'm not dreaming now, am I?" Susan asked, breaking into whatever Marcy was saying.

"What *are* you talking about?"

"Uh, I have to go," Susan said sharply.

"What's going on, Susan? Are you all right?"

"I'm fine, but I think someone from my dream is on the deck right now. I've got to catch her before she disappears."

"What? Susan, I want you to stay right there. I don't want you to go anywhere. I'll drive right up."

"No," Susan said, suddenly realizing that Marcy must think she'd flipped. She calmed her voice so that she sounded almost normal. "Really, Marcy, everything's fine. It's just that someone is outside on the deck and I want to talk to her. I'll call you later."

"Susan, I don't like this. Promise you'll call me back?"

"Yes, yes," Susan said, "I promise." She hung up the phone and ran to the sliding glass doors. The woman was gone. Dismayed, Susan slid back the screen and ran out onto the deck.

No one was there.

She ran to the front of the house, thinking the woman might have gone around to the front door.

No one was there either.

Her stomach clenched and spasmed. Welcoming the pain because it was real, she went back to the side of the house and slumped down onto the patio chair next to the glass-topped table.

The woman had stood right here in front of the table and in the shade of the umbrella, Susan remembered, her eyes focusing on the spot. She blinked, her breath catching in her throat. She leaned forward, her hand shaking as she reached out and picked up what looked to be a dark, circular stone on a gold chain from the patio table. No, it wasn't a stone, she saw upon closer examination. It was a crystal. A black crystal.

Dropping the dark crystal into her other hand, the gold chain swinging over her palm, she felt a slight tingling where the disc touched her skin. She held the crystal up to the light of the sun and frowned when the faceted gemstone did not reflect the sunlight. Totally opaque, it absorbed the sunlight rather than reflected it.

27

Obeying some deeply ingrained impulse she didn't quite understand, she slipped the chain over her head. A tingling sensation began where the gemstone rested between her breasts. Heaving a sigh and relishing the feel of peace that stole over her, she tilted her head back against the chair cushion and closed her eyes.

Opening her eyes, she saw Drew standing over her, frowning.

"Drew? What are you doing here?" she asked with surprise, hitching herself up on the cushions. "What time is it?" She glanced at her watch and raised an eyebrow. She'd been napping out here on the deck for hours.

"You didn't call Marcy back, and you didn't answer the phone," Drew said. "Are you all right?" He pulled a chair over next to hers and sat down.

Susan looked into his pale blue eyes, saw his concern, and felt a warm rush of love and gratitude for this brother of hers. She reached out and touched his cheek, aware of a feeling of relief that he had come. "I'm fine."

He hesitated for a moment and then appeared to make a decision. His eyes met hers straight on. "I don't want to act the heavy-handed brother and push you into something you don't want, but I'm willing to listen if you want to talk about it."

"There's really nothing to talk about. I'm glad to see you. It's lonely up here by myself. How do you manage?"

The corners of his lips turned up, his pale eyes sparkling with a dark and private humor. "I'm not usually alone, Susie-Q," he said dryly.

She shook her head, vaguely chagrined. "And here I was, admiring your outstanding fortitude."

"You're changing the subject," he said gravely, his grin fading. "Is it really that bad up here for you?"

"Let me put it this way—Mr. Carmine in town, you know, the old guy who runs the grocery store, well, he's beginning to look good to me."

Drew laughed. "He's sixty-five if he's a day."

"That's what I mean," she said.

"Sounds like you're in bad shape." He nodded up at the rose-stained sky. "Planning on watching the sunset?"

"Every evening," she said, settling back more comfortably. She felt good for the first time in weeks. She'd gotten some uninterrupted sleep, and Drew was here. Since their parents had died, he was the only family she had. "I wouldn't miss it. The sunsets are really gorgeous. Are you staying the weekend?"

"Yeah, I need some R&R myself," he said, shifting back into his chair. "Besides, it will give us a chance to talk. It seems as if we haven't done that in a long time."

"You hate the bugs," she said. "They'll be out in a little while."

"There are no bugs out at this time of the evening. No mosquitoes yet, anyway." He looked at her sharply. "If you'd rather be alone, Susan . . ."

"Nothing of the sort," she said, smiling at him reassuringly. "I'll make us some tea."

He reached out and caught her hand, squeezing it comfortably. "Don't move," he ordered. "Just sit and enjoy the sunset with me. I don't want to be the one responsible for your missing any part of nature's offerings."

They sat in companionable silence watching the sky turn glorious shades of rose and amethyst. The sky darkened slowly.

29

"What happened today, Susan?" Drew asked, his voice quiet but compelling.

Susan looked at him, and out of the corner of her eye caught a flicker of light in the evening sky. "Nothing much. I called Marcy because I'm still having those dreams. While we were talking, someone showed up on the deck. I hung up on Marcy because I wanted to see who it was."

"She said you suddenly flipped out."

Susan cleared her throat, shifting in her seat uncomfortably. "Yes, well . . ." She squinted and looked into the distance. She thought she'd seen something. Yes, there it was again. That flicker of bright light. Like lightning.

"Yes, well, what, Susan?" He sounded amused. "Trying to change the subject again?"

"Of course not. Did you see that?" she asked, rising to her feet, her eyes scanning the night horizon.

"What?" Drew asked.

"Over there. Flashes of light. They seem to be getting closer. Maybe it's heat lightning."

"I don't see anything. Besides, it's not hot enough for heat lightning."

"There it is again." This time the flash was much closer. She shivered and wrapped her arms around herself as she turned to look at Drew. "It's like lightning. Don't you see it?"

"No." Drew looked at her with an odd expression on his face, almost as if he thought she was seeing things.

"Then look again," she said impatiently. "If you'd look in the right direction instead of looking at me, you couldn't possibly miss it."

Drew rose and stood beside her, obviously humoring her. "Where? Where should I look?"

"There." As she lifted her hand to point, the light

flashed again, this time flashing longer, brighter, and closer.

For a strange second, Susan thought she saw the crenellations of what might have been a castle tower, and then she closed her eyes against the bright light. The hair on the nape of her neck and on her arms stood up straight, sending little prickles of energy across her skin. The black crystal tingled where it lay against her breast, and she suddenly felt dizzy. She wondered if the strange tingling sensation was some kind of backwash effect from the lightning.

A moment later she opened her eyes and she didn't have the faintest idea where she was. Everything familiar was gone.

Drew! Where was Drew? Everything had disappeared—the chalet, the deck, and Drew. She could feel her panic rising. What was going on?

It was dark, but an almost full moon cast a subtle glow over the totally unfamiliar landscape. It had been sunset a moment ago. How could it be so dark? Susan stared first at the castle tower visible in the near distance and then, looking around her, realized she stood alone in the middle of a grassy field rimmed by tall trees. The ground beneath her bare feet felt damp, but a circle of fire licked hungrily at the dew-damp grass around her.

Her hands clenched into fists at her side, and she closed her eyes, thinking that the whole strange scene would be gone when she opened them. But everything was the same as it had been a moment ago. She took several deep breaths, and then, feeling a warning tightness at the back of her neck and hearing a startled growl of disbelief behind her, she spun around in the circle of fire. A man stood not more than a few feet away from her on the other side of the flames. She recognized him immediately. The man from her dreams.

He stared back at her in startled bewilderment, his eyes Florentine gold, his hair as black as the deepest forest shadows.

"You!" she exclaimed, and the same urgent yearning she always felt toward this man in her dreams surged through her. "Who are you? What is this place?"

He reached out to her as if he intended to pull her from the circle of flames and into his arms.

She sucked in her breath, lifting her hands to ward him off. Stepping away from him, Susan felt the lick of heat against her calves. She could back away no further. Staring at him across the circle, she saw that he still held out his hand. Swallowing hard, she felt the magnetic attraction of the man begin to pull at her. Trembling with an undefined fear, she reached out to him.

There was another flash of bright light.

Reflexively, Susan blinked, still reaching out to her golden-eyed dream man. A firm grasp closed around her hand. She opened her eyes. It was Drew who clasped her fingers, who pulled her to him.

An emotion stabbed through her as Drew hauled her into his arms, and she was terrified by the thought that it might be disappointment because it was her brother who had taken her hand.

"Susan?" Drew's voice cracked as his arms closed around her.

"Drew!" she cried, feeling the solidness of his chest beneath her cheek and aware of a feeling of comfort. "Were you there?" she asked, looking up at him. "Did you see him?"

Drew's pale blue eyes were wide and shadowed. "You were gone," he said.

"Did you see the castle? Did you see *him?*" she asked, pressing her face once again into his chest.

32

It disturbed her that he shook as he held her.

"I didn't see anything. Not even you for a few moments."

Even as she sought his comfort and reassurance, she sensed his panic. "I saw him again. The man in my dreams," she said. She looked up at him and saw fear flare in his eyes.

"Drew, what's going on?"

Chapter Two

Jared si'Dakbar, second-born son of the late Simeon si'Dakbar, who had been called the Peacemaker Kamen of the Council of Glendarra, fell to his knees in the fallow field, his hands almost touching the flickering flames that had surrounded the woman but a moment ago. He sat back on his heels and watched the fire die, leaving only the smoldering grass in the shape of a black ring.

Walking the night, tormented by his private demons, he had been startled when a great wind had arisen. Lightning had flashed around him, and then the woman had appeared, standing in the ring of flames, her fiery hair blowing around her head as if each strand was a flame itself.

He had known her from his dreams; she had haunted them in the three months since Evie's death.

The sound of the dream woman's voice had swept through him like a tropical wind, hot and sultry,

34

and he had wanted her, needed her. At the sight of her, his blood had turned to liquid, burning fire, leaping through his veins. He'd had only one thought—one desire. He'd wanted this woman for his own.

She'd been lightly clad; her body had gleamed warmly in the firelight. Her hair like wildly tossing flames in the wind had beckoned, and her eyes like green leaves dappled with the gold of the sun had promised.

Jared felt his body stir in response to the memory, and he trembled as he knelt in the middle of the field. As always, the dream woman called forth the deepest, darkest desires of his soul. Desires he knew that the woman of fire would meet on equal terms with him. Desires he'd curbed with the delicate and eternally innocent Evie.

Shame and rage stirred in him at the thought of his wife. Shame, because by comparing her to the woman of fire he betrayed her. Rage, because although Evie was gone from him forever, he no longer wished to follow her into death as was the case with most of the Clan Lords. His tormented guilt drove him from the safety of his castle walls to roam the nights, seeking expiation for his reborn desire to live.

A cry thrummed in his chest and fought to be free of his throat. The sound of Evie's name rose and flew up and out over the forest, the strength of his voice causing even the night birds to cease their chitterings. Her name echoed through the night, an offering to the past, bearing witness to Jared's anguish because he desired life—not death.

Slumping to the ground and pressing his cheek to the dampness that coated each blade of grass, he dug his fingers into the charred mark of the circle. His fist closed on a clump of grass and, rising to his feet, he pulled the grass out by the roots, holding it up.

This—this was what he lived for. The earth and its slowly returning wealth and the needs of his Clan bound him to life. His love for Evie had not been strong enough for him to desire death over his love of the land and his Clan. Pressing the clump of grass to the ground where it would once again take root and grow, he looked down again at where the ring of fire had burned.

He must have imagined her after all. He'd had a sleepless night. Then he laughed—he didn't remember the last time he'd slept. Rubbing his hands over his eyes, he tried to explain the unexplainable.

If a grass fire had started, it was possible that his overactive, exhausted imagination could have tricked him into thinking he'd seen the woman he'd been dreaming of for the last three moon cycles. It was possible. He toed the dew-damp grass and simply shook his head in frustration.

Wearily, he looked to the east and saw the horizon beginning to lighten. Dawn was almost upon him. A new day was about to chase the shadows of the night, and there was much work to be done in preparation for the coming harvest.

During the long days, the strenuous work of running his stronghold had kept him sane. He worked harder than most of his people, hoping that he would be able to fall into his bed at night and sleep without dreaming instead of waking and wandering restlessly through the night. He knew that the members of the Clan who worked beside him during the daylight hours watched him with sorrowful eyes, pitying him for his restless spirit.

All knew that to wander the land at night alone and unarmed was the equivalent of a death sentence, but Jared had wandered the nights since

Evie's death and not once had he encountered a night terror. He wondered if he carried an aura that warned away the beasts of prey. Had his guilt and grief poisoned his flesh, making the taste of him unwholesome and unwanted?

Resolutely he turned to the castle, frowning when he saw light glowing in the highest window of the Keep against the dawn. The window opened on the room that had been Evie's, a private place where she had studied her small magics and mixed her healing ointments and salves.

Jared touched the key on the leather string around his neck and broke into a run heading for the castle tower, knowing an irrational hope and suspecting that he had finally gone mad.

The members of his household were barely up and stirring when he burst through the already opened portcullis and through the courtyard, throwing open the stout wooden doors of the Keep. His chest heaving with exertion and his heart pounding in anticipation of what he would find, he mounted the steps to the top room of the tower. The door was ajar, not locked, and he flung it back upon its hinges, the wood slamming against the stone wall behind it.

The woman standing at the long table turned around, her hand jumping to her throat, a startled look in her sea-green eyes. When she saw who stood in the doorway, she released a deep breath. "Jared."

"Mother! What are you doing here?" Jared roared, his voice revealing how close he was to the edge.

Magda stared at him in disbelief as she closed the book on the table in front of her, the black sleeves of her Widow's garb fluttering with the movement. "How dare you speak to me in that tone, Jared si'Dakbar." Her voice was cold and her eyes took on a deeper hue at the insult dealt by her second-born son.

"I saw the light in the window," he said, dulling his tone to a whisper and sinking his back against the rough-finished door.

She frowned at him. "You yourself gave me a key to this room to use as my own upon our return from the Clan gathering." Magda sighed, suddenly understanding. "You thought I was Evie?"

He didn't respond, only looked around the room that had been his wife's domain. If he concentrated, he might still see her figure moving in front of the table, her tiny, delicate hands moving among the vials and pots, mixing and grinding. He could almost see her impish smile when she looked up at him, the sparkle of her deep red crystal flashing at him above her soft brown eyes, her sun-kissed hair falling softly to her waist.

"She's dead, Jared," Magda said. "She'll not return to you. The dead remain dead."

"Mayhaps Evie will be different," he said hoarsely.

"Is that truly what you want? To have things as they were?" she asked.

"Yes! I want things to be the same," he cried.

"Nothing remains the same. Ever. We must always move forward. What if those ancestors of ours had wished the same? Would we ever have moved back upon the surface of the earth? Would we even now walk proudly under the sun and look with wonder upon the green that we have wrested from the desert?" Magda strode over to her son and tilted back her head, grasping his face between her long fingers. "You are mad if you believe such a thing, my son. You had the joy of her in your life for six years, but she is gone now. You must let her go. Your future lies ahead of you."

"There is no future for me," Jared said, pulling his face away from his mother's hand. "There was much I did not tell her."

"By the acid rain!" Magda exclaimed. "You wallow in self-pity until you stink with it. Never did I think a son of mine would be so fainthearted."

Stung by her words, Jared roused himself and stood tall before her. "Better one son who is fainthearted than two who are foul, madam."

Magda paled at the reference to Ruhl and turned away. "And better a hero than a coward, mewling and crying endlessly over the dead. My husband is dead. I mourned him outwardly for the prescribed time. I mourn him in my heart now, even as I mourn for your wife. But the living must continue living, and the dead must remain dead." Magda glanced at him and then turned back to the table. "I suspect that perhaps you suffer not so much from grief at words unsaid but from guilt."

He winced at the sword-thrust of her words. "Guilt is part of it. If I were a true Clan Lord, then I would wish to follow my wife into death." He could not bring himself to mention the guilt that plagued him over the flame-haired, green-eyed vision his mind continued to create.

"And you torment yourself over that?" Magda asked. "There is nothing wrong with desiring life. I think that we have suffered greatly from some of the Clan traditions and laws of late. Perhaps it is time for change."

"It seems that we shall be forced to change, Mother. I have been hearing some of what Ruhl is doing in the south. The Clan Lords who are still capable of opposing him do not because they cling to the old traditions and laws."

Magda looked toward the window. "Morning is here."

Jared approached her, knowing she was avoiding the subject he sought to raise. "What of the Prophecy, Mother?" He frowned and laid his hand on his mother's shoulder, turning her around to face him. "You will have to answer me soon. Ruhl grows more powerful every day, and the news of his atrocities are even now beginning to filter through to us. He was the one who mentioned the Prophecy to me on the night the crystal women died."

"When the time is right, you will know the meaning of the Prophecy," she said. "The time is close at hand, but it is not here yet. Until then, all is in the hands of the Widows."

She avoided his eyes, and Jared felt his ingrained suspicion of the Widows flare up within him. The Widows were planning something.

"How long will the other Widows be here?" he asked, his dark brows pulling together over his eyes as he tried to read his mother's evasive eyes. "At the Clan gathering you told me you would be returning with me here, but you forbore to mention that all the Widows would follow you." A look of ill humor crossed his eyes. He was very much aware of the presence of the Widows in their black silk tent in one of his fallow fields, their camp surrounded by the signs of ward and protection that were renewed every evening against the terrors that roamed the night.

"I was afraid if I mentioned it you would balk at the idea," Magda said with a small, rueful smile. "The Widows hold a great responsibility," she said. "Especially in times such as now. There is much unrest, the like of which has not been since the Tech Wars of five hundred years ago."

"What say the Widows of Ruhl, my twin brother?"

"We speak of many things, Jared," Magda said with a quick glance at him, "Ruhl being one of them."

"And the Widows plan," he said cynically, his mouth twisting with disdain.

"And we plan," Magda said, obviously reluctant to say more.

"What do you know of the circle of flame in the third field, Mother?" Jared asked, his voice suddenly hard.

Her sea-green eyes widened and then were veiled by her lashes. "Have you slept this night at all, my son?"

He'd had an odd feeling about the source of the circle of fire. Magda's evasive reaction confirmed his suspicion that the Widows in some way had been responsible for its appearance, although his mother would tell him nothing until she and the other Widows were ready.

He could not ask her about the dream woman. His visions were his, impossible to share.

Wearily, Jared shook his head and let his hands drop from her shoulders, accepting his mother's change of subject. "I've not slept at all these past four nights. The restlessness grows worse."

Magda turned back to the table and poured the contents of a white packet into a goblet of precious, untainted water. She offered the goblet to Jared. "Fedorra sent you this. It is a draught to help you sleep."

"I take nothing to dull my pain, madam. You know that."

Magda shook her head. "If you sleep, it will be a healing sleep. The drug will only give you the rest you need and require to function as the lord of this stronghold. The harvest is nearly upon us. You need your rest, my son, so that your holding grows and prospers to survive the coming winter."

"There is work to do today, madam. I cannot sleep or rest while the others work." His words belied the yearning in his eyes as he looked at the respite his mother offered.

"You do not sleep or rest when the others do," Magda observed reasonably, pushing the goblet to him. "What harm will this once do, Jared? Drink."

He took the goblet and stared down longingly into the water, now tinged a faint amber from the drug. To sleep if only for a full day—or a full night—would be a gift. Perhaps Fedorra had meant it as such, although he mistrusted gifts without reason, especially when they came from a Widow.

Jared stared at his mother. "I wish I had the strength to say no, but the temptation to escape for a few hours is too strong. If I am a coward, then so be it." Without reasoning it further, he put the goblet to his lips and drank deeply.

"The drug works quickly, my son," Magda murmured, gesturing to the couch against the wall on the far side of the room.

As he placed the goblet on the table, Jared already felt the lassitude creeping through his limbs. "Not here," he mumbled. He was afraid that even though the drug promised rest, if he fell asleep here, dreams of his lost Evie would torment him. Or worse, that his dream woman would appear and drive away thoughts of his wife. The memories of Evie that he retained in his mind were all he had left since her mind crystal had disappeared on the night of her death.

"What better place than a room in which you experienced happiness and love?" Magda murmured gently, pushing him down upon the bed.

His eyes were heavy, and although he desired the deep, dreamless sleep promised, he fought the effects of the drug for as long as he was able.

Magda stood beside his bed, looking down on him, her eyes gentle with the love of a mother for a child in pain. "Sleep well, my son," Magda whispered.

Jared had expected to sleep and to dream, but he did not expect the dream to come so quickly.

He walked in a wood that was unfamiliar. Sunlight spilled through crowning trees and fell to the lushly verdant undergrowth in dappled pools of yellow gold and bronze. He looked to the east to see if he could see the Keep tower, but the tall, heavily leafed trees blocked his view. He frowned to himself, suddenly uneasy. Nowhere on his lands was the view of the castle so densely shrouded with the foliage of such tall trees.

The air was rich. He took in a deep breath and was almost dizzy at its wealth. The odors of the green, growing things surrounding him were almost overpowering. He hunched to his heels and scraped away the underbrush, seeking the earth itself. Digging his hand into the moist, rich brown loam, he stared at it in wonder. Never had he seen soil so dark. He put the earth to his nose and inhaled scent so ripe with life that it almost pulsed in his hand.

Jared stood, wiping his palm down the side of his pants. He would like to dig this earth and bring it to spread over the fields that were nearer the desert, the fields that struggled year after year to bring forth the meager crops that fed his people and enabled his holding to trade with others.

He listened, hearing the sounds of life in the wood. The birds singing in the trees, the insects whirring through the beams of golden sunshine that filtered down through the trees, the peaceful lapping sound of water and human laughter not too far away.

Frowning, he started off in the direction of the sounds, treading quietly. Except for the sinkwell and fountain in the courtyard from which his household pumped their water and the deep wells out in the field used for irrigation, there was no sound of water about the castle. On days when storms threatened, the roar of the ocean pounding against the cliffs to the east could be heard, but this placid, lapping sound was strange to his ears. It was almost as if someone had brought out a large copper tub and filled it with precious water for the innocent play of children.

He hesitated at the edge of the trees, the verdant underbrush all around him, and his breath caught in his throat when he realized that what lay before him, shining and sparkling in sunlight, was a lake. Something he had never seen before. The legends said they had once existed in places in Glendarra, but no more. Never could he have imagined the beauty of such a sight.

He was dreaming, he reminded himself fiercely. He must remember that this was a drug-induced dream. A dream wrought by Fedorra, a Widow. Had she given him a gift of what his lands would look like someday, or had she given him a nightmare because he knew that, within his lifetime, what he saw before him could never be?

Jared heard laughter again, and he drew back into the cover of the trees as the voices grew louder, not wanting to be seen, and yet secure in the knowledge that he was dreaming and that everything he saw and felt was an illusion.

He believed it still when he saw his dream woman running toward his hiding place, laughing back over her shoulder. Her hair streamed out behind her in the breeze of her passage, her eyes aglow with laughter and dappled with the green and gold of the woods. He believed it even as he shrank back further into the cover of the vines and scraped his shoulder on the bark of a tree. She halted close to his hiding place.

"You were never a Boy Scout, Drew!" she called mockingly over her shoulder. "You'll never manage to light that fire with two sticks. I'm going back to the house to get some matches. We'll never have a cookout at the rate you're going."

The man laughed. "And when you get back, there won't be any frankfurters left because I'm going to eat them as soon as they're cooked."

The woman of fire laughed again, the husky sound of her voice causing Jared's heart to beat more heavily in his broad chest. She looked around and shrugged her shoulders, pushing aside the brush, setting her feet on the seldom-used path.

"Right! He'll eat them stone cold if he has to," she muttered to herself, her lips curving in a smile. "He'll cheat just to prove a point." She brushed aside the vines that hid Jared.

He stared down into her wood nymph's eyes.

She backed up a step, her face turning pale. Her eyes widened with shock, the smile faded from her lips.

Jared looked at her and felt need surge to life in his heart and in his loins.

She turned to run.

Impulsively, he caught her from behind, his hand covering her mouth when he thought she would scream. As he stole with her away from the lake and deeper into the woods, he felt her fear smolder for a moment and then burst into ribbons of flame that scorched him. The stealing of women from

45

other Clans had been forbidden for many years, although it had long been practiced in war. Jared soothed his sudden attack of conscience with the thought that, although this dream was different from his others, it was still a dream, a gift from Fedorra, Mistress of the Widows.

Or was it a dream?

He stopped, his muscles tensing in sudden confusion, and let the woman slide to the ground. She turned around and faced him, her fear still tangible, but she did not run from him. He sensed her bewilderment and he felt a common bond between them.

"Who are you?" she asked breathlessly.

"I am Jared," he answered, his eyes fastening on the parting of her lips.

"Jared." She repeated his name and on her lips it became something magical.

The need flared within him again, and he caught her to him with a groan, no longer concerned whether this woman was a dream or not. There was only the fire running through his veins. "Witch woman," he murmured, lowering his head and catching her mouth under his.

She struggled against him, and he almost let her go for fear she would force him to hurt her. But then suddenly she succumbed to him and met his overwhelming need with the fiery passion he'd sensed in his dreams of her. Her lips returned his kiss and parted beneath his mouth. He tasted the honey of her lips, his tongue thrusting deeply and exploring the sweetness of her mouth, the sharpness of her teeth. He groaned when her tongue met and mated shamelessly with his. His hands ran down her back, settling on the curve of her hips, and pressed her against him.

She pulled away unexpectedly, gasping for breath, and stared up at him, her face reflecting both the heat of passion and the confusion of suspicion.

"Witch woman," he repeated, helpless against the whispered words.

"Why do you call me that?"

He bent his head and buried his lips in her hair, murmuring as his mouth touched the strands of silk. "Because I have seen you many times before—in my dreams, in the desert wind, in the circle of fire, and because you have bewitched me. Because although I know this is a dream, it feels as real as life. Because I shall wake, and you shall be gone."

"I don't understand."

"There is nothing to understand," he said, catching the back of her head and pressing her lips to his again. "There is only the burning that needs to be quenched."

"Susan!" the man's voice called, startling Jared and the woman in his arms. "Susan?"

Jared released her suddenly, and she almost fell. He steadied her, feeling his heart beating strongly, his loins throbbing with unfulfilled need.

"We shall meet again in another dream someday, witch woman," he whispered. "And in that dream you shall be mine alone. I'll not share you with another." He backed away from her and melted in the sun-dappled shadows, his eyes holding hers for as long as he was able. Finally, he turned away.

He woke with a start in the quiet of the castle tower in the room that had been Evie's. His body felt more alive than it had since Evie's death, aching as it did with unfulfilled need and desire for the dream woman, the woman of fire whom he'd held in his arms and who had burned him with her passion.

He frowned when he saw the gloaming of the coming twilight and realized that he had slept most of the day.

Three months ago death had been all that he'd desired—to follow Evie into the light beyond death. Then, denied the comfort and lassitude of her mind crystal, his feelings had changed. He'd begun to want to live, to work the land, to bring it to green, to bring prosperity to his holding. He'd not looked for this painful resurrection of the desire for life and the feelings of guilt and betrayal engendered by that desire. He'd not looked for sexual desire to rise again, but his body was heated and he wanted his dream woman—a woman born of fire.

For a brief moment, he imagined he felt a feather-soft touch of comfort upon his cheek, much as Evie had once consoled him. Then the feeling was gone, faded into the coming of night.

Jared was left only with the fierce ache of loneliness deep inside him.

In the center of the third field, the Widows sat in the Circle of Power within the mark of blackened grass to which Susan Richards, the woman from the past, had been called according to an ancient, secret ritual prescribed by Mellissande, seeress, warrior, and crystal woman, five hundred years in the past.

There were 12 Widows, those in possession of their full powers, who formed the inner circle. The lesser Widows, 20 in all, formed the outer circle. All were protected within a ring of chalk marked by the runes of protection and ward from the evil that roamed the night.

Four of the Widows' guards, clad in the black silk of their calling, stood within the circle of protection at the four points of the compass, their backs to the women, their black crystal swords held ready.

"All is in readiness, is it not?" Fedorra asked, her lips unmoving, but her question heard clearly by all within the circle.

The chorus of yeas came softly, and yet there was not the sound of a voice in the night, only the sound of the night itself, dark and stealthy as it surrounded them, broken only by the light of the moon.

"The woman?" Fedorra asked.

Magda answered from where she sat in the outer circle. "She has been prepared through her dreams. She wears Evie's crystal about her neck. She was brought to the circle of fire as foretold by the Prophecy."

Fedorra bent her head in acknowledgment. "We witnessed her coming to the circle. Thus far has the Prophecy been fulfilled. Tonight shall we see it fulfilled further."

The women in the two circles, their minds meshing as one, the black crystals on their foreheads turning lambent with power, began, their voices rising in the dark calling the power of the night to them.

The bell-like chimes of their voices increased in intensity and traveled on the dark wind until they reached the ears of men who, shivering at the sound, knew that power was being wrought somewhere in the darkness of the night.

A column of shimmering air formed in the center of the Circle of Power.

Fedorra raised her head, the crystal on her forehead glittering with sparks of black light. "Magda, you are charged to go forth once again through the chasm between times and to bring to us the woman from Earth's past who has been chosen. The fulfillment of the Prophecy is at hand."

Magda stood and walked to the center of the inner circle. She paused before the shimmering column and then touched it, sweeping aside the air as if it were a curtain. The song of the Widows drifted into the shimmering column. A strobe of golden light from across the blackness of time answered the song of the Widows. Magda stepped forth into the freezing darkness to seek the woman called Susan Richards and to return with her.

Jared, riding his stallion several miles distant in the western desert, pulled to a halt, all his senses vibrating in resonance with the song. He frowned and turned the stallion, spurring him towards home. The Widows were up to something, he thought, knowing that if they were calling power to them in the fullness of the dark, then they were working powerful spells indeed. Spells that caused ordinary men to toss in their sleep at the uneasy miasma that crept on the night. The sooner he was home to the Keep, the better.

Ruhl, a week's journey to the south, vibrated with rage as the song of the Widows chimed faintly around him. He suspected the Widows gathered power to them in an attempt to turn him aside in his quest. He rose to his feet with a roar of rage and left the great hall. Throwing open the door of his crystal woman's chamber, he strode across the room to her side.

"The Widows work against me," he said, his voice grating with anger, his blond hair glinting gold in the dimly lit room.

Collis sat before her crystal, seeking the source of the chiming voices as they called to the power of the night to fuel their spells. Power had not been summoned thusly for hundreds of years.

She saw nothing in the crystal but an empty field to the north, but there was a shifting of the air in the center of the field that told her of the working of sorcery concealed.

Inclining her head, Collis acknowledged her lord's presence, but she did not take her eyes from the vision in the crystal. Her long, black-tipped nails rested lightly on the surface of the crystal, stroking softly with a lover's caress as if the crystal beneath her fingers were flesh instead of glass. "The Widows work their sorcery within a circle of protection."

"They work to destroy me," Ruhl snarled, his hands closing into fists on the back of her chair as he leaned forward, fruitlessly trying to see that which his crystal woman saw.

"I am not familiar with the song of power they are using. It is old. Very old," Collis murmured. "Since you declared yourself at the Clan gathering, the Widows have done nothing but work against you."

"And for that I shall rend their power from them," he said.

Collis shivered at the edge she heard in his voice. Her eyes were bleak as she turned them up to him. "The Prophecy foretells the coming of a woman."

Ruhl's golden eyes narrowed and slowly his hands settled on her shoulders and then moved up to encircle her neck. "I shall destroy this woman," he whispered, his fingers tightening. "As I shall destroy all who stand in my way. I am Kamen now, but when I am crowned King, I shall ride north. The Widows will regret what they do tonight." His voice softened. "My brother will also regret."

Collis grasped at his fingers and fought for breath. The fingers around her throat loosened and dropped away, replaced by the cool feel of Ruhl's lips against her bruised flesh.

"I shall destroy them all," he murmured softly.

Chapter Three

Susan leaned against the deck railing and sipped a cup of tea while Priscilla wound herself affectionately around her ankles. She looked at Drew where he sat, one leg draped over the arm of the patio chair. She was furious with him and trying not to let it show.

"Come on, Drew," she said tensely. "Admit it. If nothing else, you have to admit that something strange happened here the other night—to both of us. You can't suddenly change the rules and deny that something happened. What's going through that devious mind of yours?"

Drew looked up at her, his sandy hair curling in the humidity, and raised an eyebrow. "Devious?" He sounded scandalized. "Twisted, yes. Dirty, probably. But devious?"

"Don't change the subject, brother dear," she said dryly. She watched as Priscilla's attention was caught by a butterfly dancing in the long grass of the lawn. The calico cat streaked off the deck in pursuit. "We *were* talking about what happened to both of us the other night and what happened to me this afternoon by the lake. Everything's connected. It has to be," she said, frowning. "But I haven't had the dream in the past two nights."

"Yeah, but now you're dreaming during the day while you're wide awake. That's what I call a real improvement," Drew said with a snort of laughter.

Her eyes flashed with anger at his laughter, but then she saw the uneasiness shifting just below the surface of his expression. "He seemed just as real as you are. I could have sworn I wasn't dreaming."

"I've had dreams that were pretty damn real, Susan," Drew said. "But when I woke up, I knew they were dreams."

"Yeah, I'll bet," she said, imagining just the kind of dreams he was talking about.

Drew ignored her innuendo. "Instead of investing your time in a real person, you dream up this guy. For months you dream about him at night, and now, all of a sudden, you're dreaming about him in broad daylight."

"I don't understand what's happening anymore than you do." She pushed off from the railing and put her mug down on the table. "I touched him, and he seemed as real to me as you are. His skin was warm. His hair was straight and black and longer than yours. In the front it fell over his forehead and in the back it covered the nape of his neck. His eyes were gold, the dark Florentine gold of an antique piece of jewelry, absolutely the most incredible eyes I've ever seen," she said, her voice suddenly husky with memory. "He was tall, at least

54

six-foot-four. Shall I tell you what he was wearing?"

"No," Drew said, lurching to his feet and thrusting his hands into his trouser pockets. "This is crazy, Susan. You're talking as if this guy were real. He's a dream. He is not real."

"How can we be so sure?"

He cocked his head at her and frowned. "What do you mean?"

She shrugged, unsure about what she was trying to say and a little afraid of where her thoughts were leading her. "We're both assuming that what happened to me this afternoon was a dream. What if it wasn't?"

"That's crazy talk, Susan," Drew muttered.

"All right, then what about what happened the night you drove up? How do we explain that?"

"I can't," he mumbled.

"Or you don't want to," she said, suddenly understanding that Drew didn't want to deal with the possibilities.

"Maybe you're right," he said, turning to face her, his eyes blazing a deeper blue in sudden anger. "Maybe I don't want to explain any of it. I can only see two possible explanations for what's going on. I don't think you'll accept either one of them."

Her hazel eyes narrowed. "What are you suggesting?"

"I'm talking about your special ability."

"Not that again, Drew!" she exclaimed.

"You've buried your awareness of this gift so deeply in your mind because of what happened when you were a teenager that you won't even admit that it exists," he said, pointing his forefinger at her. Then he dropped his hand to his side and his expression softened with what appeared to be wistfulness. "Your gift is precious. Maybe what's happening is just another facet of your special talent. Some kind of precognition or something."

She turned her back on him. "No! I don't want to talk about this." Tension and anger vibrated in her voice.

"You've denied this talent your whole life because it made things difficult for you. It made you different. I think it's about time you admitted the truth to yourself, Susan. You are different. You're special."

"I'm not!" she cried, turning back to him. "I'm no different than anyone else!"

"Then don't ask me to tell you what I really think about all this. I don't want to hurt you, Susan." He pulled her close to him, hugging her. Suddenly, he pushed her away from him, his expression startled. "What the hell? What do you have around your neck, Susan? It nearly singed a hole in my chest."

"This?" She fumbled at the chain around her neck, pulling out the black crystal pendant from where it hung between her breasts and holding it up for him to see.

Unwillingly, his fingers touched the crystal and then let it go. "It's hot! Burning!"

"Is it?" she asked, watching as the crystal disc spun at the end of the chain. It felt warm to her touch but not hot.

"Where did you get that?" he asked.

"I found it on the table the other day. The woman who put it there looked like one of the women from my dreams." She frowned, puzzling at the sudden tangling of reality and dreams. The pendant was real; therefore the woman who had left it had to be real. If the woman was real, then . . .

He stared down at her. "Susan," he said gently, "that brings me to the second alternative."

"Which is?" She took a deep breath because she knew what he was going to say.

"That maybe Marcy is right and you've been under too much pressure lately."

"Which is a kind way of saying that you think I'm crazy." She stared down at the necklace and rubbed her fingers over it before dropping it under her shirt again.

"Not crazy," he murmured.

"All right, then. A nervous breakdown. Just being under pressure doesn't mean I'm going to cave in. We're all under pressure one way or another, Drew. And we all deal with it in our own way." Walking past him, she picked up her mug from the glass-topped table, brought it into the kitchen, wondering why she wasn't angry at Drew for voicing his "alternatives."

Standing at the sink, she rinsed out the mug. She heard Drew behind her. "I can't explain what's been happening, Drew. I don't know the answers." She turned to face him. "Yes, I have some kind of intuition when it comes to certain things, but I'm not psychic. Whenever something happens that you can't explain, you bring up that psychic stuff. I can't stand it."

Painful memories threatened: children laughing at her, her parents' looks of horror, teachers backing away, and later the testing, day after day, week after week.

Those were memories she kept deeply buried. They hurt too much. She pressed her fingers to her temples and rubbed at the pain that had bloomed there.

Drew touched her arm, drawing her back into the present. "I know you hate it when I remind you of this talent you seem to have, but that's why you're so good at your job. You sense or know things that other people don't."

She refused to discuss something that was so painful to her. It was an old argument between them. "Something else has happened that I can't explain. Do you remember that car accident I had about six years ago?"

He nodded, his eyes clearing. "You were a mess. You broke three ribs, an arm, and your ankle. And your face was cut. The plastic surgeon said you'd always have a scar."

A fine, hairline scar, but a scar nevertheless. She turned her face to the light. "Find the scar, Drew."

He grasped her chin between his fingers and turned her face one way and then the other, his eyes searching the right side of her face from her temple to under her jaw. "It's gone," he whispered in disbelief as his fingers loosened and fell away from her face. "That's impossible. A scar can't disappear like that."

"And you know something else? My ulcer hasn't bothered me since the night you came up. I haven't felt a twinge in almost three days. Explain that," she demanded.

"I've got to call Marcy," Drew muttered. "Maybe she can help explain some of this. Maybe it's some kind of self-healing."

"Wait a minute!" She reached out and grabbed his arm. "Don't you dare tell Marcy that you think I'm psychic." She was unable to control the sudden flare of anger that shook her. "How can you even think about it when you know how I feel?"

"I think it's important to tell her."

"Oh, forget it! I just can't reason with you on this." She released his arm and stepped back from him before she lost her temper completely and took a swing at him. Talking to Marcy Lanier about her dreams and the pressures of work was one thing, but having her know about—the other—was unbearable. "You go ahead and call Marcy. Tell her whatever you want and between the two of you see if you can dream up some explanation for what's happening here. Whatever it is you come up with won't be the truth."

"Take it easy, Susan," Drew murmured.

"I suddenly have a headache that's killing me. I'm going to lie down, and when I get up, I'll listen to whatever it is you and Marcy come up with, and then I'll pack. I'm going back to the city." It was an empty threat. She expected Drew to demur at the idea.

"That might be the best idea under the circumstances," Drew said quietly. "I really don't think you should be alone up here, especially after—"

"Fine," she said tightly, not letting him finish. "That's just fine with me." She stomped past him to her bedroom and, once there, threw herself on the bed. She tore off her sneakers and threw them, one at a time, into the corner of the room. She hoped he was listening.

She felt like screaming with frustration.

Trying to calm herself, she stretched out on her back and, utilizing the meditation techniques Marcy had taught her, took deep breaths, closing her eyes and extending her hands at her sides, palms up. She tried to concentrate on thinking of nothing.

It didn't work very well.

Sitting up, she threw her pillow across the room. It hit the wall next to the dresser and fell with a soft, dissatisfying *plop* to the floor.

"Drew, you are a self-opinionated, self-righteous *pig!*" she muttered as she retrieved the feather-stuffed cushion and threw herself back onto the bed, resting her head on the pillow. Despite her threat to go back to the city, she didn't want to leave the mountains. Not now.

Susan took more deep breaths, and slowly she felt herself relax. Unbidden images drifted into her mind.

The man, Jared, had held her and kissed her. She'd been frightened at her first sight of him, looming in the woods in front of her, but she'd recognized him immediately. She remembered thinking that he belonged in her dreams, that he wasn't real, couldn't possibly be real. When he'd caught her in his arms, she'd been afraid, but she'd been more afraid of herself, of the feelings she'd experienced, than of him.

His grip on her had been firm, but gentle. He'd taken her deeper into the woods and he'd kissed her, and she'd turned to flame at the touch of his lips on hers. That was when she'd begun to wonder if it were truly a dream.

No, she thought, shaking her head. He couldn't be real. He couldn't exist. It had to be a dream.

She frowned, clenching her hands into fists. And yet, if Jared wasn't real and didn't exist, then maybe Drew was right and she *was* having a nervous breakdown.

Determined to relax and ease the pounding in her head, she worked harder on her relaxation exercises. After a few minutes she fell into a doze.

The sound of singing woke her. A high, singsong type of chanting. Like wind chimes in a breeze.

She tried to ignore the sound for a minute or so, but it was too pervasive. Drew didn't have wind chimes. Sighing with exasperation, she got up and retrieved her sneakers from the corner of the room, pulling them on and lacing them tightly.

Drew wasn't in the house, and when she went outside, she saw that his car was gone.

She still heard the singing. Frowning, she stood on the deck, her hands on her hips, and tried to locate where the sound was coming from. From the direction of the lake.

Kicking some of the gravel ahead of her as she scuffed along, she walked down the long driveway that linked the chalet to the road. She crossed the road, heading for the lake, a strange anticipatory shiver coursing through her.

The lake. That was where she'd seen him in the last dream. She increased the length of her stride, following the sprinkling sunlight as it pointed out the overgrown path. Her bare legs suffered the whip of tiny leaves and the scratch of brambles from the underbrush.

Something moved in the bushes and she stopped, staring. That was all she needed—to be attacked by a gopher or ground hog. At this point, it would be likely to send her into a screaming, hysterical fit.

The underbrush rustled again, and Priscilla darted out. Susan heaved a sigh of relief and bent to pick up the cat.

"What were you trying to do, Pris? Don't I have enough problems without worrying about being attacked by strange, wild animals like you?" The cat purred her response and Susan hugged her closer. Absently, she raised her hand to the pendant around her neck, closing her fist around it, feeling it tingle against the skin of her hand.

She still heard the bell-like voices singing a strange melody. For a brief moment it felt as if the music came from all around her, encircling her, and then she pinpointed the sound as coming from her left. She stood, clutching the pendant tightly, feeling it vibrate in response to the clear tones ringing through the woods around her.

She left the path and followed the sound, walking what seemed like quite a distance, all the time conscious of the sound of the odd music, the vibrating pendant in her hand, the lashing of the underbrush stinging against her unprotected legs, and the purring of Priscilla tucked into the crook of her arm.

There was a clearing up ahead, but she approached it cautiously, her sneakers making little noise on the thick layer of organic debris beneath her feet.

The air of the clearing shimmered in the dappled sunlight of late afternoon. A woman dressed in black stood in the clearing, looking in Susan's direction. The woman smiled and then nodded.

Susan stepped cautiously, uncertainly, into the clearing.

The woman regarded her for a moment. "I am called Magda."

Susan tried to collect her scattered thoughts enough to say something coherent. Holding Priscilla tightly, she took a step backward. "You look like one of the women in my dreams," she stammered faintly. *Great opening line*, Susan thought in disgust.

"We tried to prepare you for today."

"Maybe Drew is right after all. Maybe I *am* going crazy," Susan muttered, taking a step backward.

"Don't be afraid, my dear," the woman said gently as she approached Susan. "I've come to bring you with me."

"Where?" Susan asked, her eyes narrowing as the woman came nearer.

"You must not be afraid," the woman murmured as she plucked the black crystal gemstone from where it rested beneath Susan's shirt. She held it for a moment and closed her eyes.

The Crystal Prophecy

How did she know it was there?

"We'll not harm you," the woman murmured, touching the black crystal to Susan's forehead.

Susan felt disoriented as a kaleidoscope of cascading images flashed through her mind, none of which she could grasp, none of which she recognized. Then, as suddenly as the images had appeared, they were gone.

Magda dropped the crystal, and it fell back to Susan's chest. Her forehead stung where the crystal had touched her skin.

"I'm dreaming," she murmured, knowing that was the answer. She'd been asleep just a short time ago. Susan stared at the woman, thinking that her smile seemed kind and that there was something about her eyes that inspired trust and beckoned to Susan, promising . . . something.

"We must go," the woman said, turning her back to Susan. She did something with her hand. The air began to shimmer again.

"Oh, my God!" Susan gasped as the woman took her hand and drew her closer to the shimmering air. The sound of the bell-like chiming grew in intensity around her. "This *is* a dream, isn't it?" Susan asked frantically, abruptly needing reassurance that she was going to wake up safe in her bed.

The woman reached out and folded back the air, revealing the blackness of nothing. "You're not dreaming, my dear. Stay close to me. You must put down the cat. She is not to come with us."

"What do you mean—this isn't a dream? It has to be." She peered into the darkness as she set Priscilla down on the scrubby grass at her feet. "What is that?"

"It is the chasm between times. Come, we must cross."

The past three months had acclimated Susan to strange dreams that seemed real and yet were not. She remembered mention of a chasm in her dreams.

"It is dangerous to leave the gateway open for long," the woman said, taking Susan's hand and stepping through into the blackness.

Not only was the chasm black, it was freezing cold. Susan shivered as the cold penetrated straight through her. "I'm not so sure I want to do this," Susan said, changing her mind and taking a step backward.

"Hush! The sound of your voice may bring— unwanted attention." The hesitation in the woman's voice conveyed more than Susan wanted to know.

She heard something behind her, and she looked back to see the opening to the clearing closing slowly, and in a few seconds there was nothing left behind her but blackness. Susan felt the woman called Magda tug at her arm, and, hesitantly, she followed her. There seemed to be no way to go now except forward, she thought.

Far in the distance was a glowing pulse of light. The sound of the chimes seemed to be coming from that direction.

Susan walked along slightly behind Magda. She wasn't quite sure what she was walking on in this cold, dark place, there being no delineation between what was beneath her feet and what was on either side of her or above her. Her footsteps made no sound. The blackness was quiet except for the chiming sounds of singing and an occasional rustling rush of freezing cold air.

If possible, the cold seemed to grow worse, but after a few minutes it became clear that they were headed for the pulsing light. Susan shivered as she began to walk faster, feeling a sudden urgency to escape from the cold, black hell she was traversing. The hair on the back of her neck suddenly prickled, and she knew instinctively that danger threatened and that there was no time to evade it.

"Get down! Get down!" Magda cried.

A gasp of breath escaped Susan as she dropped to a crouch, raising her arm up over her head for protection. A sudden rush of freezing air swept over her and she heard the sound of large wings beating the air.

Something slashed at the flesh of her upper arm, and she screamed as pain stabbed through her. Warm blood flowed down and chilled almost instantaneously in the freezing cold. Over the sound of her own cry, she heard the yowling of another animal, and then the deeper screech of whatever it was that still hovered over her.

Then, the danger was gone, and Susan heard someone sobbing. With surprise, she realized it was she who was crying.

Something brushed against her legs, and she almost screamed again. Before she touched it, she recognized the purr. "Pris," she whispered, picking up the cat with her right arm, glad that the cat hadn't understood that she was not to come on this journey. Susan's left arm hung limply at her side, throbbing slightly, but the deep, bone-chilling cold took away the worst of the pain, reducing it to a nagging ache.

"Hurry," Magda said, fear in her voice. "I'm afraid it will return."

Susan hugged Pris to her chest as she struggled to her feet, unable to use her injured arm for support. It seemed natural to have Pris with her, and she no longer questioned whether this was a dream or not. How could it be anything other than a nightmare?

"What was that thing?" Susan whispered fiercely.

"A Ptai, I think," Magda whispered. "Gateways into the chasm sometimes open naturally, and creatures stumble in unwittingly. But this time— I fear the Ptai was sent to stop us. Come, we are almost there."

"The light? Is that where we're heading?" Why would someone want to stop them? She didn't want to know the answer. Not right now.

"Yes. The others are waiting for us there," Magda replied.

The others. Susan didn't want to know about the others either. She walked in silence beside Magda for the rest of the distance, concentrating on listening for the noise of beating wings above the chiming singing. The light ahead grew larger, and as the two women approached the light, their footsteps quickened.

Susan only knew that she wanted to be free of this place as soon as possible, but when Magda stopped in front of what she called the gateway and gestured for Susan to go through ahead of her, Susan hesitated.

"Please," Magda murmured.

Hugging Pris tighter, Susan took a deep breath and stepped through the portal of shimmering air and light onto solid ground. She took another breath and was immediately aware that the air was thin, almost as if she were at a high altitude.

It was deep night. In the light of the full moon that hovered overhead, Susan saw that she was in the same spot as she had been three nights ago. The field was ringed by trees, the castle tower not too far away. The last time she had stood here she had been surrounded by a circle of flames. Now she was surrounded by a large group of women.

The singing stopped.

"We welcome you, Woman of Fire," an old woman said, her voice sounding almost rusty.

Woman of Fire? "My name is Susan, and I really think that I want to wake up now," Susan said firmly, deciding to make her priorities clear straight away.

The older woman ignored her remark and looked at Magda. "You were longer than we expected."

"A Ptai attacked us in the chasm," Magda said.

"I want to go home," Susan said, feeling like Dorothy from *The Wizard of Oz*.

"You will go with Magda to the Dakbar Keep. We shall speak again tomorrow," the old woman said, looking at Susan.

"Wait a minute," Susan said, stepping forward as the old woman turned away. "What is this all about? Why am I here? And where is here?"

"This is your future. Your other questions will be answered when the time is appropriate," the old woman said, and the other women followed her as she walked away.

"Future?" Susan repeated in a whisper, staring after the women.

"Come, Susan, we must go to the Keep," Magda said. "It is not safe here now."

"Safe? You talk about being safe after we walked through that black horror of nothing, and I got my arm slashed open by a whatever you called it. What could be worse than that?"

Magda grasped Susan's injured arm and turned it to the moonlight, disregarding Susan's gasp of pain. "I did not know you were hurt," Magda said, probing gently at the wounds. "I thought you screamed because you were afraid."

Susan looked down at her arm and bit back a moan. Her arm looked pretty bad. It hurt now, the numbing effect of the cold having worn off. This was one heck of a dream.

Magda bent down, lifting her skirt and tearing at her petticoat. Magda held her arm and began wrapping the cloth from the petticoat around the slash marks. "This binding will stay the blood from flowing until we reach the safety of the Keep. The smell of blood will attract the beasts of prey that roam the night."

"Beasts of prey?" Susan shifted uneasily and tried not to look over her shoulder at the moon shadows that surrounded them. "Are there very many of them?"

Magda smiled a little. "More than we'd like. When the sun sets, most men take shelter." She tied off the strip of cloth and then glanced up at the sky. "Come, the Ptai is only one of the things we must worry about."

Susan glanced at Pris, still nestled in the crook of her uninjured arm. The cat showed no signs of wanting to get down to explore, which, considering her temperament, was enough to make Susan apprehensive. Pris was a natural explorer and certainly not shy. Since they'd arrived here—wherever here really was—Pris hadn't made a sound.

"I don't even know what a whatever-you-called-it looks like."

"It is a bird of prey with a wingspan of nearly twelve feet. Its talons made the gashes on your arm." Magda led the way across the field.

"It sounds like something I don't ever want to run into again. Which way to the Keep?" Susan asked, shivering although her tone verged on flippant. Wherever she was, it would be better to be sheltered than to be standing in the middle of a field

68

in plain sight. As she and Magda walked quickly to the cover of the trees edging the field, she worried at the thought that she'd never heard of anything like a Ptai before. It sounded like something prehistoric or mythical.

"What about those other women? The ones who were in the field? Where did they go?" Susan asked, trying to keep up with the smaller woman, who seemed to be moving quickly.

"They are the Widows. Their tent is in another field."

"But aren't they afraid of these beasts of prey?" Susan asked.

"The Widows have ways of protecting themselves," Magda replied, stopping as they came to the edge of the woods. Susan stopped behind her and together they scanned the ground surrounding the walls of a fortress. There was a large opening in the center of the wall facing them with what appeared to be an iron gate over the opening.

Susan followed Magda, darting out from the edge of the woods and racing across the wide span of clear ground to the cover of the castle gate. Pressing her back against the stone of the wall, feeling the roughness abrade her skin through the insubstantial covering of her cotton shirt, she gasped for breath. The run had drained the last of her strength. Her arm throbbed. She fought against the sudden faintness that threatened to overwhelm her as searing pain knifed through her arm when she bumped it against the wall.

She heard Magda calling softly for the gatekeeper. She heard a man's murmur in response, and she heard the grate of metal on stone as the huge gate began to move upwards to allow them entrance.

"Come, my dear," Magda said.

Susan couldn't move. If she abandoned the support of the stone wall she was sure she would fall. "I can't," she gasped, and closed her eyes as Magda's face began to swim in front of her. "Give me a minute."

There was a sudden shout from above them. A flurry of activity began in the courtyard just inside the gate.

"What's happening?" Susan asked, feeling her heartbeat pick up speed.

"Someone is approaching," Magda answered.

Susan heard a note of worry in the woman's voice. "Someone or something?" she asked, opening her eyes.

Magda smiled a little. "Some*one* according to the watchman. Are you feeling better now? Can you walk or shall I get someone to carry you inside?"

"I can walk." Susan pushed away from the wall and managed to stand by herself. Hiding her fear and exhaustion was beginning to be a matter of pride. "I thought you said men took shelter at night," Susan said as they entered the courtyard. Men moved about in the strangely shadowed courtyard.

Magda nodded. "They do." She gestured above their heads.

Looking up, Susan saw the grillwork that covered the entire courtyard. Magda walked her over to a shadowed corner and sat her down on the edge of a fountain. Susan heard the gentle splash of water behind her and felt a few drops of water soak into the cotton of her shirt.

"Sane men take shelter," Magda said in a low voice. "But some men have a death wish, and they brave the night." She touched Susan's shoulder lightly. "Stay here, child, until I call you."

Susan sat in the shadows by the fountain, cradling Pris, who finally began to purr, and waited for the arrival of whoever it was who had eschewed the safety of shelter for the dangers of the night. The thundering sound of a horse's hooves striking against hard-packed earth filled the night. A streak of black galloped through the castle gate into the courtyard.

A dark figure threw himself from the back of the horse to land firmly on the cobblestones. "Widow! Widow Magda!" the man bellowed. One of the figures in the courtyard grabbed the reins from the man and led the horse away.

Susan stiffened at the sound of his voice.

Magda stepped from the shadows. "I am here," she answered quietly.

"What sorcery have the Widows been at? I heard the song of power out on the desert."

"The Widows have been about Widows' business, my son," Magda said.

He moved toward Magda and when the unshadowed moonlight struck his face, Susan gasped and clutched at Pris tightly.

Chapter Four

Susan's indrawn breath went unheard, but when she shifted her grip on Pris, the cat rebelled at the rough treatment. Pris yowled and dug her claws into Susan's shoulder, springing for the ledge over the fountain. Susan turned, hoping to catch the cat, but Pris had already disappeared into the shadows.

Susan felt rather than saw Jared's gaze as he attempted to pierce through the shadows that surrounded the fountain. He moved in her direction, and she heard his booted feet on the stones. She swallowed, fearful and not really knowing why.

"You, in the shadows," he said, his voice a low-pitched growl that sent a piercing shaft of mingled apprehension and excitement through Susan. "Are you afraid to come forward?"

She rose and with one step she removed herself from the concealment of the shadowed fountain. The moonlight played on her hair and across her face as she smiled hesitantly at the man who had occupied her dreams for months. "I'm not afraid," she answered him, her voice husky. "Not of you."

Jared stared at her. Susan heard the harsh intake of his breath and saw his face darken, his brows pull together in a frown. He spun away from her, and Susan knew confusion.

This was one of her dreams, wasn't it? He should have stepped forward and taken her into his arms and kissed her nearly senseless as he had in the woods. She wanted him to kiss her. She watched with disbelief as he walked away from her, his back rigid, to confront the woman Magda, who stood silently watching.

"What madness are the Widows attempting now?" he demanded. "What right do they have to meddle with my dreams again? Why must the Widows torment me like this?" His voice was low, but his anger vibrated on the still air.

"We have done only that which was necessary," Magda said calmly, folding her hands at her waist.

"They have no right," he said. "*You* have no right. Send her away," Jared demanded, his voice tight. "Make her disappear back into my mind, or wake me if I'm sleeping."

Susan's hands clenched into fists at her sides. The movement bunched the muscles of her arms, and the sudden stab of pain in her injured upper arm nearly took her breath away.

A dream, she whispered silently. *This is all a dream*. The cobblestones beneath her feet were roughly cut and uneven. The chill night air cut into her lungs, its thinness forcing her to take deeper breaths than normal. *A dream*, she reassured herself, and felt her heartbeat steady at the thought.

"We have brought her from her time into ours to fulfill the Prophecy," Magda said.

Jared snorted in response. "The Prophecy! I've asked you about the Prophecy, and always you've refused to answer me. The Prophecy is no more than the superstitious maunderings of some half-senile crystal woman—"

"You forget yourself, Clan Lord Jared si'Dakbar." Magda's voice cut through the shadows like a whip. "The affairs of the Widows and Clan Lords are not for the ears of your entire holding."

Jared looked around quickly, as if he had forgotten where he was. He saw the still figures of the people who stood in small groups of two or three, all their attention focused on the scene being played out in the center of the courtyard.

"I beg your pardon, Widow Magda," Jared said, his formal tone unapologetic. He cast a look at Susan. "But if the Widows choose to confront me with my unconscious fantasies, then they are the ones who could have selected a place more private."

Magda frowned. "Perhaps we made a mistake in using dreams. Neither one of you seems able to accept that this is not a dream."

"Dreams should remain sacred, Widow," Jared growled. "In bringing this woman forth from the shadows of my sleeping visions the Widows have gone too far."

Susan shivered in the chilling night air. Her senses didn't lie, and they told her that she was going to freeze to death before Jared and the woman called Magda finished their argument about whose dream this really was.

She frowned, still shivering. Her senses didn't lie. . . .

Confused, she stepped back into the shadows and collapsed onto the granite edge of the fountain, feeling the rough stone abrade the backs of her thighs. She rubbed at the roughness of the stone beneath her fingertips. Never had she had a fantasy so real—so tactile.

If this were a dream, would it be so consistent? Would it be so physically uncomfortable? Would she be struggling to breathe thin air? Would she have been so cold in the blackness of what Magda called the chasm? Would her arm be throbbing and burning with scorching fire?

"No! This must be a dream," she whispered softly, even as reality flooded her mind with the truth. This was not the world she knew. She shook her head in denial as she jerked to her feet.

"No!" she screamed, and pressed her hand to her mouth to muffle the sound as her voice echoed back at her from the high walls that surrounded the courtyard. A white blur of faces turned to her in surprise at her outburst. "No! It can't be real." And she was terrified that it was.

She ran for the gate, knowing she had to find the way back. She had to get back to where Drew and Marcy thought she was psychic, where her ulcer hurt, and where she'd once had a scar on her face.

A masculine voice shouted for her to stop, but she was beyond stopping, beyond knowing anything except that she had to escape a reality that was impossible. She ran through the gate and away from the castle walls, heading for the trees. She ran, stumbling through the woods, vaguely aware of the underbrush slashing at her, finally breaking free and running into the field beyond the trees.

She heard the thud of feet behind her and knew that it was Jared who pursued her. She heard breath rasping and realized that the harsh sound came from her in her struggle for the oxygen to fuel her run.

The moonlight revealed a circle of blackened grass and she headed for that, knowing instinctively that it was through that circle that she'd twice stepped to this impossible place.

She ran like the wind heading for that circle of fire-blackened grass as if it were a beacon in the night, running despite her exhaustion. She sent a brief prayer of thanks to heaven that she wore her sneakers rather than a pair of frivolous sandals, but she stopped dead still when she heard a screech in the air above her and the terrifyingly familiar sound of enormous wings beating the air above her.

Jared tackled her from behind, his powerful arms wrapping close around her as he pulled her to the ground. His body surrounded her, protecting her from his weight, as they rolled across the uneven ground and then finally came to a stop. Susan lay still within Jared's arms, beneath him, her eyes closed, her lungs gasping for breath, her arm burning like fire.

Again the harsh screech sounded from above. Susan felt the air around them gust at the powerful beat of the wings of the hovering bird.

She opened her eyes and saw Jared's face close to hers, his golden eyes staring down at her, his chest heaving against hers as he strained to fill his lungs with life-giving oxygen. Over his shoulder she saw the horrible creature that threatened them.

"The bird—" she gasped.

"Hush," he murmured, putting his callused hand gently over her mouth.

Another minute passed and abruptly the bird soared into the air and out over the trees as if it had been called away. Susan watched it go with wide eyes, shuddering with relief when it was out of sight. She was suddenly aware of the masculine body protecting hers. Her eyes slid to Jared's face, and he removed his palm from her mouth.

"Why did it leave?" she asked.

He levered himself up from her body and collapsed at her side. "The spells of ward and protection laid by the Widows earlier tonight linger here in this protective circle. Enough magic remains to guard us for a while longer."

"Magic," she repeated, sitting up and stifling a moan at the pain that flared through her arm. She saw that they rested in the center of the fire-blackened circle of grass. "I was here the other night. I saw you then. Was that a dream?"

"No, not a dream." He lifted himself up on an elbow, brushing the hair back from his forehead. His eyes gleaming gold in the strange light of the moonlit field, he looked at her curiously. "I saw you also that night, but it was not the first time I have seen you. I saw you in the desert one night. A glimpse, a yearning—and then you were gone. I have seen you in my dreams for months."

"And the woods? Was that a dream?" she asked, clenching her hands against her thighs as the pain in her arm quieted to a dull throb.

Jared frowned and smoothed the grass flat beneath his palm. "At the time I thought it was." He looked at her, his gaze penetrating, measuring. "The Widows have much to answer for."

Silently she agreed with him. "The gateway was there," she said, gesturing with her hand at the center of the circle. "It must still be there, but I don't know how to open it." She tilted her head to look up at him. "Do you?"

"I'm not privy to the secrets of the Widows. They keep to themselves—except when they meddle in my affairs," he said wryly. "I know nothing of any gateway in the middle of my fields."

"But you must know," she said urgently, angry that he claimed not to know. She reached out and closed her hand around his arm. "I must get back." She fell silent when he whipped his head back to stare at her with his golden eyes.

"There are no gateways," he said flatly. "The Widows brought you here, and the Widows must send you back. There is nothing I can do to help you."

She backed away from him a precious few inches, seeing the gaunt exhaustion in the deep lines that marked his face, and the haunting shadow of ghosts deep in his golden eyes.

"Then why am I here?" She glanced around the field. "Where is here anyway? What do you call this place?"

"My holding is called Corniche. The Clan holdings here in the east are called Glendarra."

"I don't understand why I was brought here. I just want to go home," she murmured. Favoring her injured arm, she fell back on the sweet-smelling grass and closed her eyes against the tears that threatened to fall. She wouldn't cry; she refused to cry. Crying wouldn't solve a damn thing. Despite her fierce denial, a tear fell.

Her eyes flew open when she felt the touch of a finger against her cheek. Jared leaned over her.

"Witch woman," he murmured, his fingers stroking down the side of her face. "Red-haired witch woman, I wish I could help you. You belong where the Widows found you. In your world where the sunlight is golden and the soil is dark and rich with life. You don't belong here in mine where the sun sucks the water from the land and turns the earth to sand."

She shivered under the touch of his hand, startled by the rough feel of his fingers against the softness of her cheek. "My world? This is still Earth, isn't it? Those women said it was the future. I'm so confused!"

"We call this planet Earth. The Techs call it Terra."

"Can you help me get back where I belong?"

"I already told you that I cannot."

If you can't help me get back to where I belong, then leave me alone." Her voice was harsh as she turned her face away from his hand. She was confused and frightened by the heat that surged through her when he touched her, and yet she knew that by turning from him she would precipitate— something.

His fingers closed around her jaw roughly and tilted her head back to face him. "No woman turns from a Clan Lord." His eyes blazed with arrogant anger as his lips descended to take hers.

Susan struggled against him for a moment, her good arm lifting to push him away, her nails digging into his chest. She struggled until the force of his lips gave way to a gentle warmth and a soft wooing of her senses. Her lips parted in response to his questing tongue, and she berated herself silently for surrendering to him even as she returned the caress of his tongue in a gentle duel.

What she had sensed in her dreams was true. He was dominant and arrogant—and overwhelming. Her hand moved up to his neck where her fingers threaded through his thick, black hair.

"Witch woman," he murmured in his deep, rich voice, moving his mouth to her jaw where he tasted the flavor of her skin and then moved down to the

79

curve of her neck where he savored the feast she offered to him.

Susan tilted back her neck to give him access, and she shivered at the touch of his lips on her tender skin. Passion rose in her swift and sure, and she marveled at the passion running through him, the awareness of every soft line and curve of her body although nothing but his lips touched her, the awareness of the glinting of her hair, gleaming darkly red in the moonlight. She marveled at the blood running hotly through his veins, pulsing with every stroke of his heart and pooling in the one place in his body where want and need overwhelmed rational thought in its quest for fulfillment.

An odd moment of disorientation overwhelmed her as Susan saw herself as he saw her, her face illumined by the soft light of the moon, her hair tangled in his strong grasp, her lips swollen with his kisses, and her eyes—her eyes half closed and slumbrous with desire. But most of all she felt his need as it hammered through his body, a pounding, relentless need that demanded completion.

She stiffened beneath the stroking of his lips against hers, realizing what was happening. "No!" she said, pushing against his shoulder, knowing that something was wrong.

"What is it?" he asked, lifting his head to stare down at her with his golden eyes, his voice harsh.

"Let me go," she cried, shifting back, her perception once again her own, and knew, as she watched his face, of the tremendous battle he fought with himself to quell the desires that fired his blood as it pulsed through his veins. His arms fell from around her. "Let me go," she demanded again, although he no longer physically touched her.

A shudder ran through him. "I'm not holding you," he said, his voice grating harshly in the quiet night air.

"My mind! Stay out of my mind! I don't want—"

She fought against him, not physically, but mentally when she felt the sharp probe of his mind against hers as he tested her, as if he himself was surprised by the odd meshing of their minds when passion had overwhelmed his conscious control.

Jared sought to scale the barriers she had suddenly thrown up against him, shaken by the knowledge that not only had he projected to her as he had once done to Evie, but that this woman had been receptive to him. Her mind had accepted his without either one of them realizing what was happening until it had already been accomplished.

"You're not a crystal woman. How can you know me?" he demanded, sitting up, his brows pulled together in a frown. "How can you know me this way?" He gripped her upper arms, lifting her from where she lay on the ground up to a sitting position.

She stiffened, caught her breath on a small broken cry, and collapsed in his arms.

Jared frowned down at the woman hanging limp in his grasp and lowered her carefully to the ground again. Surely a mind touch would not be enough to make a strong woman like this faint. Resistance and struggle from her he had expected, but not loss of consciousness.

He eased back from her and it was then that he saw it—the arm that had been hidden from him against his own body, the arm that had been wrapped in a blood-stained cloth. He bent down to pick her up and cursed himself for a fool. How could he not have known she was injured? How could he have been so blind?

But he knew why. He had been too busy being the arrogant Clan Lord in the courtyard, demanding answers, concerned only with his own discomfort at being confronted with the reality of this fey woman who so unsettled him, who had haunted his dreams since Evie's death.

Cradling her carefully in his arms, he strode across the field and toward the woods that surrounded the Keep. As he walked, he glanced down at the pale face that rested against his shoulder and wondered how their minds could have meshed. When he thought back to the moments when passion had flowed between them, he recalled the feminine sensations of arousal, the heat that coursed through her, the great gaspings of breath that she drew in an effort to pull more oxygen into her lungs.

He remembered his dream of her in the woods of her world, her time—the dream that had turned out to be a reality. The air in her world was richer. He could almost feel again the richness of the dark earth when he had bent to crumble it in his hands and the deep, satisfying draughts of oxygen-rich air he had pulled into his own lungs. He remembered the lake of sparkling water, and he suddenly felt sorrow for this woman he carried in his arms because against her will she had been torn from the richness of her time and brought into the barrenness of his.

He approached the portcullis and hailed loudly for someone to lift it. When it was high enough to admit him without bending, he walked beneath it and into the courtyard.

Magda waited for him inside the doors of the Keep, her arms crossed at her waist. "When the Ptai was sighted, I feared for you both," she said simply, her face revealing her relief at their safety.

"Widows' spells lingered in the protected circle. We sheltered there."

"Then you both were fortunate that power was wielded there tonight," Magda observed dryly. "Take Susan to the room next to mine. I can watch over her through the night."

"Susan? Is that her name?" He tested the sound of it as he mounted the stone stairs to the second level. "Why did you not tell me she was injured?"

"I hear guilt in your voice, my son. Did something happen?" Her voice was sharp with suspicion.

"There is no guilt, madam, except for not realizing she was hurt," Jared replied, waiting for Magda to open the wooden door to the dark room, then striding through and putting Susan gently down on the wide bed.

Magda walked around the room and touched frosted gray globes along the walls that sprang to glowing life under the brush of her fingers.

"Why did you bring her here?"

"The Widows made the decision. I was merely the guide."

"Don't avoid my question by quibbling over words, Mother. You know what I mean. What do the Widows require of her?"

Magda bent down beside the bed and began to unwrap the cloth from Susan's arm. "Is the question so difficult that you cannot find the answer, Jared?" She stopped the unwrapping and looked at her son as he crouched beside her.

"The Widows and their intentions have always been beyond the reasoning of a helpless male," he responded with a spark of dark humor.

Magda answered his smile with one of her own as understanding flashed briefly between them. "Make yourself useful, Jared, and bring me one of those lights. I want to look at the wound more closely."

Magda hissed when the light shined on the talon slashes.

Jared frowned and looked for himself. "By the True God, woman, why didn't you say she'd been slashed by a Ptai? I would have brought her back as soon as the Ptai left us."

Magda's glance was edged with wariness. "You were delayed?"

"I didn't know she was injured until after . . ." He stopped, realizing that he was about to say more than he intended.

"I'll need my ointments and gauzes. I'll have to stitch the wounds closed," Magda muttered, and then she looked at Jared as he paced back and forth across the width of the room. "She is untutored in the ways of a crystal woman. Whatever happened between you, I hope you were gentle with her."

"She's not a crystal woman," he said, turning to stare at Magda. "Why do you speak of her as if she were?"

"She's not a crystal woman in the sense you know, but she holds the power."

"Which she denies," Jared said, suddenly realizing why Susan had stiffened in his arms and rejected him in the field. "She denied her power and closed me out of her mind."

Magda lifted her head, amazement on her face as she looked at her son. "Your minds touched?"

"More than touched."

"You said nothing untoward occurred between you. If you have been precipitate, Jared . . ." Her voice accused him.

"We kissed," he admitted harshly. "That was all."

"Impossible! For your minds to mesh—"

"We need to be joined, and a Clan Lord can only join with a crystal woman." He hesitated, and his lips tightened as he fought to subdue the heat that suddenly flushed his cheeks. Talking to one's mother about these things was . . . awkward. "I didn't realize what was happening at first. Neither did she."

Magda looked back at Susan, who lay still and quiet on the bed. "Then even untrained and unknowing, she possesses greater power than we thought." Her voice held awe.

"To what purpose do the Widows plan to put her power, madam?" Jared asked harshly, surprised by the sudden desire to protect the helpless woman on the bed from the machinations of the Widows. He was well acquainted with the single-mindedness of the Widows when they had a specific goal in their sight.

Magda rose to her feet. "Stay with her until I return. I need my medicines."

Jared took Magda's arm, his gaze a golden, burning demand. "To what purpose do you plan to use this woman, I asked you?"

"Your questions will be answered in good time, Jared. I must tend to her. Her wounds still bleed," Magda said, removing her arm from the tight grip of his hand. "Sit with her in case she wakes and is afraid. I'll be back in a few moments." She left the room in a flutter of black skirts, the filmy veil on her head soaring out behind her on the draft of her movements.

Jared paced for a moment before he sat on the bed beside Susan, being careful not to jar her arm. "If I were you, my witch woman, I would be frightened. More frightened than I would care to admit," he murmured, carefully brushing the hair back from her forehead, his hand hesitating when he saw a faint pink mark on her forehead. Lifting the light above her face, he caught his breath when he saw that the mark took the shape of a tiny star.

The childhood memory suddenly returned to him. The Prophecy. He remembered it word for word as if it had been burned into his mind all those years ago and had merely required the sight of the star on the woman's forehead to bring it back. Jared's lips moved as he recited the words soundlessly.

Centuries shall pass before the evil comes again.
In that time men will have forgotten what threatens us today,
And so, I, Mellissande,
Have put down what I have seen of the future,
And I charge the Widows to remember and to teach the generations to come—
So that none shall forget lest the evil overcome us.

There will come a time when our world is at peace,
And when as a people we shall flourish,
Our sacred, sworn duty to restore our world our primary concern.
It is at this time, when all seems safest and most fruitful, that the evil will arise again.

From the seed of a great Kamen, called Peacemaker, twin sons will issue.
Beware the birth of twin sons for this is the sign of the evil to come.
The son of darkness and evil will be the bearer of death for all crystal women save one,
And through the talents of that one,

He will claim himself successor to the Peacemaker,
This son will cause the shadow of evil and the
promise of destruction to fall over our world.

All will look to the son of light to deliver them
from this evil,
But he, strong of heart, mourns the loss of his
crystal woman,
And without a crystal woman, he is powerless
against his brother.
Forbidden by law and tradition to issue the
Challenge of Power.

The Widows will fulfill their duty as Guardians.
They will find a woman of great strength and
loving heart,
And they will call her to us
From the darkness that surrounds us.

Born into a ring of fire, this woman,
A virgin, will be innocent of our world,
But the possessor of great powers and marked
by a star,
And she will be joined in ceremony to the son
of light.
Together, they will face the force of dark-
ness. ... .

Staring down at her, Jared frowned. So this
woman was the one. The glitter of gold around her
neck caught his attention and his eyes narrowed. He
pulled the fine gold chain, threading it between his
fingers until the small black opaque crystal dangled
from his hand.
He swore then, savagely, for he knew that the
crystal had been Evie's. He knew what the Widows

intended for Susan and himself. It was also clear that even though he would object and rail against the Widows' plans, it would be his duty to agree to their plans. Every Clan Lord, when he came of age, swore fealty and protection to the Widows. If a man valued his honor, there were no choices when it came to the Widows.

His glance slid from the crystal to Susan as she lay on the bed, still but for the shallow rise and fall of her chest. He wondered what her reaction would be to the Widows' plans for her. A skeletal grin sketched his mouth at the thought of Susan ruining all the Widows's schemes. He had touched her mind and knew she would not accede easily.

There was a sound behind him, but he did not turn, knowing it was Magda who returned. He stared at the crystal, fighting against the yearning to touch it.

"Do not touch it, Jared. The Widows—we needed Evie's crystal to bring this woman to us. It is too late for you to use it in the way it was intended." Magda's voice was gentle as she put her basket down beside the bed.

"I have not," he murmured painfully, fighting against the urge to do just that. He took in a deep breath, no longer able to muster the anger against the Widows that he knew he was entitled to feel. "The Widows took from me the only comfort available to me after the death of my wife. Should I thank them for that?" he asked sarcastically.

"It was necessary."

He knew that to argue was pointless. His sharpest pain was three months in the past. He no longer needed Evie's crystal to assuage his mourning. "I have remembered the Prophecy," he said.

"I thought you might," Magda answered. "You were fascinated by it as a child. It was as if you understood even then what it would mean to you."

"What you and the other Widows plan is impossible, you know," he said, his voice low, his eyes still snared by the crystal. It tempted him beyond endurance even though he knew it would no longer contain Evie's memories. It was now meaningless to him. "A crystal woman and her Lord are bound unto death and beyond."

Magda knelt and soaked a cloth in the bowl of water steeped with herbs. She wrung out the cloth and began cleaning Susan's wounds. "It was not always so. There was a time when Clan Lords joined again after the death of a crystal woman. If it was possible in our past, it is possible in our present."

Reluctantly and carefully, he released the gold chain without touching the crystal pendant and watched the black disk nestle in the valley between Susan's breasts. Tearing his glance away, he lifted the light so that his mother might see more clearly. "She cannot be joined with a Clan Lord. She is not a crystal woman." He knew the law. A Clan Lord wed but once in his life and then only a crystal woman. The law of the Clans could not be changed by the Widows to suit their purposes, regardless of how pure or diabolical their motives.

"Crystal women are no more," Magda said, salving the wounds with ointment. "But Clan Lords still live."

"Many of whom are already on the road to madness."

"Not all. And those that are have sons. They will inherit. Who do you suggest they join with?" Magda argued. "Who do you suggest they mate with? Who do you suggest they marry? Use any word you please, Jared, it all comes down to the same thing." Magda scowled down at Susan's wound.

"Collis lives. If she should have a girl child—"

"Yes, Collis lives," Magda agreed. "Would you join with a daughter of the Black Witch unless your soul was as black as hers? Collis cares nothing for passing on the arts of the crystal women. She cares only for power, and through Ruhl she will gain the power she craves. Through Ruhl, she will be queen."

"We have the Council," Jared said, shifting the light lower, closer to the wounds.

"And before the Council, we had kings and queens, and before that we had presidents and generals," Magda said. "Most of the Clan Lords no longer care anything for the future, and until their sons are old enough to take up their swords against Ruhl, there will be no Council."

"But Ruhl and Collis can't just—" Jared objected.

"Under our present laws they wield absolute power," Magda said sharply. "There is no one to gainsay them." She held a needle to the light and threaded it. "No one but you."

His hands clenched around the brightly lit, heatless globe. "There is nothing I can do. I am no different from the other Clan Lords. I too wait for madness and then death."

"It will not happen to you. You did not use Evie's mind crystal to prolong your death-grief as many of the other Clan Lords did. You are my son. My son who grew in my womb at the same time as my other son. Twin sons. Hold the light steady," Magda ordered as she began to stitch. "You remembered the Prophecy."

"This woman is not a crystal woman." Jared repeated the words as if they were a talisman against the Widows' plans.

"She is strong, this woman we have brought from the past. Our past. Her resonance matches yours. She has no crystal, because her power exists without the amplification of a crystal. But her power lies deep within her—dormant. We shall awaken it as slowly as we can, but our time grows short. Ruhl and Collis move swiftly in the furtherment of their schemes."

Jared looked away as Magda placed the small, neat stitches that drew the edges of Susan's flesh together where the Ptai had marked her. He turned his eyes away, angry at himself. Why should the slashes on this woman's arm affect him more than the piercing pain he remembered from past wounds of his own?

"The Widows move to advance their own plans," he said dryly. "This woman denies her power even to herself, and yet you expect her to face Ruhl and Collis?" he asked, knowing that Susan would not.

"The Prophecy says she will be one of the two who face the evil that threatens us," Magda said. "She will do it because she will know it is right." She looked up into his face. "As will you."

"You forget, Mother, that my mind touched hers. You are right when you say that she is strong. She is, but there is no reason for her to sacrifice herself to your cause."

Magda flung up her head and the crystal on her forehead sparked its black light at Jared. "Not only my cause," she said angrily. "Your cause also, my son. Ruhl will destroy our world in his pursuit of power and wealth. We have fought too hard and too long and suffered too much to rebuild our world out of the destruction our ancestors wreaked upon it two thousand years in the past. Ruhl cannot be allowed to undo our work. He must be stopped." She did not wait for his response, but bent once more to her task, and after applying another ointment, she wound a clean, white cloth around Susan's arm.

Jared put down the light and stood up. "You do not say the words, but you imply the Challenge," he said softly.

Magda sat back on her heels. "It is the only way."

He clenched his hands at his sides. "We no longer know about the Challenge. Only that it is fought on the plain behind the Council Building. That plain is so blighted that nothing will grow there. The sand has been fired beyond imagination and has turned into glass. The Widows ask the impossible of me, Mother."

"Ruhl knows," Magda said softly.

Jared stared at her. "How could he know? If the Widows do not know what the Challenge entails, then how can Ruhl?"

"The Widows suspect there is some source of knowledge which we do not know about. We believe Ruhl and Collis have discovered it. It lies to us to discover that source and utilize it ourselves."

Jared laughed, his disbelief evident. "And you think that after finding this mysterious fountain of knowledge Ruhl would leave it for someone else to find? He will have destroyed the source of this knowledge. Ruhl leaves nothing to chance. He never did."

"Neither do the Widows, Jared," Magda said in a voice so stern that Jared glanced at her in surprise. "You and Susan will be joined and together you will be our weapon against Ruhl and Collis."

"It is against the tradition of the Clan Lords. I will not do it," he said heatedly, knowing that he would, knowing that he was bound by his oath and that he had no choice but to acquiesce to what the Widows planned. "I refuse to do this."

"The Widows require it of you, Jared. You will do what is required. It is your duty." Magda's voice was implacable.

"Even if I agree—what of Susan? What if she refuses?"

"If she refuses, we shall convince her," Magda said, picking up her basket of medicines.

"And what of her place in her own time? When you are finished with her, will she be able to return? Will the Widows *allow* her to return?" he asked savagely, feeling anger on Susan's behalf at her role as pawn in a game that she didn't even know existed.

"Her return to her own time will probably mean your death," Magda said quietly. "The loss of one crystal woman you have survived thus far, but your mind is still not healed from that loss. You would not live through another loss of the mental link. Is death what you wish?"

"You know I do not willingly choose death," he murmured.

"Do you wish us to tell her that her return to her time will most likely result in your death?"

"No," he said, shaking his head. "She has been brought here to fight a battle that is not hers, to fight an evil she does not even know exists. If she agrees to the joining, I shall shield her from the knowledge of what effect her leaving will have on me. I need your promise on behalf of all the Widows that she will be returned."

"If she wishes to go," Magda qualified. "The choice will be hers."

"So be it," Jared said, inclining his head to his mother before striding from the room.

Chapter Five

Sleep seemed to take the form of cotton wool twisting around her, binding her, holding her back, part of the hideous nightmare she'd dreamed during the night. Susan fought her way through the cotton wool, layer by layer, and when she reached the top, she opened her eyes and wondered for a blank moment where she was.

The muscles of her legs were sore and aching; her feet felt as if she'd run ten miles, her arm throbbed, her head ached, and her skin itched as if a thousand mosquitoes had feasted on her, but most of all, she was painfully hungry.

The air was thin, but redolent with the odors wafting in from the narrow slit that served as a window in the stone wall on the opposite side of the room from where she lay. The odors didn't remind her of New York City or of Drew's country chalet either. These were the smells of horses and cows and pigs and hay, pungent, biting, and unmistakable. She sighed, watching the light of dawn creep from the window across the unfamiliar stone floor to the equally unfamiliar feather bed on which she rested.

It hadn't been a dream!

In the brief second before full awakening she'd thought for a moment that what had happened yesterday really had been a dream—a terrible nightmare. But this nightmare was one from which there would be no awakening. It was real. Real!

Her hand crept to the throbbing wounds of her arm. There was a clean, white bandage wrapped around it. Someone had obviously treated the wounds while she'd been unconscious. The last she remembered of last night was the flare of pain when Jared had unknowingly clasped her arm. She remembered nothing else.

The room was strange to her. Disoriented by the unfamiliarity of her surroundings, she sat up and the sheet and light blanket that covered her fell to her waist. Someone had taken her clothes. At the realization, panic welled within her. Someone had touched her without her knowledge. She felt defenseless, but she fought down the panic, knowing that it would hamper her instead of help her. Full emotional control was necessary if she was to work her way through this situation and stay sane.

"So you are awake."

Startled by the voice, Susan turned her head and saw Magda in the doorway. She looked much the same as she had last night, Susan thought. She wore the same outfit, or if not the same, one indistinguishable from the original. Her nudity increasing her vulnerability, Susan pulled the sheet up over her breasts and tucked it around her back. Pulling up her knees, she laid her cheek on her forearms where they crossed her knees and regarded Magda warily as the small woman entered the room carrying a basket.

Despite her various aches and pains, Susan was pleased to find that she felt alert and capable. As long as she kept the panic down, she would be all right. Yesterday she'd reacted to everything like a screaming ninny. Today would be different.

"You sound surprised that I'm awake," Susan observed.

Magda glanced at her, obviously disconcerted by her straightforward response, brushing at her veil where it fell over her shoulder. "During the night I laid a sleep spell on you so that you would rest properly without the pain of your arm disturbing you. You should have slept for several more hours."

Frowning, Susan remembered how difficult it had been to wake up. "Is that unusual? To wake earlier? With a . . . sleep spell?" She stumbled over the unfamiliar concept. Sleep spell?

"Not unheard of, but unusual, yes." Magda bent down and put the basket on the floor next to the bed.

Susan had to ask. "You talk about spells and things like that as if they're everyday occurrences. Are they?"

"They were until three months ago," Magda said. Sitting beside Susan on the bed and taking her injured arm gently in her hand, Magda began to unwrap the gauze.

"What happened three months ago?"

Magda met Susan's eyes briefly and then fell back to Susan's arm. "A great tragedy," Magda murmured. "I don't find it easy to talk about."

In other words, she didn't want to talk about it, Susan realized, and then another thought came to her. Her dreams had begun three months ago; she wondered if there was a connection. "I'm sorry." There didn't seem to be anything else to say.

Nodding, the Widow bent her attention on Susan's arm.

"Magda, I can't stay here, you know. I don't belong here. Where I come from—my time—I have friends, a career." She smiled a little. "I seem to have brought my cat Priscilla with me, although I don't know where she is right now."

"Your cat is prowling, hunting for food, although she has been fed. She is wary. She wasn't supposed to be here. It will take some time for her to get used to us." Magda looked at her curiously. "You don't mention a family."

"I have a brother, Drew."

"Ahhh," Magda said, nodding. "And he has his own life, doesn't he? Does he have a family of his own?"

Susan grabbed at the Widow's hand, suddenly afraid. "What do you mean? Why do you ask?"

Patting Susan's hand in reassurance, Magda spoke gently. "I was only interested, my dear. Your parents? They have passed on?"

"Yes." But Susan continued to regard her suspiciously. What if the Widow was asking about Drew for some other reason, trying to find out about him—just in case she never came back.

The Widow finished unwrapping the gauze and gently turned Susan's arm to the light. "By the True God!" she exclaimed in sudden shock at the sight of the wounds. "I cannot believe this! I worked no magic on your wounds other than protection against infection."

"What is it? What's wrong with it?" Susan asked, twisting the arm to see.

97

"Nothing is wrong. It is already half healed," Magda breathed, shaking her head in disbelief. "Do you always heal this quickly?"

"No, I don't," Susan said, frowning at Magda. "Usually I take longer than normal. I had this scar on my face that took forever. . . ." She faltered, remembering that the last time she looked, there had been no scar on her face. "Do you have a mirror?"

"In the bath chamber," Magda responded.

"Bath chamber," Susan echoed, suddenly skeptical and not too thrilled. "Are we talking about outdoor privies? A tin bathtub in front of a fireplace with the hot water carried up three flights of stairs in buckets by servants? Or are we talking something a little more modern?"

"What an opinion you have of us, Susan. We are quite civilized." Magda looked scandalized and amused at the same time.

"I'm glad to hear it," she said, wondering about Magda's definition of the word civilized. What kind of indoor plumbing could they have when they lived in a castle in what appeared to be a medieval period of history? "But I still don't know what we're talking about here. Let's face it, Magda, you live in a castle, you talk about magic, and you have flying horrors that like to eat people who stay out past nightfall. It makes me wonder if our conception of civilization is quite the same."

"Come. Let me show you." Magda moved to toss back the covers, but Susan grasped them protectively, and for a moment thought they would have a tug of war over them. Finally, Magda relinquished her grip. "Really, my dear, who do you think undressed you?" Her voice was testy, as if she were irritated by what she considered Susan's unwarranted modesty, but Magda offered her arm for support as Susan rose from the bed and draped the sheet around her for cover.

A little lightheaded, Susan leaned on her gratefully. "I was hoping it was you," she said wryly, "but I wasn't willing to bet on it. My clothes have disappeared."

"There wasn't much left of them. I'll get some things together for you while you're bathing."

"I don't want a whole bunch of people scurrying around just so I can take a bath." Susan felt hesitant about causing anyone inconvenience, having the odd feeling that making demands of any sort on the people here would tie her to them in ways she didn't yet understand.

"No one needs to scurry, my dear. Look," Magda said, walking her over to a narrow door set in the alcove on the side of the room farthest from the entrance.

Stepping through, Susan was delighted by the sight of a nearly ordinary, very familiar bathroom. "The bathtub's big enough for three people," she murmured in surprise. Constructed of stone blocks, the inside of the tub was blasted smooth. She ran a hand along it. It felt almost like marble, but a cold chill of anticipation ran through her when she saw the spigot with only one faucet. Cold water, she'd lay odds. She bent over and turned the faucet, holding her hand beneath the spigot. "Warm—water?" Her fingers rubbed at the liquid that coated her hand. It wasn't water; it was thicker and looked sticky, but when she pulled her hand free of the flow, the pale amber liquid sheeted off, leaving no residue. Her hand was dry.

Magda shook her head. "Water is too precious a commodity to use for bathing or washing. This is a compound developed by the Techs and imported by us. It's sterilized and filtered before recycling."

Janice Tarantino

"You mean someone else has already used this stuff?" Susan lifted an eyebrow, not too sure she liked the idea of bathing in a liquid that had already been used by others. But the fact that Magda knew the words recycle, sterilize, and filter reassured her tremendously. This society seemed to be almost medieval, and yet they were familiar with those terms. She reminded herself that this was the future—as impossible as that seemed.

Magda nodded and an amused smile turned up the corners of her mouth. "It's perfectly safe," she said, pinpointing Susan's concern. "Make sure that you put your injured arm into the liquid while you bathe. It helps the healing process remarkably."

"Great," Susan muttered. "Has anyone with the plague ever bathed here?"

Magda's smile widened. "Not lately. I'll leave you alone now. Call if you need me for anything."

Susan waited until Magda had left and closed the door before she discarded the sheet totally. Her fingers hovered uncertainly for a moment over the black crystal pendant, but then she decided to leave it on. Who knows what would happen if she took it off? At this point she was afraid to find out.

She had a suspicion, though, about the pendant and her newly accelerated healing rate.

The mirror was oval and hung on the stone wall above a long table against one side of the room. Susan looked at her reflection. Her hair was a mass of tangles and snarls, sticking up every which way; she was going to have the devil's own time getting out the knots.

Shoving the hair back from her face, she tilted her head at an angle, trying to catch the most light from the narrow window. Intently, she examined every inch of her face. There were no scars. Not even the one tiny mark she'd gotten from the chicken pox when she was eight years old. Her skin looked almost luminous when she'd expected to see dark circles under her eyes and about a hundred more wrinkles after what she'd been through since yesterday.

Her eyes riveted to the new mark on the center of her forehead. It was a tiny pink mark. She leaned closer to the mirror. For heaven's sake, it was a star! she thought, frowning. Experimentally she wet her finger with her tongue and rubbed at the mark. Nothing. It wasn't going to come off. She closed her eyes for a moment and remembered that Magda had touched the black crystal to her forehead in the forest clearing before they'd gone through what Magda had called the chasm between times. Her eyes snapped open. Could that touch have made the mark of the star?

Frowning, she bent and checked her appendix scar, something she hadn't done in a long, long time. It was gone. She turned her back to the mirror and looked over her shoulder at her reflection. There wasn't a mark on her body anywhere other than the cuts and abrasions she'd acquired yesterday, and those were already healing. Even the mole that had once graced her right shoulder blade was gone.

She suspected that the black crystal hanging around her neck was responsible for the changes in her body, but unsubstantiated by any qualified medical authority, her opinion would remain only that—her opinion. At least it was some kind of explanation for the physical changes that had begun at the same time she had acquired the crystal.

Hesitantly, she approached the bathtub, still not crazy about the idea of bathing in recycled bath water. But then she didn't have any options, so she stepped into the bathtub and gradually immersed herself. The amber liquid was different, she thought as she relaxed, leaning her head back against the edge of the tub. Its warmth seemed to seep through her body, relaxing her tight, aching muscles and soothing her abraded skin. She closed her eyes, determined to enjoy the one civilized pleasure she'd come across in this strange place.

How could something like this have happened? Her background didn't include much scientific theory, but she vaguely remembered reading something a long time ago about the possibility of parallel universes. Drew would know, she thought. He'd always been into science fiction.

Her hand clenched briefly on the edge of the bathtub. He would probably be frantic by now. The thought of how worried he must be put more of an edge on her determination to get free of this world and back to her own. She would insist on going home as soon as possible. She couldn't stay here, and in fact, didn't even know why she was here.

And what about Jared?

She was attracted to him, but considering the content of her dreams for the past three months, that wasn't particularly surprising. She couldn't deny her attraction, but her original guess as to what he was like hadn't been far off. He was domineering and arrogant and totally overwhelming.

And passionate. Don't forget passionate, she told herself, her cheeks burning as she remembered how his kiss had thrown her whole system into upheaval.

And autocratic. He's autocratic, she added as she felt her rational self sinking beneath the sybaritic persuasions of her emotional self.

He belongs here in this time, and you belong in yours, Susan told herself firmly. This was the future. What was happening here was not her concern. She shuddered at the thought of being trapped in this time. The air was too darn thin; she would probably die of oxygen deprivation before she'd been here a week.

If a monster didn't get her first . . .

And that was the other thing. She had absolutely no intention of staying in a world that had monsters. Birds were okay as long as they weren't any bigger than her fist. Birds of prey that looked like pterodactyls and were the size of a small airplane she didn't have any intention of coping with.

A knock on the door startled her from her thoughts, but before she could lift her head from where it rested against the tub, Magda came in, her arms piled high with clothing. Bemusedly Susan watched her as she bustled in and put the pile of clothing on the long table under the mirror.

"These clothes should fit you, my dear. Breakfast is ready when you finish dressing. Call me if you need any help." Magda sent a brilliant smile in her direction and then left.

"Thank you," Susan murmured. Galvanized by the thought of food, she washed quickly with a loofah-type sponge, and noted in amazement that the liquid she bathed in foamed with friction and acted like soap. Shrugging fatalistically and figuring that her hair certainly couldn't look any worse, she dunked her head and washed her hair. Raising her head, she finger-combed it, and was amazed when the tangles came right out and her hair was damp-dry in less than a minute. There were no towels, but she discovered when she stood up that she didn't need one. She was dry, the liquid sheeting off her just as it had done with her hair. She climbed out of the tub and pulled the plug out of the drain.

Flexing her wounded, half-healed arm carefully, she walked over to the long table and riffled through the pile of clothing, holding up one garment after another, running her hands over the silky materials. They were gorgeous in both fineness of texture and richness of color, and she would swear they were natural fibers, silk and linen and cotton. The skirts of the dress and the petticoats reached to the floor. She would be lucky if she didn't kill herself just walking across the room. The first chance that presented itself she intended to find a pair of pants and a shirt. The heck with the prom queen stuff.

Donning the featherweight underlinens, she silently bemoaned the loss of her own shorts and shirt. All these clothes were going to stifle her. When she wasn't working, she dressed casually, but this clothing was far from casual.

Dressing took forever. There were pantalets that tied, a chemise that slipped over her head, three petticoats that tied—one cream, one chocolate brown, and one black—and a chocolate brown dress that buttoned all over—down the back, at the cream lace-collared throat, and at the lacy cuffs. There wasn't even a hint that zippers or elastic existed. She double-knotted everything that tied—just in case.

Her eyes widened with dismay when she finally reached the bottom of the pile and saw the stockings and leather shoes that looked as insubstantial as a pair of ballet slippers. Grabbing up the stockings and shoes, she went into the bedroom to find Magda waiting for her. A small table held various dishes filled with delicious-looking food. Susan promptly forgot her immediate complaints about the clothing and clutched her stomach when it rumbled noisily at the appetizing smell of breakfast.

"Food! I'm starving." She looked at Magda, who was rising to her feet. Susan thought she saw a twinkle of private merriment in Magda's eyes, but she couldn't figure out if it was at the rumbling of her stomach or because her dress was gaping in the back and her feet were bare.

"How do you wear all these clothes? This is ridiculous," she grumbled, turning her back to the woman. "You'll have to do the buttons in the back. I can't reach them. Why don't you put the buttons in the front? At least that way a person could fasten their own clothes."

"Most dresses do fasten in the front, but this dress is what we call a Court dress. It's worn by crystal women on formal occasions. The number of buttons is set in multiples of three signifying the three stages in the life of a crystal woman," Magda explained as she buttoned up the back of the dress. "Childhood, womanhood, and widowhood."

"Why am I dressing in a formal gown and what is a crystal woman? And where are my sneakers? I can't wear these things," she said, brandishing the leather slippers. "Every time I step on something, I'll end up hopping." Over her complaints, she heard the sound of a horse's hooves from the courtyard.

Finished with the buttons, Magda bent and adjusted the folds of Susan's skirt. "Your—sneakers—have been put away. They are safe."

Staring down at the back of Magda's head, Susan arched an eyebrow and restrained herself from commenting at the moment.

Outside a man shouted, and Susan froze, recognizing the voice. She shook Magda's hands off the skirt of her dress and, running to the window, she leaned out, looking down into the courtyard through its framework covering of the grill. Her heartbeat quickened when she saw Jared.

The black stallion moved restively beneath his master, fighting the bit in his mouth, his hooves clicking against the stones as if he couldn't wait to gallop out the gate. As if he sensed her regard, Jared looked up to her window, one hand holding the reins, the other resting on the sheathed sword at his side.

She caught her breath when his golden gaze collided with hers and their eyes held for a long moment. Then she felt the touch of his mind in hers. She jerked in reaction and then calmed. The touch of his mind was gentle, tentative almost, and she sensed no immediate threat from him. Curious to discover what would happen, she relaxed the barriers that shut him out, and she felt his brief hesitation before he took the invitation and slid just inside the gate of her mind. She knew that if he were to move in any further, it would be by her express invitation. Holding him at the gate of her mind suited her just fine for the moment; the sensation of having another person's consciousness in one's own was strange and needed adjusting to.

"Good morning, my lady." He smiled at her, but his lips didn't move and it was a second before Susan realized she'd heard the words in her head.

She stared down at him. "We can do that?" she asked out loud.

He nodded in response. *"Try it. It's quite simple."*

Again, his words were in her mind, but the color drained from her face at his suggestion. "No! I can't," she said, shaking her head violently, as much afraid of the idea of communicating mentally as she was of the emotion she sensed behind his calm demeanor.

"Then come down and ride with me," he said, tempting her.

"I can't," she said with a backward look at Magda.

"Can't or won't?" he asked, reverting to normal speech.

"Does it really make a difference?" she asked.

The restiveness of the horse beneath him demanded Jared's attention. He stroked the horse's neck and looked back up at Susan, shrugging a little. "Perhaps not," he admitted as he firmly handled his horse.

Susan expected him to gallop off then, but he surprised her when he looked up at her once again and she heard his voice in her mind.

"I promise you that some day soon we shall race the wind together, witch woman," he whispered, his gaze holding hers with heat and promise. Then he saluted her, an odd smile on his lips and, wheeling the horse around, galloped straight out the gate.

"Oh, God," Susan whispered breathlessly as her knees sagged in reaction, afraid of what she had seen in his eyes, afraid of the explosive need that burned through her, afraid of the desire that welled within her to ride beside him wherever he was going.

But most of all she feared the sudden emptiness of her mind now that he was gone. All that remained was the faint whisper of his voice. She tried to cling to the memory of the sound, but it eluded her and faded away. Her eyes followed him as far as they were able. When she finally lost sight of him, she turned back to the bedroom with a sigh. The sooner she went home, the better. The man scrambled her emotions so badly that she couldn't think. If she wasn't careful, she would actually be considering staying here for awhile.

And yet—would it be so awful if she did remain for a few days? Perhaps to see what might develop?

She sucked in her breath and felt like kicking herself at that traitorous thought. No, she had to leave.

"He will be back," Magda said, gesturing for Susan to sit at the table and then sitting down in the chair opposite her.

"Was there any doubt that he would be?" Susan asked, her voice cold, hiding her distress that Magda had sensed something of her roiling emotions—her fickle thoughts, her sudden wavering as to how soon she wanted to go home. She couldn't afford to have the woman zeroing in on her weaknesses, and it appeared as though Jared might be a major weakness.

"Not really, although with Jared there is always doubt about those kinds of things. One never knows quite what is in his mind. He's just as likely to be gone three days as three hours. But he is very well aware of his oath of fealty to the Widows and he will do what is required of him, whether he likes it or not. He isn't happy about it, although he understands its necessity—and so he rides."

"Do I have something to do with this pressure of his?" she asked suspiciously.

"You are one of the reasons he's unhappy right now." Magda pursed her lips. "But he has many things on his mind. And today, he really does have a reason to ride out. We've received a disturbing report of trouble from one of our villages. He's going to check on the situation."

"And that's the reason for the sword? Because of the trouble?" Susan asked as she reached for a roll and some strawberries.

"He carries a sword because he is a Clan Lord."

Susan mulled over that one. Obviously being a Clan Lord wasn't all it was cracked up to be if it was a position that required the carrying of a sword. "What about guns? It seems to me that if you know about recycling and sterilizing and filtering, you should be a more technological society than you appear to be."

As she poured something that smelled like hot coffee into a cup and passed it to Susan, Magda laughed. "We're as technological a society as we want to be, Susan."

Susan's eyes widened when she sipped at the beverage. It not only smelled like coffee, it tasted like it. "You have coffee here. God, why didn't you tell me?" She savored the taste, finding it equal if not superior to the brands she'd tried at home.

"I think, Susan, that you are going to discover many things that will surprise you in the next few days, but as to your questions regarding weapons, I shall really have to introduce you to Connor."

"Connor?"

"He is a Tech who uses Jared's holding as his home base for his research travels. Although he's a Tech, at this point he's been with us so long he's almost one of our Clan. He should be able to answer most of your technical questions."

"Magda, I must go home," Susan said simply in response to Magda's insinuation that she would be here in this world for any length of time. "I mean, I can stay for another day or two, but longer than that—no."

The Widow hesitated, and then buttered a roll. "You have been summoned to appear before the Widows this morning. They await us."

"Why?" Perhaps they were ready to send her back. Perhaps they realized she would be of no possible use to them. The thought didn't bring the enthusiasm she might have expected an hour ago, and she didn't have any trouble explaining to herself why, all of a sudden, she wasn't ecstatic with the idea of going home quite so quickly. The memory of the golden blaze of Jared's eyes in the sunlight as he looked up at her took her breath away. "To send me back?"

Shaking her head, Magda avoided meeting Susan's eyes. Which didn't exactly bode well for the outcome of the upcoming audience with the Widows, Susan thought. She pushed away the cold chill of fear that shivered over her with the thought that maybe she would never go home. Forcing the fear to the back of her mind, she told herself that she had to take one day at a time. One day at a time? The heck with that. She had to take it an hour at a time. "If it's not to send me home, then why do they want to see me?" she asked.

"The Widows will explain."

Susan took another sip of coffee and watched Magda warily. When the Widows finally did get around to explaining, Susan had the definite feeling she was not going to be particularly happy about what they had to say.

Chapter Six

"Magda, pinch me if I do something wrong, okay? I don't want to ruin my chances of going back," Susan said, as they paused before the entrance to the Widows' tent. She wiped the perspiration from her face with the small, lacy handkerchief provided by Magda before they had left the Keep.

It was hot. Susan wondered why no one else seemed to be suffering as she was. All the layers of clothing she wore did absolutely nothing to keep her cool even if the garments were natural fibers and were supposed to breathe. The sun was brighter and hotter than what she was used to, and it was so strong that most of what she saw seemed to have a bluish tinge. The air, although thinner than what she was used to, was clean with a sharp clarity.

Walking over to the Widows' camp, Susan had lagged behind Magda—one of the reasons being the flimsy little ballet slippers which she'd ended up wearing after all, but the other being Susan's attempts to absorb as much of what surrounded her as she could, which had resulted in Magda hurrying her.

When they had broken from the windbreak of trees that separated the fields, Susan had gasped in surprise at the size of the Widows' camp. The main tent was an enormous affair of black silk erected in the center of the field. Around it, like the spokes of a wheel, other tents of varying sizes were pitched. The field bustled with sound and movement.

At the far end of the field, as far as possible from the location of any of the tents, horses were grazing, and beside the corral were lines of wagons and coaches. Women scurried from one destination to another, some grooming the horses, others feeding and watering them, others shoveling up the end result of the horses' natural digestive processes, which were carefully deposited into a large cart. As Susan watched, the wagon was judged full, and the driver whipped up the two horses and they moved away.

Guards were all over, some obviously coming off duty and some going on. The camp kitchen appeared to contain a full complement of staff, from cooks to scullery maids, and seemed to be where most of the activities centered.

Despite all the people moving about, Magda was the only Widow Susan noticed.

"Just pinch me, Magda," Susan repeated, taking a deep breath, trying to calm her nerves.

Magda smiled in an effort to calm her and said, "I'm sure it won't be necessary to pinch you for any reason."

"I don't see any of the other Widows," she said. Nervousness had her hands trembling, but she hid them in the folds of her skirts and hoped that no one would notice.

"They are waiting within," Magda said, pulling aside the flap of the tent and gesturing for Susan to precede her.

Although Susan was not fainthearted, she could not restrain her gasp of surprise at the two tall female guards in black uniforms just inside the tent entrance. The other guards she had seen at a distance and their size had not been quite so overwhelming.

"The Guards serve us well," Magda murmured. "It is a great honor to be chosen as one." She pulled back another curtain of silk and they were in the tent proper.

Inside was dim and cool compared to the clarity and heat of the sunlight outside the tent, and so it was a few moments before Susan, in looking about her, discovered that the tent seemed almost twice the size when inside. Globes of soft white light were suspended on stands here and there, but the predominance of light came from the blue-white glow of energy that bobbed above the head of each black-clad mistress.

At the centerpoint of the tent Widows had seated themselves in a circle on the carpeted floor amidst the bright colors of large pillows. There was space for two more in the circle. Magda sat, and Susan, her eyes wary, sank to the ground beside her, crossing her legs under her.

The oldest Widow, Fedorra, rested her gaze on Susan, who lifted her chin and returned the Widow's regard in full, sensing that she was being judged. Susan determined that she would not be found wanting.

There was a long pause, and then Fedorra chuckled. "A brave lioness, indeed." Her voice was rusty, as if she seldom used it. There seemed to be a murmur of agreement, but Susan saw no one's lips move.

"I see the questions in your eyes, my child," Fedorra said. "You are afraid and yet you refuse to show us your fear."

"My fear is my own weakness. There is no reason to share it with you," Susan said, folding her hands in her lap.

"There is nothing wrong with fear. It sharpens one's wits," Fedorra said.

"You have called me here," Susan murmured, her hands clasping more tightly in front of her.

"And you wish to know why." Fedorra's head tilted to one side and her eyes fell to Susan's hands.

Consciously, Susan relaxed her grasp. "I *wish* to go back to my own time."

"No!" The word was harsh.

Susan's breath caught at the unyielding denial of her request. "I didn't ask to be brought here. You kidnapped me."

"And did you not wish to come?"

Susan shook her head, but Fedorra would not accept the easy answer.

"Look deeply into your heart, my child, and then tell me we brought you here against your will."

"I didn't ask to come," Susan said, her own voice harsh.

"Neither did you refuse. Look into your heart and deny not the truth." The black crystal on Fedorra's forehead sparkled and a stream of light burst forth to pool in the center of the circle.

Susan shut her eyes against the image that appeared—Jared in the desert, as he had appeared the last night the dream had come to her.

"Open your eyes, child. You came because of

him. Because you knew in the deepest recesses of your mind that he waited for you here—in your future."

"No," Susan said, and kept her eyes closed.

"You are his soulmate, or as we say here—his crystal mate."

"No," she said. "There is no such thing. That's something you read about in books. It's not real."

"I thought you stronger than this, Susan. Can you not admit that one truth?" Fedorra asked.

Susan's eyes snapped open. The vision of Jared in the center of the circle was gone. "You're calling me a coward!"

"If you are not, then admit what you know to be the truth!" Fedorra demanded fiercely.

Susan took a deep breath and remembered the feeling she'd had but a short while ago while leaning out the tower window, the wave of joy that had answered his presence, the deep yearning that had called to her to follow him to race the wind, to follow him to the ends of the earth, the white-hot desire that had touched her briefly and promised so much.

"Yes," she whispered, defeated, yet victorious in that defeat. "I came because of him."

"You are the woman who is counterpoint to his point, who is white to his black, who is light to his dark, who is joy to his sorrow. You are the Woman of Fire whose coming was foretold five hundred years ago. You are she who is to fulfill the Prophecy, who will stand at Jared si'Dakbar's side and fight the evil that threatens us." Fedorra's voice grew deep with emotion. Within the tent there was no sound, and without the tent all had fallen silent, as if Fedorra's voice had traveled outside the confines of the tent and stricken silent all those who labored in the Widows' camp.

"You've laid a trap around me. I can feel it closing," Susan said, her voice breaking the unearthly quiet. She was almost, but not quite, amused. "I admit to one thing, and it follows that the rest is not so difficult to admit. What if I refuse to do whatever it is that you want of me?"

"If you refuse, then Jared faces the evil alone, and he will die, as our world, your future, will die." Fedorra's voice was old and tired again, as if the sonorous seeress of a moment ago had been but a trick of the imagination. "There is no choice, my child."

"There is always a choice," Susan objected, her voice firm. "I know nothing of your time and the evil you say threatens it. This is your world, not mine."

Another Widow lifted her head. "The singers of legends tell us that long ago our earth was green and the air was rich. Great cities rose, their metal towers reaching high. Our ancestors soared to the skies and beyond. We were wealthy beyond measure, and then the evil came, petty jealousies arose between the people, wars began and wars ended, and we poisoned the earth with our science and technology."

Susan sat quietly, feeling the sorrow that crept from Widow to Widow and finally reached her. She shuddered, realizing that Fedorra was talking about the time from which Susan had come.

"In the end, we destroyed our cities and our earth with our wars and our science. With our greed and our filth. There were few people left, and those remaining lived beneath the ground, because the earth would not suffer them to walk upon it for long. Our people came close to reverting to animals, living in burrows."

"Years passed, generations came and went," Fedorra went on. "Finally, men with courage ventured above ground to try to reverse what their ancestors had done. The ones brave enough to try to return to the surface of the earth were changed—their lungs grew large to make use of the thin air, they grew tall, much taller than the rest of their people, their eyes turned gold. They became the Clan Lords, our leaders. They became more than men."

Another Widow took up the story. "And the crystal women followed. As some of the men changed, so did some of the women—women brave enough to accompany their husbands and fathers and sons in their return to the surface. Power grew in them and they used that power to complement their Clan Lords. They were healers and wise women, and they used their power against the strange creatures that the earth had spawned since the great destruction."

Fedorra nodded. "And there lies the mystery. The power and how it was used."

"You are talking about things many years in your past and in my future," Susan said. "What does all this have to do with me?"

"There is more," a Widow said. "Perhaps the most important part." The other Widows nodded. "Those men who had gone to the stars were stranded among the stars when the storm of destruction struck the earth. At first they thought the earth was burned out, nothing left, nothing to return to, but then they and their descendants began to see pockets of green on the surface of the earth. Their hope renewed, they worked to return to the earth—to their home. Eventually they did, but what they discovered here was not to their liking. They had changed too much and the earth, or Terra as we had begun to call it, was no longer the same.

"Those of the earth were determined to bring it

117

back to its glory. Those of the stars wanted to begin again the cycle of building cities and developing their sciences and technology. All came eventually to a compromise and all signed a Pact by which we live even now."

"A Pact?" Susan asked.

"The technicalities of that Pact are not at issue," Fedorra said. "In essence it stated that the Techs would return to the stars where they were most comfortable; and the people of the earth would stay and commit to bringing Terra back to the green paradise it had once been."

Susan shook her head. "From what I've seen, you haven't gotten very far."

"On the contrary, what we sit upon, what surrounds us was once desert. We have fought the desert sand, inch by inch and foot by foot to gain as much as we have. All that was unnatural was banned from Terra's surface. The Pact provided that the Techs could come down to the surface of our planet once every ten years for trade purposes and to exchange the children of the Clan Lords and the Tech Council members."

"Exchange the children?" Susan repeated incredulously.

"For educational purposes," Fedorra said. "We sent the children of our leaders to the Techs for ten years, and they sent the children of their leaders to us. That way we could each learn about the other so as to live in harmony."

"But to send your children away for ten years!" Susan was aghast at the idea.

The Widow shrugged. "It worked. Sometimes there were unhappy consequences—an occasional child felt that the Tech way of life suited them more than the life that awaited them on Terra and remained among the stars. Tech children sometimes preferred life with us here on Terra and chose to stay. Other than those isolated instances, the Pact was rigorously adhered to by all until five hundred years ago when we discovered the crystal in the forbidden areas of the desert. Our crystals have remarkable qualities that some Techs discovered could be exploited to the fullest out among the stars.

"The Versun twins were born to a Terran woman, a Clan Lord's daughter and a crystal woman, who had decided to remain among the Techs. Twins are a rarity among both Techs and Terrans. One of the sons eventually became the High Councilman of the Techs. He secretly arranged for Tech raiders to break the Pact and descend upon us to steal the crystals from our mines. Our people refused to surrender the crystals without a fight.

"The children were held as hostages on both sides and were eventually killed. Babies. Some of them were mere babies." Fedorra's voice broke, and she gestured for another to take up the story. "Amaranthe, finish for me."

The younger Widow nodded. "Our people were forced into fighting the Tech Wars to defend not only our mines but also our future. The crystal women used no physical weapons in combat."

Susan frowned. "What do you mean—they used no physical weapons?"

"The Techs had weapons. The Terrans used the sword and dagger. Clan Lords and crystal women had only weapons of the mind. Eventually the crystal women and the Clan Lords sent the raider Techs back to the stars. Their methods have been lost to us. None of us have ever experienced the intense power the legends speak of."

Fedorra's lips twisted. "Strangely enough, the last successful Challenge was waged between the

Janice Tarantino

Versun brothers, General Jordan Versun and Lord High Councilman Jarman Versun."

Susan frowned. "I thought Techs couldn't wield the power you speak of."

"During the Tech Wars, prisoners were taken, some of them crystal women. Mellissande was a captive crystal woman. She came into the hands of General Jordan Versun and somehow convinced him that the Terrans' cause was right and just. Mellissande and General Versun fell in love and married. They returned to Terra and joined the Clan forces. General Versun was made a Clan Lord in his own right because of his service to us. In his attempt to control the crystal mines of Terra and because of his half-breed birth, Jarman was able to utilize a captive crystal woman and issue the Challenge to his brother. The General and Mellissande were honor-bound to accept and face the Lord High Councilman and his captive crystal woman in the Challenge. Mellissande and her General were victorious."

"So how do I come into all of this? I mean, so far all you've told me is ancient history. Your world is returning to wealth, slowly but surely. Why do you think you need me?"

Fedorra bent her head. "The Clans gather once a year. In times past, when a Clan Lord has grown to the point of war, there has been some hint, some whisper of the truth before the Clan gathering. This year, there was no hint, no whisper, and the Clan Lord struck at our most vulnerable point. He murdered the crystal women and children of all the Clans, and kept only his own crystal woman so that he would reign supreme by virtue of Clan law and tradition. He raised not his sword, yet he won leadership of the Clans."

Susan felt horror sweep through her. The murder of innocent women and children. "You have my sympathy," she murmured, feeling at the same time how inadequate the words were.

The Widows all lifted their heads. Susan shifted a little under the uncomfortable regard of all those eyes.

"Jared and his brother Ruhl are twin brothers," Fedorra said. "Ruhl is the one who murdered the women and children."

"I'm still not sure why you think you need me," Susan said.

"We have no crystal women left to us. A crystal woman is necessary to issue the Challenge."

"But I'm not a crystal woman." Susan became aware of an uneasy sensation prickling over her skin. There was a trap here somewhere. She could feel it. And she knew it was about to close on her.

"You are the woman foretold in the Prophecy of Mellissande. She prophesied that you will stand beside Jared during the Challenge, that you will wield your power to defeat Ruhl and his crystal woman."

"You keep talking about this power," Susan said, looking from one Widow's face to another. "I don't have any power, and I'm not a crystal woman. I don't see how I could possibly be of any help to you," she said, sensing that she had to escape before she was caught. "I'm terribly sorry, but you're going to have to look for someone else."

"There is no one else, Susan," Fedorra said. "You are the chosen one. The process has already begun. It cannot be undone."

"What do you mean?" she asked, all her fears now coming back to shiver over her flesh.

"On the night that Ruhl struck down the crystal women and their girl children, the Widows realized the time foretold by the Prophecy was upon us. We assimilated the resonance of Jared's mind and set our minds free to track a resonance that would complement his. We found you and, in the moment of finding, you were chosen. Magda tells us that you have already meshed with Jared's mind. That is unheard of before a joining. The power you possess must be greater than we suspect."

Susan froze, suddenly feeling the trap snap closed. "I have no power," she said.

"You have great power, my child. Much more than we had ever hoped for. Magda will begin to teach you the ways of the crystal women—"

Scrabbling frantically to her feet, Susan shook off Magda's restraining hand on her long skirts. "I have no power," she said, trying to keep the trembling from her voice. "I am not a crystal woman. I am not of your time, and your rules don't apply to me."

"You possess enormous powers, child." Fedorra's tone was irritatingly patient. "Why do you deny what is so true?"

"Because I possess no power. My mind is my own. Perhaps the things you are speaking of are possible here in the future, but not for me. I don't belong here. You must send me back."

"I had hoped to convince you, my child, but I can see that you will not easily bend your will to ours. Perhaps that is to be expected. Perhaps we ask too much of you too soon, but we are all so aware that we have little time left to us."

Feeling the fear rise into her throat, Susan looked at the Widow Fedorra. "I cannot do what you ask. You have all made a mistake."

"We have made no mistake, Susan. You are the one prophesied."

Shaking her head, she backed away from the circle, almost tripping over Magda, who rose to her feet as if to detain her. "I won't do it. I can't do it. And if you won't send me home, then I'll find a way to get there myself."

"You will not abandon us, Susan Richards," Fedorra said, her cracked, aging voice strong as it rose over the murmurs of the other Widows.

"Abandon you? I'm not abandoning you," she cried, a laugh strangling to stillness in her throat. "I'm escaping from you." She ran to the tent exit and, ducking through the flap, disappeared.

Magda took a few steps as if to follow her.

Fedorra raised her hand. "Magda, let her go."

"But—"

"She has nowhere to go. She is only rebelling against a situation over which she has no control. It is natural. She is strong with much spirit, and we have given her no alternative." Fedorra frowned. "But I cannot understand why she denies her power. Perhaps there is a reason we do not understand. If so . . ."

"Surely you don't intend to give her a choice!"

The Mistress of the Widows shook her head rather sadly. "She has no choice. No more than the rest of us do. I find the thought of force distasteful and the unpredictability of it makes me shudder. But if force must be used, then we shall use it and not regret its use. So, let the poor child have her few hours of rebellion against us. We shall have our way in the end."

Ruhl paced behind his crystal woman as she stared into the crystal on the table before her. "What is happening?" he demanded impatiently.

Collis held up her hand. "Wait." The silence in the room grew until it was almost unbearable. At last, Collis sat back in her chair and sighed.

"Well?" Ruhl asked.

"She has run from the Widows. As far as I can gather from her mind before she sensed my presence and brought up her mental barriers, she has refused their demands."

"Good," Ruhl said as his eyes narrowed.

"I said as far as I could tell. There is no guarantee that the Widows will not bring her around to their way of thinking."

"Then nothing has changed. The woman must be killed."

"Perhaps that is easier said than done. An assassination attempt will be expected by the Widows. They are aware that we are watching."

"But if this woman does not trust them, then they will be able to do little to stop us."

Collis shrugged. "I think that they will be able to guard her against almost anything we would try."

Ruhl stopped his pacing and frowned. "You said she has run from the Widows."

Nodding, the crystal woman began to rise.

"Then we shall kill her now," Ruhl said, coming up behind Collis and pressing her back into her chair. "She is alone?"

"Yes, she wanders the forest near the sea. Even now she has stopped to rest and has fallen asleep."

"Then send her a present, Collis, my love," Ruhl whispered. "A Ptai."

Collis sucked in a breath. "A Ptai could not maneuver among the trees, and even so—"

"I know you must become one with the mind of a creature in order to control it." His hand tightened on her shoulder. "If not a Ptai—"

"It will take me some time to prepare myself," Collis murmured.

"Then do so, my love. If this woman dies tonight, her death will save us much trouble."

Susan opened her eyes and stretched, feeling her arms scrape against the bole of a rough-barked tree deep in the woods. Faintly surprised at herself, she realized that she'd fallen asleep. She remembered running from the Widows' camp into the woods and then she'd gotten lost. She'd sat down to rest and had fallen asleep, worn out by the anxieties produced by her meeting with the Widows.

Hemmed in by trees and undergrowth, she stood up and grimaced as she took her full weight on her feet.

God, they hurt! The leather slippers had offered little protection against the leavings of nature. She would swear that she'd stepped on every rock and pebble between here and the Widows' tent.

The forest had darkened. She had no idea what time it was. She listened, her ears straining for sound, even if it was the Widows' camp, but she heard only the sound of the wind soughing through the leaves of the trees and what sounded like the crash of ocean waves. Her eyes widened with amazement when she sniffed the air and realized she smelled the sea.

Following the trail laid by sound and smell, Susan pressed on through the increasingly scraggly trees. She emerged onto wind-scoured rock that went on for a hundred feet and then ended. The gray of ocean water extended to the horizon. Susan carefully crossed the bare rock to where it fell away to nothing. She crawled to the edge, the wind plucking at her hair and lifting and tossing the tattered remains of her long skirts.

She looked over the edge and caught her breath. From the sound of the boom of ocean waves against

rock she had guessed she was on a cliff or promontory of some sort, but the actual height of the
cliff shocked her. The water was hundreds of feet
below and yet the ocean heaved itself so forcefully
against the cliff face that she felt the ocean spray
on her face.

Carefully, she edged forward a little more so that
her head and shoulders hung over the rocky edge.
The cliff face was not as smooth as she'd thought
at first glance. There were ledges and outcrop-
pings and deeper shadows of dark down to about
halfway, where the rock turned suddenly smooth,
worn so by the smoothing action of the water.

She lay on her stomach and watched the action
of the ocean as it pounded against the cliff, fascinated by the violence below her and yet repulsed
by the apparent oily thickness of the water further out, aware that something felt wrong, something in her perception was off. She wrinkled her
nose, because, this close to the source, there was
the suggestion of something slightly foul under
the salt-tanged smell of the seaspray. It was as if
the water itself were unclean. She looked out over
the sea, and it dawned on her that the ocean was
part of what the Widows had been telling her. It
was polluted and poisonous, which explained why
there was no hint of life either above or below the
surface.

There was nothing but the endless, empty swell
of a tainted ocean.

As she watched the horizon, she saw that darkness advanced. Whether it was the coming of night
or dark storm clouds, she had no idea, but she
thought that perhaps it would be smart to think
about finding her way back to the Dakbar Keep.

Reluctant to stand up so close to the barren cliff
edge, Susan crawled backwards until she felt it

was safe. Pushing up with her hands, she stood up and groaned when her weight was full on her sore feet.

Stupid, useless shoes! When she got back to the Keep, she intended to demand her sneakers, and she wasn't going to relinquish them until she got back home.

After throwing one last wary glance at the approaching darkness which she was afraid was nightfall, she turned and froze in terror at what met her sight.

Chapter Seven

Jared rode the black easily, ignoring the dust that kicked up from the dry road. The stallion knew the way home as well as Jared himself, and judging by the way he pulled at the bit in his mouth, Gaeten wanted to get home as quickly as Jared did.

Almost home, Jared thought, enjoying the feeling of anticipation he felt at the thought of arriving at his Keep. Without probing too deeply into his feelings, he knew they were due to Susan's presence there. Their discourse of the morning had unnerved him with its depth; he wondered how it had affected her. Had she thought of him during the day as often as he had thought of her? Had images of him tormented her even as images of her had tormented and distracted him?

"Susan," he whispered, and then chuckled when Gaeten's ears pricked up at the sound of her name, almost as if the stallion recognized it. Jared patted the stallion on the neck as he squinted at the horizon and shifted his shoulders, feeling his shirt stick to his sweat-dampened skin under the leather armor. Nightfall was approaching.

He wondered how Susan had fared today. How was her wounded arm? Had she adjusted to the changes that had confronted her? Or had she thrown herself on the bed and spent the day weeping? Shaking his head with sudden conviction, Jared knew she had not spent the day in tears. In fact, he'd bet half the horses in his stable that she'd had the Keep turned upside down within a couple of hours of his departure this morning. Despite his efforts to concentrate on his investigation regarding the men disappearing from the village, his thoughts had dwelled too long and too often on the woman with the hair of fire.

"She's quite a woman, Gaeten. If only she was from our time, then perhaps . . ." For a moment his thoughts departed from logic and common sense, weaving a brief fantasy that almost, but not quite, convinced him that what he dreamed was possible.

"Ach! What's the use in dreaming, Gaeten?" he exclaimed. "She'll leave and go back to her own time. Compared to her's, my world is a barren place indeed." In sudden disgust at his thoughts, he drove his heels into the stallion's sides, urging him into a canter. He had enough to worry about without tying himself up in knots over a woman who would never consent to what the Widows planned and who would return to her own time as soon as she could convince the Widows to send her back.

He rode, harder now, Gaeten's hooves drumming against the hard-packed earth of the road, raising a cloud of dust behind them, and soon the tower of the Keep came into sight. Breathing hard, sweat trickling down his back between his shoulder blades, Jared pulled up the stallion, and his eyes moved swiftly over the battlements of the castle walls as he considered where to place additional sentries.

The news at the village today had not been good. Men were disappearing from all the villages along the desert's edge, and although rumor and speculation were rife, no one had been able to tell him anything definitive.

Jared was sure renegade Techs were behind the disappearances, and he was also sure there was more than one band of raiders involved. Too many men were disappearing for it to be one small group of raiders.

The name of Orsin had been whispered more than once today, and Jared had been shocked at the feelings and memories that the name of his former Tech teacher had brought back to him. Orsin's name invoked fear certainly, especially among his former students, for he had been antithetical to the peaceful Tech norm. No Tech and no Terran had been fiercer than he. Jared's body still carried the scars of Orsin's physical training. Orsin had broken away from the presently conservative Tech government after being castigated and stripped of his rank after the death of one of his students during a routine training session.

The word was that Orsin had sought refuge from his detractors among the dregs of Tech society. Pursued by Tech lawkeepers, Orsin had presumably moved his operations to Terra.

If the rumors were true and Orsin led the renegade Techs, then Jared knew his difficulties had just begun. He would have to come up not only with a plan of defense but with a plan of offense against the renegade Techs.

Jared dug his heels into Gaeten's sides, frowning when he saw the group of people gathered in front of the open portcullis despite the lateness of the hour. Nightfall was almost upon them, and the gate should have already been closed. Jared spurred Gaeten closer, and he frowned down at his mother.

"Jared, she is gone," Magda said, and Jared felt the trembling of her hands when she laid them on his knee. "We have searched, but we cannot find her anywhere."

"How long has she been gone?" he asked briefly, surprised by the flash of panic he felt at the thought that Susan was without the protection of the Keep with the coming of nightfall. He was also achingly aware that both he and the stallion were exhausted.

"Since early this afternoon," Magda replied. "The Widows met to talk to her and she—"

His eyes gleamed down at her in the half darkness while an unwilling smile played at the corners of his mouth. "She didn't fall in so easily with your plans, did she?" He couldn't help the feeling of rather perverse pride that shot through him at the thought that Susan had resisted the Widows exactly as he had thought she would. "Which direction did she head off in?"

Magda shrugged helplessly. "We don't know. The Widows' Guard thought she went north, but the stablehands said she went east. We have had men searching in all directions but have found no trace of her. With the coming of nightfall we had to call them back."

He stared down at her for a moment, his mind racing. A woman alone and unused to the dangers of the night stood almost no chance of surviving. He felt Magda's fingers tighten on his knee.

131

"Your minds have touched," she whispered, her face pale with strain. "If there is anyone who can find her, it is you."

He nodded, turning Gaeten from the gate.

"Jared!" Magda called and he turned back to her. "She is indeed even more special than we thought. You saw her wounds last night. They were nearly healed this morning."

"That's impossible. No wound could heal that fast," he said, frowning down at his mother, and then his anger rose. "And the Widows drove her away?"

"She ran," Magda answered simply.

Jared nodded. "I'll find her." He nudged Gaeten in the direction of the Widows' camp.

Their camp was quiet. Three Widows stood in front of their tent as if they waited for him.

"Have you found any trace of her?" he asked, fighting to keep his anger out of his voice.

Two of them shook their heads, but the younger spoke up hesitantly. "The sea, perhaps," she said, frowning. "I can smell the sea."

The oldest Widow hushed the younger. "She has closed her mind to us. How can you know she's by the sea?"

The younger shrugged, but her eyes flashed defiantly at the older Widow. "I only know I smell the sea."

Jared flashed a smile at the younger woman's bravery in the face of disapproval. "Did anyone reach as far as the sea in their search?"

All three Widows shook their heads. "We were sure she hadn't gone so far, and then dark began to fall."

"Then I shall start there," Jared said, his stomach muscles tightening at the thought of Susan alone by the sea at dark. He gathered the reins into his hand, but paused when he felt the claw-like grip of the oldest Widow on his thigh. He narrowed his eyes down at her. Seldom did anyone touch a Clan Lord without permission, particularly a Widow. Clan Lords and Widows usually kept their distance from one another under normal circumstances.

"She must be found, Lord Jared. She is our only hope," the Widow said.

His lips tightened. "I seek a young woman who is unfamiliar with our ways and who is frightened by the strangeness of our land. I seek not a woman who is the last hope of the Widows."

The old woman narrowed her pouchy eyes, the jewel on her forehead sparkling for a moment at his audacious response. Then she chuckled, a dry, old woman's laugh, and her fingers loosened and dropped from his thigh to rest on the head of the cane she carried. "You are angry with us, Lord Jared. You fight us and that is good because it brings you back to life after the tragedy we all suffered three months ago. But despite your anger, I don't think you'll fight so hard nor rail so strongly against the Widows on the night of your joining to this woman whom we, the Widows, have found for you."

"Mithra!" the younger Widow exclaimed. "The joining is a sacred ceremony between a Clan Lord and his crystal woman. It's not something that should be referred to in such a distasteful manner."

"Lewd manner, you mean," Mithra said, cackling and peering with poor sight at the young Widow. "I'm old now and entitled to say what I think and to think what I wish. Young Lord Jared knows what I mean." She cackled again and slapped Jared on the thigh.

Gaeten shied, taking a few prancing steps away from the old woman. Jared found his mouth stretching in an unwilling grin as he brought Gaeten under control. He'd never thought to find a Widow with a sense of humor—and a slightly bawdy one at that.

The oldest Widow sent a sly grin in the direction of the younger Widow. "Don't try to convince me that you've forgotten the night of your own joining, Gersta. I heard tales told from your mother-in-law." The Widow chuckled again, gesturing at Jared. "Oh, but to be a fly on the wall on the night to come. By my reckoning there'd better not be a piece of crystal within two hundred meters that night, else it be shattered to splinters. Find her, Lord Jared. She is special and will bring you much joy—both in and out of bed." The Widow hobbled away, leaning heavily on her cane.

Jared felt his face flush with heat at the old woman's words, but he candidly met the eyes of young Gersta when she turned to him, blushing herself. Her husband, Clan Lord Kalin, had died last year when he'd been thrown from one of his prize stallions and had broken his neck. He and Jared had shared the same passion for breeding horses and had spent a fair amount of time together trading experiences. Jared also remembered a few evenings spent quaffing ale in front of Kalin's glowhearth and some of the stories Kalin had told about the night of his joining. In deference to the young Widow, Jared kept his lips from twitching.

"Forgive her, Lord Jared," Gersta whispered. "She is old."

Jared felt the sense of urgency that suddenly pulled at him, but he smiled down at Gersta. "But not so old that she's forgotten what it's like to live— and love. Reassure the Widow Mithra that I shall find Susan." He spurred Gaeten on to the woods that edged the field and there he threw his mind open, searching for that particular resonance of the essence that was Susan. Gaeten moved restlessly beneath him, anxious to continue, but held back by the light touch of Jared's strong hands on the reins.

There! His mind touched on golden shimmer far distant and yet close enough to read the streaks of blue despair that threaded through the gold. The shimmer of Susan's mind was evident to Jared, but it was muted as if she had erected mental shields.

Jared nudged Gaeten and they moved forward carefully through the woods, following the thread of golden luminescence that led to Susan. Jared, not wanting to frighten her, held his mind back, although he wanted nothing more than to wing toward her and drive the blue threads from her mind. Then he grinned, mocking himself. What reassurance did he have that his presence would do any such thing? More than likely, she'd run from him faster than she'd already run from the Widows.

The smell of the sea, brought to him on the wind that presaged the fall of night, grew stronger as he moved deeper into the woods. He knew he was close, but he remained careful not to project his presence to Susan, sensing instinctively that if she knew he was close, she would escape him. When he heard the boom of the sea against the cliff, he dismounted and, moving close to the stallion's head, stroked Gaeten's neck, whispering for him to stay and wait quietly.

Quickly and yet not making a sound, Jared made his way through the underbrush to the clean, clear sweep of rock that lay between the trees and the edge of the cliffs. He had almost reached the edge when he felt the barriers that Susan had erected to protect her drop and her essence burst forth in a brilliant flare of gold that quickly turned to the dark violet of fear. His mind touched hers and he felt the sheer physical terror that trembled through her together with disbelief and absolute revulsion at what confronted her.

At the same instant, Jared was assailed with the smell of an animal. Tremillium! One of the most difficult of the night beasts to overwhelm. Engagement of the reptilian-skinned, catlike animal usually required at least two men, one to play decoy and the other to wield the sword. But he was alone and Susan was in danger. How far was he from giving her aid? Moving forward quietly but quickly, he reached the edge of the woods.

The Tremillium was halfway between him and the edge of the cliff, and Susan was only a few feet beyond the beast.

Nearly at the edge of the cliff, she stood tall and unmoving except for the stirring of the wind in her hair and the fluttering of her torn skirts about her legs.

"Be still!" Jared projected the thought to her, together with a touch of reassurance. He saw her jerk a little at the impact of the words in her mind and saw her eyes move as she tried to find him, but she did not reply to him. He pressed his lips together grimly as he reached for his sword, sending quick, decisive instructions to her mentally as he freed the sword from its sheath at his belt with a faint *hiss-ching.* He wanted her well away from the battle that was about to commence, and he told her so in no uncertain terms. When he found no resistance in her mind, he assumed that she understood the instructions.

136

Moving quickly, silently, he made his way unseen in the underbrush upwind of the Tremillium, knowing that his scent would alert the animal to his presence. As he moved, he gripped the hilt of the sword more tightly, watching the swaying of the long neck of the curiously repulsive predator.

Susan couldn't know it, but the creature was preparing to strike. The strike would result in either her jumping back and falling over the edge of the cliff or in her being impaled by the fangs that carried the poison used to paralyze its victim.

Although he tried not to think of the consequences if he made a mistake, he was unable to control the light sweat that broke out on his brow at the thought of all that could go wrong in the next few moments.

Jared sought Susan's mind to give her warning of his impending attack, and found to his amazement that she had her fear well controlled and solidly contained behind the shields that were once more in place, although he sensed they were not as high as before.

The beast should have sensed his presence by now, Jared thought with a frown as he moved into position slightly north of the animal. Just then the Tremillium swiveled its long neck in his direction and hissed, moving forward on its ungainly legs with lightning speed.

Jared burst out of the trees and crouched in plain sight with plenty of fighting room around him.

The Tremillium moved forward in a weaving, darting path and attempted to strike again, but Jared had moved with panther-like quickness off to the side and struck with his sword at the vulnerable neck of the scaled creature. The predator squealed with pain at the gash that suddenly opened under the flashing blade of Jared's sword, and the darting head swiveled to strike at the source of the pain. Jared rolled away and sprang to his feet, feeling exultation as he saw the wound he had inflicted spew glowing green ichor.

The green blood of the Tremillium was as poisonous as its viperous bite. He had to stay clear of the wound while attempting to inflict others. Jared circled, avoiding the striking head, watching for an opening as the Tremillium hissed and struck at the air a scant foot in front of him.

Jared backed away cautiously, his eyes narrow, his mind gauging the possibilities that were left to him. It would be difficult to strike again since he had no decoy.

He feinted to the right and recoiled, feeling the impact of the beast's fangs on the sword shudder its way up to his shoulder. He couldn't lose the sword! He feinted to the right again and withdrew more quickly. Jared frowned as he watched the wounded Tremillium's head swing from the center to the right and back to the center, anticipating Jared's next move.

Moving as if to feint to the right, Jared quickly pulled back and sped to the left, swinging his sword and gashing the left side of the neck to match the right. He spun in a tight ball to escape the striking fangs as the Tremillium suddenly and painfully caught on to the game.

Jared unrolled and sprang to his feet, ready once again to face the hissing, pain-maddened predator. The next wounds would be harder to inflict because the quadruped would no longer be cautious. The animal would no longer seek to protect itself; it would merely try to inflict as much damage as possible before it died. If only there was a decoy, Jared thought as he gasped for breath and stumbled back several steps as the hissing head snapped at him and almost caught him.

His eyes darted to the sudden flutter of movement at the edge of the trees. *"No! No!"* he cried at her silently as she moved out to divert the attention of the Tremillium. Hadn't she heard him earlier? He could have sworn that she'd heard him.

And then it was too late to think of anything except the danger she was in.

Hissing virulently, the beast swung in her direction and with that curiously ungainly swift movement pursued her, sensing she was the easier prey. Jared was presented with a perfect target as the predator moved past him, and he swung his sword straight down, cleaving the thick, sinuous neck from its short, squat body.

A piercing shriek rent the air.

Jared jumped away from the twitching carcass, avoiding the glowing mess of green blood that spilled onto the rocky ground. Raising his sword, adrenaline throbbing through his veins, he threw back his head and screamed his Clan's victory yell to the darkened sky. The sound of his voice flew out over the forest and for a scant second all was quiet, and then as the scream of victory faded away, the sounds of the night resumed.

Jared brought his sword down and leaned on it, feeling his heart pump the blood through his veins, his gaze stabbing the night as he searched for Susan.

She stood a few feet away from the head of the Tremillium, staring down at it, her eyes filled with horror. "That sound . . ."

He watched her through narrowed gold eyes, fighting down his anger, sensing the horror in her at the sight of the beheaded creature, but also sensing something else stirring in her—but it was gone before he could pin it down.

"You fool!" he thought at her and watched with satisfaction when she flinched at the raw fury of his anger as it echoed in her mind.

Susan looked up at him then. "You needed me," she said simply.

"You could have been killed," he said, his voice hoarse with the remnants of exertion and with an undefined emotion as he used her preferred method of communicating.

"And you could not have been?" She lifted what remained of the hem of her skirt clear of the blood of the conquered beast and moved around the head, approaching him. "What is it called?"

He looked down at her, restraining the impulse he had to reach out and grasp her by the shoulders and shake her until she was dizzy. "I am used to the dangers of my world. I know what a Tremillium can do. What it will do when attacked. I know its quickness of movement. I know what it does when it's about to strike. I know how it kills."

"And now I know about a Tremillium too," she said. "I merely responded to what you needed. Your mind kept crying decoy at me. I was in no danger. I knew what you intended to do."

Her voice was so reasonable that he caught himself doubting his own right to be angry. "What if I had missed my aim?" he asked, appalled by the trust she had in him and yet intrigued by the admission that she had known his thoughts. When she had run out to decoy the deadly quadruped, he had wondered if she had understood him after all.

"You would not have missed, Lord Jared," she said, using the formal method of address, attempting to put a certain amount of emotional distance between them.

He turned away from her, willing for the moment to give her the distance she needed, and wiped the blade of his sword carefully on the bits of grass that grew on the crag. When he was convinced that his sword was clean of the poisonous green blood, he thrust the blade into its sheath.

"Come," he said, extending his hand to her, silently breathing a sigh of relief when she took it, and scanning the now black sky with his golden eyes. "We must get back. There are many people anxiously awaiting us both at the Widows' camp and at the Keep."

At his words he felt her resist as she pulled back against his hand. When he turned to her, he saw her toss her head, her thick hair flying behind her like a flag in the breeze. He was conscious of faint amusement when her lips firmed.

"I'm not going back to the Widows," she said.

Observing the way she'd planted her feet on the rocky promontory, Jared had the feeling it was going to take some effort to move her. He scanned the night sky again. He didn't want to frighten her unnecessarily, but there were dangers. His gaze moved back to her face and he found that she was staring at him.

Hesitantly, she tilted her head to the side and glanced heavenward herself. "What . . ."

"My world is unfamiliar to you, Susan. And there is something strange about this night that not even I understand," he said, seeing her gaze swing back and fasten on his face. He ignored the clutch of tightness in his belly when her tongue moistened her lips. "The cry we heard as the Tremillium died is not a sound it makes. I am afraid that something other than a simple predator stalks us. We must reach shelter."

"I won't go to the Widows," she insisted.

141

He chuckled. "We shall only stop to let them know you are safe. Then we shall go on to the Keep." He tugged at her hand and led her into the trees, moving carefully, alert for any noise that would indicate danger.

"Why can't you just send a mental message?" she asked. "Oh!" she exclaimed, startled by the dark shape that loomed in front of them.

The stallion nickered a soft welcome, butting his head against Jared's shoulder. "Everything's fine, Gaeten," he murmured to the horse. "It's time we were gone." He mounted, and then reached down, taking Susan's hand and gesturing for her to step on his stirruped foot.

He grasped her around the waist and swung her up in front of him sideways with her legs resting over his thigh, smiling in the dark at her gasp of surprise and the sudden clutch of her hands on his forearm.

"Gently, my lady," he murmured in her ear, tucking her closer against him. "Gaeten is a proper gentleman. He'll do nothing to alarm you." His smile widened to a grin when he gathered up the reins and felt Susan trying to inch forward away from him. Tightening his arm around her waist, he pulled her firmly back into the cradle of his thighs. He nudged the stallion forward with his heels.

A short distance further, he felt her stiff muscles give a little, but he made no overt moves to distress her. He found himself spreading his perceptions over a wider range in an attempt to identify any dangers and also in an attempt to distract himself.

Holding her close, feeling her lean into his chest, and drawing in deeply the scent that laced her hair where it tangled around his neck proved too much of a distraction for him, and he felt himself sinking swiftly into a sensual dream that was shattered suddenly by the sound of her voice.

"Why can't you send the Widows a mental message telling them we're safe?" she asked, her voice tense as she stiffened and leaned forward away from him.

Soundlessly he groaned as he realized that his traitorous body had transmitted his thoughts all too blatantly. His voice was rough as he sought to control his response to her nearness. "I can't send them mental messages. What made you think I could?"

"You spoke to me that way this morning and yet again a short while ago." Surprise tinged her voice.

Frowning, he sought the words that would make her understand, and yet even as the words left his mouth, he knew they were inadequate and not really the truth—at least not with regard to her. "A Clan Lord can only mesh minds with his crystal woman. There is a special bond that occurs at their joining that permits it. I cannot mindmesh with anyone I choose."

By the True God, it was an effort to keep from closing his arm tightly around her waist and burying his lips in her hair. Although he kept his mind from touching hers, he could sense her thinking about what he had just said.

"I don't understand," she murmured, and he could hear the frown in her voice. "Everyone keeps talking about crystal women. I mean, I can see *what* a crystal woman is and why she's called that, but I don't know what her purpose is. And then everyone keeps talking about this joining, but you tell me that you can only mindmesh with a crystal woman after joining."

"It's rather difficult to explain."

"Yes, it seems so," she agreed, "especially when the rules don't seem to apply to us. Lord Jared, you are obviously a Clan Lord, but I am not a crystal woman. And yet we seem to have mindmeshed—at least I keep hearing your voice inside my head—and you tell me that's impossible because you can't mindmesh with anyone but a crystal woman to whom you are joined." She paused and drew a deep breath.

They came to the edge of a field where the forest fell away. Jared reined Gaeten in as he probed the field and the sky for predators. "We'll travel the edge of the field," he said in sudden decision, inexplicably uneasy at the thought of crossing the open field. "We take a chance on something being in the trees, but I'd rather chance that than be caught out in the open with no cover at all."

"How much further do we have to go?" Susan asked, her eyes darting from side to side in the darkness. "Why is it so dark? I thought there was a full moon last night."

"The moon hasn't risen yet," he murmured. "In about another hour, you'll see it rise on the western horizon." He urged Gaeten to keep to the edge of the trees as they circled the field, and for a few moments the only sound heard was the creak of saddle leather.

"It's so quiet," Susan whispered.

"Something is abroad," he murmured in her ear. "Something that causes even the night birds to still their songs." He extended his awareness, but still sensed nothing but the uneasy quiet. Even the crickets were silent.

In a few moments they had reached the other side of the field and as they entered the windbreak trees, the feeling of danger faded. Jared exhaled, unaware that he had been holding his breath. Susan relaxed against his chest.

"There was something terrible in that field," she said, her voice hushed.

He nodded. "I think so. I don't know why it didn't attack us. Perhaps it had just fed."

She shuddered, and he whisked his cheek across the top of her head in comfort.

"Tell me about crystal women," she demanded.

"Crystal women have the power," he murmured, keeping his awareness extended and alert even as he spoke. "They are born with it, although it doesn't develop until age five or so, when the crystal forms. It acts as an amplifier, and it increases and focuses whatever power the child possesses. Crystal women are the healers of our Clans." He hesitated. "They are also our hearts," he murmured, thinking momentarily of Evie.

"You keep talking about this joining."

He nodded. "Only Clan Lords can be joined with crystal women. As a result of the joining, a part of each is . . ." He hesitated, searching for exactly the right word. "Lodged in the mind of the other. Not physically," he hastened to add when he heard her small sound of what he interpreted to be disgust. "A part of the essence of that person is always with the other. It's like a constant awareness. A knowing that you're not alone."

"Don't these crystal women ever join with anyone else other than a Clan Lord?"

"It's not possible. The word joining specifically refers to the mindmesh. A crystal woman may enjoy a sexual relationship with someone other than a Clan Lord, but it is rarely done. There is no specialness, no advantage to the liaison, although there may be love. Or pleasure." He was aware that he was explaining it badly, but the relationship between a Clan Lord and a crystal woman was so different that it was almost impossible to explain.

Susan was silent for a moment. "In my time love would be enough."

"Here it is not. A Clan Lord is responsible for the lives and welfare of many. He must have every advantage possible to ensure the continuation of the human race and the fight to restore our planet."

"How does a Clan Lord use a crystal woman to give him those advantages?" she asked, resting her head on his chest just below his neck. Her voice sounded sleepy to his ears.

"In the past crystal women were warriors and they stood beside their Clan Lords in battle. They were able to channel their power and use it as a weapon. We no longer know how it is done. Now a crystal woman is a healer who holds the magic of the Clan, but even more than that, a crystal woman is the only one who can bear a crystal girl child." He looked down and saw that her eyes were closed.

"Magic," Susan murmured. "I haven't seen any magic yet."

"You will," he promised her. "You might not have seen it, but you have experienced it. Remember the circle of last night?"

"Oh, yes," she said. Her eyelids flickered and then she sat up straight. "Is that light I see ahead?"

"The Widows' camp."

The corners of her mouth turned down. Jared smiled down at her, entranced by the mobility of her expressions.

"Let's skip right by them and head for the Keep," she suggested.

"We must stop."

"Then not for long."

"No, not for long," he agreed. "Merely to let them know we are safe."

"It seems to me that if they have all this power, they should know that," she said, her voice sharp.

He shook his head. "They couldn't find you earlier. They had no idea where you had gone." He frowned down at her then as a thought occurred to him, something that was so obvious he should have asked about it before setting out on his search for her. "But you're right. They must have a scrying crystal. They should have been able to track you, even as they are probably tracking us now." He almost regretted that their journey was about to end. He enjoyed the feeling of her warm, pliant body snugged up against his.

An escort of four Widows' guards met them one field away from the camp.

"The Widows don't wish to detain you, but they need to speak with you about something, Lord Jared," one of the guards said.

Jared looked at him curiously. "They knew we were coming? A scrying crystal?"

The guard nodded, and Jared's frown grew deeper. He didn't understand, but then there was no time to wonder. They entered the camp, and were escorted directly to the small group of Widows who stood in front of their tent.

Fedorra inclined her head slightly. "Lord Jared, we are pleased to welcome you safely back."

"Mistress Fedorra," he replied, bowing in return. "I wished only to inform you of our safety before continuing on to the Keep. Your guard informs me that you have tracked us in a crystal."

"Part of the way, Lord Jared," Fedorra said, peering up at Susan's face, which was still and cold under the Widow's regard. "But I wish to ask you about what happened in the first field after the cliffs. Something strange happened that we cannot explain."

Gaeten moved restively and Jared tightened the reins. "I have my own questions, Mistress Fedorra. Why did you not attempt to track Susan in the scrying crystal before sending me on my search? Why did you not send the search parties after her in the direction of the cliffs?"

The old woman raised an eyebrow at him. "We would have if we had been able to see her in the crystal. There was no sign of her. The child is evidently skilled at throwing up mind shields."

"Mind shields," he repeated, remembering the barriers in Susan's mind that he had sensed before she had dropped them in her encounter with the Tremillium. He bent down a little to Fedorra. "There was something in the first field, was there not? I sensed something, but couldn't pinpoint it."

Fedorra scowled up at him. "We watched your battle with the Tremillium, Lord Jared. It was only then that we were able to see Susan. She had dropped her mind shields then. But as you approached the first field, you faded from sight. We could not find you. Although there was the suggestion of movement along the edge of the field, we could see no clear picture. We feared for you. It was not until you had passed another field that you became visible again in the crystal."

Jared straightened and looked at Susan, the frown still creasing his brow. He knew he was incapable of doing what Fedorra was suggesting. And yet Magda herself had said that Susan was much more powerful than they had at first thought. "Susan, while we were edging that first field, did you do anything?"

"What do you mean?" she asked, avoiding looking at any of the Widows.

"Did you try to hide us in some way?"

"No!" she exclaimed.

He looked back at Fedorra. "There was something there, wasn't there?"

Fedorra nodded. "A Fergon. Crouched in the center of the field, hiding in the corn."

Shuddering at the idea of a Fergon, his arm tightened around Susan's waist. "You must have done something, Susan," he said softly. "Because a Fergon lets no man pass him whether he's recently fed or not."

"She cloaked you," Fedorra said. "She has tremendous power. We have made no mistake in our choosing of her."

Susan jerked forward, and if Jared hadn't grabbed her, she would have slid off Gaeten. "I have no power, Widow Fedorra. I have nothing that you want."

Fedorra's eyes found Jared's, ignoring Susan. "Surely you must admit that we are right, Lord Jared. There can no longer be any doubt in your mind about the rightness of what we have done."

"She is not willing," he said, his voice deep with reluctance.

"She has no choice," Fedorra said. "Tomorrow."

"You're sure there is no other way?" Jared asked doubtfully, and yet his heartbeat quickened and his blood heated at what the Widow was proposing.

"What's she talking about?" Susan asked, tugging at his sleeve.

"Tomorrow," the Widow intoned. "Word has already been sent to all concerned."

Jared inclined his head. "Then I shall uphold my oath to serve the Widows in whatever way they demand." He wheeled Gaeten around and urged him forward to a trot.

"What's going on?" Susan asked, twisting to look him straight in the face and trying to maintain her seat. "What's tomorrow?"

Jared slowed the horse to a walk, groping for the words to explain what the Widows required of them both. He had grown up knowing of the joining, knowing and expecting that he would be joined when a crystal woman had been chosen for him. When Evie had died, he had thought that part of his life was over. He had never heard a whisper of the possibility that a Clan Lord could join again. He knew it was impossible for the crystal women to join with another Clan Lord—that was why the Widows existed. He watched as a stunned half-comprehension dawned in Susan's eyes.

"You didn't answer me, Jared," she whispered. "What was Fedorra talking about? What will happen tomorrow?"

He sighed, realizing that their relationship was about to take a turn for the worse regardless of the intimacy the Widows planned for the morrow. "As much as you want to deny it, you are evidently the closest thing to a functioning crystal woman as exists in our world. The Widow Fedorra was informing me that tomorrow we shall be joined."

Chapter Eight

"I won't do it!" Susan repeated for the fifth time as they finally reached the Keep courtyard. Her tone was as rigid as her body, and she intended to keep it that way. There was no way anyone was going to manipulate her into doing something she was dead set against. Especially something so nebulous and threatening as this joining thing.

"Susan, we have to talk about this," Jared said, his voice deep and steady although she heard the strained undertone that marked his words.

"I don't care," she said. "I don't care what you say, I'm not going to do this—whatever it is." She struggled against his grip, and finally found herself sliding over Jared's thigh down the long length of the stallion and finally feeling her aching feet land on the cobblestones of the courtyard.

"You don't understand," Jared began, dismounting and handing the horse's reins to a stable hand.

She whipped around to glare up at him. "You're

darn right I don't understand. I don't understand any of this. I don't understand what joining means—although to tell you the truth I think I have a pretty good idea."

"I can explain."

"I don't want you to explain anything," she cried. "I just want to go home where I belong."

Jared gripped her arms tightly, forcing her to listen to him. "And you will go home, Susan. You will. I promise you that. On my life I swear to you that you will be returned to your time, but you must understand that I cannot stop this."

"Of course you can," she said. "You're the Clan Lord here. You are the one who makes the decisions."

"And when I took my responsibility as a Clan Lord, I swore fealty to the Widows as all the Clan Lords do. It was an oath of honor which I cannot break." His grip on her arms loosened, but did not fall away. "As long as what they require of me does not harm this world, or my holding, or pose danger to my people, I am honor-bound to accede to their wishes. If I do not, the Council, which has also sworn the same oath to the Widows, can strip me of my holdings, my rank, and my life. They can take from me whatever the Widows demand."

"Why do the Widows have such control?"

"They are the guardians of our world. They make sure that none of the natural laws are interfered with." He glanced around and saw the courtyard crowd hanging on his every word. His every move mirrored his exasperation as he pulled her toward the Keep. "What we have to say to one another on this subject is between the two of us, Susan. I have no wish to air my personal life and opinions in front of everyone in my Clan."

Her fury with him rose even higher, and she

leaned back against the pressure he was exerting on her. No one was going to manhandle her and tell her what to do or where to do it.

"Ach, woman, have you no sense?" he asked, obviously reaching the end of his patience.

He swung back to her, not relinquishing his grip on her arm. When she saw the look in his golden gaze, her eyes widened in panic and she tried to release his grip on her arm. She kicked him, hurting her foot more than his shin, and gasped when it became clear that he intended to ignore her assault to pursue an assault of his own.

His dark head bent to her, but it seemed like forever before his lips touched hers. She trembled with anger, and then with the heat that flashed through her, when he made it clear that he was the one in command and that he intended to take all that she had, whether she was willing to give it or not.

In the space of a breathless sob, Susan became aware of a black fury that pulsed through her, doubling the intensity of the fierce desire that demanded surrender and no retreat, regardless of the consequences. The heat grew and blacked out the awareness of the people in the courtyard who were witnessing this shameful scene between a Clan Lord and his soon-to-be lady. She felt the strength of her hand grasping a softly indented waist and the beginning curve of buttocks, the other hand tangling with the soft long curls at the nape of a feminine neck.

Suddenly, she realized what was happening, and she reared back, breaking the contact with Jared's mouth, gasping with relief when she found herself once again in her own mind, not his. The lungs that inhaled air were hers, the blood pounding through her veins was hers, the heart beating triple time was hers, and the warm heat that dampened her was female, not male. Still snared in his angry arms, Susan almost fell with the sensation of relief that weakened her knees, but Jared held her and did not permit her to fall.

Her awareness of the surroundings came back to her in a rush when she heard the encouraging shouts, stamps, and whistles of the stable hands in the courtyard. Mortified that he had made such a spectacle of the two of them, she reacted without thinking, swinging her hand up to strike his face. He caught her wrist when it was halfway to its mark, and she felt the awesome strength of his fingers as they clamped around the fragile bones of her wrist and forced her hand down between them. With a shrinking feeling of horror at her lack of control, she saw that his face was flushed with fury.

"Oh, God, I'm sorry," she cried in anguish, appalled by her action.

Without a word he bent down and clamped his arms around her thighs, tossing her up high and over his shoulder. The blood rushed to her face in the upside-down position and her only view was that of the leather that covered his back. Although she was furious, she felt no fear as he walked, taking long, ground-eating strides.

Anger. Excitement. Anticipation. Yes, she felt those emotions, but she felt no fear that Jared would really hurt her. She thumped on his back. "Put me down!" There was no response. "Put me down, I say!" she demanded again. Experimentally, she tried to kick him, but her feet flailed uselessly at the air.

"If you keep that up, you'll end up looking even more ridiculous than you already do slung the way you are over my shoulder like a sack of grain,"

Jared said, obviously not strained in the slightest bit by her weight.

Susan thumped his back again—this time with feeling. "Put me down."

"I'm not putting you down until we reach the privacy of my apartment," he said. "We can talk there—without being disturbed."

At that threat, she shivered with what she pinpointed as excited anticipation, but inexplicably she renewed her frenzied attack on his back regardless of how ridiculous she looked. "I don't want to talk or anything else," she cried, thumping him right above the kidneys and feeling immense satisfaction when she heard him grunt in response. Someone opened the door to the Keep, and she was aware of the change in light levels from the dark outdoors to the brightly lit interior, but no one moved to save her from her ignominious position until they were halfway across the great hall.

"Jared!"

Susan picked up her head and saw Magda, but seeing the expression on the Widow's face, Susan wasn't sure if she was relieved or upset at being rescued by Magda.

Jared slowed, as if deciding whether to acknowledge Magda's interference or not, and then he sighed and turned around to face the Widow, as if her demand for his attention was stronger than any defiance he might have wished to exhibit.

"What is the meaning of this—spectacle?" Magda asked, her voice cold with disapproval.

Jared bent from the waist and deposited Susan gently on the stone floor of the hall, but he held onto her hand, making it clear that he had no intention of allowing her to escape him. "Spectacle?" Jared asked, his eyes narrowing as he looked at the slim figure of his mother. "Susan and I were

155

merely searching out a private place to discuss a slight difference of opinion on what's to happen tomorrow."

"Spectacle," Magda said firmly. "I heard noise in the courtyard and went to the window to see if you had found Susan. While standing there I was subjected to a vulgar display of temper and an absolutely shameful exhibition of ill-timed passion which was also witnessed by half the Keep. Have you no shame, Jared? Have you no conception of the dishonor that you do Susan by subjecting her to the whistles and catcalls of the stable boys and the laundresses? You bring disgrace upon the Clan and the woman who tomorrow will be your wife."

"Wife?" Susan repeated faintly. She had suspected that what Jared kept referring to as the joining had some sexual connotation, but never had she imagined that it meant marriage. Marriage denoted a commitment, a long-term commitment, and if there was one thing she was unwilling to do, it was to commit to anything long-term in this time.

"Now, wait a minute," she began, looking up at Jared and seeing the dark flush creep along his cheekbones.

"You accuse *me* of bringing disgrace upon our Clan, Mother?" Jared asked pointedly, completely ignoring Susan's protest. "It seems to me that your accusation could well be directed at another, one much more worthy of your reproach."

Susan saw Magda's face drain of color as the woman clutched her hand over her heart. Susan frowned, wondering why such a simple statement could bring so much distress, but seeing the look on Magda's face, there was no possible way that she was about to ask for an explanation.

Jared continued, his tone almost disinterested. "Our little disagreement was on precisely the subject of the joining tomorrow, Mother. Susan was rather insistent about discussing the matter in the courtyard. I decided to search out more private quarters in which to continue our discussion."

Although Magda remained pale, she seemed to regain possession of her poise. "In anticipation of your finding Susan and knowing that neither one of you had eaten, I arranged for a light repast to be prepared. I shall have it served in the tower room, where we can discuss this further."

"Not the tower," Jared said, seemingly jolted out of his indifference.

"The tower is private, Jared," Magda said. "Where would you suggest if not the tower? Your room? Impossible. Susan's room? Even more impossible. Not even a chaperone such as myself could protect you from the gossip and erroneous conclusion that would arise in the Clans under those circumstances."

"Since when have we been worried about the gossip of the Clans?"

"Representatives of most of the Clans will attend the joining tomorrow. There must not be a breath of scandal or any question that the joining has been anticipated."

"Anticipated? What does she mean—anticipated?" Susan asked Jared, trying to find an anchor point in a conversation that found her superfluous and reluctant to address the question to Magda, who seemed to be unapproachable.

Jared pinned his gaze on his mother, although the pressure of his grip around the flesh of Susan's wrist increased subtly. "She means that we cannot be alone lest I lose control of my good sense and submit to the sensual urges that are screaming at me to bed you." He swung his gaze to her, and she had to will herself not to flinch away from the molten gold of his eyes.

"Oh," Susan said, swallowing with difficulty at the possessiveness she read in his gaze.

"Come," Magda said and walked regally to the staircase that led up to the tower.

Jared followed, still holding her wrist, and Susan limped after him, suppressing the groan that threatened to escape her lips at the idea of climbing the stairs. At the foot of the steps, Jared turned and before she could object, he swept her up into his arms.

"Your feet are sore and tired," he said by way of explanation. "Surely, Magda, there can be no objection to me helping my lady up the stairs to the tower room?"

Susan caught a glimpse of Magda's lips as they pressed together. In that moment, if she had ever had any doubts that Jared was his mother's son, those doubts would have been dispelled. The expression was one that she'd seen on Jared's face a multitude of times, both in her dreams and since she'd come to his world.

"There is no objection to that, Lord Jared," Magda replied formally, turning and continuing up into the tower.

Susan lifted her arm and curled it around Jared's neck, smiling up at him uncertainly when he looked down at her. Her heart lightened when he smiled back, the warmth in his eyes and on his lips reminiscent of the heat of the sun at noon.

His warmth eased some of her uncertainty, and she felt more comfortable even as they headed for that unknown tower room. She was aware when they passed the level where her bedroom was located, and she spared a brief thought for the comfort of a bath and clean clothes. Regretfully, there wasn't much left except tatters of what Magda had called a court dress.

They passed another level before reaching the room at the top of the tower. Magda pushed open the door and Jared carried Susan in and deposited her on a bed off to the side. He knelt on the floor in front of her and picked up one foot, easing the slipper off. He *tsked* under his breath when he saw the condition of the stocking where it clung in a few places by threads, his face intent in the sudden light that glowed in the room as Magda walked around and touched the glowlights.

"Push down the stocking, Susan. Mother, get someone to bring a bowlful of the bathing liquid and some gauze."

"It'll be okay," Susan said, still basking in the warmth that had radiated through her at his smile. "It's mostly just scrapes and a few bruises."

Magda came over to look over Jared's shoulder. "Scrapes and bruises! Child, how did you walk?"

Susan smiled. "I didn't walk. Jared carried me."

The Widow went to the door. "I'll be back shortly."

Susan sat quietly while Jared eased off the other slipper and shook his head. "Push down the stockings, Susan," he ordered. She looked at him strangely, and watched as the lines around his mouth bracketed more deeply. "If I touch anything but your feet right now, we're both lost, and the Widows would never forgive me my loss of control."

A blush burned in her cheeks as she reached under the tattered remains of her long skirt and pushed the stockings down from her thighs. His words evoked a picture in her mind that was hard to ignore.

Janice Tarantino

"I don't understand everything that you and Magda were talking about," she said hesitantly. "This joining you keep mentioning is actually marriage?"

He nodded. "Essentially, yes, but it's a bit more than that—as I explained to you. Common Clan members marry. Clan Lords and crystal women join."

"But I'm not a crystal woman, Jared," she insisted quietly, anxious now that he understand what she was trying to say. "I can't help you if you need a crystal woman."

"You don't carry a crystal on your forehead, Susan, but you carry the star."

She frowned at him. "The star? Oh! You mean that mark on my forehead. I noticed that this morning. I couldn't figure out where it came from." Her fingers moved up to touch the place where she knew the star was. "The only thing I could think of was that Magda touched my forehead with this black crystal before she brought me here." She fished under the neck of her dress and brought out the black crystal on its gold chain.

Jared turned his head for a moment, and then he turned back to her, but his eyes avoided looking at the black crystal that swung from her fingers. "I knew you had the crystal. I saw it last night while you slept after being wounded by the Ptai."

"But would such a thing make the mark of a star?"

Jared got to his feet and walked to the long, scarred table that stood to one side of the room. "I don't know."

"What is it, Jared? What's wrong? It's the crystal, isn't it?" Susan looked down at the crystal where it swung from her fingers and frowned. Jared had

160

closed up tighter than a clam at the sight of it. Why?

"The crystal belonged to Evie, my wife."

Susan had a horrible thought. "You mean she wore it on a chain around her neck like me," she said, hoping she was right.

Jared shoved his hands in the pockets of his trousers and turned to face her again. "Evie wore no chain."

The crystal dropped from Susan's fingers and lay against her chest. "No! Tell me what I'm thinking is wrong, Jared," Susan cried. Her fingers clawed up and fastened around the crystal.

He moved back to her swiftly and his hand closed around hers over the crystal before she could tear it from her neck. "This was my wife's mind crystal. It formed on her forehead when she was five years old, and shone like a sparkling white diamond until she reached puberty. Then it slowly changed to green, indicating that she was ready to be joined. She was sixteen summers old and I was twenty-six. The crystal turned red then. At her death it became this opaque black." He gently pried her fingers open.

The crystal rested in her palm, slick, black, and opaque. Still Jared did not touch it. "A Clan Lord uses the mind crystal of his wife in a singular way after her death. The crystal retains the memories of the crystal woman and by holding it and rubbing it a Clan Lord can access those memories and, in a way, relive the happiness of the past. But in doing that, the Clan Lord forgets to live in the present. He does not eat. He does not sleep. He does not let the mind crystal out of his hand, because if he does, then the real world will crash in upon him again and with that reality comes the realization that his wife, his crystal woman who was part of him, is dead."

Janice Tarantino

"But . . ." She fell silent and squeezed her hand closed over the crystal again.

"So a Clan Lord lives in the past through the mind crystal and eventually dies because there is nothing in this world to hold him."

"But if I have your wife's mind crystal, that means you didn't have it."

His eyes met hers, and she almost cried out at the depth of torment and sorrow she saw there. It was this torment and sorrow she had seen in his eyes when she had seen him in her dreams.

"No, I didn't have Evie's crystal. It would have eased my grief at her passing and allowed me to eventually follow her into death."

"Well, I'm glad they didn't give it to you!" she cried. "I'm glad you didn't die." After a short moment, she fumbled for the clasp at the back of her neck. "But the crystal isn't mine. I shouldn't have it."

"It is your mind crystal now, Susan," Magda said from the doorway. "Everything you experience—your perceptions, the way you see things—is being recorded in that crystal. There is no longer anything of Evie about it." She came into the room and placed the bowl of bathing liquid on the floor near where Jared knelt.

Susan looked at Jared. "But you don't want to touch it."

He shook his head. "If I touched it, I would feel its emptiness. It would be painful for me."

She frowned as he picked up one of her feet and eased it into the bowl.

"The Widows had to keep Evie's crystal from Jared," Magda said, obviously feeling the need to explain her actions. She beckoned for a serving girl carrying a large tray of food to come in, and directed the placement of the food on the table

162

even as she continued. "Jared, out of all the Clan Lords that terrible day, had to live."

"Because of this Prophecy thing you Widows told me about?" Susan was aware of a blessed feeling of coolness as the liquid began to work its healing magic. When the odors of the food drifted in her direction, it became clear that she was starving. She'd thought herself beyond hunger.

Magda dismissed the serving girl. "Yes, because Jared is the one foretold in the Prophecy. He is the only one who can challenge Ruhl and stand a chance of survival. To do that, he must have a crystal woman. All the crystal women save Ruhl's were murdered, including Jared's Evie."

Susan frowned. "And so you had to find someone to act as a crystal woman. I still don't understand why he needs a crystal woman."

Magda shook her head. "The only way to defeat Ruhl is to issue a Challenge. Throughout the long centuries the ways of the Challenge have been hidden from us. All we know is that a crystal woman is needed because of the power she wields. How that power is to be used, we do not know."

Susan looked down and saw Jared lifting her foot from the bowl and carefully wrapping gauze around it. "All that you say may be true, Magda, but I am not a crystal woman."

"You are not a crystal woman as we recognize one in our world. But you have the power. The mind crystals merely amplify the power that resides in the mind. If the necessary amount or facility of power exists without a crystal, then an amplifier is not needed."

"I have no power."

"You do not want to admit that you have it, and because of that, you don't realize how strong you really are." Magda stood behind Jared and

163

watched critically as he wrapped Susan's foot.

"How do you expect to defeat this Ruhl if you don't know what needs to be done?" Susan asked, trying to move the discussion to something other than some elusive mythical power she was supposed to possess.

"Somewhere the knowledge exists. The Widows have been doing much research into the problem in the last few months."

Jared looked up over his shoulder at his mother. "You haven't mentioned this to me."

"It was still speculative," Magda said softly. "Until we had something concrete there was no point in mentioning it."

Jared turned his attention back to Susan's foot. "The Widows' plan to overcome Ruhl will never work unless the ancient knowledge is discovered."

"But we must attempt to stop Ruhl in any case. We have had several disturbing intelligence reports come in about his activities in the south," Magda said. "The Widows will continue to search for the knowledge of the Challenge, but you and Susan must try to discover a way to implement the power by yourselves. We're trying to approach this problem on both levels."

"What intelligence?" Jared asked, his voice sharp.

"Ruhl intends to declare himself king. He traffics with renegade Techs. Contrary to our agreements with the rational and peaceful Tech government, there have been reports of ships landing in the Western Desert. Likewise there have been reports of people disappearing. The conjecture is that they are unwilling conscripts to Ruhl's intensified mining of the crystal."

"The village I visited today mentioned seeing bright lights in the desert. Out farther than they dared to investigate. The village chief said several men had disappeared." Jared frowned, his hand closed around Susan's ankle. "It may be Orsin and his band of miscreants. You know Orsin is looking for revenge for losing his rank and standing at the Academy and in the military."

Magda shrugged. "We'll not know until more reports come in."

"If Ruhl himself is dealing with Orsin's Techs, then he has put himself beyond the laws and traditions of the Clans," Jared said thoughtfully. "Perhaps the Widows were not so wrong to follow the course they did."

"Our world is in deep danger, Jared. Did you think the Widows would act so decisively if it were not? Did you think we were doing all this for our amusement?" Magda asked, her voice surprised and tinged with anger. "Ruhl is a danger to us all, and more than that, if he is trafficking with malcontent Techs, there is the possibility that he is importing substances declared illegal on our world. Substances that could prove harmful to our returning ecology. Substances that could destroy all that we have gained."

"You will go against him?" Susan asked, looking at Jared. "What will happen if you don't have a crystal woman?"

"With or without a crystal woman I shall go against him." His hand trembled against Susan's ankle before he let go and rose to his feet. "The food is getting cold."

Susan allowed him to lift her and set her in one of the wooden chairs at the end of the long scarred table. "Is Ruhl such a terrible person? Can't he be reasoned with?"

"Ruhl is a monster!" Magda exclaimed, seating herself across from Susan. "He seeks only to satisfy his own desires. He cares nothing for anyone else. He is a murderer."

Jared froze, his hands tightening on the back of his chair. "You have proof?"

"We found a Tech who swears that he sold Ruhl a disrupter," Magda replied.

"A disrupter?" Susan asked, frowning.

"I want to speak to that Tech," Jared demanded, sitting down.

Magda stared at the table. "He is dead."

"But his testimony was reliable?"

"As reliable as it could be under the circumstances," the Widow answered.

"What circumstances?" Susan asked.

Jared stared at his mother for a moment, his golden eyes narrowed. "Torture," he replied in a low voice.

Susan pushed back her plate, suddenly nauseated. "Torture?"

"If that Tech had even the slightest part in the slaughter of those innocents, then he deserved the method of dying," Jared said implacably, fixing his golden eyes on Susan. "And since Ruhl is the one responsible for their deaths, I shall be his executioner, with or without a crystal woman, with or without the support of the Council, with or without the blessings of the Widows. If I die in the trying, then so be it. But Ruhl murdered one hundred and three women and children whose greatest sin was to bear a half-inch crystal on their foreheads. He will die even though he is my brother."

Susan stared at him in shock. Thoughts of her own brother Drew passed fleetingly through her mind, filling her with an overwhelming love, but she pushed them aside. "How can you even think of killing your brother?"

Magda lifted her head, tears sparkling in her

eyes, the black crystal on her forehead gleaming. "My firstborn son. The Chief of the Dakbar Clan, and murderer of innocent women and children in the name of power. Would that he had died within my womb."

"But you're talking about killing your brother." Susan simply could not fathom the idea.

"Death is the result of the Challenge of power. Yes, I am talking about killing my brother," Jared said. "You do not understand. Ruhl is capable of reducing this planet to a cinder, a spark of nothing revolving around our sun. We are not talking about one death here, we are talking about the deaths of millions of people and animals. The death of our planet. Ruhl will squeeze this world until it is dry and then move on."

"Collis knows about the chasm between times," Magda said. "I suspected as much when the Ptai attacked Susan when I was bringing her over."

"She and Ruhl know?" Jared asked, horror and a strange kind of fear in his voice.

"We believe that Collis has made at least one trip across," Magda said. "Fedorra is terribly afraid that Ruhl and Collis will move through the chasm to another time. Their workings would not be recognized until it was too late, and there is nothing that the Widows can do to prevent it."

"Do you mean that my time may be in danger just because Ruhl and Collis know about it?" Susan asked. "Why didn't you tell me this earlier?"

"You were assimilating many things during your meeting with the Widows. I didn't think it right to burden you with such knowledge then. But it appears that you need this information to be committed to our cause. I believe Ruhl and Collis would prosper in your time and eventually gain

167

power." Magda stared across the table at Susan.

"My time is too sane for that. No one would believe in their magic or power."

"And that is exactly where the danger lies. In the denial of either their magic or their power. Their use of it would not even be recognized before it was too late to stop," Magda said.

"Is this true?" Susan demanded of Jared. "Is what she saying possible? I remember that Fedorra said something about it, but she didn't say that anyone else had actually crossed that godawful chasm."

"I remember being in your time, Susan," Jared said softly. "The air was crisp and heavy with oxygen. The earth was dark and rich and fertile. You must have many other riches there." He nodded. "Yes, I think that if he could, Ruhl would forsake our time for yours."

Susan stared down at her plate for a moment before she looked up, her decision made. "Then I guess I'm in. You understand that I don't believe I can help you in the way you think I can—with this power nonsense—but if the slightest chance exists that my time is in danger, then I have to do whatever I can to prevent that from happening."

Magda closed her eyes in what appeared to be relief. "I knew you wouldn't disappoint us, Susan."

"Let us understand each other, Magda," she said, her voice suddenly turning hard-edged. "I will do what I can to help you, but I must go back to my time. I have a brother there. A brother who's probably worried sick about me. I have a job. I have a life." She looked from Magda to Jared. "I must be permitted to go back."

It was as though a veil fell over Jared's face and there was not even a whisper of his presence in her mind. She was unable to sense his reaction to her words, unable to tell what he was thinking.

But she wasn't able to dwell on it, so deep was her panic at the mere thought of never seeing her brother again, of never returning to her work, her world. She had to make them—him—understand how she felt.

Even though Jared knew the mind-probe he felt was inadvertent on Susan's part, he withdrew from her as far as was possible. Something close to fear stirred within him at the idea of joining with this woman only to be ripped apart from her. But she must never know this. She must never know that her leaving would mean his death. Even after the joining he would have to conceal the knowledge from her.

Not trusting himself to speak, he simply nodded his agreement to her plea.

"You have our promise," Magda said, drawing Susan's attention. Silence fell around them as each became lost in their thoughts of the near future.

Finally, Susan looked at Jared, wondering at the sudden flare of heat she felt when she thought about what her agreement to the plans of the Widows meant. "This joining thing tomorrow—is it really necessary?"

"Our minds have already meshed a few times," Jared said, addressing his mother. "You know more than I about this. Is it necessary?"

Magda nodded. "It is imperative. Each time your minds have meshed, your bodies have been sexually stimulated in some way or you have been in danger, is this not true?"

Susan rolled her eyes. Great! Not only was she being railroaded into this whole situation, but her sex life was now going to be verbally scrutinized—with Jared's mother, no less.

Jared nodded, and Susan thought she detected a faint stain of red high on his cheekbones. So, he wasn't so happy discussing this kind of thing with Magda either, she thought, repressing a grin.

"From what we can tell, the joining will enable you to mesh your minds at any time, not just under the stimulation of sensual energy," Magda said, seemingly undeterred by the subject matter.

"Then we could just make love and accomplish the same thing, couldn't we?" Susan asked, struggling not to stutter and blush at what she was suggesting. "I mean, under the circumstances I'm not so anxious to make a commitment like marriage. I don't even know if you have such a thing like divorce here, although if you have marriages, you must have divorces."

"Divorce?" Magda asked.

"Uh-oh," Susan murmured, seeing problems ahead. "Divorce is when the marriage breaks up."

"Marriage is until death," Jared said quietly. "Joining is to death and beyond."

"That is not necessarily so, Jared," Magda pointed out.

"Wait a minute," Susan said, holding up her hand. "I can't commit to something that can't be undone. I intend to return to my time when this is all over."

"I think there's something you don't understand, Susan," Jared said, looking at her, his golden eyes gleaming. "It is not a foregone conclusion that we shall win against Ruhl. The Challenge guarantees nothing. We may die, just as Ruhl and his crystal woman may die."

Susan's hands clenched in her lap. She had known. She just hadn't wanted to admit it, but Jared was evidently determined that she make this decision with her eyes wide open, damn him.

"I understand, Jared," she said softly, her eyes lifting and meeting his. "All I want is your promise that if we defeat Ruhl, I have the option of returning to my world—to my own time."

Jared pushed his chair away from the table and rose to his feet. "You have my word, Susan. When Ruhl is defeated, you shall be returned to your own world. Marriage or no. Joining or no. The traditions and laws of our world have no claim on you once you have returned."

"But they do," Susan objected. "Even if you let me go back, I can't leave you here married or joined to me or whatever you want to call it. Then you wouldn't be able to marry again, would you?"

"It will make no difference, Susan," Jared said, walking over to the window. Magda followed her son with her eyes, and Susan thought she saw sorrow in them.

"But it has to make a difference. If there are no crystal women left, I understand that you won't be able to join with them, but you might want to marry again. It seems to me that we'll have to be divorced or something before I go back."

"Do not push the issue, Susan," Jared roared, spinning on his heel, his eyes blazing at her. "I'll not join or marry again after you leave us."

"It is imperative that you join with Jared, Susan," Magda said. "The Clans will not accept that you and Jared fulfill the Prophecy unless you are treated as a crystal woman. There are certain specifics laid out in the Prophecy and if even one of them is ignored, then we will have no support in our countermeasures against Ruhl's actions before we institute the Challenge."

"You keep talking about this Prophecy, but I haven't the slightest idea what it is." Susan asked. "What specifics?"

"The woman of fire will come to us from a time

unknown, the mark of the star upon her forehead. She will be a virgin of great power—"

"Hold it!" Susan said, feeling her cheeks flush, but knowing she couldn't let this go any further. Apprehensively she looked at Magda and then at Jared. "If you need a virgin for this particular ritual, then you have a very serious problem."

Chapter Nine

Susan stood by the window in her bedroom in the tower, Pris purring in her arms. The cat had wandered into her room last night and settled down on the bed with her as if they'd never been separated. Susan decided that Pris had a satisfied look about her that made her wonder about cross-breeding across the centuries.

Glancing out the window and down into the busy courtyard, Susan suppressed a shudder. "I'm awful nervous, Pris," she murmured to the cat. "They're all coming to see me get married to Jared. God, there are hundreds of people down there!" She stroked the cat behind the ears where Pris liked it best. "If you get pregnant, I'll never forgive you, you know, and if I get pregnant, I'll never forgive myself."

She recalled the blank look in Magda's eyes when she'd asked about birth control and shuddered when she recalled the answer.

"You didn't see the look in Magda's eyes, Pris. I did. And I thought Jared was going to go right through the ceiling at the idea. They seem to be very progressive in some ways here, and totally backward in others. We'll just have to hope for the best, I guess." And at the rate her luck was running, she and her cat would go back to her world pregnant. She frowned. If they got to go back at all.

Not that she doubted Jared's promise to her, but the more she thought about this Challenge thing that everyone seemed to hope would kill Ruhl, it seemed to her that the chances seemed equal that it could also kill her and Jared.

The only thing that she had going for her in this whole weird situation was the fact that her mind appeared to resonate with Jared's. She interpreted that to mean that there was some mighty powerful sexual chemistry at work here. The idea that she had any of this power that everyone ranted and raged about, she dismissed.

"A few glimmerings here and there, Pris. That's all. Faint premonitions. A few dreams. Certainly not something that could be used to destroy someone." Susan turned uneasily away from the window. The idea of killing or destroying another living being worried her. She had trouble swatting insects.

Magda had told her to stay in her room until someone came for her. She was not to see Jared until the actual joining ceremony, which was to take place at noon.

This ceremony troubled her. She'd asked Magda if there were any books or anything that would describe the ceremony so that she would be prepared. But she'd seen the look that Magda had sent in Jared's direction. She'd also seen the slight shake of his head that had indicated no, and she'd been left wondering whether he'd meant there were no books or she was not to be given them.

Magda had simply replied that she would be guided through it. The marriage ceremony would be performed on the steps of the great hall where all could see, but then they would proceed indoors and only Clan Lords and the Widows would be permitted to witness the actual joining ceremony.

What was so secret that only select people could witness it? Just thinking about it made her nervous. And she was sure what she was imagining was ten times worse than the actual ceremony. And this waiting was a hundred times worse than anything she'd ever imagined.

She'd woken at dawn, and despite Magda's injunction against leaving her room, she'd opened the door cautiously and had nearly jumped out of her skin when she'd seen the Widows' guard standing outside her doorway. He'd made no response to her greeting. For heaven's sake, he hadn't even looked at her. So she'd closed the door again and taken to pacing.

Her feet had healed during the night. That was another strange thing. The quick rate at which she healed here. Back home, some of her crazy friends were into crystals and their different properties. Did the mind crystal have some kind of healing power?

Thoughtfully, she picked up the crystal from where it rested on her breast and held it in her palm.

It sparkled a brilliant emerald green back at her. She blinked and stared at it again. The crystal had been black and totally opaque when she'd gone to sleep last night. It had been the last thing she'd looked at, wondering about Jared's first wife, Evie.

Susan frowned. Was this change in the crystal something that normally happened? Who could she ask? Jared had said something about the crystal being clear and then turning to green at puberty. She smiled a little to herself. At 28 she was definitely past being pubescent.

But what else had he said? Something about after being married, the crystal turned red? If she carried the correlation a little further, she could make a connection between marriage and sexual experience. If that was the case and the crystal was, as Magda had said, reflecting her state of being and not the dead Evie's, then the crystal hanging around her neck should be red, not green.

Why wasn't it red?

There had been too many changes in the past 36 hours. All the scars on her body had disappeared, even the one on her elbow that she'd acquired as a child when she'd fallen constantly on her roller skates. But on second thought, the changes had been occurring in a longer time frame than the past 36 hours. The scar on her face had disappeared the day after she'd started wearing the crystal necklace.

"Why isn't the crystal red, Pris?" Susan asked, and then grinned to herself. Her question about birth control hadn't been the only bombshell she'd dropped on the Widows' plans last night. Her comments on her lack of virginity had shocked Magda, although after his initial shock Jared had seemed to take the news in stride. He had told his mother that the moral code of one time could not be expected to apply to another, and that he'd known of more than one crystal woman who'd worn a veil at the joining ceremony to disguise the blood red color of the crystals on her forehead. Magda had muttered something about arranging proof and

176

that had been the end of that. Only now did Susan wonder what proof Magda was going to arrange.

Pris meowed and jumped down from Susan's arms, prowling around the bedroom door.

"Is someone finally coming or do you just want to go out?" Susan asked.

Pris rubbed her head against the door.

She opened it and Pris darted off, but four Widows stood outside along with several young girls behind them carrying what Susan surmised were her bridal garments. She swung the door wide and everyone filed in. What had originally been a spacious bedroom shrank to the size of a crowded bathroom. The young servant girls deposited the clothing on the bed and then left without saying a word.

One of the younger Widows stepped forward. "We have come to prepare you for the ceremony, Lady Susan. I am called Gersta." She gestured to each of the Widows. "This is Amaranthe, Lila, and Mithra."

Susan smiled tentatively. "I probably don't need much help unless the dress you brought has as many buttons as the last one Magda brought me."

Gersta looked shocked at the suggestion. "It is our duty to prepare you, Lady Susan. It would be against the tradition of the Widows to do otherwise. Amaranthe will prepare your bath. Lila will dress your hair. I will assist you in the gowning."

Susan looked askance at the old Widow named Mithra.

Gersta cleared her throat. "Mithra is to supervise."

"What color's your crystal, girl?" Mithra asked.

"This?" Susan asked, holding out the emerald green crystal on the gold chain.

"Green?" Mithra cackled. "Now that surprises me."

"Mithra!" Gersta exclaimed.

"Go on, Gersta. I remember the night of my joining. I'm not senile enough to have forgotten it, but you act as if a Clan Lord never pricked your nether regions. You wouldn't be a Widow if one hadn't, and don't you forget it." The old woman peered at Susan, who was trying to keep from choking with laughter. "I am surprised that your crystal's still green. Knowing Lord Jared like I do, I would've sworn it would be red by now. His Evie was my grandniece. I've known him since he was a boy. He was always in some sort of trouble."

Susan couldn't help herself. She grinned at the old woman. "Actually, I'm rather surprised that the crystal's green myself."

Mithra cackled again. "Had a few close calls, have you? I knew it." She slapped her hand on the knee that was disguised beneath layers of skirts. "You'll be a rare match for young Lord Jared, you will."

"Lady Susan," Gersta pleaded, "please don't encourage her."

Gersta was a prude, Susan decided. She rather liked Mithra. At least the woman spoke her mind.

The old woman waved her toward the bathroom. "Go on. Let Amaranthe give you your bath, but be quick because we're running out of time."

In the bathroom, Amaranthe began to fill the tub.

"I really can do this by myself, Amaranthe. I don't need any help," Susan said.

The Widow held out her hand for Susan's nightgown. "This is our custom, Susan. I won't intrude any more than is necessary."

Susan sighed and tugged the nightgown over her head, dropping it into Amaranthe's outstretched hand. She bathed quickly, but Amaranthe insisted on washing her hair.

"Mithra likes you," Amaranthe said. Her voice was tinged with laughter.

"Is that unusual? For Mithra to like someone?" Susan asked, trying not to feel self-conscious when the Widow began to wash her back.

"Yes, Mithra despises most of us. I get along with her all right, but poor Gersta just can't cope with her. Mithra knows it and deliberately plagues the girl. She says things that she knows will shock Gersta just for the fun of it. Mithra's really not that bad. She just pretends to be. She's been a Widow for a long time, but she was deeply loved by her Clan Lord. She still grieves for him after all these years. Not every joining carries such deep devotion. Not every joining is as perfect as theirs must have been."

Susan frowned. "Then a joining doesn't have to be a love match?"

Amaranthe helped her from the bath and handed her a soft robe. "Joinings have always been arranged between families. Frequently what has been arranged turns to love. Sometimes not, but there is always deep respect and reverence. Lord Jared adored Evie. We never really thought he would go along with this scheme of . . ." The Widow's eyes widened in dismay. "Oh, dear, I shouldn't have said that. Not with you about to join with him."

"No, that's all right," Susan said quickly, at a loss to explain the sudden tight feeling in her stomach. "The more I know the better I'll be able to cope with the situation. Jared didn't want to do this?"

179

Amaranthe shook her head. "A second joining has never been done before that we know of. He was dead set against it, and he gave Magda a terrible time the night you arrived."

"What changed his mind?" Susan didn't dare admit, even to herself, what she hoped Amaranthe's answer would be.

"His oath to the Widows and his sense of honor and duty. He never had a choice. Not really." Amaranthe looked closely at Susan. "I shouldn't have said anything."

"No, really. It's all right." Susan looked away, shocked by her reaction to Amaranthe's words. Surely she wasn't foolish enough to think that Jared might feel something for her, was she? She had known from the beginning that Jared would go through with this joining only because it was what the Widows demanded. He had never given her any reason to think otherwise. She frowned. Why did she think it should be different? Why did she wish it to *be* different?

"No, it's not all right, but what's done is done and what's been said has been said. The only thing we can do is go on from here." Amaranthe opened the door to the bedroom. "Lila will do your hair now."

Mithra's face brightened when she saw Susan. "Here she is now. As bright and pink as the day she was born. And as perfect. You are really lovely, child, with all that white skin and red hair. Sit in the chair, Susan. Lila is wonderful with hair. You won't recognize yourself when she's finished with you."

Susan sat quietly, thinking, while Lila brushed her hair.

"See those crystal strands, Susan?" Mithra asked, pointing to the heap of sparkling crystals on the table. "Lila will twist them into your hair and they'll turn as green as the crystal around your neck."

"Green," Susan said, knowing she had to ask. "What does the green color mean, Mithra? Truly?"

Mithra frowned a little and got up somewhat painfully from her chair by the window. "Truly, child? Truly the green color stands for innocence. The crystal can't be tricked. It reflects the true essence of the wearer. Some say the green crystal stands only for virginity, but I believe it reflects also the purity of the heart." Her voice grew softer as she approached where Susan sat and the crystals were heaped.

Susan watched as the old woman reached out and touched a strand of crystal on the table. As she looked, Susan saw the crystals swirl and take on a dark tinge that changed slowly to black but with a hint of green in their centers. The old woman bent down and looked into Susan's leaf green eyes.

"Has no one explained to you what will happen today, child?"

Susan shook her head and then stopped, aware that Lila was twisting one of the strands into her hair. "Not really. Magda told me that the marriage ceremony would take place on the stairs outside the great hall and then certain people would move inside where the second ceremony will be performed."

"And that's all they told you?" Mithra's eyebrow raised and then she chuckled softly. "Perhaps that's for the best. Perhaps." She touched Susan's hand with her own wrinkled one. "Don't be frightened, child. Whatever happens, don't be frightened. Remember that no crystal woman ever died from a joining ceremony. Not one ever came close." Mithra's gaze lit mischievously as she looked in Gersta's direction. "Except maybe Gersta. I've heard tales that she cried and screamed through the entire ceremony because at the end she knew she would lose her precious virginity."

"I did not, Mithra!" Gersta said, her cheeks staining red.

"What? Cry and scream? Or lose your virginity? Which was it, girl?" But her hand was gentle on Susan's as she nudged it good-naturedly. "Jared's a good lad. He'll treat you right."

Susan stared down at her hands and told herself that she wasn't afraid. She'd made love before, regardless of what the green crystals were telling everyone. She knew what it was like. There was no reason to be afraid.

But she was. From what Mithra said and from what she had already gleaned, there was more to this joining ceremony than just the uttering of a few words. This was a different society. Suddenly, she pressed a white-knuckled hand to her mouth to prevent herself from telling everyone that she'd changed her mind and didn't want to go through with this after all.

Gersta hurried over and knelt on the floor beside her. "See what you've done now, Mithra? You've frightened her." Gersta brought Susan's hand down from her mouth and closed her fingers tightly around Susan's. "Truly, Lady Susan, there is nothing to be frightened of. The ceremony is probably just different from those in your time." She glanced over at Mithra and then lowered her voice to a whisper. "It will be all right. If I survived it, you certainly will. I'm a coward, although I refuse to let Mithra know that." Gersta smiled ruefully. "I think she suspects, though."

"What are you blithering about?" Mithra asked. "It's getting late. Let Lila finish her hair, Gersta."

"I'm doing just fine, Mithra," Lila said serenely. "I'm almost finished."

"Good."

Silence fell in the room. Amaranthe stood quietly by the door, Lila twisted more crystal strands into Susan's hair, and Gersta began to fiddle with the clothing laid out on the bed. There didn't seem to be much of it, Susan noticed.

"There," Lila said, giving Susan's hair a final pat. "I'm finished, and it does look lovely, doesn't it, Mithra?"

Mithra got up again from her chair and circled Susan, reaching out and touching her hair here and there, but finally she nodded. "It's perfect. These crystals are priceless. The Techs are willing to pay fortunes for the few we sell them. Wars have been fought over these crystals, although most will deny it and tell you that there were other reasons for the fighting. But it all comes down to the crystals. Don't let anyone tell you different." Mithra stood up, and Susan would have sworn that she heard the old woman's bones snap and crackle with the movement. "Let Gersta dress you now. It's nearly time."

Gersta held up a chain that was studded with clear crystals and waited expectantly. Susan stared at the chain and then looked at Gersta. "What is it? A necklace?"

"No, it's a maiden chain. You don't have these in your world? Open the robe, Lady Susan," she instructed. Susan hesitated for a second and then resignedly opened the robe.

"We fasten the chain around your hips so," Gersta explained, "and then we lock it with the crystal stone in this ring." She applied the ring to the lock. Susan watched her movements, and raised an eyebrow when the crystals on the chain around her hips glowed green.

"Now the gown," Gersta said, turning to the bed and picking up the emerald green material. She waited while Susan shrugged off the robe and clenched her teeth while Gersta seemed to take forever getting the gown up and over her shoulders.

"Where are the rest of the clothes?" Susan asked, even as she realized the significance of the color green in this world. These people struggled and dedicated their lives to make their world green again and so they translated the color of green, growing things to their ritual ceremonies.

"The rest?" Gersta looked at her blankly. "Other than the veil and the slippers this is all. Let me seal the clasp on the dress and then you're ready."

"Other than the veil and the slippers?" Susan asked, unable to keep the tinge of sarcasm from her voice, as Gersta pressed the ring to the one clasp on the dress, that one at the waist. The rest of the sleeveless dress gathered and flowed around her. She looked down as she moved her leg to take a step forward and saw her leg. "I need a pin."

"A pin?"

"Either I need a pin or I need some underwear. I refuse to go out in front of all those people without any underwear in a dress that's slit down the front and held together with only a clasp at the waist. What if it falls off?"

Mithra's cackle of laughter startled her, but the Widow didn't say anything.

Gersta frowned. "This is the traditional marriage gown, Lady Susan."

"How do I know the clasp won't break in the middle of the ceremony? How do I know a stiff

184

breeze won't come up? Forget it, ladies. I'm not moving until I get a pin or some underwear. Preferably both." Susan looked at each Widow defiantly. Mithra was still laughing, Lila held her hand over her mouth, Gersta looked dismayed, and Amaranthe's lips were parted in a genuine smile.

Amaranthe opened the door. "I'll let Magda know of your objections."

"We might as well finish dressing you," Gersta said, sighing. "To add anything else will be flaunting tradition, you know. All that you wear has been supplied by Lord Jared, including the crystal clasps and the key to them, which is the ring. All three were part of the same crystal. During the ceremony you will signify your consent to the proceedings by giving this ring to Lord Jared." Gersta slid the ring onto Susan's thumb.

"Don't lose that ring, child," Mithra cackled from her corner. "Lord Jared is like to be a mite upset if you do. We'd have to cut you out of the dress. Don't worry about it falling off."

Susan grinned wryly in response. "Well, that's a relief." She ducked her head as Lila approached her with the white diaphanous veil that covered her hair and touched the floor in the back. Over the veil a circlet made of intricately wrought gold and studded with clear crystals was settled so that it rested on her forehead. Gersta knelt at her feet and helped her slip on the green leather slippers.

Amaranthe arrived back in the room and smiled, holding up a tiny gold pin. "This was all Magda would consent to. She was very upset, but Lord Jared calmed her down." She handed the pin to Gersta, who fastened the gown together at mid-thigh. Amaranthe's blue eyes shone with amusement. "Lord Jared laughed and asked me to tell you that he's been to many joinings and unfortunately for the men in attendance never once has a stiff breeze been a problem."

Smiling at Amaranthe was difficult, because Susan found that her lips were trembling with anxiety. "Thank you, Amaranthe," she whispered.

Sudden concern shadowed the Widow's eyes. She slipped closer to Susan. "Bear up, my dear. You'll do fine. You look lovely."

Mithra walked around Susan and inspected her from every angle. "You'll do," she said. "It's late. Are the others ready?" she asked Amaranthe.

A few minutes later Susan walked through the empty hall, flanked by Widows and the Widows' guard. Amaranthe hurried ahead and threw open the enormous double doors leading out to the courtyard.

A breeze swept into the great hall, ruffling Susan's skirts open below her knees, and the veil lifted and flew out behind her. Susan darted a glance at Amaranthe as she passed the Widow. Amaranthe's eyes were wide as she saw the dress trying to separate, held only by the tiny gold pin. Mercifully, Mithra made no comment and only a small chuckle escaped her.

"Darn good thing you got me the pin," Susan whispered to Amaranthe, and walked to the top of the stairs leading down to the cobblestones of the courtyard.

When she appeared at the top of the steps, a murmur rose from the gathered crowd, and Susan almost reeled back against the Widows standing behind her as the seething, confused mental emanations from the crowd in the courtyard struck her. She gasped and struggled to right herself, totally confused and disoriented by the experience. Quickly, she closed her eyes and concentrated on blocking out the silent noises. After only a moment she was able to ignore the mute efflux projected by the crowd and focus on what was happening.

The sun was high above them, beating down mercilessly on the throng gathered in the courtyard, the grid above the courtyard casting long, lean intersecting shadows, and the odors of perfume and incense and not-too-frequently-washed humanity wafted in the thin air. The crowd was a colorful one and banners hung along the edges of the grid, flipping and flapping in the unpredictable breeze.

The murmurings and rustlings of the people around her suddenly quieted, hushed into silence, and they parted, crowding themselves even more, but leaving a clear path to the open portcullis at the other side of the courtyard.

Susan looked out along the path—the fear within her suddenly unfurling like the sail of a boat on the open sea—and she saw three figures standing beneath the archway of the gate.

Her breath shortened as her eyes focused on the center figure, the tallest of the three. It was Jared, and although she knew him, he was strange to her.

He looked taller, his shoulders wide, his chest broad and tapering down to a narrow waist and hips. The powerful muscles of his thighs flexed against the constraints of tight-fitting trousers as he walked the path that led to where she stood on the granite steps leading to the great hall.

His complexion was dark against the pure white of his short, sleeveless jacket that was adorned only by intricate gold embroidery. His hair was straight and as black as a raven's wing, a lock falling over his forehead. A gold earring pierced the lobe of his left ear.

Funny, she didn't remember ever noticing that he had an earring before. He looked almost piratical now. A stranger. And despite the sheer physical impact of his appearance, his eyes, as gold as cold metal beneath the black slashes of his eyebrows, were what held her in thrall as she stood and waited for his approach, for his eyes did not waver from her, although she could not tell his mood from looking into them.

He finally stood at her side, his gaze holding hers even as he reached out and took her icy fingers into the warmth of his grasp. A shiver ran through her at the heat of his touch, at the feel of his rough, callused, sword-nicked hand closing around hers. The contrast between the heat of his flesh and the coldness of his eyes stunned her. A dread feeling of uncertainty invaded her every pore as she met his eyes. She could not find even a flicker of warmth in their depths.

Didn't he want this after all? she wondered. Had he reconsidered? Did he resent being forced into this marriage?

She broke her gaze away from his to study the two who had accompanied him down the stairs.

The regal-looking woman of an indeterminate age was Magda, her hair silvered, her face unlined, her gown for once not of black but of brilliant turquoise falling from her shoulders straight to her ankles. Her bearing exuded a sense of great strength and tranquillity. Susan searched Magda's face for some reassurance, and was rewarded when the Widow inclined her head slightly and smiled. But Susan's sense of relief was short-lived when her attention turned to the man who had accompanied both Jared and Magda to her side.

He was old, his face wizened with the wrinkles of time. His body was stooped into a posture of great age. His sharp black eyes peering out from under folds of drooping flesh were hostile as he stared at her, his mouth merely a slash in the lower part of his face.

The priest, for that was what he must be, Susan decided, stood below them on the stairs and they stood facing the crowd. The priest mumbled and muttered and prompted both Jared and Susan to respond in the appropriate places.

Susan didn't understand a word the priest said, and Jared had to prompt her several times, his voice deep and dark and like velvet in sharp contrast to the bright noonday sun. In spite of the breeze, the heat began to press on her, making her head ache, and she felt as if she was wilting.

Jared's hand squeezed her elbow. "We're finished."

Blinking as if she was just awakening, Susan became aware of the cheering throng, and the precious few flowers that were thrown at her feet. Carefully, using Jared for balance, Susan bent down and picked up the colorful blooms, fighting a wave of dizziness.

Forcing herself to smile, she held the flowers high above her head and then she bowed to the crowd. The wave of emotion that flowed from the people and battered her as a result of that gesture threatened to drop her to her knees. Sensing her weakness, Jared slid his arm around her waist and pulled her close to his side. Susan looked up at him, meaning to thank him, but the words died on her lips unspoken.

His eyes were still chips of golden metal and he was pale. He looked down at her as if he wasn't sure who she was. And then Susan knew that this ceremony, obviously a repetition of the one performed when he was a young man, had confused him too. Bits and snippets of conversations came to her as she watched him. A Clan Lord had never remarried before. Jared was the first. No one, not Jared and not the Widows, even knew if it was going to work. She was aware of a sense of fear and despair. If all this was for nothing—

Jared's eyes suddenly cleared. "Come, we need to go inside. My landholders and villagers will be feasting for the rest of the day. You and I have another ceremony to endure."

And then she knew that he dreaded this next ceremony almost as much as she did—perhaps even more so.

He turned her around and together they led the way into the great hall, followed by the Clan Lords that were left after the tragedy of three months ago, their sons and heirs, and the Widows. They were the only ones who would witness this next ceremony—the ceremony of the crystal women.

Once Susan was out of the breeze, the long, sleeveless green gown behaved, clinging to her body and falling in graceful folds around her feet. Jared walked back with her into the great hall, but he abandoned her almost immediately. Smoothing the silken material of the gown under her somewhat unsteady hands, she sank down onto one of the benches that flanked the tables where most of the household evidently ate its meals. She hadn't participated in a household meal yet, but perhaps she would after today.

If she survived, of course. The ceremony to come next frightened her the most because she didn't have the slightest hint what it would entail.

Testing the atmosphere around her, she found that fear hung around her like a pall, invading every pore of her body, and she shook with it, but in glancing around she realized that the fear was not coming from those around her, but from herself and from a point distant across the room. She lifted her head and saw Jared standing alone, staring broodingly across the hall at her.

Susan didn't need any kind of extrasensory perception to know that both she and Jared were feeling the same paralyzing dread of what was to come. An unknown future that held both of them tangled in the web devised by others.

A pressing, painful tightness across her forehead caused her to raise her fingers to touch the circlet that bound her head. She pressed her temples just below the gold circlet, attempting to push away and protect herself against the intrusive clamorings of those around her.

The projected thoughts and emotions of the now-much-smaller group around her worked insidiously at crumbling the protective barrier in her mind. These people inside the great hall were more powerful than those outside, and even though their numbers were smaller, their impact was greater. She wondered at her sudden sensitivity to the mental emanations of others.

For out of the morass of mundane thoughts and petty emotions she was also able to filter their doubts of the success of the venture she and Jared were about to embark on. She knew that most of them, Clan Lords as well as some of the Widows, believed that Jared would not be able to go through with this ceremony.

"Drink some wine, my lady." A gruff voice came from over her shoulder and a hand waved a crystal wineglass in front of her face.

She looked up startled as one of the Clan Lords came around from behind her and sat down at the table across from her. Reaching out and smiling her thanks, she took the wineglass from his hand and sipped at it.

"This drink is more than likely going to make me drunk," she said with a little laugh. "I don't have much of a head for wine."

"You'll feel better for drinking it," he assured her. "Garrett si'Lemaldin's the name."

She lifted the wineglass to him. "It's a pleasure to meet you, Lord Lemaldin." He had the typical look of a Clan Lord. He had the golden eyes, although his were faded with age, and before he'd sat down she'd gotten the impression of great height. Garrett si'Lemaldin was a big, barrel-chested man, and although she would have expected a man of his size to move awkwardly, he moved with a fluid grace that belied his bulk.

"You were looking a trifle pale. I expect the sun outside didn't add to your comfort," the big man said.

She smiled at him, although she wasn't able to put much warmth into it. "No, I don't think the sun helped."

"I was watching you pretty closely, my Lady Susan. You had a rough time of it." He narrowed those pale gold eyes at her. "They say you're a crystal woman."

"That's what they say," she said noncommittally.

"Yet you have no crystal," he said, his voice sharp.

Susan knew she was being tested. She fumbled at the odd neckline of the wedding dress and pulled out Evie's green crystal. "I have this."

"But do you agree with the Widows?" Lemaldin asked. "That you're a crystal woman?"

"It isn't up to Susan to agree or disagree," Jared said, coming up from behind Lemaldin. "The Widows have decided that she is."

"And you, Jared?" Lemaldin asked, looking up at his peer. "What do you think? Are you going to be able to do this thing the Widows have asked of you?"

Jared raised a dark eyebrow. "Would you be able to do it, Garrett?"

The older man looked at Susan. "I don't know. I think perhaps I might. I think I would do almost anything to dispel the darkness in my mind."

Susan reached out and covered his hand with hers. "The tragedy struck you?"

"I lost my wife and two girl children," he murmured, his gaze dropping from hers. "At times I've been tempted to just give up, but I can't." He looked rueful. "Marion's crystal is on the shelf in my bedroom, but I avoid touching it. My Clan and my holdings need me more than Marion and the two girls do."

"I wish you peace, Garrett," Jared said quietly.

The older man nodded. "And although I wish you joy in your new marriage, I don't envy you your ultimate task. I stand behind you. Let me know if there's anything I can do to help." Garrett got to his feet and, with a nod in Susan's direction, walked away.

"Poor man," Susan murmured.

"He was testing you," Jared said.

"Are they all like him?" She glanced around the great hall, noting the men of impressive size with gold eyes.

"Garrett is probably one of those who are in reasonably good shape. He chose not to touch the crystals, although he probably dies a little every day anyway because he won't let himself seek their comfort. But he's right. We need him to hold his Clan together."

"Jared . . ."

He turned to her and their eyes met and she saw in his bright gold eyes a certain defensiveness that she hesitated to breach. He held out his hand. "It's time, Susan. They're ready."

She left the wineglass on the table and took his hand, rising to her feet, knowing Jared was having a difficult time, knowing he had no comfort to spare for her. Her gaze traveled in the direction of the dais, where the Widows waited.

The Clan Lords sat in ornate chairs in a half circle in front of the dais, leaving an aisle of only enough room for two people to walk between. What was left of the families of the Clan Lords, mostly earnest-looking young boys, sat on benches behind them drawn from the trestle tables in the room.

Jared brought her down the length of the great hall to the foot of the stairs leading up to the dais. There he stopped, and Susan stood next to him, her hand clutching his arm for support and courage.

She closed her eyes for a moment and silently told herself that she was doing this for a reason. The world she knew was threatened by the evil in this one.

She opened her eyes to see Fedorra, flanked by a Widow on either side, descending the steps from the dais until the Widow stood on the step just above Susan and Jared.

"Our world is in danger," the Widow began, and Susan heard a rustling noise from behind her, as if the Widow's words caught everyone by surprise and they sat up to pay close attention. "We mourn the dead, but we must live. We as a people have dedicated ourselves to bringing back our precious earth to its ancient glory. The choice that each of us made is in jeopardy."

Fedorra hesitated and looked around the great hall, her sharp, raisin-dark eyes falling on each Clan Lord in turn. "This time of evil was foretold long ago by a crystal woman who was also a warrior. I speak of Mellissande. She foretold the deaths of our crystal women and children. She foretold the taking of power by the son of darkness. But she left us not without hope for the future of our families, our Clans and our world. In the foretelling, she also gave us the answer to defeating the son of darkness, provided we were strong enough to implement it."

Susan felt Jared's hand tighten on her forearm.

"We, the guardians of Terra, the Widows, were strong enough to do what was required of us, even in the face of great uncertainty and doubt. We brought forth the Woman of Fire as foretold in Mellissande's prophecy. Now, we call upon the courage of the Clan Lords.

"Lord Jared si'Dakbar is called upon to break with our traditions and customs of centuries and take to him the Woman of Fire whose essence burns with the power necessary to fuel the defeat of the son of darkness." Fedorra looked down at Jared. "Are you willing to do this, Clan Lord?"

A heavy stillness fell over the great hall. She sensed an overwhelming anticipation of Jared's answer, the kind of breathless hush that precedes great tragedy or great joy.

She did not dare to look at him, but out of the corner of her eye she saw him lift his chin. His voice was firm when he said, "I am willing, Widow Fedorra."

Susan reeled a bit under the emotional backwash that struck her from the people in the hall who seemed to exhale their relief all at once, but Jared's hand steadied her. She held her breath when she saw the Widow's eyes shift and settle on her.

"And you, my child," Fedorra asked gently, "a stranger in our world, are you willing to perform this great service for us?"

She hesitated, distracted both by the gentleness in Fedorra's voice and the tension in Jared's hand as he dug his fingers into her forearm. "I am willing, Widow Fedorra," she said, using the same words as Jared had, forcing her voice to be strong so that it could be heard by those behind her.

Fedorra bent her head. "So be it." Then her gaze fell once again on the Clan Lords who sat in witness. "But in their quest Lord Jared and his lady need your help. The Widows need your help. We ask that when you return to your holdings, you search your libraries and your archives for any mention of the Challenge. Send word to us and we shall come to you. All are bound by Lord Jared's promise. We must all stand together to defeat the son of darkness before he destroys us all." Fedorra waited while Clan Lord after Clan Lord nodded, acquiescing in her request. "So be it. All are committed. The time of the Prophecy is at hand. Let us commence."

She motioned to the Widow at her side, who opened the long wooden box. Inside on a bed of white silk lay a dagger, its blade wrought of gold, its hilt of amethyst crystal.

Fedorra took the dagger from its bed and she lifted it above her head for all to see. Light flashed off the golden blade and sparkled in the faceted hilt.

A visceral spasm of fear and self-preservation shook Susan to the core at the sight of the gleaming naked blade. As she moved instinctively to take a backward step, she felt the hand of the man at her side, her husband already, tighten around her waist and hold her still.

Chapter Ten

Slowly Fedorra lowered the blade and held it between her two hands at chest level, chanting in a high, singsong voice, her body swaying slightly, her words unintelligible to Susan's ears.

When Fedorra paused, Jared extended his left arm to the Widow, palm up.

Susan stared at the old scar running down the inside of his forearm, plainly visible in the light. Her gaze flashed up to the Widow who held the knife, and Susan, suddenly making the connection between the knife and the scar, was afraid. She felt her fear take on a tangible form when she saw the golden blade descending toward Jared's naked forearm.

The old woman moved suddenly and decisively, the blade slashing down the inside length of Jared's forearm.

Susan gasped, her own flesh searing with heat

and burning at the shallow cut, although she was untouched by the blade.

Jared did not flinch. As his blood welled and dripped in spatters on the marble floor, he turned his golden eyes to her, his right hand sliding around her and grasping her right forearm as he guided it up and forward, holding it tightly, palm up.

She strained against his iron grip on her forearm, even as her eyes traced the slow upward movement of the golden knife, its edge now traced with his blood.

"Oh, my God," she whispered into the silence, and was aware that Jared's hand tightened on hers painfully, holding her still.

The blade hesitated at the apex for an agonizing moment before arching down and slicing her tender flesh. The cut welled forth, rich and red, spattering first against the green of her gown and then the marble floor. She trembled at the pain but retained enough presence of mind to stand still and fight back the blackness that threatened her and the nausea that clutched at her stomach. One of the Widows took her wounded arm and placed it against the slash on Jared's arm, binding their forearms together with a strand of clear crystal beads, wound to wound, so that their blood flowed from one to the other.

Susan struggled with the burning pain, shocked and horrified by the barbaric ceremony that required the spilling of blood. She understood now why no one had told her in advance what the ceremony entailed. She knew with certainty that the Widows had been afraid she would balk. She also knew that Jared had thought she would not be strong enough to face the experience.

I was wrong, Jared's voice echoed in her mind.

"About what?" Susan silently asked him, the

voiceless method of communication suddenly seeming right.

"About your strength. You have the valor and strength of a warrior," he responded. She felt his hand tighten on her elbow as a flash of brilliant light strobed. *"Look,"* he said, *"it begins."*

Startled, Susan looked down to where their arms were bound together. The strand of crystals sparkled with beams of light so strong it hurt the eyes. She shut her eyes against the bright shimmerings and forgot to speak to him with her mind.

"What does it mean?"

His voice in her mind was like a velvet caress. *"It signifies the beginning of the mindmesh. All the crystals you wear are doing the same. The strength of the light emitted by the crystals is indicative of the strength of your power. Since the light is close to blinding, we have to assume the Widows are pleased by the results of our joining."* The final statement was tinged with a shadow of sarcasm that dulled the pleasure she'd first felt from his words of praise.

Fedorra reached out and rested her hands on their shoulders. "The rings, Lord Jared," she said. "It is time to exchange the rings."

He nodded and removed a sparkling ring from his pinky and slid it onto the ring finger of Susan's hand where it rested on his arm. She noticed with amazement that the heavy ring that Amaranthe had used to seal the clasps of her gown was sparkling with lights as bright as those of the strand still binding their arms. She took it off her thumb and then slipped it onto Jared's ring finger.

Fedorra lifted her head and her voice rang out rich and clear, untouched by the tremor of age. "The ceremonial joining is complete. What is done cannot now be undone by man."

Can't be undone? she thought. That wasn't what they had told her. What did it mean? She was confused by the strobing lights of the crystals that seemed impossibly bright. Joy and happiness flooded through her, and it was a moment before Susan realized they were not her feelings, but emotions that belonged to the other people in the great hall. Her only feeling was one of exhaustion and relief that the worst was now over. *"What happens now, Jared?"* she asked. *"I don't know if I can take much more of this. I don't feel very well."*

"After one of the Widows removes your veil and replaces the circlet, it's over," he said. Gently he urged her to turn.

She felt hands move lightly over her head, and when those hands lifted the tight circlet from her head, she felt the diaphanous veil fall softly away.

"The star! Look at the star on her forehead! It glows!"

Susan tried to locate the one who had called out, but she could not see past the flashing of the crystals. The circlet was replaced on her head.

"Come, Lady Susan," he said, swiftly unwinding the brightly glimmering crystals that bound their arms together. "It is time to retire to our private chambers." He guided her quickly through the Clan Lords who had risen to their feet, holding the bloodied crystals high above his head so that all could see.

Words of congratulation and promises of support assaulted her on all sides, and it seemed to Susan as if those present all tried to touch her in some way. She thought she managed to smile in response to most of them, but she wasn't sure. Her exhaustion was growing more overwhelming, and reality forced her to admit that she was probably in mild shock. She needed food, and she needed sleep.

Jared's chuckle, a full, rich, throaty sound, rolled through her mind. *"I can do something about the food. That is customary, but I'm afraid that sleep is not part of ritual. Not at this point, in any case."*

She stopped. "You aren't serious? Surely you wouldn't—"

"Wouldn't what? Susan, the public ceremony is completed. The private one is about to begin, and that is what seals the bond between us. It is not something that can be put off."

They had finally reached the staircase that led upwards. Jared helped her up the stairs and led her to his bedchamber. He reached around her and locked the door and then led her over to the canopied bed, where he sat down and then pulled her gently down next to him. Strangely enough, she wasn't the slightest bit frightened anymore. She was merely confused and exhausted.

She smiled a little. Maybe she was too tired to be frightened, but when she looked up at Jared's face bent so intently near hers, she knew that wasn't the answer. She trusted Jared. Simply trusted.

The crystals that had bound them together were still flashing in Jared's hand. Although she understood more now than she had this morning, there was still much she felt was hidden from her. She cradled her injured arm, not daring to look for the moment.

She watched Jared as he held up the crystal strand to stare at it for a moment. She wondered how he managed to look at it when it was still strobing so strongly.

"At least this strand tells the truth," he murmured, rising and putting the string of crystals on the small table over by the window. A covered tray rested on the table.

She frowned, fighting the drowsiness that stole

over her now that she was sitting down. "What do you mean?"

"That strand reflects the strength of your power. You are very strong." He sent her an odd glance. "Didn't Magda tell you what she planned to do with the other crystals?"

Susan shook her head.

"The green crystals. Magda arranged for green crystals to be substituted for the clear ones that would have turned red when they came in contact with you. Red crystals would have given the game away as far as the Prophecy is concerned. Magda wasn't about to jeopardize the other Clan Lords acceptance of the Widows' belief that together we shall fulfill the Prophecy."

Frowning, she rose. "But the crystals were clear."

"Magda said she would substitute green ones."

Susan shook her head. "Mithra brought clear crystals. When she touched them, they turned black."

His frown evinced his bewilderment. "But you said you were not a virgin," he said slowly, his golden eyes fixing on her with unrelenting steadiness. "The crystals only turn green for a virgin."

She pulled out the crystal on the chain for him to see. "Then explain this."

He raised his eyebrows. "Magda was thorough. She even thought to replace Evie's crystal with a green one."

"I'm telling you Magda didn't replace this," Susan said, staring down at the sparkling green crystal. "This was the black crystal."

"I don't understand," he said.

She laughed. "Now you know how I feel most of the time."

"I'll have to ask Magda later." He sat down on

the bed next to her. "We're about to experience the first test of your power, Susan. You must heal the joining wounds."

"You're kidding!"

Jared shook his head and a smile tugged at the corners of his mouth. "No, I'm not. It should be child's play for you."

She looked at him doubtfully. "I know that you all think I have this power, but I just don't think . . ." She let her voice trail. Then her eyes searched his. "What if I can't do it?"

"Just try. Being successful at this might be just the thing that convinces you that you do have power. Crystal women are primarily healers."

"What do I do?"

"Put your hand on the wound and concentrate. Visualize it the way the skin should be when it is healed." He shrugged. "That's all I know about how it's done."

Hesitantly, she reached out and took his proffered forearm, somewhat gingerly pressing her fingers on the shallow wound, afraid of hurting him. She didn't really believe she could do this.

"You can do it," Jared reassured her. *"Don't be afraid to hurt me. You can't."*

Strengthened by his reassurance, she closed her eyes and concentrated on the tactile sensations being translated to her mind from her fingertips. Gently, she felt the edges of the wound, her fingers feeling the stickiness of the blood that had already stopped flowing. She felt the slight stiffness of the sprinkling of hair on the back of his arm and the smoothness of the skin of his inner forearm, and she felt the raised ridge of that old scar. For the rest of his life Jared would carry the proof that he'd been Joined more than once.

Then she felt him in her mind. He remained

in the background and did not interfere with her exploration. She sensed that he was willing to let her explore this new, rather extraordinary power she was supposed to possess.

In her mind she pictured the wound, and then she pictured it fusing together, healing from the shallowest part, slowly moving down to the deepest, which required more concentration because she found that she had to delve beneath the surface of the skin to knit together the tissue structure there. Her fingertips warmed with the heat that flowed down her arms from her shoulders and sank into Jared's skin.

It was the strangest sensation, she thought, almost as if she was generating tremendous heat and channeling it to the wound. Finally, she thought she was finished, but she was afraid to open her eyes to see what she had done.

"Open your eyes, Susan," Jared said in a normal voice, and she could hear his amusement at her reluctance.

"Did anything happen?" she asked apprehensively.

"Look and see."

It was perfect. She stared down at his forearm in amazement. Other than the smears of blood, all that remained of the wound was a thin, smooth white line. Her eyes shining, she looked up at him. "I did that?"

He nodded. "Now you must heal your own wound."

"I don't think I can do that," she said.

Jared slid off the bed onto his knees in front of her. "I'll help you as much as I can. Yours is shallow, and you've already had the practice of healing mine."

Encouraged, she closed her eyes and put her

hand on the wound on her own forearm. She jumped when Jared closed his hand over hers, and she felt him in her mind at the same instant. Gently he encouraged her to begin.

She found the sensation of him being present in her mind and physically touching her at the same time . . . odd. It was almost as if he, in surrounding her, protected her. Almost without realizing it she found herself visualizing her arm and Jared was there, reinforcing the image in her mind.

The heat began to flow through her and she channeled it, seeing the wound heal in her mind. She projected the image of healing flesh to Jared and felt him jump a little at the first touch of the image, but he joined her then in actively channeling the energy with her.

When Susan opened her eyes, she looked down at her arm and saw only the faintest trace of a white line. Delighted with the accomplishment, she grinned at Jared. "How wonderful!" she exclaimed. "There's barely a mark left. I can't believe it."

"Believe it, Susan. It's a skill common to crystal women, but I have the feeling you're better than most at it."

She traced the old ridge of scar tissue on his forearm. "This?"

"Evie. She wasn't as skilled as you, although like you, it was her first attempt at healing. Her power was nowhere near as strong as yours is. When Evie and I joined, the binding strand of crystals twinkled brightly, but they did no more than twinkle." He took her hand and twined his fingers between hers. "You may deny it, Susan, but you possess great power."

"But until we figure out what to do with it, it won't do us a lot of good against Ruhl."

He stood up and drew her to her feet, keeping

his fingers twined with hers, an odd smile on his face. "Oh, but I can help you figure out what to do with all that power, Susan. There are—interesting—ways to use it before we confront Ruhl."

She frowned at him, a little puzzled, and then the frown cleared. Tossing back her head, she laughed. Her exhaustion had drained away with the use of the healing power. It was almost as if she'd been rejuvenated. "Interesting ways, huh?" she asked, teasingly.

Catching her against him, he brushed his lips across her forehead. "In an odd sort of way, Susan, I'm rather glad I won't be the first. Joinings are frequently very traumatic experiences for the two involved. You at least know what to expect during this part of the ritual." The smile faded from his lips. "I want you to know that there will be some mental discomfort at one point. At least you won't be distressed by bodily discomfort."

She backed away from him, suddenly shy, although she knew she shouldn't be. For however long this situation lasted, this man was her husband. "I'd like to wash," she murmured.

"The bathing chamber is through there," he said, nodding at the door at the other side of the room.

She escaped and closed the door behind her, taking a deep breath when she was alone and at a loss to explain the incredible shyness she suddenly felt. Bending down, she unfastened the tiny gold pin that had saved her from embarrassment. She fumbled with the fastening of the dress at the waist, frowning when she couldn't undo it.

"Oh, for heaven's sake," she muttered, stepping over to the basin and settling for washing the dried blood from her arm. She inspected the thin scar and shook her head in wonder. It wasn't something that was easily believable.

Looking up, she stared at her reflection in the mirror above the basin, startled by the pinpoint glimmerings and sparklings of the tiny green crystals threaded through her hair. She looked . . . different, although it wasn't something she could pinpoint. The star shape on her forehead was a little larger and certainly a darker pink. She smoothed her fingers across it. How was she going to explain this to Drew when she returned?

Thoughts of her brother instilled a deep longing in her to see him. But she pushed the emotions to the back of her brain. This was a time of celebration, not sadness.

Susan sighed. Since she couldn't bathe fully clothed, there was no choice but to ask Jared for his help in divesting herself of the dress. She opened the door and stepped out to see Jared standing at the table and running the string of still-brightly-glittering white crystals through his fingers. He looked pensive.

"Jared?"

He looked up, a sad smile touched his mouth. "All finished?"

She shook her head. "No, I'd planned on bathing, but I couldn't get the dress off. This clasp seems to be stuck."

Jared grinned then, a genuine smile of amusement. "No, you wouldn't be able to get it off. The clasp needs the application of my ring."

"You're right. I do remember Gersta saying something about that. Give me the ring." She held out her hand.

If anything, his grin grew broader. "That's not quite the way it happens, Susan." He walked closer to her, and to her surprise, she found herself backing away from him. He halted and the smile faded from his lips. "I've given you as much time

207

as we can afford to spare, Susan." He gestured back at the crystal strand that lay on the table. "The next part of the ritual must be completed before the crystals stop glittering. Already their brightness has begun to fade."

Susan felt suddenly awkward.

As if he sensed her discomfort, he approached her again slowly, his hands reaching out and resting on her shoulders for a moment before trailing down her arms and smoothing the sides of her hips, catching there and pulling her to him, inch by slow inch.

"I'll not hurt you, Susan d'Richards si'Dakbar," he murmured, bending his head down and touching his lips to her neck. "This is something we've both wanted from the moment of our first meeting in our dreams. And although we've both had to subdue our response to each other up until now, you're still my witch woman. The Woman of Fire whose touch makes my body flame with desire. For you."

She shivered at the soft touch of his mouth on the sensitive skin of her neck and admitted the truth of what he said. Lifting her arms, she curled them around his neck, wordlessly giving him the answer he sought.

With an inarticulate murmur, he brought her body firmly against his, and through the thin silk of her gown she felt the hardness of his thighs and knew that he desired her in the same way a man from her own world desired a woman. Another of her fears fell away from her.

One hand firm against the small of her back, Jared cupped her breast through the silk of the green gown as his lips traveled from her neck, across her jaw to her mouth. As his thumb stroked across the firm nipple, Susan took a deep breath, trying to control the sudden heat that surged through her body, a heat similar to that which she'd experienced during the healing. Sensing that she would be quickly out of control, she tried to back away from him, to remove one of the stimulants to her senses.

But he held her firm. His hand at her back tightened and the hand at her breast shifted and moved down, brushing aside the material of her skirt and touching the soft inner skin of her thighs.

Her breath caught at the heat lightning that strobed through her at his touch, and her knees threatened to buckle. His lips left hers and he turned her around so that her back rested against his chest, abdomen, and thighs. His breath rasped harshly in her ear.

"You mentioned something about unfastening your gown," he said, a tinge of amusement in his husky whisper. His left hand slid upward and Susan, her head leaning back against his chest, saw the green crystal pulsing. Jared pressed the ring against the crystal in the clasp at her waist and the gown suddenly parted. He reached under her arms and cupped her full, firm breasts.

"Beautiful," he whispered, gently releasing his hold and turning her around to face him. "You are absolutely beautiful, Susan." He pushed the dress off her shoulders and it drifted down her arms and, once free, the thin silk pooled on the floor at her feet.

Susan was conscious of standing before him, bare except for the thin chain slung about her hips. He grasped her chin and tilted her face up so that their eyes met, his a lambent gold, hers a shy green.

"Not afraid, are you?" he asked, daring her to answer yes.

"I'm not afraid," she answered, and as she said the words, she realized she wasn't, she was merely hesitant, and now even the time for hesitancy was gone. "I was just wondering if your clothes were as tricky to get out of as my dress was."

He laughed, a deep rumble that vibrated against her when he swept her into his arms and twirled her around and tumbled back with her onto the huge canopied bed. "They are, and that's why I made sure you had the ring that unlocks them."

Holding her hand up before her, she twisted the ring so that the crystal stone faced inside against her palm. "It seems to me an awkward way to dress for a wedding day." She smiled down at him wickedly, her tongue darting out to moisten her lips as she levered herself up to kneel by his side.

He watched her curiously as if he couldn't figure out what she was about. "What we wear is traditional. It used to be worse than this."

She touched the ring to the first button on his jacket and then she slid the button from its buttonhole, bending down over him and touching her lips to the bare skin she'd uncovered. Lifting her mouth from his skin and sliding her hand down to the next button, she murmured, "How could it be worse?" After unlocking it, she unbuttoned it and again touched her lips to his firm, tanned flesh.

He sighed with pleasure, one hand closing on the back of her neck in encouragement, the other reaching for her breast. "In times past warring Clan Lords sometimes stole the crystal brides from their enemies right from under their noses. The crystal-locked dress became customary, and believe me, it was much more elaborate than what you wore."

His words rose and fell around her, but she barely heard them, so intent was she on finishing her self-imposed task of undressing him. All her concentration was aimed at bringing both of them the maximum amount of pleasure from the preliminary moves that would bring them together eventually, and she moved down, unbuttoning his jacket and caressing the flesh she exposed. His hands caressed her body in return, and she felt the white heat burn hotter in her core and begin to flow out to her skin's surface until she thought that every nerve ending in her body was on fire.

When she reached the closure on his trousers, she was aware that Jared seemed to hold his breath until the button was unfastened. She watched him, seeing his half-closed eyes turn from gold to deep amber as she slid her fingers delicately under the waistband of the trousers and his undergarment, exploring the hair-roughened flesh of his abdomen. He groaned deeply and arched against her hand when she touched him, dragging her up the length of his body, pulling her head down to his and fastening his mouth over hers, his tongue thrusting deep into her mouth.

He gathered her up against him and rolled over so that she was on her back beneath him. She quivered in protest when he tore his mouth from hers and rose to his knees on the soft bed, ripping his jacket off and tossing it over the side of the bed. She reached up to caress him, her fingers trembling through the light sprinkling of dark hair that arrowed down to the gaping waistband of his trousers, hesitating once or twice to investigate the scars of wounds that marked his flesh.

Groaning, Jared pushed away from her and stood at the side of the bed, shoving his trousers down over his hips and kicking them off. Quickly he walked over to the table where he had placed the strand of clear crystals, catching them up and

211

winding the still shimmering strand around his hand. He came back to the bed and stood there, looking down first at the strand of winking crystals and then at her, his hesitation clear.

With intense interest and pleasure, she observed his male beauty and how naturally and how freely he wore his masculinity, but even as she admired him, she knew something was wrong. "What is it, Jared?" she whispered.

He came down beside her on the bed, holding the crystal strand where she could see it. "I don't want to seem the impatient bridegroom, Susan, but the glimmerings grow weak. We must consummate this joining before the crystals return to their natural state."

She looked at the weak glitterings of the crystal and then into his eyes and knew that he spoke the truth. She didn't understand the relationship between the strand of crystals and the consummation of their marriage, but she was willing to admit that he knew more than she did about it. "Then I guess we'd better do something about it," she murmured, holding out her arms to him.

Jared fell onto the bed beside her, all hesitation and indecisiveness gone. Now, he was all aggressive male, his hands closing on her soft flesh, his mouth fastened on hers, his tongue exploring the moist recesses of her mouth. His body was heavy on hers, but she welcomed it, knowing it was the prelude to something she suddenly realized that she had wanted since the first time she'd seen Jared in the dreams brought by the Widows.

His knee separated her legs and she felt him settle himself in the cradle of her thighs. His blunt shaft, an intriguing mix of velvety softness and iron hardness, probed her feminine flesh gently.

"Susan," he gasped, his hands cupping her buttocks as he touched his forehead to hers. "Remember. There will be some mental discomfort."

In answer all she could do was clasp him closer to her, straining towards the peak she knew without doubt that she would reach with him, and yet she was aware of several small discomforts that seemed minuscule in comparison to the deep pleasure that rocked through her as he prepared to enter her. She was aware that where his forehead rested against hers, her skin burned. She was aware of the dig into the firm flesh of her buttock of the crystals on the strand that was still wrapped around his hand. Despite that, she urged him forward—and stiffened in shock when he hesitated at the entrance to her softness, barred by a barrier that should not have been there.

"No! Wait!" she cried frantically, seeing her own shock reflected in his golden eyes and also seeing the strength of purpose there as he gathered himself to thrust past the barrier.

"We can't wait, Susan," he whispered harshly. "It must be done—and quickly." He held her tightly as she writhed in protest against the warmth of his body, and he thrust past the thin barrier, sinking deeply into her with a groan that was partly pain and partly passion.

She arched against the pain that shot through her at his entrance, and a shrill involuntary cry escaped her throat as she felt herself caught in the maelstrom of white heat that pulsed through her veins, welling and spilling forth, engulfing both of them in blinding white light.

She gasped in protest and dug her nails into his back, where they inflicted their own pain. Her skin where his forehead touched hers burned like flame, and then suddenly, he was in her head, his essence intertwining with hers, until their minds were wonderfully, inseparably woven together. He was in her mind and in her body, his thoughts fused with hers, his body fused with hers. He engulfed her, surrounded her, and penetrated her. In that moment he was truly one with her, and she suddenly knew the true meaning of the joining. She knew and shared his every thought, his every emotion, his every hope, his every fear. Just as he shared hers.

"Easy, Susan. Easy! The effect will lessen in a moment," he whispered reassuringly, his hand moving up to caress the side of her face.

She squinted at him against the strobing of the suddenly rejuvenated crystals comprising the strand twined around Jared's hand. She did not need sight to know he was as disconcerted as she was about the joining. It was as if his thoughts were her thoughts, and in that moment when all his barriers were down and their souls meshed, she discovered two things.

She loved him and had perhaps done so since the beginnings of her dreams of him. She also discovered that although Jared was fascinated by her, felt affection for her, felt passion and felt desire, he did not love her. He had gone through this marriage to her in the name of duty toward the Widows and his world.

As Susan's essence poured into his mind, she knew the empty places she filled had once been inhabited by Evie. Even as she fought against the joining, she wept for Jared's pain as those voids in his mind were filled by her. She felt him try to hide his pain from her, to spare her, but the soul-searing joining allowed them no defenses against one another and no secrets.

Thinking to make a noble sacrifice to save her world, she had consented to this marriage, only to discover that she really hadn't made any kind of a sacrifice at all. Her decision to go along with the Widows had been a purely selfish one. The threat to her world had been the acknowledged reason she'd acquiesced, but it had been only part of the reason. In the space of a couple of days she'd fallen deeply in love with Jared si'Dakbar. It was almost incomprehensible that he should not feel the same about her.

Sobbing, she sought to push him away, trying to hide her own truth from him and knowing that it was impossible, knowing that he already knew what she had just realized.

Gently but firmly, he stilled her frantic movements, his lips touching hers soothingly, and although she felt his tenderness, his caring for her, she sought in vain for the love she wanted desperately. She tried to build a barrier against him in her mind, but found that she could not keep him out. He was infiltrated solidly in her mind; he was part of her.

He moved against her experimentally, and as his body thrust into hers, striving for the completion of what they'd started, she could not bank the fires he raised in her, and she felt the insidious stirring of that white heat they called her power.

It began in her mind and then slowly seeped to burn through her veins, her breasts, her loins and transmitted itself to Jared.

His need drove him into her time after time even as the fire of her power burned him, consumed him, and finally lifted him beyond the possibility of control. Susan, unable to resist the insidious flare of the power through every cell in her body, responded to Jared's movements and followed him, giving the only thing she had to give—

her love—as her power engulfed the two of them in its hot, hot light.

He arched over her, a deep groan breaking from his throat as he flew into the light, spilling his seed deep into the darkness of her womb. She flew after him, following him into orgasm, her body spasming and accepting his offering. It was like nothing she had ever experienced before. It was as if she were a virgin both mentally and physically.

He collapsed on her, breathing heavily, his chest heaving against her breasts. He touched her face in reassurance, but she turned from him, closing her eyes against the remaining pulse of the energy that still flickered over their nude bodies.

Moving off her to the side, Jared pulled her head into the crook of his neck and carefully stroked her hair with his hand. *"I'm sorry, Susan,"* he said quietly in her mind.

"Let me go, Jared," she said, her voice breaking on a sob. She felt mortified and humiliated by the fact that he knew precisely how she felt about him, even as she knew precisely and in great detail how he felt about her. He was in her mind, and she wanted him to go.

"I cannot leave you now, and you can no longer block me out," he said, reaching out to the chain of glittering red crystals that encircled her hips. The stone in the ring that he pressed to the crystal lock also glittered red. The chain opened and, reluctantly it seemed, fell free to the bed below Susan's hips. *"I shall be with you always, as you will be with me."*

"Under the circumstances, I don't think that I shall be able to stand that," she said quietly.

He withdrew from her and sat up, staring down at his hands as he folded them in front of him. *"Unfortunately, this has happened to many crystal*

*women and Clan Lords. We cannot always choose
where we love. Susan, perhaps with time—"*

"Time!" she said. "Time? That's something neither one of us have, Jared."

"That does not mean we can't come to an agreement about our relationship, Susan," he said out loud, giving up the mental communication when she showed no sign of reciprocating. "Damn it, Susan!" He strode away from her and stood at the window in naked splendor. "You knew the rules when you joined the game at the Widows' urging. You can't claim foul now." He turned and strode back to her, towering over her as she lay on the bed. "No one promised you love, Susan. No one. Not even the Widows."

"Leave me alone, Jared," she whispered, swearing to herself that she would not cry. "I can't take any more."

Reaching out, he pulled her into a sitting position. "Susan," he said more gently, "I knew what to expect from this joining. You did not. This total honesty and knowledge of the other is part of the magic of the joining whether we like what we discover or not. We were both surprised and shocked by something we did not expect to exist. You said you were not a virgin."

"But I wasn't," she cried. "I wasn't."

"I know. You did not lie to us, but for some reason, somehow, in coming to this world your body changed. You became a virgin once again. Perhaps it has something to do with the way your body has been healing so quickly."

She sighed, her heart aching. "Perhaps."

Rising to his feet, he looked down at her. "I'll leave you alone for a while. At dusk we must go down again to the great hall." He walked to the bathing chamber, but he hesitated on the threshold and turned back to her, the words almost reluctantly leaving his lips. "Despite what we thought, Susan, and despite our attempts to interfere, the Prophecy demanded a virgin. The Prophecy has been fulfilled so far in every respect."

She lay there, staring up at the canopy over the bed, not giving a damn about the Prophecy for the moment, and clenching her fist as a tear slid down her cheek.

She turned over onto her stomach and muffled a tearful sob in the pillow. She was married and desperately in love with a man who did not love her.

Chapter Eleven

Susan frowned and bent over closer to read the small print of the ancient book that was spread open on the scarred wooden table. Magda referred to the book as an herbal medicinal.

Rather doubtfully Susan looked at the disgusting-looking mess she'd been grinding up using a mortar and pestle for the past hour or so. It was supposed to be a paste that could be applied to a wound to prevent infection. Susan thought the thin green liquid looked more like bile than something she would want applied to a wound. She shuddered at the thought. There was no way she'd ever let anyone put something that looked like this on her. Hadn't anyone here ever heard of penicillin?

In the week since she'd become Lady Susan d'Richards si'Dakbar and a crystal woman, she had struggled under Magda's direction with the making of ointments and salves and medicines for healing and the relief of pain. Magda had told her she must know these things if she was to be perceived as a true crystal woman, but Susan was aware that Magda was quite frustrated with her lack of talent in the creative healing arts of a crystal woman.

"But why do I have to know this stuff?" Susan had asked after one particularly spectacular failure. The pain relief draught she'd been distilling had spontaneously combusted with a torch-like flame and had burned merrily in the glass beaker until there was nothing left. "I can just heal the way I did for Jared."

Magda had looked at her as if she were not too bright. "Healing takes a great deal of power. You would be exhausted if you employed that method of curing day after day. Why put yourself at risk when a simple potion or salve will do the job in a satisfactory manner?"

Susan hadn't had an answer for Magda and had quietly gone back to working on the potions and salves. She had come to the conclusion that she had not come to this world to spend most of her day making up goos and extracts when someone else could do it with a higher success ratio than she.

But having come to that conclusion, she'd also decided that she wasn't physically equipped to protect herself in this world. Her confrontations with the Ptai and the Tremillium were still fresh in her mind. Back home if she'd felt the need for self-defense she would have gone out and bought a gun. Then she would have taken shooting lessons to make sure she knew how to handle her chosen weapon.

There were no firearms here so she'd done the next best thing. She'd cornered the master of arms,

Fenil, one morning and demanded that he teach her to wield a sword and dagger.

A stocky, broad-shouldered man with arms as muscled as a weight lifter's, his hair as burnished with the gleam of silver as the swords in his charge, Fenil had thrown his head back on his thick neck and bellowed with laughter. She'd stood in front of him, her hands curled into fists, and waited for his laughter to subside.

"I'm serious," she said when he showed signs of stopping, but her words set him off again.

"Does Lord Jared know what you're about, Lady?" he gasped finally gaining some control of himself.

"What does that have to do with anything?" she asked. "I want to learn how to handle a sword. Why does Lord Jared have to give me permission?"

"Because you're his Lady wife," Fenil said, his voice suddenly as serious as hers. "And he would have my head if any harm came to you because I was so bold as to accede to your request." His eyes flickered over her shoulder.

She turned to see Jared leaning against the doorway. As usual, just the sight of him was enough to steal the breath from her lungs. She recovered from her surprise quickly, but not before he had caught the backlash from the warmth that flooded through her at the memories of the past week of long nights spent in his arms. He nodded at her, his eyes warm gold, and suddenly a kaleidoscope of erotic images spilled into her mind. She blushed, and Jared grinned at her, but his grin faded when he felt the sadness that welled in her a moment later. He turned his attention to Fenil, but Susan felt his lingering regret.

"Fenil, I came to see what or who had my Lady in such a state that her anger began an ache in my head so severe that I fear I'll have to consume a crystal woman's remedy." His eyes questioned Fenil silently.

"Lady Susan wishes me to instruct her in the art of the sword and dagger," Fenil said, his eyes darting between his Lord and Lady.

"And you said her nay?" Jared lifted an eyebrow.

"He said I should ask you for permission!" Susan said, recovered from the poignant sharing she had experienced with Jared a few moments ago, and now practically sputtering with renewed fury.

Jared was silent for a moment, his golden eyes narrowed. Then he nodded and looked at Fenil. "If Lady Susan wishes to be instructed, then you are to do so." He turned his attention to his wife. She was surprised by the fact that he made no attempt to probe her mind for the reason she wished to undertake instruction with Fenil. "Watch the blade, Susan. I do not wish you hurt." With that, he was gone and Susan turned back to Fenil to see a strangely resigned look in his eyes.

She smiled at him sweetly, and was pleased to see him blush and turn his eyes away. "I would have rather won my victory alone, Fenil, without Lord Jared's intervention, but having his permission—when can we start?"

Now, after several days of Fenil's instruction, she stood up and stretched, arching her back, feeling the sore muscles of her arms and shoulders pull. Fenil had found her a sword suited to her height and her strength, and he had begun to instruct her in a warrior's art. She worked twice a day with the sword. In the morning her lessons were combined with those of the young men and women who were guards, and in the afternoons, she worked alone with Fenil. She'd become used to the ache and pull of the sore muscles in her body, finding them almost comforting. Sore muscles meant she was working and not just taking the easy way out.

Taking the easy road would have been simple. She could have retired to this room that had been Evie's and done nothing but study whatever Magda gave her. It had been the room in which Evie had done her mixing of ointments, salves, and potions—the same things Susan was doing now, but there was no doubt in Susan's mind that Evie must have been much better at it than she was. Susan knew for a fact that she was ten times better with the sword and dagger than she was with making herbal remedies.

Wandering over to the narrow window, she looked out. From the top room of the tower, the lighter and darker greens of the fields and forests seemed laid out with unnatural precision. Which they had been, as Jared had explained to her when she'd asked. When the holding had been granted by the King to the second son of the Dakbar Clan hundreds of years in the past, every foot of land had been planned for hundreds of years into the future. Jared had shown her the master plan.

At the thought of her husband, Susan's vision became glazed. Jared was never far from her conscious thoughts because by now he was firmly entrenched in her mind, entwined with all her thoughts and feelings. He was with her constantly, as she was with him. There was always one part of her mind that was aware of him. She didn't know if she'd ever get used to the sensation of being so close to another human being that she was aware of his well-being, his moods, his emotions.

It wasn't as if she could read his mind, because she couldn't, although she suspected she'd come close a couple of times. Certain strong emotions came through, and she perceived what he felt, but unless he actually projected his thoughts to her, she didn't know specifically what he was thinking. And the mental barriers each of them had been erecting since the day of their joining had grown stronger and higher.

On that day almost two weeks ago both of them had been so surprised by the intensity of their physical and emotional reactions to each other that they'd left themselves wide open, enabling the other to know, with painful preciseness, what the other was thinking and feeling. She had realized that Jared's heart was still given to his first wife, and he had realized that she had expected much more of him than just a partner in bed every night. But after that first traumatic moment of the total mindmesh, Susan no longer sensed Evie's ghost in Jared's mind—not because Jared had changed his mind, but because he had hidden all his emotions regarding his first wife behind that tall, impenetrable wall in the center of his mind. At the time of their joining, Susan hadn't known that the complete openness of their mental union was only a temporary state—that it would be possible to carefully construct a wall in her mind to protect her most secret thoughts and emotions from Jared.

Just as now Jared could not know, but could only sense, what her feelings were with regard to him, because she had taken those aching emotions and hidden them behind the wall of her own making, and it was entirely possible that her barrier was higher and stronger than his.

Leaning on the stone embrasure of the window, Susan smiled a little as she stared out over the checkerboarded fields. Despite the landscape's austerity, it was quite beautiful. There was beauty in its very starkness, and the pockets of lush green growth gave hope for the future. The air might be thin, but it was clean and fresh with not a hint of pollution.

Her eyes scanned the horizon, and she pinpointed the field where the Widows had made their camp. The Widows' black tent was gone now. They had moved on to the holding of another Clan Lord, one who had informed them that he had an extensive although ancient library. Magda had been left behind to help Susan while the Widows continued their search for the secrets from the past.

Susan understood now that the Widows truly were frantic about what was happening. Their world was threatened with extinction if the proper balance was not restored. She could almost, but not quite, forgive them for snatching her away from her own time to help them, although she was still of the opinion that there wasn't much she could do.

The joining had convinced her that she did have some kind of power as the Widows claimed, but how strong it was and how effectively it could be used still remained a large question in Susan's mind. So, although Jared had been after her to stretch and expand and test what she could accomplish, she had been hesitant to take the first step.

If the Widows expected her to develop her power and then save their world in one stunning exhibition, they were going to be sadly disappointed.

Susan suddenly flinched as a blast of anger ripped through her mind and left her gasping. Wherever Jared was, he was furious about something. Shaking in reaction, she uncurled her hands and discovered her nails had left crescent indentations in the fleshy part of her palms.

From what Susan had deciphered last night during the after-dinner conversation between Jared and his headman, a sinkwell responsible for the irrigation of several northern fields had gone dry.

He had taken a group out to one of the northern fields to find another likely site where they would find water and drill a new well.

What could be so wrong that Jared was so angry? she wondered, toying with the idea of sending him a message in return protesting the fact that he'd made no attempt to shield his anger from her. But even as she considered it, she felt him bank his emotions. A small smile tugged at her lips as she sensed an apology from him, wordless, but there nonetheless.

About to turn from the window and try once more to make the bilious paste, she hesitated and frowned when she saw a cloud of dust rising in the distance along the road. Even as she stood there watching, she heard the voice of the sentry on the battlement call out a warning. So, whoever was coming was not expected, she thought, wondering at the odd feeling that trembled through her. The news this man brought would be bad. She knew without knowing how she knew it.

Almost hesitantly, she opened her mind and directed a call to Jared.

"Jared!"

"What is it?" His response was tempered and without the anger that had flooded him but moments before.

"A horseman comes fast from the west. Something's wrong," she told him. *"I feel—"* Unable to transmit her feelings in the soundless words of the mind, she relayed to him her feelings of uneasiness. She turned, distracted, when she heard the door open.

"Do you know who's coming, Magda?" she asked.

Magda shook her head. "No, but we expected no one. Whoever it is travels quickly." She moved over to the table and began gathering jars and bottles, carefully arranging them in a basket she took from a shelf.

"He's coming from the west," Susan observed. "The desert lies in that direction."

Magda nodded and came to stand beside Susan, her brows pulled together in a frown. "I am worried. So much seems to be happening all at once. The Widows are beset on all sides by requests and demands for their presence."

"Why is that?"

Shrugging, Magda went back to the table and packed some more medications. "Most of us think it is because the time foretold by the Prophecy is upon us."

"The rider is almost here," Susan said, unable to leave her watchpost at the window. Magda joined her at the window again.

"He's riding one of Jared's horses!" Magda exclaimed, turning from the window and hurrying to the door. "But he's not from the Keep."

"What does that mean?" Susan asked, bending out over the windowsill, watching the horse and its rider thunder through the portcullis and into the cobbled courtyard.

"The only one I know of who has a Keep horse is Connor. He's about due back. There must be trouble for him to send someone back here at a gallop and not come himself. I'm going down to find out."

Susan left the window embrasure to hurry after Magda. "Wait! I'm coming with you."

Together they quickly descended the stairs and found the rider on a bench in the great hall being tended to by the woman who ran the Keep's kitchen and surrounded by several of the guard and Fenil.

"What message does he bring?" Magda asked, her voice sharp as the snap of a whip.

Fenil looked up at her, his eyes darting to Susan and then back to Magda. "None yet, Widow. Bette from the kitchen is trying to bring him around. He is wounded and was tied to the saddle. He fainted when we cut him loose."

Fumbling in a pocket in her voluminous skirts, Magda brought forth a small vial.

Susan got her first clear view of the unconscious man when Magda bent over him to wave the vial beneath his nose. She caught her breath at his condition. What appeared to be burns covered the left half of his body from his head down to his knee—the flesh blackened and bubbled, the side of his face bearing the burn marks, his features a shapeless mass of flesh that no longer bore any resemblance to being human. Susan shuddered to think of the pain he must have endured during his journey. No wonder he had been tied to the saddle. He wouldn't have been able to stay astride if he hadn't been.

His body jerked, and he moaned as his one good eye flickered open. His lips parted and the sound of his scream of pain brought tears to Susan's eyes. She stepped forward, knowing only that he had to be helped, but Magda held up her hand and stopped her from approaching.

"He'll need to be immersed in the bathing liquid," Magda said, loudly enough to be heard over the man's screams. "I have something that will relieve his pain without putting him to sleep." She turned to one of the serving maids and spoke to her in a low voice. The girl nodded and ran off.

"Magda, I can help him. I know I can," Susan protested at not being allowed closer.

The Widow shook her head. "Trust me in this, Susan. There is not a Widow nor crystal woman who could heal a man injured this grievously."

228

"But he's hurting."

"Attempting to heal him could cause your own death, Susan," Magda said. "You cannot risk it."

Susan felt her anger flare. She was beginning to grow tired of being told what she could and could not do. "You and the other Widows insist that I have this power. Let me use it. If you do not, then this man will have suffered when he could have been helped."

The Widow shook her head.

"What of his message, Magda?" Susan persisted. "The man must have a message. In his condition he can do nothing but scream and who knows how long he can do that without fainting again, or worse yet, dying. We must relieve him. How can you allow him to suffer like this?"

Magda gripped her arms. "There may be twenty-five more like him lying in a cornfield. Will you attempt to heal them all? At what cost to yourself? Your death? We cannot risk you. Better one man dies rather than risk forfeiting our only chance to save our world. I forbid you to do this, Susan."

Shrugging herself from Magda's grasp, Susan gently moved the older woman aside. "I'm sorry, Magda, but I am not subject to your orders. If I can help this man, then I must do so." Gritting her teeth, she knelt on the cold stone floor at his side.

He turned his head, his eye catching hers, and she saw the tormented plea there. Hoping to reassure him, she lay her hand on his shoulder and her body jerked at the flood of sharp, burning pain that coursed through her, flowing from the body of the tormented man through her hand and through her own body. She gasped and took her hand away, staring down at it, for a moment seeing the flesh of her own palm and fingers blackened and bubbled as if it had been burned.

Her body trembled at the thought of putting her hands back on the man and attempting to heal him. She closed her eyes tightly and took a deep breath. When she opened them, she reached out both her hands and, leaning across the man, put them both on his leg above the knee.

Her body quivered at the first jolt of fiery agony and she closed her eyes and clenched her teeth tightly. It was almost impossible to remember what she had to do. She fought against the pain, her head tilting back as she tried to concentrate on healing the distressed flesh. Her fingers moved slowly, her breath came in harsh gasps, her body shook with tremors, but she did not remove her hands.

The man's keening faded to the distance and she was conscious only of a vague roaring in her ears—the sound of her own blood moving through her body, she thought. And then she realized she was close to losing consciousness herself. She struggled against the life-stealing, soul-eating drain of the man's hungry flesh, but the ominous blackness rushed in to overwhelm her and she felt herself falling, falling, falling into the black, bubbling pit of agony.

Jared spurred the stallion, turning the horse toward the Keep. Susan's projected sense of unease flickered at his awareness, and a fear of his own grew in his mind.

Perhaps her fear had been set loose in reaction to the blast of fury he'd felt when he'd viewed the three northern fields he'd expected to see affected by the dried-up sinkwell.

What he had seen had not been the effects of too little water on his crops. The fields had not been destroyed by natural means. He recognized the remains of laser fire when he saw it. The tall, proud corn-bearing stalks had been cut down to stubble.

The men with him, his engineers and drillers, had drawn back from his fury and had gone on with the work they had come to do. The destruction of the field was a curiosity to be sure, but they were not responsible for the solving of the mystery of how or why it had been done. That was the responsibility of the Clan Lord.

That responsibility weighed heavily on Jared as his bleak golden eyes surveyed the damage done to years of effort. This was the first year these particular fields were to have yielded anything but alfalfa grass. For years, he'd nursed these fields from black sand to the acceptably rich soil they were now. The sinkwell had gone dry because of the demands put on it, the constant feeding of the precious water to the fields that had drunk thirstily, absorbing the water as soon as it fell.

What was left to him this year? Nothing except the promise of a rich harvest next year. The stubble and stalks would need to be plowed into the earth until spring, when seed could once again be planted.

But now, as he rode toward the Keep, Jared wondered why renegade Techs had struck at his northernmost fields. Was he being decoyed? Were renegade Techs even now descending on the Keep, knowing that in all probability he was too far away to get there in time? He shook his head.

No, if something was happening at the Keep, Susan would be able to tell him. The strange horseman would not be a forward scout sent to occupy the Keep dwellers until the main force could arrive. Perhaps the horseman was a messenger from one of the outlying holdings. Perhaps he was bringing word of more odd happenings from the edge of the desert.

Just as Jared caught sight of the Keep tower, he was almost rocked from Gaeten's back by the backwash of pain that flashed into his mind. He groaned, falling forward over the stallion's neck, and the sound of his own voice was like broken glass grinding into his flesh. Then the moment passed. With pain-dazed eyes, he lifted his head and, although shaking a little from the aftermath, kicked the stallion to move toward the Keep at a gallop.

He was afraid now of what he would find on his arrival. And just as he thought that, a second wave of pain flooded through his mind, this worse than the last and unremitting. Jared thought it would fade as the first one had, but this one kept on and on and on. As the pain continued, Jared felt himself more able to control it, to ignore it, to push it into the background so that he could still function. He galloped into a courtyard curiously devoid of people with the exception of a young stable hand.

Throwing himself from the back of the horse before he had come to a stop, Jared sprinted across the courtyard and threw open the doors to the great hall. He paused on the threshold, his breath coming harsh in his chest, the pain flaring through his mind, his eyes scanning the group gathered at the far end of the hall.

Striding quickly, he crossed the hall, pushing people aside ruthlessly and without apology as he made his way through the crowd. When he reached the small center clearing, he hesitated for a second as his mind assimilated the images before him.

He saw his wife of almost two weeks kneeling on the stone floor, her head thrown so far back, her slender neck looked in danger of snapping, her glorious mane of red hair falling down her back. Her entire body trembled and shook with the pain that pounded through her.

Did she know? Jared wondered. In the throes of her healing did she even realize that he was experiencing everything she was? He forgot his questions when he saw her sway and begin to crumple. Two strides brought him beside her, and he knelt, his arms sliding around her and pulling her to him, supporting her from falling. Wedged securely himself, he closed his eyes and sent his mind spiraling into hers, and found himself falling after the bright light that was her soul as it plunged down the dark tunnel toward death.

He swept after her and caught her scant feet from the horribly boiling black pit that threatened her. Without hesitation or weakness he turned his back on the death below and brought them both back, up toward the sun, up toward life. Once there, he stayed with her, holding her, supporting her, adding his strength to hers. With careful dexterity, he wound his strength with hers and beat back the pain, protecting her from it, so she could finish her healing and remain whole herself. Her gratitude and her joy at his presence flooded him and filled him with tenderness, for he knew she had been sorely unprepared and frightened by what she had undertaken.

At the end, after she had healed the ruin that had once been a man and was once more, he felt the shudder that ran through her fragile body as her hands dropped away from the man's face and fell limp to her sides. Her body seemed to collapse on itself. Opening his eyes, he lifted her into his arms as if she were a breath of wind that bore no weight at all. Carefully and with great tenderness, he carried her away. The members of his Clan parted before him and provided a path to the tower.

Magda followed him up to his bedchamber, hurrying to the bathing room for a bowl and a cloth as Jared placed Susan on the canopied bed and loosened her gown. Magda returned, placing the bowl on the table to one side of the bed, and prepared to help Jared remove the rest of Susan's clothing.

His hands still shaking, he glared across the bed at his mother. "You allowed this?"

Magda reared back, the crystal on her forehead sparking in indignation. "I forbade it. It was too dangerous. He was too badly injured."

"And yet she did it?"

An eyebrow raised, Magda allowed a dry chuckle to escape her lips. "Does that surprise you, my son?"

Wearily, he shook his head, not surprised at all. Since the joining, he had learned much about his wife. "Leave us."

"She needs to be cooled. She is burning with fever."

"I'll do what needs to be done. I wish to be alone with her."

Reluctantly, Magda backed away. "Call me if you need anything. I shall stay close."

"When the messenger has recovered and he is able, send him to me. I shall hear what he has to say then. It's trouble, I fear," Jared said, his hand smoothing the curling tendrils of hair back from Susan's forehead. "He suffered laser burns."

"Then the villagers were right. It is renegade Techs," Magda said flatly. "I shall send word to the Widows."

Jared looked at her. "Perhaps not just a band of renegades this time. I suspect they're more than an

organized band of malcontents seeking the richness of our crystals and our women."

"Then what else?"

He shook his head. "I don't know. When the
messenger is able to speak, we'll know more. In
the meantime, leave me with my wife."

He waited until he heard the door close behind
Magda before sitting down on the bed beside
Susan. He picked up the cloth and after dipping
it into the bathing liquid, gently he sponged her
body.

Examining her creamy white skin for signs of
trauma, he found none. Remembering the seething
black pit that had represented death, he feared the
damage would be to her mind. He had never known
of anyone attempting to heal such a grievously
injured man.

"And you, little one, had to be the one who tried
it—against the orders of a Widow no less. You are
a valiant warrior, my crystal woman."

She mumbled something, her words unintelligible, her head tossing from side to side on the
pillow.

Jared glanced at the window. It was close to
dark. No matter what the messenger had to say,
it would be too late to act on whatever information
he carried until morning. Moving the cool, damp
cloth over Susan's body, he remembered what she
had told him of her world—that people were not
afraid of monsters at night. They were free to walk
the roads and the forests of her world, wary only
of predators who were human and whose prey
were human. He wondered which world was more
frightening. He thought perhaps that Susan's was.

A knock at the door interrupted his thoughts.
After covering Susan with a bedsheet, he walked
over to the door and opened it, staring at the

young man who stood, strong and hearty, in the hall outside. Jared stepped out into the hall and gravely looked down at the man.

"Your lady? She will recover?" the young man asked hesitantly.

Jared nodded. "After some rest, she will be fine."

The messenger seemed to detect the hesitation in his voice. "I am sorry for any pain I caused her. If she had not done a healing on me, I should be dead now. Forgive me, my Lord, for putting your lady at risk."

"Lady Susan chooses her own path. There are none to gainsay her. Not even me," he added with light amusement, his lips curling in a rueful smile. "You bring a message?"

"I am called Percy. I bring you an urgent message from a Tech called Connor."

Jared nodded. "We've been expecting him. What happened?"

"Renegade Techs descended on us with their weapons. Our swords and pitchforks were like nothing against the weapons of the Techs. The battle continued as I left. Connor organized my people, but he begs that you come at first light and help us," Percy said, meticulously relaying the message he had been given.

"How many Techs?" Jared asked, already calculating what he would need to bring relief to the beleaguered village.

"A hundred, perhaps more. All of them have weapons. We cannot get close enough to fight them. Our people have retreated within the village walls and Connor is directing the defense."

"There's none better than Connor," Jared said thoughtfully. He looked at the young man. "Will you accompany us back to the village in the morning?"

Percy started, Jared's question evidently stunning the young man. "Then . . . then you'll come?"

"Did you think I would not?" Jared asked, his voice cool. "Your village is under my protection, and even if we are all to die on the morrow, you are entitled to whatever aid I can render. Such is my vow to your village chieftain and such is his vow to me."

Percy hesitated.

"What now, boy? Have I not satisfied you?" Jared asked impatiently, anxious now to return to Susan.

"Does your lady travel with us in the morning?"

Jared frowned at him, surprised by the question. "Why?"

The young man floundered, searching for the words and yet obviously sincere. "Your lady healed me when all forbade her to do so. She took my pain and made it hers. I have never known a kindness such as that."

"Bravery recognizes bravery, boy," Jared said quietly. "Your courage touched her."

Percy touched his fingers to his face, his expression one of wonder. "And even so, she did not merely take my pain. She restored me as I was before. If she rides with us, I should like to have a minor place in her guard. If danger threatens her, I should like to have the opportunity to defend her."

Jared touched the boy's shoulder. "Then you shall ride in her guard, whether or not she chooses to come with us in the morning, Percy. If she does not ride to the village, then neither shall you. Subject to my lady's desires in this matter, you shall be her guard from this day forward."

As Percy bowed in acquiescence, Jared saw the red blush of hope fulfilled on the young man's face.

Janice Tarantino

"See the Widow Magda, Percy. She shall see you settled for the night. Rest well." He watched as the boy walked quickly down the hall and disappeared from sight. Turning, Jared went back into his bedchamber and sat at his wife's side.

He stared down at Susan as she slept the sleep of exhaustion. Reaching out to her, he stroked his hand down the side of her face, his fingers lingering on the strong line of her jaw.

His wife was a woman of strength and courage—more strength and courage than he had ever seen in a woman, even in a crystal woman. Evie would never have been able to do what Susan had done today; she would never have even thought of it. His mother's word would have been law.

Susan had defied Magda and had done what she had perceived as the right thing. He knew instinctively that she had plunged into the healing without even considering the danger to herself. He knew that she would have done so even if she had known that her own life might have been forfeit. Their joining had taught him that once Susan committed herself she never reneged.

And she loved him.

His hand clasped around hers where it lay beside her. Slowly, her fingers curled around his hand. He looked down at the soft milkiness of her skin where it contrasted with the dark olive of his. She was beautiful, his wife, his crystal woman.

Something inside him, something buried deep behind the high wall in the center of his mind, cried out in pain as he stared down at her. If only things were different . . .

"I would find it too easy to love you, Susan," he whispered softly, his thumb stroking the tender skin of her hand. "But in the end you will do naught but fly from me. Better it remain this

238

way. In your world you will recover and love someone else." He leaned down and pressed his lips to where the star marked her forehead. "I hope that you will remember me with love, and yet I pray for both our sakes that you will forget."

Chapter Twelve

Susan had hoped to be mounted on the horse Jared had given her as a wedding present before he discovered her intention to accompany him on the journey. He had been gone this morning from their bed when she had awakened, but she remembered seeking his warmth in the night. Jared had held her close, and in his arms she had found comfort and peace.

But this morning, she'd sought to evade him until the war party was on its way.

Her luck ran out when he found her in the arms room along with the other members of the Guard as they prepared themselves for the foray to the village on the desert's edge.

She was buckling her sword belt around her slim waist when she caught sight of his long shadow out of the corner of her eye. She continued to arm herself as if she was not aware of his presence. When she turned, he stood in front of her, his golden eyes staring down at her, his hands on his hips, his broad chest barring her way.

"Well, madam," he said slowly, his eyes traveling over Susan's trousers and tunic, the leather vest that served as light armor, and the heavy belt that held her sword and dagger safely sheathed. "I recall telling Fenil to instruct you in the arts of the sword and dagger, but I don't recall telling Fenil or anyone else to outfit you as a member of my Guard."

Lifting her chin, she returned his regard, making it clear that she would refuse to yield an inch in her decision to accompany him. She attempted to probe his mind, seeking his true disposition this morning.

He successfully parried her attempt, his mental barriers rising up, a faint smile curling his lips.

"I'm coming with you, Jared," she said firmly. "You'll not change my mind. Fenil has merely followed my instructions."

"Surely you have not progressed so far in your lessons as to take your place as an equal of any member of my Guard. Fenil gave me no such report on your progress," he said, the smile still tarrying at the corner of his mouth.

She stared at him, carefully gauging his mood and wondering how far she could push him. "Fenil has given you no report at all," she said finally. "I asked him not to. But as to your other question—no, I have not progressed so far as to take a place in your Guard. Far from it in fact, but I wish to accompany you. I'll not hold you back nor cause you any anxiety, Jared." She paused, wondering what else she could say to prevent him from forbidding her to ride with him.

He stared down at her for another long, endless second and then to her surprise he nodded.

"You may accompany us, but on one condition, madam."

Here it comes, she thought ruefully. She should have guessed that no concession from him would be free of penalty.

Jared beckoned behind him and called forth the young man whom she had healed yesterday. "Percy wishes to act as your personal guard."

Opening her mouth, she started to object, and then she saw the hopeful, half-bashful look on the young man's face. She snapped her mouth closed and narrowed her eyes at Jared, trying to figure out his motives. "Instruct me, Jared. You know I don't know what's customary in a case like this."

He laughed. "There are no cases like this, madam. You are a law unto yourself. I am merely trying to guarantee your safety in light of my ignorance as to your skill with the sword and dagger. Since Percy has requested the honor, I see no reason to deny him, if you have no objections." His eyes and voice softened. "It would ease my mind, Susan, if I knew he was at your side. He tells me he is versed in the use of a sword, and he has no reason to lie, knowing it might mean your life. He is a brave lad who would die for you if necessary."

Looking at Percy, she smiled and made up her mind. "I would be very upset if you felt you had to die for me, Percy. But if it is your wish, then, yes, I would be honored to have you as my guard."

The young man blushed and stammered, "The honor is mine, my Lady."

"See Fenil about getting kitted up quickly, Percy," Jared said. He turned back to Susan, and she felt her cheeks grow warm under his intense regard. "I was worried about you last night. Are you sure you're up to traveling?"

She sucked in her breath as her eyes flickered over his broad chest. Just looking at him and remembering their nights together was enough to drive every coherent thought from her mind. "I'm tired," she admitted, and then she frowned. "But I have the feeling I must go. I can't explain it, Jared."

He nodded. "So be it, but you will obey me without question if I require it of you, will you not?"

"Yes," she answered without hesitation, knowing instinctively that, once having given his blessing to her presence in his war party, he would not interfere if he did not need to, and knowing that if he did, it would be only for her own safety—or perhaps his own.

A short time later, she mounted Desert Moon, her white mare, and was concentrating on keeping her seat when Jared moved Gaeten to stand at her side. Controlling the enormous stallion with only his heels, Jared leaned over and pressed the same gold circlet she'd worn during the joining ceremony over her unbound hair, centering the crystal over the star on her forehead—the star she barely noticed anymore when she looked into a mirror.

He looked down at her and reached out to clasp her hand for a moment, bringing it to his mouth for a brush of his lips. "The circlet will make it clear to all that you are my lady." Without another word he spurred the stallion and rode ahead to take his place at the head of the column of 20 guards, squires, grooms, and pack mules loaded with provisions and medical supplies.

The Clan flag was unfurled by the Captain of the Guard and with a shout they were on their way at a fast pace. As Susan fell into line ahead of the pack mules, Percy joined her but stayed several paces behind her. Regardless of her smile and gesture for him to join her at her side, he shook his head and refused.

"The place beside you is held for Lord Jared," Percy said. "He will join you at some point during the journey. It would not be seemly for his place to be filled."

Riding alone, Susan every so often lifted her hand to finger the filigree gold of the circlet that rested on her brow and marveled at how wearing the circlet seemed to bring her perceptions into sharper focus. Even her sight seemed sharper. She had experienced the same kind of clarity on the day of the wedding but had not understood it at the time. Vaguely, she wondered if, had she been wearing the circlet yesterday, she would have been so affected by the attempt to heal Percy. Perhaps in some way the crystal set in the center of the circlet enhanced whatever mental acuity she had.

She had not admitted to anyone yet, least of all Jared, how shaken she had actually been by the healing. She realized now that she had not truly expected to be able to heal Percy so completely. She had sought to ease his pain, but she had been caught up so completely by the young man's agony that she had instinctively reached to heal all—his body as well as his mind. She had also known, subconsciously perhaps, that if she had left him crippled and maimed he would have died a slow and tortured death of the spirit.

Sunk into her thoughts, she at last admitted silently to herself that she possessed some kind of power, the strength of which had yet to be tested, although it appeared as if the Widows had been right all along. The extent of her power, based only on Percy's healing, appeared to be formidable. That it could be enhanced was also obvious; she just had to observe the effect of the golden circlet with the great crystal, glittering red now, that rested over the star on her forehead. Her mental shields had become stronger almost without her realizing it, and when she wore the circlet it was a rather simple matter to screen out most of the peripheral awareness of the people around her.

Involved deeply in her thoughts, she looked up with surprise when Jared suddenly joined her. He rode at her side in silence at first, and then with a glance first at Percy, he fixed his gaze on her face, his eyes worried. "How are you faring?"

She smiled at him, touched by his concern. "I'm fine. Just a little tired. Stop worrying. I promise if I don't feel well, I'll let you know." She smiled ruefully as her hand rubbed at her hip. "The only problem that I foresee is going to be a sore rear end. I'm not that used to riding yet, although I've done some every day. Back home, my riding was limited to once or twice a year on some very safe bridle paths in New York."

He was silent for a moment. Then he said, "Tell me about how you lived in your world. It is clear that many of our ways surprise you." He smiled a little and gestured toward her outfit. "Magda's shock at your garb was something you couldn't understand. I felt your confusion when she taxed you with her objections."

Susan nodded. "In the last twenty or twenty-five years, it's become commonplace. The women's movement did a lot for . . ." She saw the look of polite confusion on his face and laughed. "Let's just say that women wearing pants is a relatively common occurrence in my world." She glanced at him quizzically. "Haven't you ever seen a woman in trousers?"

"Tech women wear trousers." His eyes looked down at her sneakered feet in the stirrups. "Their grav boots are similar to your footgear."

"These are sneakers," she said with a laugh, appreciating the odd incongruity of the white leather high-top sneakers against the copper-colored silk trousers she wore. In her tunic of copper and with her red hair topped by a circlet of gold, she would be hard to miss on a battlefield. She'd wanted something simple and dark, similar to what the men and women of the Guard wore. But the seamstress and Magda, once she had agreed to the venture, had been aghast at the idea that Susan would array herself as a common soldier. She'd succumbed to their wishes only because she'd won on the more important point—the pants. "And you wouldn't believe the time I had getting Magda to return my sneakers. She kept telling me they were made from forbidden materials. They're made from leather and rubber. What's so forbidden about that?"

He shrugged. "The leather is not, so she must object to what you call rubber. We don't have that substance here."

"You don't have rubber trees?" She fell silent for a moment. "No, I guess maybe you wouldn't. Explain to me about this forbidden-materials law."

"It is simple really. Nothing is permitted on the face of the planet that cannot be returned to the earth or recycled in some way. There is no waste here."

"But you use metal for your swords. These stirrups are metal."

"Metal rusts and eventually returns to the earth, but most of the time it is reforged when necessary."

"But what about the technology that you do have?" she asked. "You have many things that the people of my time don't have."

"The Widows and the Council together oversee the introduction of anything new to the planet's surface. They regulate the trade with the Techs. Everything must be beneficially biodegradable, and there cannot be any harmful waste or byproducts from its use." He looked at her with amusement. "But we've moved off the point. You were telling me about life in your time."

She sighed. "But I'm here in your time, and the more I find out, the more I realize I don't know. And if I'm to help you, and ultimately my own time, then I have to know as much as possible." She looked out past the road and saw the fields, their perimeters marked by trees and undergrowth. "I want to take back to my time as much knowledge of this place as I can possibly absorb."

His face changed subtly, and it suddenly seemed to Susan as if he drew back from her, his eyes and mind shuttered. "Let us hope that it will not be too long before the Widows can safely return you to the past." He bent his head to her as he gathered up his reins. "I must confer with the captain. I'll check back with you later." And with that, he galloped along the column, raising a cloud of dust in his wake that made Susan cough.

She blamed her suddenly watering eyes on the dust. It was a convenient excuse, although she didn't think she fooled Percy. She knew she didn't fool herself. Jared's sudden withdrawal from her had hurt, and it had hurt even more because she didn't know what she'd done to provoke it.

After Jared left her, the line of horsemen moved more swiftly. It was mid-morning when the column crested the hill that had been taking shape before them all morning.

Susan had seen the billowing black smoke rise from the far side of the ridge. Bursts of light had

Janice Tarantino

been visible against the louring sky as the crest of the ridge had become more defined the closer they came. Now, nearly at their destination, Susan assumed the sights and sounds were the signs of battle.

She spurred her horse to take the ridge, and rode up beside Jared with Percy trailing behind her. She understood how hard Jared's people fought for the green and growing things on the land they'd wrested from the earth, and when she looked down the other side of the hill, she could have cried aloud at the devastation and death spread out before her.

Below them lay a small village protected by high stone walls. Around the walls, laid out in the now familiar checkerboard pattern, were fields, once green and growing, now marked with black swathes of destruction. To the south, a field burned, the yellow fire dancing across what was once green and consuming all in its path. Even as she watched, the flames jumped to the young and tender leaves of the line of young trees that acted as a windbreak. The column of black smoke rising from the field widened until it became a barrier past which nothing of the desert in the distance could be seen.

Jared turned to look at her as the Guards formed horizontally across the ridge behind them. "Stay here." He sent Percy a dark, gold look. "See that you keep her safe, Percy, until I send word. But if you receive no word from me, ride back to the Keep as swiftly as you can and have Magda alert the Widows."

"Percy and I will stay with the mules," Susan said, looking back to the bottom of the ridge to where the mule handlers were setting up some kind of camp.

"No," Jared said. "The picket will be one of their targets if things go badly for us. It's our source of supply, and the Techs will seek to cut us off from it. Wait there." He pointed to higher ground.

Susan hesitated for a moment and then wheeled her horse, heading as Jared had instructed for the stand of straggly trees to the northeast. Behind her she heard a wild cry that was familiar. It had a certain musicality and cadence that was barbarically beautiful, especially when taken up by the rest of the Guards.

"'Tis the Dakbar war cry," Percy explained, his breath coming short as he pulled up beside her.

"I know. I've heard it before," she murmured, remembering the night Jared had defeated the Tremillium. She turned and watched, her heart in her mouth, as the castle Guard led by Jared charged down the sloping ridge into the battle below.

It was easy to tell who belonged to which side in the battle. The Techs wielded the guns and lasers. The farmers and villagers wielded swords and pitchforks, and now they had the horses and swords of Jared's castle Guard. Susan knew the castle Guard were good, but she had the sinking feeling that they weren't going to be enough. It was amazing to Susan that the meagerly armed farmers had held out a day and a half as they already had. Taking into account the superior weapons of the Techs, it seemed impossible for the fighting to degenerate so swiftly after Jared's arrival to hand-to-hand combat.

Frowning, she watched the horses of the castle Guard weave through the clusters of fighting men, hacking and slicing with their swords and, in some cases, hatchets, as their horses reared and wheeled and responded to the commands of their riders' heels alone. It was as if the scene laid out before her was some sort of hideous, bloody ballet. It was very clear to her that she was watching a consummate fighting force practiced in evading the superior weapon fire of the enemy while inflicting maximum damage.

Growing stiff from sitting on Desert Moon, she slid from the horse's back and looped the reins around a sapling. Vaguely she was aware that Percy did the same.

Her gaze searched, and she found Jared. She refrained from touching his mind, for fear of distracting him. Although she knew he was aware of her presence, she was also afraid to try to pierce the pulsating aura of violence that enveloped him. Somehow, she knew that if she tried to touch his mind, she would be engulfed by the same thirst for violence that shuddered through him now. She would feel what he felt when he swung his huge sword and made contact with a Tech's blood and flesh. She knew that she would feel the warm spray of blood that flew forth from mortal wounds to spatter Jared's exposed flesh with each blow that struck true. She had already experienced the coppery taste of her own blood when she'd bitten her lip during her weapons training. She would bet that the flat, metallic taste of blood was in each warrior's mouth and that it grew stronger with each blow struck.

As she watched, she became aware of an inner urging. She had the feeling she should be doing something—something to contribute to the battle, although she didn't have the slightest idea what.

Watching even more closely than before, she thought she could detect a pattern to the movement of the battle. Techs rushed forward, firing their weapons, and then retreated, leaving behind the fallen bodies of both comrade and enemy, which were then swept with laser fire by those Techs who held stationary positions. The defenders, despite the aid of Jared and the castle Guards, were doing little more than meeting the offensive each time it came and trying to defend their positions.

And they were losing. Even as she watched, she saw them surrender several feet of the battlefield as they retreated back toward the ridge and to the north closer to the stone walls of the enclosed village. If the focus of the battle did not shift, perhaps Jared would be among those slain. As it was, too many had already died.

Moving forward a few paces, she stood on the crest of the ridge and stared out, past the front battle line, past the desert's edge. Her sight limited her. She closed her eyes and reached out with her senses, her awareness, and found something new. An inner sight that was not bound by the physical limits of her eyes. She found her sight skimming along just above the desert surface—out further and further. With a gasp she opened her eyes. The crystal disc on the golden chain around her neck burned where it rested under her tunic.

Was this farsight something all crystal women had? She frowned with concentration and closed her eyes again, determined to use this newly discovered ability to Jared's advantage. Her vision skimmed out above the desert surface again. Finally, she found what she was looking for.

Out in the desert beyond the first dunes of black sand, an enormous vehicle hovered several feet in the air above the sand.

She saw figures behind the smoked glass, and she focused on one figure in particular—a tall man with silver white hair, his face lined and pitted. He bent over a table, his gnarled, nicked, and scarred fingers moving across a map.

Suddenly, as if he sensed he was being watched, he lifted his head and Susan saw his eyes, deep, dark cesspits of sadistic cruelty. He frowned and moved over to the wide glass, looking out, his eyes staring in the direction of the ridge where Susan stood. It seemed as if he sensed her ethereal presence.

And then she shuddered and broke the odd contact, opening her eyes once again, seeing the hovering craft as a dark speck far off in the distance, but still feeling the dark, cold sensation of the touch of evil. She knew without a doubt that somehow that man knew she stood on the crest of the ridge. And there wasn't any question in her mind that he knew who she was.

And she knew who he was. Without understanding the process of her knowing, Susan was certain his name was Orsin. He was the orchestrator of the battle. She also knew that if Jared was to have any chance of winning this battle at all, the control craft and its personnel had to be put out of commission. There was no chance that Jared could spare any manpower to attack that craft, and even if he could, Susan knew the craft would be heavily armored and weaponed. None of Jared's force would stand a chance.

Again she was aware of the nagging feeling that there was something she should be doing to help.

Her eyes were drawn back to Jared. So far he was faring well, although she sensed that he was tiring. Even as she watched, she saw the guard fighting beside him fall, victim of a laser blast.

Jared's anger suddenly broke through his mental barriers and the force of it, blood red and burning hot, nearly rocked her off her feet. She staggered and caught her breath in horror as Jared wheeled Gaeten and charged in the direction the laser blast had come from.

"No, Jared! No!" she screamed, knowing that the Tech was leveling his laser weapon, aiming at Jared's chest, his finger tightening on the trigger. She knew when the Tech's finger passed the point of no return on the trigger. She saw the thin beam of light and in instinctive reaction, she threw up her hand, palm forward, to ward off from Jared the burning light of death as it sped toward him.

No one was more surprised than she when a shield of shimmering transparent gold appeared in front of Jared a fraction of a second before the laser beam reached him, deflecting the beam, sending it back in the direction from whence it had come. The laser beam struck the cover where the Tech was hiding, and in an instant the Tech was a blackened lump of burned flesh and charred bones.

Susan felt Jared's startled question in her mind, but found herself unable to answer him, frightened and sickened by what she had accomplished, all unknowingly.

"My Lady," Percy whispered. "Look below! They've circled the picket."

Reluctantly, she tore her eyes from Jared and looked back to where the pack mules were located. She was almost convinced Percy was mistaken when she saw a flicker of movement along the perimeter of the camp.

"They must be warned," she murmured, and then hearing the sound of a cry choked off, she spun on her heel, startled.

Four men dressed in khaki jumpsuits stood between her and the stand of trees and the horses. Percy hung in the grasp of one of the men, and even as she watched, the Tech let Percy slide to the ground.

Dead or unconscious? she wondered, her eyes flickering over Percy's body, searching for injury and finding none. Unconscious then.

Her hand flew to the sword hilt at her waist, but fell away when the weapons held by all four men threateningly followed her movement.

"We're to bring you to Orsin," the tallest man growled in a guttural voice. "Unless you want the same treatment as your pretty boy here, you'll come with us and give us no trouble."

She concentrated on the weapon he held, trying to determine whether it was in reality a stun gun or whether it was one of the death-dealing lasers.

The tall man with the graying hair smiled at her as if he knew what she was thinking. It wasn't a pleasant smile. "The lasers have several settings."

She didn't answer the man, focusing her concentration instead on the weapon in his hand. In a moment, the gun was too hot for him to hold. He cursed and tossed the weapon away from him, staring down at his burned hand in amazement and then staring at where the melting mass of metal had fallen in the tall grass. Swiftly, the three other men followed suit as their guns began melting in their hands.

After the fourth and last man had dropped his weapon, she drew her sword, hearing with satisfaction the sibilant *hiss-ching* of metal on leather as the sword slid smoothly out of its sheath. She felt the balanced weight as she gripped the hilt of the sword. She sank into the fighting crouch that Fenil had taught her and stared at the men, silently daring them to come closer.

They drew short daggers from their belts, and then began to advance on her.

She felt the fear then, rising and lodging in her throat, nearly choking her as she realized this was not sword practice with comrades in arms. This was real, and she knew with a sick feeling in her stomach that someone was going to die before this confrontation ended. She didn't intend to be the one to die.

All four rushed her at the same instant.

She slashed with the sword in a half-circle, trying to keep them away. The razor-sharp blade of her sword caught one in the belly, gutting him. His scream of agony was high-pitched, and she shuddered when she saw the blood on the sword. The other three drew back for a moment, as if surprised that she had been effective, before they widened the distance between themselves and then rushed her again.

This time, one of the men impaled himself on her blade, and she struggled to pull it free as he fell. Then there was no more time for thought or strategy. The other two fell on her and she reacted, fighting now for her life.

Originally, with the length of the sword against their daggers, she'd had the advantage, but she wasn't skilled enough to keep it. She pivoted to meet the threat, but the men had flanked her and she could only fight in one direction. The second man grabbed her from behind and with an arm around her neck, pulled her back tight against his body.

The sour smell of his sweat engulfed her as he pressed the point of his dagger to her throat hard enough to draw a tiny rivulet of blood. She froze.

"Drop the sword," the man rasped in her ear.

She did as she was told, furious with herself for not foreseeing or knowing how to cope with the flanking maneuver they'd pulled on her.

The other man reached forward and plucked the crystal handled dagger from her belt.

Susan stared at the throat of the man who'd just taken her dagger, a sudden idea coming to her, not knowing if what she planned to do would work, but also knowing that at this point she had nothing more to lose. If she miscalculated, she knew that it wouldn't take much for the man who held her from behind to draw the dagger all the way across her throat. She was terrified, but desperate enough to try anything.

Mentally, she pictured his windpipe as it slowly closed, cutting off his supply of air.

It was a moment before the man realized what was happening. He dropped her dagger and grabbed at his neck, his breath rattling and wheezing as he tried to force it past the obstruction in his throat that Susan's mind had created.

Growing more bold, Susan then wove in the reality of the man behind her, linking him to her illusion. In a matter of seconds, he too began struggling for breath and his grip around her neck loosened and the pressure of the sharp dagger point against her throat lessened.

Susan frowned with the concentration required, feeling the dull thud of a headache begin at the base of her neck and across her forehead, almost as if a vise was twisting tighter and tighter, but knowing that her life was at stake, she ignored the ache and focused on bringing what she had begun to its inevitable conclusion. Barely two minutes later, the two men lay on the ground at her feet, dead from suffocation, marked by the power she wielded. Beyond them, the other two lay dead, bloodied with the violence of her sword, the manner of their deaths in striking contrast to the two who almost appeared to be sleeping at her feet.

Sinking to her knees in the high grass, Susan trembled and brought the thin air into her lungs with deep gasping breaths.

She, who had always hesitated to kill a spider, had just killed four men.

Shocked by her actions, she shook, suddenly feeling sick to her stomach, although she knew that any one of the dead men lying around her would have killed her without any more compunction than if she'd been an irritating insect. She had seen the reality of her own death in their eyes when they had first approached her. She also knew that Jared needed her in this battle.

These warlike Techs, so different from the people Jared had described when speaking of his ten years among the stars, would fight to the last man for whatever motivated them. A fair fight obviously meant nothing to them since they were using technologically superior weapons to the swords and pitchforks of the defenders. They meant to win by fair means or foul.

Her back stiffened as she knelt there, her eyes narrowed as she looked down at the battle that was turning against the defenders of the village. She searched out Jared, and with a gasp found that he had been knocked from his horse and lay on the ground, struggling to rise and trying at the same time to avoid being trampled by Gaeten's hooves.

Power surged and ebbed within her, fighting against the restraints her subconscious had put on it. The power within her knew that it was needed. She had only to allow the power to flow through her and find its way to the heart of the enemy, where it would destroy whatever it found.

Stretching her hands out in front of her, palms facing her, she saw the reflection of something strobing and pulsing off the white skin of her palms. The red flashes of light came from the crystal set in the filigree circlet bound around her head.

Slowly, she rose to her feet, her hands still stretched in front of her, the palms facing outward now. She stood there, focusing now on the hovercraft, the control center of the enemy, where it hung over the black sand of the desert. She felt the power build within her as she forced back the feeling of fear that built along with the power.

A thick miasma of cold shadow seemed to condense around her, pressing close, making it difficult for her to breathe and sucking the power from her almost as quickly as it built. With sudden clarity she realized that there was power other than hers at work here. Someone was projecting a field around her, seeking to contain her power, seeking to prevent her from using that which she must, draining off what she was building within her.

Although it was hard, she ignored the shadow and struggled to focus on the enemy's hovercraft. She visualized the hovercraft up close as she'd seen it earlier, her gaze fixing on that black speck in the desert. Again, she sensed Orsin's awareness of her power, and then strangely his presence was gone from the control room. She felt only the confusion and sudden terror that reigned when others realized their leader had left them.

She took a deep breath, and as she exhaled, she released the energy. Physically she felt its heat as it traveled through her body. Finally, with a blast of flaring red light, the force escaped from her hands, burned through the cold shadowy mist that surrounded her, arrowing along her line of vision to where the vehicle waited. She saw the streaming red light of her mental energy strike the hull of the vehicle, flicker, and spread across the metal, seeking a weak point. Barely a second later, the hovercraft exploded in a glorious burst of yellow light, red flame, and black smoke.

The shadows that surrounded her and sought to bind her burst away, as if affirming that she had won. Whoever had wielded their power on her had been aware of the death she had flung at the enemy.

She stood there on the crest of the ridge, staring down at the battle that had suddenly broken. The Techs, obviously shocked by the destruction of their control center, had broken from the engagement and were retreating toward the desert as fast as they could. Jared, the Guard, and the villagers pursued the Techs as they tried to escape from the battlefield.

Susan found herself unable to do anything but watch with cold, almost unseeing eyes the final cleanup of the battle. Vaguely she heard Jared mentally calling to her, but she retreated from the sound of his voice as it echoed through her mind, and hid behind the highest mental wall she could build, closing herself off from feeling, from caring, from the shock and horror at what she had done. She gathered herself, the essence of what she was, into a tiny ball and hid in that central core of her mind, silently weeping and sobbing at the carnage she had caused.

Turning finally, she walked over to where Percy lay still unconscious and sat down, placing his head carefully in her lap. She had no strength left. She felt like a hot cinder that had flared and burned itself out in one last spark of flame.

Chapter Thirteen

Jared had promised to send someone for her when the battle was over, but he came for her himself.

He dismounted slowly. Susan saw his eyes flicker to where she sat quietly, her fingers tangled in the hair of the still-unconscious Percy, stroking the silky brown hair of the young man she'd saved only the day before from death. Jared looked at her and then at the four dead men who surrounded her, and without a word, he bent down and lifted Percy away from her, giving the unconscious young man over to the care of the Captain of the Guard.

Jared knelt in front of her and looked into her eyes for a long moment, and then his hand reached out and stroked her hair gently. "You did what you had to do, Susan," he said, his voice pitched for her ears only.

She looked at him mutely, her face expressionless, and she knew her eyes reflected the pain she felt. "Did I?" she asked. "Or did I merely do what was expedient?"

He frowned at her. "These men threatened you. You reacted in self-defense. That is one of the reasons you are studying under Fenil."

Shaking her head, she closed her fingers around the strong bones of his wrist. "I asked to study under Fenil because I wished to defend myself against the animals in your world, not the humans."

"These four men would have killed you," Jared said.

"And what about the twenty in the hovercraft out in the desert? I murdered them, and they never even suspected they were about to die. These men at least saw death coming. They made their choice when they attacked me. Those out in the desert had no choice at all." Her grip on his wrist loosened and fell away.

"You were the one?" His gold eyes blazed at her as his hands snapped out and gripped her upper arms, his voice taut with barely controlled excitement. "You mean to tell me that you were the one who destroyed the control center?"

Puzzled by his reaction and the strange expression in his eyes, she nodded.

"I knew something strange was happening when that shield of gold sprang up in front of me just when that laser was about to hit me," he murmured. "You did that too, didn't you?" She nodded. "There was so much going on around me at the time I didn't have time to think about it. When their control center blew, I thought one of their reactors had overheated or malfunctioned for some reason. I never thought you had anything to do with it."

"My Lord Jared," the Captain of the Guard said, saluting as he came to a stop several feet away.

"Two of these men died of sword wounds, but we haven't been able to find any wounds on the other two."

Jared stared at her. "Susan?"

"They suffocated," Susan whispered.

"Suffocated," Jared repeated in an odd, tension-filled voice. Suddenly, he rose to his feet and, bending down, he picked Susan up in his arms and strode over to where Gaeten waited, lifting her on the stallion and swinging up behind her. He turned his attention to his Captain. "Take care of the bodies and then come down to the village. We'll rest there tonight and return to the Keep tomorrow morning." Without another word, he turned the horse toward the high walls of the village.

Susan sat before Jared, afraid of what she had seen in his golden eyes a few moments ago. Her use of the power to destroy the Tech control center had meant something to him—something important. She was afraid of what her sudden use of such enormous destructive power would mean.

As they rode along slowly, she worried at the questions in her mind. It was obvious that her power was growing stronger. As it grew, and if indeed it continued to do so, would she be able to control it? Would she be able to avoid what she had done today?

The numbness that had enveloped her until Jared's coming fell upon her again. Too much had happened to her today. Too much had happened *because* of her.

She felt Jared's arms tighten around her waist, aware that his embrace held her on his horse. She was aware when Jared issued orders to the Guard to bring the wounded to the village center for treatment. She was aware when he told them to carry the dead within the village walls to be prepared for burial at the desert's edge in the morning. Her eyes saw the grimy, weary, injured villagers also carrying their dead and wounded through the safety of the gate.

She saw it all, but she felt little. The part of her that experienced emotion had retreated, overwhelmed by too much sensory input. In essence her system had shut down. She knew it, and she welcomed it. She no longer wanted to feel anything.

Jared sat behind her, saying nothing, and she was grateful for the peace he allowed her.

They approached the wall, and Jared brought Gaeten to a stop beside the gate, watching and waiting as his Guard and the villagers filed past them. Susan, too, watched, and she saw the khaki-clad, slight figure of a man in his early thirties come through the gate and join them where they waited outside the wall.

"Jared!" the man said, his hand closing on Jared's knee, his face lighting with a smile.

Jared reached down and covered the man's hand with his own. "Connor. I'm glad to find you alive and well."

"I almost wasn't." Connor grinned up at him. "I just made the shelter of the village before those Techs found me. I think they were tracking me." His pale blue eyes shifted in Susan's direction and one eyebrow lifted.

She stared back at him. So this was Connor. Magda had mentioned his name to her several times. Jared's mother claimed this man could answer many of her questions regarding the technology of this time. She looked at him more carefully.

He was an unprepossessing man. Smaller than

Jared, with pale brown hair and pale blue eyes, he was the type of man she could pass a hundred times in New York and never take a second look at. In this world, he practically faded into the background. If it hadn't been for his khaki coveralls, so different from the garb of the villagers, who were clad in brightly colored garments, and the fact that he had approached them directly, Susan knew she would never have noticed him. But once he was noticed, there was something about him that demanded a closer look. What was it, she wondered, that drew her to him?

"This is my wife," Jared said. "Her name is Susan."

Connor looked quickly at Jared, his eyes puzzled. "A crystal woman?"

Jared nodded. "We have much to catch up on, Connor. You've been gone for weeks."

"I've discovered some interesting things too." Connor said, seeming to be satisfied by Jared's promise of a later conference.

Jared nudged the stallion through the portcullis, followed by Connor, who signaled for the gate to be lowered. "We'll have to get everyone settled before we have a chance to talk, Connor," Jared said. "Judging by the damage done this day, I doubt we'll find time for ourselves before we get back to the Keep. Where is the head man of this village?"

"Dead," Connor said. "An old warrior. He held a defense line against the Techs and was one of the first to fall."

Dismounting, Jared reached up to lift Susan from the saddle. "We'll need a place to sleep. I want Susan to rest. All the medicines should be gathered into one place so that the injured can be treated."

"The village square," Connor said.

"I can't rest while everyone is working," Susan objected, swaying on her feet but fighting the exhaustion. "I may be able to help some of them."

"There'll be no healings by you," Jared said firmly.

Despite what Jared ordered her to do, she knew there would be no rest for her during the coming night. Her memories would haunt her.

He bent as if he would pick her up into his arms, but she evaded him, holding him off with her flattened palm against his chest, shaking her head. "I'll stand on my own, Jared. I have no wish to be considered weak in front of your people."

The gold in his eyes went suddenly dull as if she'd said something that had cut him deeply. "Where is the head man's house? We'll stay there."

"This way," Connor said, gesturing toward the outer wall of the village.

As they walked over to where a tiny cottage nestled in the shadow of the stone wall, Susan wondered what she'd said to hurt Jared. But she saw no lingering sign of his hurt when he made her sit down in a chair at the well-scrubbed table in the one room cottage.

"Connor and I will see to settling the village and then we'll be back," Jared said. "I don't want to see your face outside this cottage. Do you understand?" He stared at her for moment as if he were unwilling to leave her. "Let's go, Connor, before it gets too dark to accomplish anything. You know the layout of the village. What do you suggest . . ."

Their voices faded as the two men left the cottage. Susan waited for a few minutes, then opened the front door and looked out. There was no sign of either Jared or Connor. She had no intention of

sitting around while there was work to be done—
when she might be able to help someone.

Making her way in the direction that most of the
people seemed to be traveling, she thought that
she would have to keep an eye out for either Jared
or Connor, but especially for Jared. If he found out
that she had ignored his instructions, he would be
furious.

As she resolutely walked toward what she thought
must be the center of the village, her attention was
caught by a young girl who darted from person to
person in the crowd. The child seemed to be begging
for something, but she was being shrugged off by
those passing.

The child slumped against the wall of one of the
cottages and rubbed her fists into her eyes. With
sudden decision, Susan walked forward.

"What is it?" she asked. "What's wrong?"

The child started and dropped her hands from
her face, pushing away from the wall.

"What's wrong?" Susan asked again, noting that
the girl was older than she'd thought at first, probably about 13 or 14.

"Lady!" the young lass whispered, her gray eyes
wide.

Susan frowned, unsure whether she'd been recognized or whether the word was a term of address.
"You're upset," she said, deciding to avoid addressing the subject. "Do you need help?"

"Lady, my mother's time's come early."

"Her time?" Susan asked, her frown growing
deeper.

"The babe," the girl answered impatiently, and
yet Susan could detect the fear in her voice.
"Mama's been laboring since early last night. She
says something's wrong. I'm afraid for her."

Oh, hell, Susan thought, and rather absurdly

remembered the line in *Gone with the Wind* uttered by Butterfly McQueen about not knowing anything about birthing babies. She suddenly knew exactly how the maid had felt.

"What about a doctor?" Susan fumbled for another word—one that might be familiar to the child. "A midwife? A healer?"

"The healers are all in the square tending the wounded."

Where I should be, Susan thought. "What about your father?" she asked.

"Dead. He was killed in the fighting yesterday."

Susan heard the stark horror in the girl's voice, and was sure that the child had seen her father die. "Come on then, honey," Susan said, making her decision. "Let's see if there's anything I can do."

"You'll come then?"

Susan nodded. "I know the basics about how babies are born, but not much more than that. I don't know what help I'll be other than holding your mother's hand."

"Lady, that'll surely be more than she has now," the girl said.

She followed the young girl off the main path to the right. She looked behind her and marked the cottage with a window flower box with a few bravely struggling pink flowers to fix in her mind a landmark so she could return the same way. As she turned to follow the girl, a furtive movement caught the corner of her eye. Susan stared at the spot, her gaze probing a few shadows, but she saw nothing more. Finally, shrugging, she moved on to follow the girl, marking the incident down to an overactive imagination and exhaustion.

"What's your name?" Susan asked when the girl paused in front of one of the larger cottages.

"Cammie, Lady," the girl said, ducking her head

in a short bow, her hand resting on the latch of the cottage door.

"Well, my name's Susan," she said.

"Yes, Lady," Cammie said, opening the door.

Susan mentally shrugged, and followed the girl over the threshold into the dim interior of the cottage.

Four solemn, young children greeted her, all standing in a row, in order of size from tallest to smallest. The little one had a thumb firmly anchored in her mouth.

Susan stood and returned their regard. All four were girls, and all four were gorgeous, with the same dusky curls and gray eyes of their older sister.

"The Lady came to help Mama," Cammie said to the other children as they awkwardly curtsied to Susan.

"She's bad," the oldest of the four said, stepping forward. "She's been crying."

"The Lady will help her," Cammie said stoutly, beckoning to Susan.

The implicit faith of children, Susan thought resignedly. At this point she was convinced that she'd made a mistake in coming alone. She didn't have the slightest idea what to do, and if something did happen to the expectant mother, Susan realized she was going to be the one who would have to deal with the consequences.

But when she stepped into the darkened bedroom and felt rather than saw the soundless sobs of the exhausted woman on the bed, all her doubts fell away. She'd done the right thing in coming, even if she couldn't do anything more than comfort the woman.

Cammie ran to the bed and knelt. "Mama? I've brought the Lady to help you."

Her eyes straining in the dimness, Susan saw the woman's hand stroke her oldest daughter's dark hair.

"You did well, Cammie," the woman whispered. "Now, go and stay with the other children."

Cammie kissed her mother's hand and then quickly left the room, but Susan saw the tears in the girl's eyes as Cammie passed her.

"Come closer, my Lady," the woman on the bed whispered.

Realizing she was standing in the middle of the room like a fool, Susan approached the woman. "What can I do for you?" she asked uncertainly. "I know nothing of babies."

"Light the lamp," the woman said, her voice thin and papery.

Susan touched the glowlight on the small table beside the bed, and saw the woman's face bathed in light.

The woman looked at her in wonder. "So, it is true after all," she said.

"You know me?" Susan asked.

The woman reached out and touched the star on Susan's forehead. "Word came to us that Lord Jared had joined with the crystal woman who was not a crystal woman. The villages all along the desert's edge have been whispering of the coming of the time of the Prophecy."

"Did your daughter know who I was?" Susan asked curiously.

The woman nodded. "She knew who you were the moment she saw you. There are none here with hair the color of fire. She did well to bring you." She caught her breath and her face contorted, her hands falling to her belly. When the spasm had passed, her voice was weaker. "Always before, my sister would come to help me birth. None of my children have come into this world easily or willingly."

"She couldn't come this time?" Susan asked, looking around for something to wipe the perspiration from the woman's brow.

A moment later, Cammie appeared with a small bowl of water and a cloth. Susan took the bowl without questioning how the girl had known what she wanted.

"She died. She was Garrett Lemaldin's crystal woman."

Susan's hand froze for a moment over the woman's forehead, remembering what Magda had told her of that night months in the past—the night her dreams had first begun. "She died at the gathering of the Clans," Susan said.

The woman nodded. "Yes, she died with all the others. I despaired even then of this birth, because always before I needed her with me."

Susan silently watched as the woman suffered through another labor pain.

"My children, all girls, fight against being born," she continued. Her laugh was a breathy whisper. "Perhaps they know what is awaiting them here. But there will be no more children. My husband is dead."

"I can ease your pain if that is what you want," Susan offered gently, not sure if her offer was an acceptable one.

The woman grasped her hand and squeezed it tightly. "No, my pain is nothing. I need you to bring the child from my womb safely."

"I'll help you all I can," Susan said, "but I don't know what to do."

"You don't understand, my Lady. You must touch the child's mind and calm her so that she may be born safely. She is afraid."

Susan sat back on her heels. "How do you know that?"

"Look at my forehead."

Susan took the glow light and held it over the woman's forehead. There was a round scar there, in the center, about a half an inch in diameter. "A crystal?"

The woman nodded. "I was born a crystal child as was my sister, but when I was but four years old, a fever came and destroyed my power and the crystal when it was first forming. My sister escaped the fever and so became a crystal woman. I was condemned to the life of an ordinary woman."

"But you still retain some of the powers of a crystal woman?" Susan asked, frowning in bewilderment.

"No, none of the powers, except for a sensitivity to very strong emotion and the ability to touch the minds of those closest to me. Because of this I sense the babe's fear of being born."

"And you want me to touch the mind of an unborn child?" Susan asked incredulously.

"I can't ease the child's fear because she knows my pain and feels her own. To the child, her intelligence yet unformed, she knows only sensation, and through me she senses that the world is a painful place. She knows only the safety and security of the womb." The woman gasped with exhaustion. "Please, my Lady. It is almost too late for her. She will die."

Not knowing if what the woman asked of her was possible, and without thinking about the matter any further, in response to the woman's plea Susan placed her hands on the swollen belly, closed her eyes, and sought the mind of the child.

Janice Tarantino

She found it at once, and she jerked back at first, taken by surprise at the violence and chaos that swirled in the mind of the babe in the darkness of the womb. Regrouping, she mentally approached again, this time projecting thoughts of calm and peace, seeking to soothe the child.

She felt it herself when the woman began to have another contraction, and Susan fought to maintain control over the child's mind. The woman's pain was palpable. It was no wonder that the child was frightened almost to the point of insanity. The baby was poised feet first and frantic to retain its position in the womb.

"Come, my child," Susan crooned silently. *"Come out into the world. It is not so painful. The world is a beautiful place. It is lovely to be alive."* She projected thoughts of green, spreading trees, and fields of gently stirring, fragrant flowers, and swift-flowing streams, bubbling white water over rocks.

Acting carefully, Susan blocked the projections of pain emanating from the helpless mother, and was rewarded by the child's slow relaxation and acceptance of her guidance in the journey to the world.

Suddenly it was over and the mind link was broken by the sudden loud squall of the child Susan held in her hands. She blinked, her eyes adjusting to the light of the bedroom. She saw the flow of dark red blood, and her mind flew swiftly to the mother's as she put the child on the bed and moved her hands back to the woman's belly to try to heal her. But she was too late. Even as she touched the woman's mind, she felt it fade, although she felt the touch of gratitude and could have sworn she heard a whispered word of blessing.

The child, Susan thought, pulling away from the

woman's mind. The child would need attention.

The baby was crying loudly, and now her cries were joined by the cries of the children in the next room. Susan stared down at the baby. The umbilical cord. That had to be tied and cut. She saw on the table next to the bed a plate that held some string and a sharp knife.

Her hands shaking, she did what was required, and for good measure, not knowing what the requirements were for sterilization in this world, she added some of the healing power she was already familiar with to her fingers as she tied and cut the umbilical cord. Just in case, she thought blankly, picking up the crying baby and pulling the bed linens up over the woman.

Walking over to the doorway, the baby in her arms, Susan wondered what she was going to say to the other children. "Cammie," she said, seeing the older girl surrounded by the four other girls. They were all crying. They knew their mother was dead. But how? How did they know? Susan wondered.

Cammie looked up and nodded. "Come, girls. Our new sister must be tended to, and we need to say good-bye to Mama. Each of you must wish her well on her journey and kiss her so that she may take our love with her to light her way to her soul's resting place."

Cuddling the newborn, Susan accompanied the girls back into the dark bedroom and watched as the children said good-bye to their mother, barely able to hold back her tears at the poignant farewells. After a few minutes, Susan gently urged them out of the room.

With Cammie's help, Susan washed and dressed the infant, finally wrapping her in a light blanket. The three younger girls watched.

"Well," Susan said. "I don't know what the procedure is now. Do you have any relatives? Anyone who can take care of you now? Who do we tell so that they can take care of your mother?"

The second oldest frowned at Susan, looked at Cammie, and then turned back to Susan. "We belong to you now."

Susan shook her head. "I'm afraid that's not possible. You must have someone—"

"She's right," Cammie said. "We have no one. It's the custom that the one who is present at the moment of—going away—assumes the responsibilities of that person."

Feeling suddenly numb, Susan stared down at the baby in her arms and then at each one of the older girls, starting with the youngest and working her way up to Cammie.

"That's why no one else would come to help," Cammie said. "No one wanted to be responsible for us after Mama died."

Remembering the sounds of crying she'd heard at the moment of the woman's death, Susan asked, "How did you know your mother had died? You did know, didn't you? You all began crying."

Cammie nodded. "We just knew. We felt her leave us."

Sighing, Susan acknowledged that she was out of her depth. She didn't know what was the custom. Jared would know, and she had the feeling he would be furious with her. She rose to her feet. "We'll have to find Lord Jared. He'll know what to do. In the meantime, the baby will have to be fed soon. Do you have any ideas, Cammie?"

"Several of the women in the village have had babies recently. Surely one of them will nurse her."

"Come," Susan said, holding open the cottage door and waiting until the children had filed past her into the dusky evening. "Lord Jared will be coming to the head man's house at some point this evening. We'll wait for him there."

Cammie walked beside her, the other girls in front.

"You knew who I was from the beginning, didn't you, Cammie?"

The girl nodded. "We heard that Lord Jared's new wife was a woman with hair of fire and a star on her forehead. I have never seen hair like yours before. And your thoughts were kind."

The baby mewled in her arms. Susan looked around. She didn't recognize the area as one she'd passed on her way to the woman's cottage.

"Are we going the right way?" she asked.

Cammie nodded. "The head man's cottage is but a short distance from here. We'll cross the field by the gates and then we'll be there."

Susan looked up at the sky. "It's almost dark."

Cammie looked also. "It's best we be inside soon."

Ahead of them and across the commons Susan saw the pale light in the window of the head man's cottage, and she was dismayed when she realized Jared must have already returned. There were going to be a few explanations to make before she would get to sleep this night. She wondered how Jared was going to take the revelation that she'd somehow or another acquired five children in the past few hours.

There was a flicker on the grass ahead of them, and Cammie stopped dead still in her tracks. Susan stopped, seeing that the other three girls had also frozen in place.

"A firefly?" Susan whispered hopefully.

Cammie shook her head.

Susan stared at the flicker and clasped the baby

275

closer to her chest, uneasiness pervading her mind. There were too many unexpected surprises in this world, she thought irritably. Just when she thought things were going reasonably smoothly, something unusual or threatening happened.

The flicker of light suddenly shot tall and straight into the air in front of them, reaching for the night sky, forming a swirling, flickering column of flame.

Susan thrust the baby into Cammie's arms for safety and ran forward to pull the other children back. "Run, girls. Get back," she urged, not understanding the danger, but knowing suddenly that the column of fire threatened them all. The children obeyed unquestioningly, and without a sound disappeared into the shadowed stand of trees behind her.

Susan stepped back a few paces, her eyes darting past the column of fire to what she could see of the head man's house. The fire cut her off from that illusory haven. She saw the front door open and two men run out, one tall, one shorter.

The column of flame suddenly shrank to nothing, revealing the figure of a woman, her arms spread wide, her gown of white silk blowing about her, her dark, waist-length hair rippling with motion although there was no wind. What startled Susan most was the blood-red sparkle of the crystal on the woman's forehead.

Susan knew then that she was looking at the last existing crystal woman—Ruhl's consort.

The woman looked directly at Susan and her red lips formed into a smile that was distinctly unpleasant. "You will die, crystal woman," the woman said, her voice reverberating around Susan.

Frozen with indecision, Susan watched as the woman's arms swung from her sides together in front of her level with her chest, her palms pointing directly at Susan. Jared shouted something to her, but she didn't understand him. The woman laughed as a blazing white bolt flashed from her palms directly toward Susan.

Instinctively, Susan raised her hands.

The beam of frenetic energy hit Susan's palms. Susan felt the jolt and experienced a flash of pain. For a brief second she thought she was dead, but then she realized that the lightning flash had been deflected by her palms and had spent itself harmlessly in the dirt at her feet. The smell of ozone was strong around her.

Shocked, she stared at the woman.

"So, it is true," the woman said, lifting her chin, her dark hair flowing down her back. "You are indeed a crystal woman, although you bear the mark of a star rather than a crystal. It begins. You have come a long way to be defeated. I have visited your time and found it beautiful. I shall look forward to ruling there as well as here," the strange woman said. She turned her head toward where Jared stood on the edge of the commons opposite Susan. "Ruhl awaits your Challenge. All shall be as foretold in the Prophecy, but delay not, else Ruhl will seek you out."

The woman stretched her arms out again and the column of flame rose up around her with a roar. When the flames died away a few seconds later, the woman was gone.

Susan discovered that her knees had turned weak and wouldn't support her any longer. She sank down on the ground and dropped her head into her hands, fighting the shaking that trembled through her. She didn't believe what had just happened. She couldn't believe it.

When the touch came on her shoulder, she jerked

away and stared up at Jared, fear in her eyes.

"Are you all right?" he asked, hunching down beside her, his hands cupping her face gently. "You weren't hurt, were you?"

"What the hell was that all about?" she asked. "Was that who I think it was?"

Jared raised an eyebrow at her tone, but when he answered her, his voice was tight. "That was Collis, my brother's crystal woman."

"Does she do this kind of thing frequently?" she asked, her tone acid with shock and reaction.

"Not that I know of. Her powers have grown." He reached out and grabbed Susan's hands, turning them palms up. "But it seems to me that your powers as a crystal woman equal hers, if they don't already surpass them."

It all seemed suddenly too much for her. She balled her hand into a fist and struck at his shoulder. "I'm not a crystal woman, damn you! I'm a stockbroker! I don't understand any of this! Why did you bring me here?"

"You are a crystal woman!" Jared's hands tightened on her wrists and he forced her to look at her palms. "Look, Susan! There's not a mark on your hands. Ruhl and Collis are afraid of you. They're afraid that you'll be too powerful for them to beat. They're trying to force us into issuing the Challenge before we're ready."

"I'm a stockbroker! I understand money and the stock market and in my time I could make you rich! But all this craziness, columns of fire, women appearing out of nowhere, I don't understand—"

Rising, he yanked her up with him and caught her to him, cutting her words off when his mouth closed over hers. It was as if he realized she could not deal with tenderness and gentleness, because his lips were like fire on hers, urgent and demanding. Suddenly he was in her mind, surrounding her, catching her up in the passion that always took her so much by surprise and yet seemed so natural between them. It was impossible for her not to respond to him, and with her response she lost all sense of the present and the danger that had threatened them all just a few minutes before.

When he finally released her, she almost fell. He scooped her up into his arms and strode with her in the direction of the head man's cottage.

"Wait! Wait!" she said suddenly, escaping the sensual haze that had dulled her mind, struggling to look behind them.

"What is it?" he asked, looking down at her, his voice low and rough.

She gazed up at him, seeing impatience, desire, and passion all mixed up in his gleaming, golden eyes, and for a moment she almost lost her tenuous control over her own desire. She wanted nothing more than to be taken to bed and to be surrounded by the heat of his passion, to be held in the safety and strength of his arms, to be sheltered from the horrible reality of all that had happened in the last few hours. But then, over his shoulder, she saw the children coming out of the shadows behind them, the five children, walking in order of size, the oldest carrying the youngest.

"Turn around, Jared," she said softly, and hesitantly she smiled up at him. "I think I've become a mother."

Chapter Fourteen

Alerted by the softness of Susan's voice, Jared spun around, his eyes narrowing when he saw the four young girls and the baby. Holding Susan tightly in his arms, he stared down at the quiet, obviously apprehensive children.

"Where's their mother?" he asked, although he instantly comprehended the situation and felt a flickering sense of sadness for another family torn apart. A curious feeling of rather amused resignation flooded him.

"It appears that there was a Clan tradition I didn't know about," Susan said, her voice unsure. "A little while ago their mother died giving birth to the baby."

Glancing down at her in surprise at the uncertainty he detected in her voice, he realized with lingering regret that Susan expected him to be angry.

As well he should be, he told himself sternly,

pulling his brows together in a scowl. But even though she'd deliberately disobeyed him and left the cottage in the first place, his anger was unconvincing. When Susan's tense body relaxed in his arms, he knew she'd seen through him.

"Don't think I'm not upset, Susan," he said. "Not about them." He nodded his head in the direction of the children. Loosening his hold on her, he allowed her to slip down the length of his body until her feet touched the ground. "I'm upset with you. I told you to stay in the cottage. I'll bet I was barely out of your sight before you left." He knew he'd hit on the truth when he saw a faint blush of rose touch her pale cheeks.

A wave of tenderness flooded him at the sight of her chagrin, and for a moment he forgot to hold back his emotions from her. Brushing the hair back from her eyes, he smiled down at her ruefully. "Do you have any idea of what I felt when I came back from the square and found you gone?"

He knew he'd made a mistake when her green eyes went soft and liquid as they did when he made love to her. His body tensed involuntarily and he sucked in his breath with surprise. Merely thinking of making love to the fragile-appearing woman in his arms made him grow hard. He didn't dare admit to feeling more for her; he *couldn't* let himself feel more for her.

He knew that since their marriage, Susan had sought for some sign from him that she meant more to him than merely being the means chosen by the Widows to fulfill the Prophecy. He had not been able to give her what she wanted. If he admitted that something more than mutual need and desire existed between them, he was afraid that he would not be able to let her go when it was time for her to return home. Dissatisfaction swept through him when he realized that the only time they came close to being totally honest with each other was when they made love.

Gently, Jared set her back from him, regretfully seeing the sadness rise and shimmer in her eyes. If he said the words out loud, there would be no turning back for either of them. He had to remain silent for both their sakes.

"What of the children, Susan? Who did you try to help?" he asked gently.

"Then it's true? It really is a custom?" she asked, looking at the children.

He nodded his head. "Yes, among some of the Clans, not all."

"I told them that we should come to you. That you would know the answers," she said, her hand moving up absently to rest against his chest. "I had to try to help them, Jared. No one else would."

His chest burned where her hand touched it, and he found himself struggling to concentrate on what Susan was saying instead of concentrating on the soft moss-green of her eyes and the moist richness of her lips. He frowned down at her. "No one would help them other than you?"

Mutely she shook her head.

"Is this true?" he asked of the oldest girl, who handed the newborn baby to the next oldest sister before stepping forward and curtsying to him.

"Yes, Lord Jared," Cammie said softly. "No one would come with me to help my mother except your lady."

He was disturbed by the information. The custom had originally guaranteed that the survivors of a tragedy would be taken care of. The thought that some of his people were refusing aid to anyone because of fear of being saddled with additional responsibility worried him. He looked at Susan.

"No one should have refused."

"But they did. I couldn't do the same," she answered.

"No, you wouldn't have," he thought at her, and smiled at her warmly before addressing the oldest girl. "And is there no one here in the village who would care for you and your sisters?"

"None who would do so willingly, especially now," Cammie answered.

"The woman said her sister had been crystal woman to Garrett si'Lemaldin," Susan said softly.

Jared frowned again. "Garrett si'Lemaldin is a good man. We'll detour on our way back to the Keep and stop at his holding. If he does not take you into his household, then, as custom demands, you and your sisters will become part of mine." He accepted the fact that if Garrett did not accept the children as his kin then, after Susan left him to return to her world, he would have these five feminine reminders of her softheartedness to torment him with memories.

His lips firmed. If he was fortunate, his torment would not last long after Susan left him. As Magda had said when this had begun, his mind might not be able to withstand the shock of the loss of a second mind link. He would die, but he would most likely go mad first. He repressed a shudder at the thought.

"Thank you, Lord Jared." The girl curtsied again, but not before Jared saw the look of relief in her eyes.

Feeling vaguely guilty because he had suggested Garrett si'Lemaldin as a solution to the problem, he gestured for Connor to approach. "See about putting the children somewhere for the night, Connor. There isn't enough room in the head man's cottage for all of us. And Connor"—Jared lowered his voice—"see that someone takes care of the mother's body." Connor nodded.

Jared turned back to Susan, but he froze when he saw the expression on Susan's face as she watched the children being shepherded out of her sight. Her delicate features were suffused with such a glow of tenderness and longing that his heart suddenly beat faster and the blood throbbed hotly through his veins at the thought of giving her a child of her own to love and cherish. For a Clan Lord, the continuation of his line was all important, and although he was bound by oath to do nothing to prevent the conception of children, the thought of giving Susan a child who would return with her to her time made him burn with strange feelings of possessiveness and anger at the situation in which they both found themselves.

The Widows had not taken into account the reality of human feelings when they had put their plans into action. He felt impotent anger at the perennial callousness of the Widows. They had acted strictly as strategists, seeking the solution to a problem, never considering the side effects of their machinations.

The children disappeared into the darkness, and a sudden sadness pulled at his heart. He only hoped there would be no child of his union with Susan, for if there were, the pain he would feel would be increased a hundredfold. And yet he knew that he would never be able to deny Susan her right to the child even though his line of the Dakbar Clan would die when the child passed from his world to Susan's with its mother.

Evie had desired children desperately, but had never been able to conceive. A frown creased his forehead when he realized how seldom he'd thought of Evie in the past week. During their marriage he had loved Evie unreservedly; she had been the star around which his life had revolved. But he knew with a sudden flash of insight that if it had been Evie standing on the ridge today, she would never have found the strength of purpose to kill in her own defense. Neither would Evie have been strong enough to face the trial that was predicted for him and his crystal woman by both the Widows and the Prophecy. Evie had been his wife, his companion, his most trusted friend, but he knew without a doubt that she would have shrunk from the task that now lay ahead of him and Susan.

At that moment of realization, the gates of his mind opened, and he freed the last remnant of Evie's soul that he'd kept trapped in his inviolate inner core. Evie had been the wife of his youth, and he would remember her always with the passionate love of the young.

Susan was the wife of his maturity, and as he looked at her, he knew a terrible longing to grow old with her at his side. He needed her deep well-spring of strength for sustenance of his life. Without her there would be nothing for him. When she returned to her world, he knew that nothing would hold him to this existence—not the soil, not his Clan.

Susan sighed. "The children will travel with us?"

He nodded in response, and knew a wounding sadness that what he desired with all his heart would never be. Susan, for all her strength of purpose and will, for all her turbulent emotions, for all her commitment to the saving of both his world and hers, longed to return to her own time. His golden eyes blazed down at her, and he swore silently that, whatever the consequences and regardless of what was destined for him, Susan would go home.

He took her arm and, from the look in her eyes, knew she was puzzled by the tight possessiveness of his grip as he led her to the tiny cottage. Despite his feelings for her, and perhaps because of them, he was still angry that she had disobeyed him. Not because in doing so she had flaunted his authority, but because in doing so she had put herself into danger.

Momentarily, he relived the moment when he had seen the flicker of light in the grass become the column of flame. He had known immediately that danger threatened her. Subconsciously he had been expecting some move by Ruhl and Collis against either Susan or himself ever since the ceremony that had joined them, but Collis's appearance had caught him by surprise.

Shutting the door behind him, he folded his arms across his chest and leaned back against the door. "Now, madam, perhaps you will explain to me why you disobeyed me." He saw the exhaustion and strain on her face, but he had to drive home his point now, while some of the shock of Collis's attack still lingered. That Susan might have been injured or killed with him helpless to come to her aid horrified him.

"If you knew me at all, Jared, you would know that I could not sit here and rest while others worked, not while there was the slightest chance I might be able to help someone or do something constructive."

"I'm beginning to believe I know you too well, Susan," he said, a sudden lopsided grin coming to his lips in spite of his annoyance with her. "I think I knew you would not willingly rest yourself, which was why I was so strong in my insistence that you do." The grin faded from his mouth. "But what just happened was the reason I wanted you safe. As long as I had no crystal woman, Ruhl considered himself safe from the fulfillment of the Prophecy. But when I not only married you but joined with you, I sent him a message saying that I considered you a crystal woman in every sense of the word."

"I won't be locked away just to be safe, Jared," she said, putting her hands on her hips and glaring at him, her eyes burning with green fire.

"If you hadn't reacted so quickly in deflecting Collis's blows, you would have been dead!" he said, trying to keep his anger under control. "You have no idea of how much danger you were in."

"As far as I was concerned, Lord Jared," she said coldly, "I was in about as much danger as I've been in all day. What difference is there between being threatened with death by four men and being threatened with death by a woman who's crazy enough to spin herself into a column of fire?"

"The difference is that the four men were exactly that. Men. Collis, on the other hand, is a crystal woman who has rediscovered the way to use powers that have been lost for centuries." Jared saw the mulish expression on Susan's face and knew he wasn't getting through to her. He again experienced that spark of excitement he'd felt out on the ridge after the battle when he'd realized what Susan had done. "In defending yourself against those men you utilized powers that crystal women barely remember."

"Whatever I did was instinctive. I didn't know what I was doing. Everything just happened." She shrugged. "It was like pulling a rabbit out of a hat."

He frowned at her for a moment, his anger subsiding, diverted by the image of her pulling a rabbit out of a hat. "Why would you want to pull a rabbit out of a hat?" His voice held a curious quality.

A small, involuntary chuckle escaped her and the tense muscles in her body relaxed a little. "It's one of the tricks magicians do in my time. What I was trying to say was that I don't know how I did the things I did today."

"Crystal women in past times possessed awesome powers. They were powers of the mind, although they manifested through the body. What Collis exhibited tonight was an example of that power. Just as you used the same kind of power to defend yourself against those Techs."

"And to destroy their hovercraft?" Susan shook her head and wrapped her arms around herself as a shiver visibly shook her. "I don't think you appreciate how difficult all this is for me. Admitting that I have power is one thing. But realizing that I can use it to kill frightens the hell out of me."

"You have to believe in yourself, Susan. You have to believe that you can control the power you possess." Quickly he approached her and grasped her upper arms, forcing her to look at him, willing her to understand, somehow knowing that right now she balanced on a thin edge. "Visualize for yourself what the center of your power looks like."

She frowned and closed her eyes, appearing to delve deeply into herself. There was a long pause before she spoke. "It's like a shining light." She opened her eyes and looked up at him. "But—it's incomplete," she faltered. "I don't know why I feel that way, but I feel as if it needs something to be . . . whole."

"What kind of things do you think you can do as a crystal woman?"

She stared directly up at him, her eyes soft and lost. "I can direct energy, as I did this afternoon with the hovercraft. I can kill. I can sense things. The power can be good or evil." She paused a moment, searching within herself. "Yes, the power can be perverted. At this point I can turn it to evil as much as to good."

His hands tightened as he heard the words. Somehow he hadn't thought the power she possessed could go either way, but then he realized how naive he was being. Obviously, with Collis the power had turned to evil. "Can you control it?"

"Yes," she said, looking surprised at the definiteness of her answer, and then she hesitated, as if searching for the source of the sudden uncertainty she felt. "For the moment I can. I don't know what will happen if it gets stronger."

"What else? What else can you do with your power other than blow up hovercrafts and kill people in self-defense?" he asked, regretting the necessity for the cruelty of his words when he saw her face drain of color. But he had to make her see that she could do almost anything, even simple things. He had to make her see that eventually she would have the choice instead of being forced into doing things that went against her nature. He let her go and picked up a glowlight. "Can you make this move? Can you make it rise from my hand and suspend it in the air?"

She glared at him. "Of course." She stared at the glowlight cupped in the palm of his hand, her brows drawing together in concentration. Slowly, the light lifted above his palm several inches, then, carefully, she let it down again. She looked at him triumphantly. "I was able to do things like that even when I was a child—" She stopped and her hand flew to cover her mouth, her eyes darkening with what appeared to be horror.

He reached for her, wanting to protect her from the memory that so obviously frightened her.

"He was right," she whispered, burying her head in his chest. "Drew was right all along."

"He was right about what?" he asked gently, enfolding her into his arms. He felt distress quiver through her body, and he probed gently at her mind.

She pulled away from him. "Don't do that! I have to think. I . . ."

Jared caught her in his arms, not wanting to let her suffer alone whatever it was she was feeling. "I can help," he whispered, stroking her hair back from her face. "Let me share whatever it is. The pain will be less if you share it with me." He lifted her chin and forced her to look at him. When her liquid-drenched eyes met his, he lowered his lips to hers, gently taking possession, and deliberately, his mind reached out to hers.

This time she allowed both the physical and mental contact, and Jared found himself lost in a swirling mass of colors and long-suppressed memories. Scene after scene caught at him, and it seemed to him that he was Susan, and he experienced her memories as if both he and she were one.

He felt her hurt when schoolchildren, cruel because of a difference they sensed about Susan, taunted and jeered. He felt her insecurity when disapproving adults pursed their lips with outrage because Susan knew too much about their inner thoughts.

And time after time, a man and a woman appeared along with an older boy. Instinctively Jared knew these were Susan's parents and her brother. Even he disappeared, and was replaced by a parade of serious-looking, stern-faced men and women, but the face of one man overshadowed even those. It was then that Jared felt her fear.

By the time the images stopped, Jared knew why Susan had denied that she had the power of a crystal woman and knew he would have done the same if he had been like her—trapped with nowhere to go.

He broke free of her mind with a gasp and caught her as she swayed, almost falling but for the strength of his arms around her. There was a noise behind him and he turned quickly, still somewhat confused by what he had just experienced, but sheltering Susan from any danger.

Connor stood hesitating on the threshold of the cottage, his expression uncertain.

Jared nodded to him and scooped Susan up into his arms, striding over to the bed in the corner of the room, gently laying her down on it. "Sleep now, Susan," he said quietly, covering her with one of the blankets.

Her hand closed over his wrist. "Don't go," she whispered.

He sat down on the side of the bed, waiting. She had trusted him with the most intimate memories of her past, and although he hadn't understood some of what had happened to her, he had understood enough. "You need to rest. You need to come to terms with your memories. You buried them deeply for many years because it hurt to remember."

"I didn't remember," she whispered, her face pale, her eyes sparkling like emeralds up at him. "But Drew remembered, and he tried to tell me all these years, but I couldn't believe him, because then I would have remembered that it was all the truth." She shivered beneath his hand where he stroked her shoulder. Her eyes moved to where Connor stood by the table. "Connor is waiting. I'll be fine."

"Connor can wait." Jared looked down at her and his eyes sparkled enigmatically in the dimness of the room. "Who were those people at the end of your memories, Susan? Who was that man? I felt your fear of them. The rest I understood. You were resigned to the children teasing you, making fun of you, the anger of the adults in your life when you did something they didn't understand, but those people at the end of your memory frightened you."

She was quiet for a moment and then drew a deep, shuddering breath. "Yes, I was afraid of them. I was nothing to them but an experiment, an object for them to poke and prod and test. They didn't care about me at all."

He waited, knowing that she would tell him, knowing that she only had to find the words to overcome the fear she still remembered.

"My parents died in a car accident when I was almost fourteen, but before that my mother had been taking me to a psychologist because she was so worried about me and what I could do. She didn't understand. She thought there was something seriously wrong with me. This psychologist, Charles Lamb, was affiliated with a government-sponsored program, and he was fascinated by what he called my talents." Her voice was bitter. "He was working to get custody of me even before my parents died. He had my mother half convinced that she wasn't competent to take care of someone like me. When Mom and Dad died, Drew wasn't able to convince anyone that he should have custody. He was twenty-three.

"Drew fought them as hard as he could, but the court awarded custody to Lamb." She frowned. "Thinking back, something must have been going on behind the scenes. Maybe money—maybe some other kind of pressure. I don't know. I was tested constantly, experiment after experiment, day after day. In all the months I was with Lamb, he only let Drew see me a couple of times, and even then he never left us alone together. Drew looked at me once," she whispered, her voice breaking a little. "I could tell his heart was breaking at what they were doing to me. He asked me in a funny voice if I was really different. Could I really do all that they said I could?"

Jared clasped her hand in his and squeezed, trying to help her, trying to give her strength.

"That's when I started thinking, which was what Drew had tried to get me to do. If I couldn't do these things, then I wouldn't be of use to anyone. So I stopped doing everything. It drove Lamb crazy. He did everything he could think of to make me perform all my little tricks for him again, but I wouldn't."

Jared remembered the sensations of hunger he'd experienced during the memory flashback he'd shared with her, and he knew that this Lamb she kept talking about had withheld food at the very least in his attempts to get her to work with him again.

"I convinced myself that I couldn't do any of the things Lamb wanted me to do, and then finally, I really couldn't do them. Eventually, Lamb let me go. I was an expensive research project that had stopped producing results. Lamb couldn't justify the expense of the project. One day he just let me go. I suppose there were legal papers and things involved, but no one ever told me anything. Drew just picked me up one day and brought me home with him. I remember he hugged me and said what a good job I'd done all by myself. I remember looking at my brother and wondering what he was talking about. At that point, I had blocked so much out. It's only now that I realize how much. I was fourteen years old." She shook her head on the flat pillow. "I lost so much time."

"It was over a long time ago, Susan," Jared said, tamping down the anger he felt on her behalf. "You weren't ready to remember before. You can cope with the memories now. They don't have any power to hurt you anymore. They're just that—memories." He loosened his grip on her hand. "Sleep now." He waited until she'd closed her eyes before he stood and joined Connor at the table.

"Everything all right?" Connor asked, concern etched on his face.

"It will be," Jared said quietly. "Today has been nothing but one trauma after another for her, but she's strong. Stronger than even she realizes. At least now she fully accepts the fact that she does have the power of what we call a crystal woman. In her world they have not discovered the potential of a crystal woman, although it appears that some of them suspect the power exists." Jared chuckled a little and shook his head at Connor's look of bewilderment. "That's right, Connor, you don't know what I'm talking about, do you? You've been gone from the Keep for months."

"A very lucrative few months it's been too," Connor said with a quick smile. "At least as far as my research project is concerned. But tell me what's happened with you first, and then I'll fill you in on what I've discovered."

Swiftly and concisely, Jared explained.

Then raising a booted foot and resting it on the chair, Jared stared down at Connor. "So, do you think this attack is the beginning of Ruhl's moves against us here in the north?"

"What else could it be? You know yourself from the messages I've sent you that there's trouble in the outlying villages. Men disappearing."

"I've heard stories about men disappearing from some of the villages," Jared said, his brows pulling together in a frown. "But no one seems to have any idea what's happening to them. Where they're going."

"Rumor is that the renegades are forcing prisoners to work the crystal mines for them. Considering the price of Glendarran crystal off-world, the rumor seems entirely possible."

Jared nodded. "The price of our crystal is reason enough to go to war."

"The renegades are evidently taking the crystal off-world with Ruhl's blessing. Up until now the Council has controlled the amount of crystal that leaves the planet's surface, but now the Council no longer exists—by decree of the King." Connor saw Jared start in response to his information. "Ruhl's been busy. It looks as if the renegades are going to flood the market. Economically, that's not good."

"I'm beginning to understand some of what's had the Widows so upset for the last few months. If Ruhl is regularly dealing with the renegade Techs and they're shipping crystal off-world, then that means their ships are landing and taking off without regulation."

Connor nodded. "The residue from the ships landing and taking off is going to accumulate, and sooner or later it's going to affect your ecological balance. Right now you don't notice any effects because all the activity is taking place out in the desert. I would guess that you're going to start noticing changes very shortly."

"So what's the answer, Connor?" Jared asked.

"You know the answer as well as I do, Jared," Connor said.

Jared nodded resignedly as he removed his foot from the chair and stood straight. He'd known the answer to the problem as soon as they'd started talking. Things were even worse than he'd thought and the urgency that had existed before had now tripled. He cast a glance in the direction of the shadowed corner where Susan slept. They weren't going to be granted the time they needed.

Connor followed the direction of Jared's glance and knew his thoughts. "Isn't there any way you can speed up your search for this knowledge you need? Have you tried to contact the Tech Archives? They may have some information. Surely whatever information they have about the Tech Wars will have been declassified."

Jared stared at him in amazement. "I never thought of it, Connor. Do you think they might know something?"

Connor shrugged. "I can't be sure, of course, but I do know that the crystal women fascinated my people at the time of the Tech Wars. From what I remember of my history, I think they captured a few crystal women over the years both during and after the war." Connor grinned. "Not that they were able to keep them for long. Those women escaped as fast as the Techs could catch them." His grin faded. "But there was one crystal woman who married a General. She was the one who eventually drafted the treaty that both sides signed."

"Mellissande," Jared breathed.

Snapping his fingers, Connor nodded. "I remember now."

"Our legends say that she fell in love with your General Versun during her captivity. She was a warrior crystal woman and a seeress. It is said that she saw the future and helped shape it. She is the one who spoke the Prophecy that shapes our lives even now." Jared looked at Connor. "It is possible that she left records with the Techs. Is there any way we can find out?"

Connor shrugged. "I have a friend in Archives." He tapped his overall breast pocket. "I'll contact her when the space station's overhead in the morning. If anything's up there, she'll find a way to get it to us."

Nodding, Jared reached out and grasped Connor's shoulder. "I'll take responsibility if your friend can commandeer a shuttle to land and bring us the information." His face clouded. "I can explain the necessity to the Widows."

Connor rose. "We'll talk some more in the morning during our journey to Lemaldin's holding. In the meantime, we both need some rest. I feel as if I haven't slept in a week."

"You did a fine job here, Connor."

"We would have all been dead if you hadn't come and brought your crystal woman."

Narrowing his eyes, Jared stared down at Connor. "Have you heard them speculate on who's behind these raids?"

Connor nodded soberly. "Orsin."

"You know what that means," Jared said.

"If it's true then this could get a hell of a lot worse before it gets better."

Jared opened the door and nodded. "Just pray that your friend finds something in your Archives, Connor. If she does find something, then maybe— just maybe, we'll have a chance."

Connor left and Jared closed the door after him quietly, thinking over all that had been said. He hadn't realized things were so bad in the south, but maybe he hadn't wanted to know. He'd been so wrapped up in his guilt and grief over Evie, just as the other Clan Lords had been over their dead crystal women. Suddenly, he saw it all very clearly. The Clan Lords in the south, suffering the same guilt and grief as he had been, had looked to anyone who was willing to lead them. Ruhl had stepped in to fill the gap and the Clan Lords, relieved that someone was able, had handed Ruhl all the power he had needed, without a fight.

With a deep sigh, Jared admitted to himself that he probably would have done the same if the Widows had not made their demands on him. The Widows—and Susan—had saved him.

"Jared."

Her soft voice came from the corner.

"I thought you were asleep, Susan," he said, walking over to the bed and looking down at her, seeing the gleam of her eyes in the dimness, seeing the spill of her glorious red hair cover the pillow.

She shook her head. "No, I was listening. Things sound bad."

"Yes."

"Come to bed, Jared," she said, lifting the blanket and making room for him.

"I have to think, and you need to sleep."

"The two are mutually exclusive?" she asked, sudden laughter in her voice. "You'll think better after you've slept. Lay beside me, Jared. You comforted me earlier. Let me comfort you now. This is your world, and you see it being destroyed around you. Let me share your pain as you shared mine."

He saw her smile as she reached up and tugged at his hand, drawing him down beside her.

"Let me love you, Jared," she whispered, her voice throaty with desire.

He resisted no further and sank down on the bed beside her, sighing with pleasure when she reached for him with soft, eager hands.

His mind merged with hers almost effortlessly and he felt her love surround him, cushioning him from the worst of his thoughts, and for once, whether from exhaustion or from something undefined, he allowed his feelings to go free to entwine with hers. But he retained enough of his self-possession even as passion claimed him to remember to hold back the words. Feelings and emotions while in passion's grip could be misinterpreted. Words voiced in the warm night could not be denied in the cold light of day.

Even so, their lovemaking had left him breathless and shaking with its intensity.

She lay in his arms now, sleeping. Her unspoken words, wrested from her control and whispered in his mind at the height of their passion, kept him from resting. *"I love you, Jared."*

He bent his head and his lips brushed her forehead. Would he be able to let her go when the time came for her to return to the past?

He had to. He had given his word.

Jared's eyes were bleak as he stared into the darkness.

Chapter Fifteen

Susan tightened the saddle cinch on Desert Moon, patted the horse on the rump, and stood back. Shading her eyes against the glare of the sun, she searched for Jared. Although she was ready for the trip to Garrett si'Lemaldin's holding, judging by the unorganized gathering of all the people, castle guards and villagers alike, around her, it didn't look as if anyone else was.

She saw Jared finally, standing beside Connor upon the battlements of the wall surrounding the village. His shoulders were wide under the protection of his well-worn leather vest, his hips narrow in the close-fitting fawn-colored trousers, his booted feet spread wide.

As she watched, she saw Connor palm something and then put it into a pocket of his coveralls. Connor clapped Jared on the shoulder and then descended the ladder to the common area. Susan lost sight of him in the milling crowd.

Jared remained on the battlement looking out to the desert, the wind ruffling the dark hair that fell over his forehead. He'd been gone from their bed when she'd awakened this morning. She'd dressed, then had gone searching for him. She'd found him organizing this morning's caravan to Garrett si'Lemaldin's holding. When she'd actually caught up with him, Jared not only had been busy commandeering a cart and donkey from the supply picket to carry the five children Susan had acquired, but he'd also found a wet nurse for the newborn baby.

She'd watched him then too. He'd moved with an easy grace and vitality that belied the exhausting and almost totally sleepless night he'd had. He'd stood in the bright sunlight and issued commands without hesitation, bringing order out of chaos with no apparent effort. He'd personally seen that the children were settled comfortably. Jared had placed Percy in charge of them temporarily, although Percy was still shaky from the stun he'd received the day before.

As Susan settled on her head the gold filigree circlet that Jared insisted she wear, she thought that her husband looked very much the conquering hero surveying his prize as he stood alone on the battlements.

Her husband. She savored the words, feeling the heat of a blush rise in her cheeks. He'd had much the same look in the early hours of the morning when his golden eyes had blazed down at her, consuming her with their heat and passion. During the night she'd sensed the tender and passionate feelings she'd been searching for in him so fruitlessly since she'd come to this starkly beautiful world, although he'd still said nothing out loud to her. For some reason, the words seemed so terribly important.

He'd laid himself open to her in the hours of darkness, and she'd taken the tentative tendrils of his emotions and wrapped them tightly around her, clinging to them, afraid they might disappear in the cold light of day. In response, she had unfolded her emotions like a rose, one unfurling velvety soft petal after another until her center had been exposed to him in all its beauty. He'd drunk the nectar of her blossoming love. Although he'd stubbornly refused to say the words, she'd sensed them in his gaze, in his kiss, in his touch.

Frowning, she stared at him where he still stood on the wall of the village and saw his chest heave in a sigh. Jared had closed his mind and walled off his emotions in response to her probings. Her night fears that his emotional openness would disappear in the light of day had been grounded in reality.

She tried again to touch his mind, but although he turned and his golden eyes found her in the crowd, he wouldn't let her past the barriers he'd erected, refusing to let her in. In the bright sunlight, Susan suddenly wondered if the night had been a dream, if she had imagined everything.

"Never doubt that he loves you, my Lady."

Susan turned, startled, to find Cammie standing at her side with the new baby in her arms. "How is the baby this morning?" Susan asked, smiling at the young girl.

"The baby is fine. Lord Jared loves you," Cammie said insistently, her deep gray eyes meeting Susan's. "More than even he knows."

"How do you know?" Susan asked, her voice a whisper.

Cammie shrugged. "His thoughts are clear. His eyes follow you, he smiles when he sees you, his hands are tender when he touches you. Everyone must know that he loves you."

"I wish I could believe that."

"He's afraid," Cammie said, rocking back and forth, soothing the fretting infant.

"Jared afraid?" Susan asked, wondering what she was doing discussing her love life with a child of 14. But the idea of Jared being afraid was not a totally alien one. She'd sensed in him on several occasions a vague sensation of fear that kept a barrier between them.

"He's afraid to love you too much because he thinks you'll be going away." Cammie looked at her, sadness deep in her eyes. "Are you? Going away?"

Once again Susan glanced up at Jared where he still stood alone on the wall of the village. "I don't know, Cammie."

"You love him. He loves you. People who love each other should be together." Cammie turned and watched as the wet nurse was helped into the cart by Percy. "Will you ride beside us a little during the journey?"

Smiling, Susan nodded. "Of course."

With a final smile in Susan's direction, Cammie went back to the cart.

Susan waved at Percy where he sat on a small perch on the front of the cart. He waved back at her, and she almost laughed at the carefully controlled look of horror on his young man's face when one of the little girls plucked at his sleeve with what was obviously a sticky hand. When Susan had visited his family's cottage this morning to receive his mother's heartfelt thanks for the healing of her son, she'd discovered that Percy had four younger sisters. The poor boy probably knew in exacting detail what he was in for on this trip.

Struggling to control a grin, Susan looked back up at the village walls, but Jared was gone.

Knowing that they would be on the way soon, Susan checked her sword and dagger, settling the weapons belt more comfortably around her waist. She stood by the head of her horse and patted Desert Moon's nose, waiting for the order to mount.

The castle Guards began to form up in a column, but there were fewer than there had been the day before. They were leaving their wounded behind in the village. Their dead they had already buried on the desert's edge.

At first Susan had been amazed by the lack of grief exhibited by the Guards. It was not until she'd been tacking up her horse side by side with one of the more hard-bitten-looking members of the Guard that she'd gotten up enough courage to ask.

"Being a Guard is our life," the guard had said before adding with a mumble that his name was Cossan. "We train for it from the twelfth summer. We live to protect our lord and his lands, and when it is our time to die, we pray that it be in battle. Our fallen comrades died with honor. Why should we grieve? They fulfilled their destiny as the rest of us will when comes our time to die. We gave our comrades a proper send-off and buried them with their weapons so they'd have them when they enter the Crystal Gates and offer their service to the True God." Cossan had spat and fixed her with a baleful eye. "The crystal plague on those who don't believe."

Susan had offered a shaky smile and had thanked him for the information, but she was determined to ask Jared about this crystal plague at her first opportunity.

The order came to mount, jerking Susan to attention, and she swung up into her saddle after a brief fumble with the sword that seemed intent on tangling with her leg. She was thankful the sword was sheathed. She gained the saddle finally and settled in, wincing a little at the soreness of her buttocks and thighs.

The people of the village formed a ragged line on either side of the column, pressing closely in some places, some smiling, some weeping. Gifts of thanks and farewell were passed to the castle Guards: articles of clothing, canteens, food, and, in a few instances, young maidens giving brightly colored scarves that were immediately tied to the pommels of the saddles of the recipients.

Turning her attention to the front of the column by the now-open gate, she saw Jared's stallion prancing and pawing at the ground. Jared looked as if he was part of the horse.

In addition to the Dakbar Clan flag which led the column, gilt-edged banners and flags of various bright hues were unfurled and held by the leading Guards. Another shout and the column, amidst the musical jingling of spurs and harness links, began to move forward.

Susan looked behind her as she gently kicked Desert Moon, making sure that Percy had joined the column. She smiled and waved over her shoulder when she saw him guiding the donkey in the midst of the pack animals. She laughed as the girls jumped up in the ramshackle cart and waved back at her. Percy was going to have his hands full keeping the girls from overturning the cart with their rambunctious jumping and jouncing.

But the laugh faded from her lips when the cool shadow of the gate lintel engulfed her and she saw the cloaked man standing deep in the shadow of the gate. His features were barely visible in the shadowed darkness of his hood, but his eyes gleamed as the column passed him. For a moment, her eyes caught his and a shudder passed through her at the icy coldness and hate she saw there. When she leaned forward, frowning, for a closer look, the man was gone, as if he'd melted into the shadows.

The man had been frighteningly familiar, she thought, settling back into the saddle and wincing once more at the raw feeling of her thighs. But where had she seen him? She'd seen so many new faces in the past week that she was lucky she still recognized her own.

The column had moved a substantial distance down the dusty road before she remembered. In the remembering, she wondered how she'd ever forgotten. She'd seen him as he'd bent over a map on a table, his silver-white hair gleaming in the dim, directed light of a control room.

She pulled Desert Moon out of the column and galloped to where Jared led the column, Connor at his side.

"What is it, Susan? Is something wrong?" Jared asked, and although his voice was sharp, his eyes were concerned as he pulled Gaeten to the side of the dusty road.

Susan drew back on Desert Moon's reins. "There was a man. In the shadows. I think it was Orsin."

"You're sure?" Jared's eyes flashed to hers and he frowned. "You've never seen Orsin."

"I saw him in the control room of the hovercraft. I've seen him in your memories—a silver shadow of darkness and pain."

"Stay here," he said, and wheeling Gaeten, he rode to the head of the column and called a halt. He held a low-voiced conversation with the Captain of the Guards. A small party of Guards rode back to the village with Connor. Jared returned to Susan's side.

"We'll wait until they return," he said.

"You don't think they'll find him, do you?" Susan observed shrewdly.

"No, I don't think they will." His face was pensive. "He's a soldier and a spy. He's skilled at blending into a crowd and disappearing. The Guards won't find him." He fell silent and looked out to the desert again.

Here, the road ran close to the desert. A few spindly trees struggled in the sandy earth for survival. Scrubby-looking bushes dotted the sand as far out as Susan could see. She felt the heat from the sun-baked desert carried on the breeze that caressed her cheeks and stirred her hair. The heat was wretched here along the road; she couldn't imagine what it would be like to be lost in the desert with no respite in sight.

"You've been avoiding me this morning," she said in a low voice, looking everywhere but at him. "I get the feeling that there's something going on that you don't want me to know."

He was silent at first, and then he grinned at her with genuine amusement, his golden eyes sparkling, his mobile lips forming a flashing smile. "Well, that'll teach me to try to keep a secret from you. I told Connor it wouldn't work." Jared chuckled.

Although a little annoyed by his amusement at what she suspected was her expense, Susan was surprised at the feeling of delight that shivered through her at the sound of his laughter. She couldn't help the responding smile that crept across her face. "What were you trying to keep a secret?"

Janice Tarantino

The grin faded from his lips, and he glanced around them as if to make sure no one was close enough to overhear him.

"Early this morning Connor made contact with a friend of his in the Tech Archives. This friend managed to put her hands on some material about crystal women that dates back to the Tech Wars and Mellissande. Connor and I are pretty sure that the information is what the Widows have been trying to find for months. Connor's friend has arranged to bring a shuttle in, and we'll meet her at a rendezvous point in the desert by midday."

An odd feeling crept over Susan as she listened, a feeling of bleakness, a feeling of loss. Something was going to happen. Something bad. "Don't go, Jared," she pleaded, shifting her weight as Desert Moon became suddenly restless under her. "It feels wrong."

"I have to go," he said patiently. "No one but you, me, Connor, and his friend know about the rendezvous."

She shook her head. "Something's going to happen. I feel it."

"The information this Tech woman is bringing may be our salvation, Susan. It's about the Challenge. What if it describes the procedure in detail? Detail that both you and I need if we're to survive against Ruhl and Collis. Our time is running out. Collis made that obvious last night."

She fought back the shiver of fear that trembled through her at the idea of facing Ruhl and Collis. "Don't go, Jared. Arrange this meeting someplace else. Another time. Not today."

Jared looked toward the village, shading his eyes from the sun. "I'm afraid I don't have a choice. Connor and I will keep the rendezvous in the desert. We can't afford to let any chance

308

slip past us. You heard what Connor said last night. Ruhl's going to destroy our entire planet ecologically and economically if someone doesn't stop him."

"But if something happens to you, then who's going to save your world? According to this Prophecy, you're supposed to be the one. No one else. What happens if you die?"

Jared edged Gaeten closer and, reaching out, he covered her hand with his, smiling gently. "I thought I was a dead man before you came to me. I hated what the Widows required of me, what my honor as a Clan Lord demanded of me. And then you came into my dreams and into my life. Against my will, I found myself wanting to live, wanting to fulfill my obligations to the Widows. To my Clan. You called me back from the edge of madness and death, Susan. Do you think I would chance giving that all up now on a whim? For nothing?" He shook his head and let her hand go.

"But what if—"

"Nothing will happen, Susan," he said firmly. Then he shrugged. "And if it does, then be assured that I shall not die easily."

"But how will I know—"

He looked at her, and for a fleeting moment she saw a trace of the pain she'd seen in his eyes in the beginning when he'd been nothing more than a dream to her.

"If I die, you will know. There will be no doubt in your mind that I am dead." He hesitated for a moment. "And if I am dead, then, Susan, you have an enormous task in front of you. Both your time and mine will still be in danger. It will be up to you and whatever help you can find to try to defeat Ruhl."

Susan felt whatever color was left in her face drain away. "Don't you even dare think about it, Jared. Just remember that if anything happens to you, I'll never forgive you. Do you understand me? Never!"

With a furious scowl she pulled on the reins and turned her horse, thinking to return to the place in the column where Jared felt she was safest. Then she stopped, her mind racing. Without another word or another look at her husband, she once again turned Desert Moon and slowly moved to the head of the column. She heard the thud of Gaeten's hooves behind her.

"What are you doing?" Jared asked, puzzled.

She sat tall in the saddle, schooling her face not to reveal any emotion. "I'm taking my rightful place as your wife and as your crystal woman. I belong at your side, not in the back of the column with the pack animals."

"Susan," he said warningly, his voice a low growl.

She knew the eyes of his Guard were on them, and she knew he was aware of it also. Lifting her chin, she looked at him. "When we rode to battle, did I argue with you, Jared? No, I took the place you indicated was safest for me then."

"Madam—"

Susan touched the left side of her chest, over her heart. "Now, when my heart feels that you'll be riding into danger, perhaps even to your death, will you deny me my right to ride beside you as your wife for the short time we have left?"

She had won. She saw it in his eyes a second before he pressed his lips together tightly and nodded his concession to her demand.

"Pray that neither one of us regrets this decision," he said.

"There's no danger on this road to Garrett si'Lemaldin's," she replied. "The danger comes when the road is abandoned for another path."

He nodded. "So be it." A sudden shout from the rear of the column caught their attention. "Connor's returning."

A few minutes later Connor rode up on Jared's left side as the column began to move forward.

"Orsin is gone, but he'd been there. Others saw him. They thought him a member of our party."

"Why would he be here?" Susan asked. "Wouldn't he have retreated to safety after being defeated?"

Jared shook his head. "Not necessarily. If he thought he could gain information, he would risk capture."

"What would he be looking for?" Susan asked, thinking that, as a large group, their movements were not exactly a secret.

"Our movements. Our plans." Connor stared out over the desert sand. "Our appointment to meet a Tech shuttle craft."

"But we were alone when we made those plans," Jared objected.

Connor shrugged. "There are all kinds of devices, Jared. Most of them are illegal, but that wouldn't stop Orsin from using them."

"Then our trip to meet your friend could be an ambush."

Connor nodded.

"I want to come with you, Jared," Susan said.

"No! Connor and I go alone."

"Jared, please, there may be something I can do to help you, just in case."

He shook his head. "You'll continue on with the column to Garrett si'Lemaldin's hold. Connor and I will meet the shuttle as planned. If all goes well, we should join you at sunset."

Janice Tarantino

"And if you don't?"

"We've discussed that eventuality," Jared said. He looked sternly at Susan. "I don't want you getting any ideas about following us. I can't risk walking into a trap with you anywhere around."

Susan frowned at him. "I can take care of myself, Jared."

"He means that he can't risk both of you being taken prisoner," Connor said. "They would use you against him."

"But . . ."

Jared shook his head. "We know Orsin. We know what he's capable of."

"But he's a renegade Tech."

Connor rubbed his left forearm with his right hand. "He wasn't always a renegade, Lady Susan. Both Jared and I knew him. He was our combat instructor at the Academy."

"The Academy?"

Jared pointed skyward. "I spent ten years with the Techs at their Academy. Most Clan Lords send their sons. Some even send their daughters."

"You were one of the children?" Susan asked, her eyes widening. The Widows had told her it had been done in the past. She'd had no idea that the custom still continued.

"That's where we met," Connor said. "We were ten years old, and the administrators put us together in the same room. Our psych profiles showed that we'd balance each other." Connor looked at Jared and grinned. "I still think the computer was on the blink the day they ran us through the psych tests."

"You're probably right," Jared agreed, his face lighting up with a boyish grin. "Do you remember the time we breached the security on that airlock?"

Connor nodded. "The automatic systems should have kicked in to isolate the area."

"They didn't?" Susan asked with a raised eyebrow.

"No, we nearly decompressed the entire installation before they got the manual systems to work. Caught hell for that one, didn't we, Connor?"

"Couldn't sit down for a week," Connor recalled.

"All the administrators had a crack at us, if I remember correctly," Jared said.

"So, you've been in space," Susan said softly, remembering adolescent dreams of being a woman astronaut. Dreams turned in and traded for a more pedestrian career. "What's it like out there?"

Jared closed his eyes and thought for a moment. "It's beautiful," he said, his voice low. "Stark and clear and absolutely beautiful. The distant stars are like diamonds." He opened his eyes and looked around him. "But nothing grows. Death is all around you, waiting. One wrong move and not only are you dead, but most likely so is everyone else who's with you. I prefer my oxygen produced naturally. I need to see the green of spring, the cycle of growth. The hope for new beginnings."

Connor looked at Susan. "He hated it every moment he was up there. He couldn't wait to come home."

"I used to talk to my mother and father on the comlink. I would beg them to bring me home," Jared said. "Mother would cry, but my father told me that being among the Techs was one of the rites of manhood for a Clan Lord's son. He thought that if ten years among the Techs could be survived, then anything could."

"Was he right?" Susan asked, sensing a multitude of memories and emotions in Jared. She had no trouble picturing the brave little boy he must have been.

"I think maybe he was. Sometimes I'm not sure. But one good thing came of it anyway." Jared reached over and clapped Connor on the shoulder. "I met Connor. Without him I would have disgraced my family name. There's nothing worse among the Clan families than being sent to live with the Techs and not being able to make it." He looked at Connor. "We're just about there, aren't we?"

Connor nodded, and Jared motioned for the Captain of the Guard to take the head of the column while the three went to the side of the road and watched as the column passed them slowly.

"I want you to ride in the back behind the Guards, Susan," Jared said.

"The danger is not to me," Susan said. "I'll ride at the head with the Captain."

Jared looked at her and saw the determination on her face. He smiled a rueful little smile and shook his head. "At least promise me that if you're ambushed, you'll take cover and won't lead any attack charges."

Susan tried to restrain the amused twitch of her lips, but wasn't successful. "That I can promise you." Her smile faded. "Please don't go."

"Get to Lemaldin's Keep," he said, and with a flick of his hand in a salute he was off in the direction of the desert, Connor galloping behind him.

She watched them go, a dark foreboding stealing over her soul. Then she sighed and rode to the head of the column, falling in a little behind the Captain of the Guards. She was quiet, her mind turned inward to the link with Jared.

There was danger ahead for him and Connor. She could taste it. She was determined to keep in contact with Jared, whether he liked it or not.

She reached out and touched his mind. *"Don't shut me out, Jared,"* she said mentally. *"I plan on being with you every step of the way on this one."*

"Not all the way, Susan," he said. *"If this is a trap and something happens to me, sever the mind link immediately. You won't be able to stand the shock."*

"Shock?" she asked, not comprehending what he meant.

"Come closer," he said in her mind, his mental voice as low and soothing as his physical voice. *"I want you to understand."* Gently he guided her to a dark place in his mind. The place that he normally guarded carefully from her sight.

Hesitant now, she clearly sensed what he wanted her to know, and she physically and mentally recoiled from the dark, chilling, empty place in his mind. She knew without being told that this was where Evie had resided. She knew this black emptiness was where his link with his first wife had been.

She backed away from the despairing place. *"I understand,"* she whispered softly to him. If something happened to Jared, her mind link to him would be severed and would result in the same empty, nothing place in her mind as existed in his. She couldn't imagine the pain of such a sundering, and she wept for the agony he had suffered at Evie's death. She had not understood until now what it must have been like for him.

"I'm sorry to have shown you that, Susan," he whispered to her, *"but it's for your own protection."*

She retreated to her own place in his mind and waited quietly, her senses alert and wary. The danger signals beat at her, but she kept them to herself. Jared did not need her screaming in his head that there was danger.

The afternoon passed in slow agony for Susan as she mentally tracked every step of Jared's journey

Janice Tarantino

even as she continued on her own. She sensed his uneasiness as he and Connor proceeded further into the desert. A dark jumble of rocks cast no shadows. She could feel the heat as the thin atmosphere veiled the sun only minimally; she could feel the hot itchiness of the sweat as it soaked through Jared's shirt and stained his leather vest. She was aware of the two men waiting and searching the sky. Through Jared's eyes she finally saw the sharp pinpoint of light against the darkening firmament that marked the approach of the shuttle.

Danger! Danger! Danger! The word beat at her mind, and she bit her lip until it bled to keep from crying out a warning. Jared knew there was danger around him. He knew, she told herself.

The shuttle landed and she could almost feel Jared heave a sigh of relief. He and Connor dismounted, tying the horses to a bit of scrub, approaching the shuttle on foot. The shuttle door opened and Susan caught a glimpse of the young woman standing in the doorway, gesturing urgently.

Then Susan saw the blackness coming. It was like a great, dark evil cloud, obliterating all as it traveled through Jared's mind toward her swiftly. Before she had time to call a warning to him, the horrible cloud engulfed her and forced her out of conscious contact with Jared's mind.

Frantically, with her mind she beat at the leading edge of the haze, trying to pierce its darkness to reach Jared's mind, but the cloud was too thick. She couldn't reach him. He was gone beyond her reach, separated from her by the cloud of stygian darkness.

He is not dead, she thought frantically. Not dead. He'd said there would be no doubt in her mind if he was dead. He was not dead.

She slumped in her saddle, the mental effort to reach him so draining that it affected her physical body. Without the mind link she'd begun to depend on, she felt . . . abandoned and so very alone.

Chapter Sixteen

"Come!" Garrett si'Lemaldin gestured to her expansively. "We have some news!"

Susan felt her heart pound in her chest as she hurried to the dais where Garrett and Magda sat waiting for their dinner to be served. There was no sign of the children, although they were the light of Lemaldin's life. He had welcomed them with open arms and spent as much time as he could during the day with the girls.

"Have you heard anything about . . ." Susan asked sharply as she took her place at Garrett's right hand across from Magda.

Lemaldin shook his head. "Nothing about Jared, unfortunately. No, I'm afraid my news is a little more prosaic. The Widows have camped about five miles south of us. They should arrive tomorrow."

"There are several Widows who have the talent for farseeing," Magda said. "They've already begun the search for Jared and Connor."

Susan led her own search every day into the desert. She allowed rest only during the worst heat of the day. Tents were pitched, and everyone rested beneath the dubious shelter of the canvas, the heat draining their bodies of strength, the sand abrading their sweat-dampened skin. After the rest period, Susan bullied the men and women to their feet and onto their horses. At nightfall they headed back to the safety of Lemaldin Keep.

Lemaldin had looked at her sadly that first day of searching as they had stood at what had been the shuttle landing site. "The Techs have him. A Tech is the only one who would know how to move a shuttle."

"We'll get him back," she'd said confidently, not doubting that they would be able to do it.

But as the days passed, Susan's certainty that they would find Jared eroded. Although her confidence waned, her hope did not. Although physically she spent her days in the desert, she spent her nights sending her mind winging out over that same desert, searching for her love.

Garrett's voice brought Susan back to the present.

"The question is whether farseeing will be able to find them when Susan hasn't been able to. That is, if he's even still alive," Garrett said doubtfully.

"He's alive, Garrett," Susan said, her hand unwittingly clutching at the crystal she wore around her neck.

Magda nodded.

"I know Jared still lives," Susan said, fighting to keep her voice even. "The place where he resides in my mind is shrouded in darkness, but it isn't empty. He's still there. I just can't reach him."

She glanced at the heavy gold of the ring on her finger, the rich color of the red crystal glowing in the evening light. Nervously twisting it around, she reminded herself that the color of the ring crystal on her finger and the color of Evie's crystal around her neck correlated directly to Jared's life. As long as the two crystals glowed and sparkled red lights, Jared lived.

She would find him, she promised herself fiercely. He was still alive, and she would find him.

"A question plagues me," Magda said, her brows pulled together pensively. "Why would Orsin want to take Jared prisoner rather than kill him? If one believes in the Prophecy, then Jared stands as a threat to Ruhl and anyone who follows him."

Garrett tapped his forefinger on the table. "Perhaps Orsin has his own agenda and Ruhl is not a part of it."

Susan said thoughtfully, "The night before we left to come here, Connor and Jared talked about crystal mines."

"The crystal mines! Of course," Garrett exclaimed, his face lighting up with sudden comprehension. "Our crystals would provide these renegades with the power and wealth on more than just our world. By controlling the crystals, Ruhl himself would gain in power and wealth. And if Orsin did away with Ruhl, then Orsin would control the supply."

"I think you may be right, Garrett," Susan agreed.

"Economically the mines are our lifeblood. The type of crystals cut from our mines cannot be synthesized or duplicated offworld. Depending on the cut and the color, our crystals are priceless. They're used in everything from jewelry to comlinks. They're even used in Tech starship engine drives." Garrett nodded. "I think the renegade Techs would do anything to get their hands on a continuing source of our crystal."

"But that wouldn't answer the question as to why Jared has not been killed," Magda said.

"Orsin probably plans on using him as a bargaining chip. Ruhl is obviously using the renegade Techs for his own purposes. I see no reason why the Techs would not do the same." Garrett pounded his fist on the table. "By the True God! It all makes sense."

Susan leaned forward in her chair. "But why can't I find Jared with my mind?"

"From what you describe, it could be that Orsin has access to a magic-user," Magda said. "A simple spell could place a barrier around Jared's mind and make it difficult for you to find him. But the only magic-users left are the Widows and Collis and you, Susan."

"An even simpler explanation would be a Tech shielding of some sort," Garrett suggested. "Considering their level of technology, it might be quite a simple matter to accomplish."

"What kind of indication would I get if Orsin had surrounded Jared's mind with the spell you're suggesting?" Susan felt as if the answer to the puzzle was just within reach of her grasp. "Is it this shrouded darkness? This cloud in my mind?"

Magda looked at her in surprise. "You would get nothing. There would be a blank spot in your mental vision."

"Could we trace that darkness?" Susan asked, her mind racing. "If I can see all around this one place that won't let me in, then doesn't it make sense that the blank spot or clouded spot is what I'm looking for?" she asked, her spirits rising. "Where are these crystal mines?"

"At least three days hard riding out into the desert," Garrett said. "But no one but miners go there, Lady Susan. It's too dangerous."

"Why?"

"No one really knows what the deep desert contains," Magda said. "And for the unwary and unprotected it holds death."

"From what?"

"The crystal plague for one thing," Garrett said. At Susan's look of surprise, he smiled. "I spent my ten years among the Techs. I studied under their masters the same as Jared did. One of the things I learned was that the Techs are just as susceptible as we are to the frailties of our bodies, so it makes me think that they've found some way to deal with this crystal plague. Otherwise they would not be living in the desert. Our miners have methods to protect themselves, but their herbal protections only last a matter of months. Then there are other strange things that go on in the desert. The miners tell stories among themselves about strange creatures, although they hesitate to speak of them to strangers."

"If we assume that Jared is being held in the crystal mines and we go in after him, how can we protect ourselves?" Susan asked.

"Assuming that we will be in the desert only a short period of time, a few days at the most, we can use the same methods the miners use," Garrett said, his glance suddenly attracted by the fast movement of a Guard approaching the dais. The Guard bent to Garrett's ear and whispered. Garrett's face suffused with red and then he nodded and dismissed the Guard.

"The Widows are not the only ones with my keep as their destination. Ruhl has just passed the Widows' encampment and intends to spend the night within my walls. I have been ordered to make ready for him." He rose to his feet and bowed to Magda and Susan. "I must see to several things before Ruhl arrives." Garrett gestured to the Captain of his Guard and together they walked quickly from the hall.

"Come," Magda said. "You must get ready. You cannot face Ruhl for the first time dressed as you are."

Susan looked down at the plain yellow gown she wore. "You have something different in mind?"

Smiling, Magda nodded. "Very."

And so the Widow did, as Susan found out a short time later as she stared at herself in the full-length mirror. The gown Magda had produced was like an elaborate wedding gown, complete with train. The difference was that this gown had been made of gold thread spun into cloth.

Raising her hands, she slowly pushed the mass of fiery red curls back from her face, studying the fine bones that had emerged with the loss of about ten pounds. With the hard desert riding of the past two weeks, the daily combat exercises with the Guards, and the minimal rations she'd barely taken time to eat, her body had slimmed and her muscles had toned until her flesh was as solid and lean as that of the female Guards.

She doubted if her brother Drew would even recognize her now. She looked different, nothing at all like the person she had been. Her light auburn hair seemed brighter now, glinting with deep fiery sparks, growing thick and springy in a mass of tangled curls. Her skin was tanned to a deep gold, the result of hours spent under the hot desert sun in anguished search for any trace of Jared.

With a heavy sigh, she dropped her hands from around her face. In some ways the mirror was too revealing. She saw things in herself she didn't want to see. She was turning into a different person, one she barely recognized. In some undefinable way she was becoming a creature of the world around her. If she became one with this time, how would she be able to go back to her own? Would she be able to go back? In the end would she even want to go back?

Of course she would want to go back! She had family back in the twentieth century, a loving brother. She had—she shook her head. It wasn't the time to consider those questions. The answers would come later, after she found Jared.

"Where did this come from, Magda?" Susan asked, pushing all her questions to the back of her mind. She stroked the heavy, but soft, gold material.

"The Widows found it packed in a trunk in one of the storage rooms of the keeps they were searching for information about the Challenge."

"Who did it belong to?" Magda's silence alerted her, and Susan turned her attention from the gown to look at the Widow.

"It was found in Lord Rudd's Keep. His is believed to be one of the oldest. His family is also believed to be descendants of Mellissande. The Widows believe that this gown was Mellissande's wedding garment."

As Susan looked at her reflection with wide-eyed astonishment and carefully lifted the filigree coronet, placing it on her forehead, there was a knock at the door. Magda hurried to answer it. When Magda closed the door a moment later, she held a scrap of paper in her hand.

"Who was it, Magda?" Susan asked, apprehensively looking at Magda's shaking hand. She lifted her gaze to Magda's face, which was suddenly pinched and white. Bad news, Susan thought.

"Amaranthe. She was sent by Fedorra to bring you this paper," Magda said, still standing by the door. "The formal words of the Challenge. The Widows found them in Lord Rudd's archives. You are to issue them to Ruhl tonight."

Susan stared down at the scrap of paper and frowned. "I am to issue the words of Challenge? I thought the Clan Lord was the one who . . ." Magda avoided her eyes. "What do you know that you're not telling me, Magda?"

"The Widows with farsight have picked up traces, very faint traces, of Jared."

Susan stood, breathless, as she waited for Magda to continue.

"They feel he might not live to issue the Challenge."

Susan felt as if a knife had slashed at her heart, the pain sharp and unbearable. "No! You told me yourself that the crystals I wear don't lie, Magda. He is alive. The crystals prove it."

"Look at the crystals, Susan," Magda said. "Look at them closely."

Taking a deep inhalation, Susan lifted her left hand and looked at the ring crystal. It glowed and sparkled on her finger as always. She released the breath with a rush of relief. "It's red, Magda. It's the same."

"Look deeply, Susan. Look deeply into its center. The center will tell you true."

Biting her lip, Susan looked to the center of the ring crystal, schooling her eyes to ignore the reassuring red of the sparkling surface facets. It was a little like hypnotism, she thought as her gaze dove deeper into the crystal.

And then she found it. The dark center, the deeper, almost black red, its tendrils moving slowly, infinitesimally slowly outwards. She sobbed. "No!" She denied the evidence of her eyes. But even as she watched, the dark red turned darker by a shade.

She broke her gaze free and stared wildly at Magda. "It's not true."

"He is dying."

"No!" Susan cried, her voice strong with denial. "I'll not let him die."

"How can you prevent it?" Magda gestured to the ring crystal. "He fails even as we speak. He may be too close to death to pull back."

Susan drew herself up stiffly. "Then we must move even more quickly than we have." She clutched the paper. "These are the formal words of Challenge? They shall be spoken tonight in Ruhl's presence. Afterwards, I'll take my Guards and we'll ride into the desert to find Jared and bring him back."

"The night terrors, have you forgotten them?" Magda asked.

"Tell the Widows to figure out some way of protecting us. If they do not, I'll hold them responsible for contributing to Jared's death."

Magda drew herself up regally and her eyes turned cold. "You overstep yourself, crystal woman. You cannot order or threaten the Widows."

Susan was aware of the sudden barrier that had sprung up between them. She returned Magda's gaze.

"You and the other Widows brought me here to assist your son in the saving of your world. Your son is my husband, Widow Magda. I love him, and I shall do all that is in my power to save him, regardless of the consequences. I must live up to the promises I made him, even if that means alienating the Widows. It might be smart to remember that if Jared dies, then I will be a

Widow. I promise you that I'll be a force to reckon with. Remember, Magda, both your time and mine are on the brink of disaster. If you allow something like protocol and precedence to stand in the way of their saving, then you are the fool."

Magda pressed her lips together, and then, just when Susan had about given up, the Widow nodded. "You're right. These are strange times. I shall send word to the Widows. They will find some way to protect you."

Susan inclined her head. "That is all I ask." She gathered up her skirts. "Judging by the noise in the courtyard, I assume Ruhl has arrived. He doesn't believe in giving much notice, obviously." Susan knew that the short exchange had changed their relationship forever. She had confronted the power of the Widows, challenged it. And she had won.

Opening the door to the hall, Susan allowed Magda to precede her, and it was when she saw Magda's face that Susan also knew she had lost something that had been very important to her. Magda had been a friend, and now it was something she could no longer be. Susan knew instinctively that Jared's mother would leave the Lemaldin Keep this night and join the Widows. The Widow Magda would no longer stand by Susan's side to smooth her way in this world.

In the hall below, Garrett si'Lemaldin, his face stiff and without expression, met them and, taking Susan's hand, led her to the dais, indicating that she was to take the chair in which he normally sat as Clan Lord. "Lady Susan, as of this moment, my entire holding is under your command, myself included. I and everything I own are yours to command as you see fit. Therefore the seat I normally occupy is yours. It is you who must deal with Ruhl, not I."

Garrett bowed, and Susan felt tears prick behind her eyelids. She fought to hide them, knowing that to show weakness at this point would be disastrous. She didn't argue, but simply took her place on the dais, although she did not sit. She wished to receive Ruhl while standing. An escort of four Guards took their places, two on either side of her and slightly to the front so that she formed the center of a V. Magda stood behind her on her right, and Garrett took his place to her left. And then Susan smiled when she saw Pris jump from the stone floor onto the dais and sit just in front of her as if the cat herself were choosing sides.

Garrett's castle Guards were lined up along the sides of the great stone hall, fully armed, and Susan saw from the alertness of their stance that they were ready for any contingency.

Susan's fingers closed around the piece of paper she still held. The words were already committed to her memory and had been from the first reading. It was a simple statement on which hung the fates of this time and hers. Crumpling the paper in her hand, she dropped it to the dais behind her. She squared her shoulders, standing tall, and looked to where Ruhl would enter the great hall.

His Guards entered first. They formed a double line down the center of the hall.

Susan found herself holding her breath in anticipation and with a murmur, she forced herself to breathe normally. The man she was about to meet was Jared's twin brother, son of the Widow Magda. How evil could he truly be? Obsessed with power, yes, that much was obvious from his actions ever since she'd been in this world. But evil?

Orsin, leader of the renegade Techs, she had seen and touched mentally. He was an evil man, a mean man sunk into depravities and petty cruelties for the simple joy of them. How much worse could Ruhl be?

Collis, she had met also, and although their confrontation had been brief, Susan knew the woman was cold, with little human feeling and compassion. How much worse could Ruhl be?

Absorbed in her thoughts, Susan suddenly became aware of a crawling feeling at the nape of her neck. She focused her gaze on the figure standing beneath the arched entry to the great hall of the Lemaldin Keep.

He was a golden man. His blond hair shone like a golden halo around his head in the artificial lighting of the glowlights. His skin was pale and white as if he never saw the sun. His face was the face of an ascetic, an impression belied by the richness of his clothing. The glowlights picked up the threads of gold in his black jacket and trousers and sparked off the gleam of his black boots. He was as tall as Jared, with wide shoulders and narrow hips.

In fact, he was every woman's dream of the perfect male, Susan thought, until she looked into his eyes. His golden eyes, so like his brother's, were the eyes of a Clan Lord.

His eyes were gilded whirlpools that led directly to the inky recesses of his essence. Susan, without thinking, followed the path to his soul with her gaze. The malignant blackness surrounded her on all sides, sucking her in, drawing her on, further and further.

At the last moment, the moment just before being absorbed into the dark corruption of Ruhl's being, she realized what was happening and with a twisting movement of her head, she tore her eyes free of his hypnotic embrace. Her breath came fast when she realized how easily he had almost overcome her, and she shuddered when she recalled the loathsome, depraved images that she had seen in his mind.

The man, if he could be called that, was the essence of all the diabolic, repellent evil in this world. He was like a vampire, feeding upon the depravity and wickedness around him. A magnet, attracting the sinful frailties and noisome strivings of the humans around him, magnifying them, and reflecting them back. His soul was a brackish mirror of putrid corruption, making a mockery of all that was good and pure.

He advanced slowly into the hall, stopping exactly halfway. A curious smile pulled at his well-shaped lips. "None have ever seen so clearly as you, Lady Susan. But even you, seeing and knowing, are in danger of succumbing to me."

She dipped her chin in one brief nod, admitting to the truth. "I underestimated you. It won't happen again."

"Dismiss your servants," Ruhl demanded. "I would speak with you alone."

Susan heard the murmurs of protest of those around her. Her gaze scanned Ruhl's Guard, and for the first time she noticed Collis, who stood behind him. "There is nothing you can say to me that cannot be said in front of everyone here."

"You are afraid," he said softly, tauntingly.

"I would be a fool if I weren't," she replied, straining to keep the fear from her voice. She *was* afraid.

He shrugged. "Very well, then. You realize that your effort is all an exercise in futility. I shall win, and you shall lose. It's as simple as that." Ruhl took a few steps forward. "But perhaps we could change things. Perhaps I could persuade you—"

Before she could protect herself, she felt the touch of his mind on hers, and she cried out at the darkness that shrouded her for a moment, clutching at Garrett si'Lemaldin for support. Susan struggled to put up a mental barrier that would hold back the darkness from overwhelming her, but the effect of Ruhl's mind on hers was too heavy and strong for her to fight. She felt herself mentally falling back further and further, retreating from Ruhl's advance, unwillingly abandoning more and more of her mind to the black corruption that threatened her.

She was losing the battle before it had even begun, she thought, gasping in despair, and it was a moment before she even noticed that four tiny motes of light in her mind had stopped Ruhl's advance. Even as she realized the little lights existed, a fifth joined the other four. The five lights formed a protective matrix that slowly but tenaciously forced Ruhl back and finally out of Susan's mind.

Her eyes snapped open wide and she first looked at Ruhl, who stood there with as surprised a look on his face as she knew she had on hers. It was clear that he was as off balance as she. Susan looked up to the balcony that hung over the arched entryway to the hall, and there she saw Percy with Garrett si'Lemaldin's nieces. All five of them were there, the baby held tightly in Cammie's arms.

Five motes of light. Five girls. Susan made the connection and was dazed by the implication. She saw Percy move the girls quickly and protectively from the balcony back into the shadows of the upper hall. She looked back at Ruhl. His lips were drawn back in a half smile, half snarl. Susan had a sudden, swift impression that he was in pain and striving to conceal it.

"So," he said softly, "I have my answer."

"What do you want, Ruhl?" Susan demanded, feeling her strength flow back now that the darkness had receded. Instinctively she knew he would not threaten her again that way.

"I have waited for the Challenge to be issued by my brother, but I have waited in vain. I sent you word that if the Challenge was not issued soon, I would come myself to press the issue."

"Your brother, my husband, has been taken by the renegade Techs."

"What will you do if Jared is dead, Susan?" Ruhl asked, a cruel smile pulling at his lips. "Will you challenge me? Do you have the courage to do that?"

"Jared is not dead."

"Look at your crystals, Susan. What do they tell you?" Ruhl asked.

Even though she knew it was a trick to undermine her confidence, Susan couldn't help but look at the ring crystal on her finger. She knew it was a ruse, some magic on his part, but still she felt sick when she saw the slick, barren blackness of the crystal set in her wedding ring. With a trembling hand, she pulled Evie's crystal from beneath her gown and saw that it too was stark black.

A trick or not? She searched her mind in the place where the link with Jared was placed and found it still and dark and shadowed, but she felt no sense of loss, no pain. A trick or not? In reality, it did not matter, because her reaction must be the same under any circumstances.

Her head bowed, she took a deep breath. Then she flung her head up and back, her eyes meeting Ruhl's. In a clear, strong voice she said, "In the name of the unnamed source of power and in the name of purity and innocence, I issue the

Challenge of Power to you, Ruhl, master of evil and the dark arts, the battle between us to end only with the consignment of one or the other to the blackness of infinity, the coldness of nothing."

As she spoke the words, she felt the flush of power surge through her, rejuvenating her, ripping away the shrouded veils in her consciousness.

"Beloved." She heard the faint, sad whisper in her mind, and then there was nothing. It had been Jared's voice; she knew the resonance of his mental voice.

Frantically, she reached out mentally, trying to follow the voice back to its source, and frowned in bewilderment when she found that Jared's voice had not traveled far at all. In fact, it was very near.

Ruhl threw back his head and laughed, the sound echoing at him from the buttressed ceiling of the hall. "So, you have the courage after all. I have something of yours, and now that I've gotten what I wanted—the Challenge—I can afford to be magnanimous."

"You have nothing of mine," she countered, still feeling the tingle of the power rushing through her, but thrown off balance by the voice that had reverberated in her mind.

Negligently, Ruhl turned and, raising his hand, gestured indolently. "Somehow I don't think you'll deny ownership."

Susan gasped as three sets of Ruhl's Guards came into the hall, each set dragging a body between them. One after the other, his Guards dropped a body to the stone floor and retreated. Susan's heart jerked in an irregular rhythm and then resumed its ceaseless beat.

Ruhl walked over and with the toe of his boot flipped over one of the bodies. He looked up at

Susan. "This appears to be my brother. Do you want him or shall I take him away again?"

She refused to humiliate herself by answering his question.

"Leave us, Ruhl," she ordered, her voice suddenly harsh with emotion, fighting the urge that demanded she run to Jared's side.

But Ruhl stood firm.

Jared stirred, his moan a faint sound that barely stirred the air in the suddenly silent hall. His eyelids flickered open, and Susan nearly cried out at the dark, pain-filled gold color of his eyes. His hazy attention focused on her and she fought back a sob when the corners of his mouth quivered in a faint smile.

"Beloved Susan, you issued the Challenge?"

"Yes, Jared," she whispered to him softly, silently, gently. *"I challenged him."*

"You have the courage of a lioness, my crystal woman," Jared replied, and his eyelids closed over the gold of his eyes slowly, reluctantly, as if he were loath to bar her from his sight. *"Be easy, Susan. All will be well."* His voice faded from her mind, and Susan knew he was unconscious once more.

On either side of her she felt both Garrett and Magda start forward, but although it was the hardest thing she had ever done, Susan held out her hands and stopped them. This wasn't finished yet. Ruhl would exact some price for his gift. "Leave them all, Ruhl. I claim ownership. I had thought they were in the possession of renegade Techs."

Ruhl raised an eyebrow. "I took him away from the Techs. His kidnapping was overzealousness on Orsin's part." He turned away from Susan to stare at Collis, who backed away from him. "A slight miscalculation, you might say. I'll have to see to it that Orsin won't be making any more of those."

Susan heard a startled gasp and saw that Collis had covered her mouth with her hand, her face suddenly white. It was obvious to Susan that the crystal woman was just finding out about Orsin. Was it possible that there had been something between Orsin and Ruhl's crystal woman? It seemed impossible to her, but—

Ruhl's attention focused once more on Susan.

"Of course there must be some penalty for keeping me waiting for the Challenge," Ruhl said in a conversational tone. "And I find that the persons guilty of that transgression are this Tech"—he booted Connor roughly—"and his woman friend."

Ruhl snapped his fingers, and a Guard rushed forward with a sheaf of papers and a small pyramid of frosted glass. Ruhl took the papers, held them for a moment, then dropped them onto the stone floor. He turned the compact pyramid in his hands. "This was found on the Tech woman. Perhaps it means something. Perhaps not." He tossed the glass to the floor disdainfully. The pyramid bounced once but did not break. "The information the woman brought is yours, although it will do you no good. Perhaps it will make our meeting in the Challenge more—interesting. No matter what aid you procure from any source, you'll not win against me." Ruhl's voice was contemptuous, as if he believed Jared and Susan had no chance at all in the battle to come.

Susan couldn't stand his haughty, supercilious attitude. "Be careful that you don't underestimate us, Ruhl."

He laughed, the sound an arrogant assault upon Susan's ears.

"You still don't understand. You have no chance. I shall win the Challenge. My power is great and growing stronger with every day that passes. My crystal woman has studied her art for many years." His features sharpened with impatience. "Why do I waste my time with you? The result of the Challenge will be clear in a few days. And now, for the guilty ones."

But for the first time since Ruhl had stepped into the hall, Susan was ahead of him. She raised her hand and a shimmering gold shield sprang up around each of the three bodies on the floor. "Touch them not, Ruhl. You have your Challenge. You need nothing else," she said fiercely. "Certainly not their lives."

Ruhl stared at her for a moment as if weighing whether this was the time to test her. The heat of his golden glare was suddenly banked. His decision was made. "The Challenge of Power will take place at the Clan Gathering site the fourth dawn from tomorrow. Before it is over, you will call me your King." Ruhl turned and strode from the hall, his Guard forming behind him and following him out.

Susan quickly ran down the stairs leading from the dais. Apprehensive as she knelt by Jared's side, the heavy gold of her gown billowing around her, she glanced at the crystal on her finger, afraid of what she would see, remembering the momentary anguish that had flared through her when Ruhl had somehow turned her crystals black. The crystal glowed a dark red, but its center was now as black as an obsidian stone.

Her eyes flaring with panic, her hand grasped his jaw and she bent to whisper in Jared's ear. "Don't you dare die on me and leave me here alone, Jared. I'll never forgive you if you do." She took a deep breath, aware of the trial on which she was about to embark.

"Magda," she said, looking up at Jared's mother, "we'll need the Widows most skilled in healing. They must accompany us to the place mentioned by Ruhl, and they must try to heal Jared and the others on the way." Her eyes pleaded. "Can this be done?"

"You intend to try to heal him now?" Magda asked, brushing the back of her hand across her forehead, obviously trying to conceal the fact that her eyes were flooded with tears.

"I intend to dispel the blackness from the crystals. I don't know if I can do more than that. I keep remembering what happened after I healed Percy. I was weak for days, and I can't afford the weakness now—not if we're to meet Ruhl."

"Do what you can for him," Magda said. "I shall summon the other Widows."

Susan looked up at Garrett. "You'll see to Connor and the woman?" When he nodded, Susan looked down at Jared, frightened by his pallor and apparent lifelessness. What had been done to him? Could she save him? Did she have the strength to heal him?

With a soft sigh and a gathering to her of the power that a few weeks ago she hadn't known she possessed, she rested her hands on either side of Jared's waxen face. Deliberately, consciously, she began the spiraling descent into his mind to attempt to initiate the healing that would hopefully bring her lover back from the threshold of death.

Chapter Seventeen

Jared had retreated from her. She pursued him
through the dark maze of his mind until she realized she was driving him closer to the dividing line
between life and death. She stopped, sobbing her
despair.

"Let me help you," she whispered.

"I don't want you to see—to suffer . . ."

She thought for a moment, seeking a compromise. He was strong-willed and decisive enough
that he would step into death rather than submit
her to the memories of whatever tortures had been
inflicted on him. *"Let me take away some of the
pain then. Not all. Just enough."*

He was silent.

*"Jared, please. You must allow me to do this. Too
many people are counting on you. Your world is
counting on you."* She stopped, another sob claw-
ing at her throat. *"I cannot let you die!"*

His sigh was deep, as if he heard the desperation

338

of her cry. *"Then do what you must. Do not drain your power. Do enough only to ease me a little."*

Taking advantage of his assent, she moved forward.

The contact with her husband's mind shook her. Pain coursed through her, convulsing her muscles, draining her strength. Frightful images filtered through to her, as if from behind a gauzy curtain. A human shape, but not human—the roughness of scales, the soft, slithering sound of movement, the draining, the weakness. And through it all, rising above all else, Jared's voice repeating her name as if it were a mantra, an anchor of hope.

Weakened by the horrible images and sensations, Susan took on as much as she could bear of Jared's experience and then moved on to the physical healing of his body. She didn't accomplish as much as she wanted to—there was too much damage. And she didn't dare risk herself. Weeping because she could not do more, she emerged from the healing trance.

Exhausted by the ordeal, she stroked Jared's face with her fingertips, wishing she could lend him more of her strength. She knew she couldn't. She glanced up. "Magda, make whatever arrangements we need. We leave for the Clan Gathering site as soon as we're ready."

Sitting on a blanket on the dusty ground, Susan leaned her back against the wagon wheel behind her and shifted her grip on the glowlight. The sun had set over two hours ago, and she squinted her eyes as she tried to read the ancient writing on the dry, brittle papers brought in the shuttle by Connor's Tech friend. The papers were priceless, written by the crystal woman Mellissande during the Tech Wars. Susan handled the papers carefully, but was distressed because they were so old and brittle that they chipped and broke with every touch.

Her eyes were too tired to study any longer. She put the papers down on the blanket beside her, weighting them with the glowlight. She picked up the squat little pyramid in exchange. Thus far she hadn't been able to puzzle out the purpose of the glass object.

Her fingers slid along the smooth surfaces, probing for something to push or pull. It was a most exasperating puzzle, because she was sure the pyramid represented something important. But if she couldn't trigger it, then it was worse than useless to her.

"Bah!" Disgusted, Susan tossed the pyramid into the dirt. After a few minutes, she laughed softly to herself and got to her knees. She reached for it, taking it back into her hands and wiping away the dust.

What had she expected it to do? Burst into song? Susan settled back again and crossed her legs, holding the mysterious glass loosely in her hands.

Susan looked into the night, sadness stealing over her. The Tech woman who had piloted the shuttle and brought the papers had died two nights ago. The Widows hadn't been able to save her, and Susan herself had been too weak from the effort she'd expended on Jared to help the woman. Had the Tech woman known how to use it?

She looked back down at the pyramid. Would Jared know what to do with it? Did Connor know how to use it? Both men were still unconscious, their bodies continuing the healing process she and the Widows had begun.

Closing her eyes and cupping her hands around the cool frosted glass, Susan leaned her head back against the wheel, feeling the hard rim dig into her scalp as she listened to the sounds around her of the camp readying itself for the night.

The encampment was large. The perimeter was patrolled, and Susan had been assured that the Widows had marked the camp for safety against the night terrors.

Opening her eyes, Susan stared into the darkness, seeing the shadows of small groups of people huddled around the comforting glowlights that gave off heat as well as light. Night terrors. Those strange creatures that hunted in the dark were the least of her worries at this point.

They'd been two full days on the road. She worried about getting to the site of the Clan Gathering before dawn of the fourth day as Ruhl had issued, although Garrett had assured her they were making reasonable time. At this point in their journey, everyone was tired, and the wagons slowed them down.

The wagons were like Gypsy wagons: rectangular boxes on wheels with a ledge in the front for a driver to sit on and a narrow door and a couple of tiny steps in the back. These belonged to the Widows, and many were painted in what Susan had been told were the colors of the Clans into which the Widows had been born. Some even bore painted Clan crests. The wagons hauled provisions for the journey and carried not only Jared and Connor, but also Widows who were too old to ride or walk.

The Widows watched her. She'd felt their eyes on her constantly during the two days the caravan had spent on the dusty road heading south. She felt as if she were being tested by them. Surely the ultimate test would come the day after tomorrow when she faced Ruhl and Collis. Her fingers knitted together tightly around the glass in her grasp.

She was afraid.

Her breath exited her lungs with a loud rush of air. With it went a great deal of her tension. There. She'd admitted it. She was afraid of the confrontation to come—afraid not only because she might lose, but, in a strange way, also afraid because she might win. Staring blankly out into the night, she wondered what she would do if she won. Most surely she would be faced with a choice.

Susan heard the soft pad of Pris's paws only a second before she felt the cat rub against her side, purring. Reaching down, she stroked the cat and in a moment of whimsy, held out the glass pyramid to the cat. "Do *you* know what this is for?"

Pris sniffed at the glass delicately, her whiskers twitching, and then curled up beside Susan and began to groom herself.

The glowlight was still on the ground beside Susan and suddenly, from this angle, it seemed as if the center of the pyramid was lighter than its geometrically correct edges. Her hand tightened around the cool glass. Perhaps it was her imagination. She looked more closely.

No, the center was definitely brighter. She frowned.

Lifting the pyramid closer to her face, she stared down at its center. Focusing on the glass shape, she blanked out not only the muffled night sounds of the camp around her but also Pris's purring. She stared at the center of the frosted glass, concentrating.

The image in the glass formed so suddenly that Susan almost dropped the pyramid. Despite her loss of concentration, the image remained and didn't fade, as if once triggered, it could not be stopped.

The face of a young woman smiled at her from the depths of the frosted glass, a wild mane of red hair curling riotously around her heart-shaped face, a deeply red crystal shimmering on her forehead. Her eyes were the deep turquoise of a summer sky and her full lips were a lush, shimmering pink.

Susan heard a voice, and knew she was not hearing the voice with her ears but with her mind.

"This message can only be heard once so you must listen well, sister of the future. Although I don't know your name, I know you are from the time already past. This much I have been granted to see.

"I have not been able to see what the future holds for the memory of my existence, but I do know that if you have been given this Tech recording device, then I have not been completely forgotten. I am Mellissande, a crystal woman as you are, although you bear the mark of the star on your forehead and not a crystal."

Her voice was soft and musical, like the chiming of bells in the far distance, and yet Susan had no trouble understanding the words. She sat quietly, all her concentration on the picture in the glass.

"Since you hear this message, the time I have foreseen must have come to pass. You have been brought to my future by the Widows in fulfillment of the Prophecy. I gave my vision unto their keeping with instructions to teach it to the generations that follow. They must know how to recognize the time of danger and know what to do.

"There is one thing that you must understand completely. The danger you were brought to fight is real and terrible." Mellissande's voice was solemn. "The birth of two children from one womb at the same time has always been cause for terror in

343

my time. We can only be thankful that this type of birth happens only once every five hundred years or so.

"This aberration of good versus evil from one womb was what brought my world to the state in which you find it now. We have struggled for two thousand years on the edge of annihilation. The Tech Wars are also part of this cycle of evil. It was to combat this recurring evil that the Challenge of Power was created far in our past.

"The Challenge is not something about which I can talk freely. I can give you very little help, but perhaps enough to make the difference between your success and failure.

"The Challenge of Power is exactly that: a challenge of the power of good against the power of evil. No one who enters into the Challenge knows beforehand precisely what it entails. It is different for each. That is partly what safeguards the process against corruption. The Challenge must take place in the arena at the Clan Gathering place. The arena has been specially designed for the purpose of the Challenge and is safeguarded.

"If all has gone as planned, you have been joined in marriage and mind with the twin who represents all that is good in our world. Your minds and bodies have meshed, and you have come to the fullness of love and the realization of that love. Utilizing your love for your husband is the only way you can win the Challenge. If you have not reached that point, then do not enter into this battle, for you will surely lose, and in losing you will unleash upon our world a destructive force that may annihilate the entire planet, for the victors of the Challenge absorb and assimilate the powers of those who have been defeated, and you, my sister of the spirit, are truly powerful.

"Crystal women are the true holders of the power which is necessary to win this battle and that is why crystal women have always been so necessary to the Clan Lords. A Clan Lord can be used as a reflector or a magnifier of your powers. Look to yourself and the love you hold for your husband. It will be your source of strength in your battle to come, and if your love for your husband is as strong as my love is for mine, then you will be invincible. Remember that nothing is precisely what it appears to be and that the answer—the key—lies within you and no one else."

Mellissande smiled gently. "The task laid upon you is a heavy one, my sister, but I have seen your image in my seeking for the truth. You seem to be much like me, and if that is so, then you will do whatever you must to be victorious. That is your nature, as it is mine. Remember also that if, for some reason, it appears that the evil will win and you are about to die, then you must— you must—attempt to bring the evil with you into death.

"Believe in yourself, crystal woman, and believe in your love—for that is what will save you and your Clan Lord—and our world."

The image faded slowly and was gone, but not before Susan saw a dark shadow appear behind the legendary crystal woman and, as the shadow reached out with a loving hand to caress her delicate shoulder, Mellissande looked up and smiled as she beheld the face of the person who Susan knew had been her husband and lover.

Susan drew a deep, shuddering breath as the last hint of light winked to darkness in the pyramid, and it was once again merely a piece of frosted glass with an ageless shape.

Slowly she got to her feet and picked up the

papers penned by Mellissande, the glowlight, and the blanket. Now she understood why the papers Ruhl had tossed at her told her so little about the Challenge. The most important information had been in the glass pyramid.

Opening the narrow door of the Gypsy-like wagon, she mounted the two tiny steps, quietly placing the blanket and the glowlight on the floor just inside the door.

A Widow sat in a tiny chair by the head of Jared's narrow bunk. She glanced up when Susan stepped inside.

Susan stood in the narrow aisle that ran down the center of the wagon and looked down at Jared. "How is he, Amaranthe?"

The Widow shrugged. "He seems to be mending. More than that is hard to judge. I think whatever pain he feels now is more of the mind than of the body."

Susan nodded.

"He has been restless these past few minutes. Perhaps he is close to waking," Amaranthe said, rising to her feet. "I'll leave you alone now."

Impulsively Susan put her hand on Amaranthe's arm. "Amaranthe, can you tell me something?"

"If I can," the Widow answered kindly.

"I have felt the Widows watching me since we left Lemaldin's Keep. Do you know why? Can you tell me?"

"There are different factions even among the Widows. Some of us believe you will fail the Challenge. Some believe Lord Jared is too weak. These women believe that if and when you fail, our world will change. They are frustrated because they are powerless to change the situation."

"And the others? Surely there are some who believe I'll win," Susan said, desperately aware that she needed the assurance that someone believed in her.

"The others believe you will defeat Ruhl. They are curious about a woman from another time, a time long past, who fits so well into ours. They are fascinated by a woman who has stronger powers than most of them can conceive of. It is only natural that some of them are jealous. And many of us are just frightened. We have never witnessed a Challenge of Power."

"Which faction do you belong to, Amaranthe?"

The Widow raised an eyebrow and she smiled. "I am one of the believers. I am certain you love, and because you love, you can do nothing but emerge victorious from the field of Challenge."

Susan felt a deep jolt of joy as a familiar and beloved presence flooded her mind.

"Perhaps she loves too strongly, Widow Amaranthe," Jared said, his voice but a hoarse croak, his eyes gleaming gold from the darkness of the bunk.

"Jared!" Susan cried, falling to her knees beside him. She reached out and clasped his cold hand tightly, relief surging through her when he returned the pressure of her fingers.

"There is no such thing, Lord Jared," the Widow said.

"She wasted precious strength healing me when she should have conserved it to face Ruhl," Jared said, his voice growing stronger as he spoke.

Amaranthe pursed her lips primly and shook her head, clearly disapproving but just as obviously not desirous of an argument. "I'll leave you now."

"Thank you for staying with him, Amaranthe," Susan whispered as she rose to her feet, watching as the Widow carefully stepped to the ground.

"He is still weak, although he probably won't

admit it," Amaranthe whispered. "Don't keep him awake too long."

"I won't," Susan promised. She waited a few moments and watched the Widow disappear into the darkness before closing the door and returning to Jared's side. She knelt on the floor beside his bunk and rested her cheek on his shoulder, her lips brushing the smooth skin of his bare chest. "How do you feel?"

He smiled down at her and lifted his other hand to stroke her hair back from her forehead. "Do you want the truth or a lie?"

"I don't know," she responded. "Which would give me greater confidence?"

"The lie," he answered so promptly that she laughed.

"Seriously," she demanded.

"Seriously then," he said, tugging gently at a lock of her hair. "I feel better. How soon before we meet Ruhl?"

"Garrett tells me that we'll arrive at the site of the Challenge late tomorrow if we keep up the same pace as the past two days," she said. "Do you think you'll be strong enough?"

He was silent for a moment, and when he finally replied, his voice was grave. "I'll have to be, won't I? The Prophecy specifically states that the two of us will meet Ruhl together." His voice turned wry. "So far the Prophecy has worked out so well without anyone's help that it would be a shame to change it all now, wouldn't it?"

"Most definitely," Susan agreed. Her lips quirked up a little at his gentle sarcasm, and she wondered if this was a good time to tell him about what she'd discovered from the frosted pyramid. But what he asked next drove all thoughts of Mellissande's message out of her mind.

"How are Connor and Lordana?" Jared asked.

"Lordana? Was that her name?" Susan asked unthinkingly. She regretted her response when she saw his face. His dark brows pulled together into one slash above his gold eyes, and his jaw clenched in sudden realization. "I'm sorry. There was nothing we could do for her."

"Lordana was Connor's betrothed. They were to be married when he returned from this research trip." Jared looked away from her for a moment as if trying to control his emotions, and then turned back, hesitating for a moment as if building his courage to ask. "Connor?"

"He's still unconscious. The Widows are attending to him. He's in good hands." She looked directly into his eyes. "What happened, my love? What did Orsin do to you?"

He didn't speak for several moments, and in the quiet Susan heard his teeth grind together harshly. When he finally spoke, his voice was under control.

"You were right about the ambush. Orsin and his Tech soldiers were waiting for us. As soon as Lordana stepped from the shuttle, they were all over us. We fought them, but there were just too many of them. We were taken out to one of the crystal mines. The Techs set up their base there, close enough to be able to do damage to the border villages, but far enough into the desert to discourage our pursuit of them."

"Garrett and Magda both felt you were being held in the mines," Susan said. "What about the crystal plague? Garrett told me about it."

"None of them seemed to be worried about it. No one wore protective gear." His voice roughened. "After a few hours, the plague was the least thing we were worried about. What kind of injuries did you find on Connor and Lordana? We were separated almost immediately."

She hesitated to tell him, and he read her hesitation for what it was.

"Susan, I need to know even if you're afraid that it will upset me," Jared said, tightening his grip on her hand.

She sighed, reluctant to cause him more pain. "Well, Lordana had serious burns. When I saw them, I thought they were like the burns Percy had suffered. And then there were bruises and cuts." Susan felt the tears she'd struggled against for days start to well in her eyes. "The poor woman, she must have suffered terribly." She shifted her thoughts away from the ill-fated woman. Her attention now was needed for the living—for Jared, who must heal by the time they reached the place of Challenge. "You had a bad gash in your side that had become infected."

"Dagger wound," Jared stated tersely, and he plainly didn't intend to add any more. "What else?"

Susan frowned with the effort of trying to describe the hideousness of the evidence of the most bizarre atrocity she'd found on their bodies. "Strange marks, and I found them on you as well as on Connor and Lordana. Round marks about this size." She formed a circle with her thumb and forefinger. "They were almost like bruises, and yet they were more than that. Dark purplish marks, mottled. All over your body." She brushed her fingertips across his chest. "You still have many of the marks, although they're beginning to fade now. I couldn't spare the strength to heal them when you had so many deeper injuries."

He closed his eyes, and Susan suddenly realized that he was attempting to conceal a strong emotional reaction from her. Mentally she reached out to touch his mind, but his hand shot out and grasped her upper arm in a grip strong enough to leave a bruise.

"Don't," he gasped. "You've done enough."

"But perhaps I can take away your pain," she protested.

"And assume it yourself." He shook his head. "No more."

"What was it that I saw? What kind of creature made those marks?"

"A Cornelian. They have sucker-like pads on their hands and can suck a human body dry of liquid in about thirty-six hours. I know that after the first session, I wasn't anxious to repeat it."

"But what did Orsin hope to gain from torturing you?" Susan asked, her brows pulling together in a frown. "We thought he meant to use you in some way against Ruhl."

"Orsin wanted whatever information we could give him about the Challenge of Power. He confiscated what Lordana brought on the shuttle. He's a dangerous man." His eyes glittered in the darkness, questioningly. "How did you get us away from him?"

"We didn't," she said. "Ruhl brought you to the Lemaldin Keep. He indicated that Orsin is his prisoner."

"Ruhl took us from Orsin?" he asked, his voice deepening in disbelief. "Then Orsin is more of a threat to him then I even guessed."

There was a moment of silence between them, and then Jared's eyes flared gold in the dimness. He reached out to her and smoothed the back of his hand against her cheek and then down the side of her neck. Gently, he urged her closer to him.

She stared directly into his eyes, their warmth causing heat to rise in her body.

"I dreamt about you," he whispered. "I dreamt about you and thought about you constantly. Your memory was what called me back from the edge of madness time and time again."

His warm breath brushed her lips, and she quivered against him, recalling the sense of loss she'd experienced at being cut off from him. "I couldn't find you," she whispered. "And I felt lost without your presence."

"I was there, but there was some sort of shield I couldn't pierce—that you couldn't pierce. Yet I knew you were searching for me." He urged her into the bunk to lie beside him, his warm hands moving over her body, stroking and smoothing, and reassuring himself that she was real.

"I knew you weren't dead," she said, reaching up and resting the palm of her hand against his cheek, reassuring herself that he was once again with her. "Our link still existed, and I felt no pain. Just a sense of loss."

"And now?"

"And now I feel . . . complete," she said, a sense of wonder tingeing her voice. "You're in my mind once again, and you're safe, and you're with me, and we're alone. How can it get any better?" she asked, unable to hide the overwhelming choke of emotion in her voice.

"I could make a suggestion," he said wryly, and then it seemed as if he realized what the odd sound in her voice had implied. "Susan?" He touched her face with his forefinger and it came away wet. "What is it?"

She smiled down at him through her tears as they rose and then fell unbidden. "I always thought when people said they were crying because they were happy that they were crazy. Now I know what they were talking about." Her voice turned suddenly fierce. "Don't leave me like that again, Jared. Take me with you the next time."

His hand tightened at the nape of her neck, and he pulled her to him, his lips closing on hers with bruising urgency.

Truly he practiced magic, she thought when they were both naked. She hadn't even been aware of his hands removing her clothing or his. But even though she felt the urgent heating of her blood and the pounding of her heart, she remembered that he'd been injured, that he was still recovering.

"We can't," she said, the words coming in breathless gasps when she felt the furnace-like heat emanating from his body and the gripping passion that emanated in waves from his mind.

He ignored her protest, and Susan sensed that he needed the physical link with her as much as they both needed the mental link. As his mind and his body tangled with hers, she slid once again into the sensual sensations engendered by the curious mind link. Jared urged her over him and, as she sank down onto his hard flesh, she threw back her head and gasped, overwhelmed by the need and desire that he projected and her own passion as it rose to meet his.

They made love with a single-minded intensity that was strange to both of them, each fully aware that their time together might come to an abrupt end the day after tomorrow. Their knowledge of that possibility somehow made each sensation sharper and more intense.

Jared arched beneath her, a groan torn from his throat, and he clutched at her hips, bringing her with him into the black night that was pierced by a million starpoints that rushed past them faster and faster until they were illumined in a sparkling waterfall of shining light.

As Susan sank down and rested against him, still joined to him physically and mentally, she heard him whisper the words she thought she would never hear from his lips.

"I love you, Susan, my crystal woman, my life."

"As I love you, Jared," she whispered in return, sighing and touching her lips to his, carrying his words with her into the dark peacefulness of sleep. For the moment they were together and, in each other's arms, they were safe, regardless of what the morrow would bring.

Chapter Eighteen

"No," Susan said, standing in the Widow's wagon with her hands on her hips as she inspected and then rejected the gold-threaded gown held by the Widow Magda. "I won't be hampered by a dress. I'll wear what I have on." She indicated the spring-green trousers and sleeveless tunic she had put on a few moments before Magda had shown up with the gown the Widows had decided she should wear on this auspicious occasion.

"But it is customary—"

"Magda, no one knows what's customary when it comes to the Challenge," Susan said impatiently, aware of the passage of time as she stood there arguing with Jared's mother over what to wear. "There hasn't been one in hundreds of years. I really don't think anyone cared what the crystal women were wearing."

Magda's voice was chilly when she responded, laying the gown down on the bunk carefully. "I was going to say that a gown like this is customary on an occasion of great note. I would say that this is such an occasion."

Susan gentled her voice, aware that each of them in their own way was trying to cope with enormous stress. "Yes, Magda, and under normal circumstances I would agree with you, but these aren't normal circumstances. I'm going to participate in a proceeding that no one even understands. Perhaps the gown would be more appropriate afterward." She shivered, not voicing what she was thinking—that the gown would be appropriate for either a celebratory ball . . . or a funeral.

But Susan didn't say it out loud, because as removed from the situation as Magda tried to appear, the fact remained that her only two sons were about to face each other in a battle from which only one would emerge victorious. The other would be dead. Susan looked at Magda with compassion.

"Magda, have you had a chance to speak to Jared this morning?"

The Widow turned away and shook her head, her black veil sliding across her shoulders with the movement. "He does not need for me to add to his burdens today."

With a shake of her head Susan grasped Magda's shoulders and turned her around. "You are his mother and he loves you. Surely telling him that he bears your love is not adding to his burden. It is one more layer of goodness and protection that he can add to the shield he brings with him into the battle. Go to him, Magda." Susan's hands tightened on the Widow's shoulders. "And then go to your firstborn son and say to him what is in your heart—whatever that might be. It is the only way you will live in peace with yourself for the rest of your life."

Magda ducked her head away from the penetrating hazel of Susan's eyes. "But the other Widows will say—"

"Who cares what they say?" Susan asked fiercely. "Ruhl and Jared are not the sons of their bodies, as they are of yours. Surely none will deny you your right as a mother to speak with each of your sons on this day." And it seemed that Susan had said the right words, because Magda nodded.

"But what of you? You need my help—"

"Magda, I'm already dressed." Susan urged the Widow the few steps to the back door of the wagon. "Go to your sons. Don't worry about me or about anyone else." She watched as Magda descended the stairs and hurried without a backward glance into the pre-dawn darkness.

Susan looked to the east and saw a faint lightening of the horizon. The time was almost upon them. Dawn was the designated time for the Challenge to begin.

And then, like a razor-sharp knife, fear sliced through her. She gasped for breath as it welled and then crashed within her, like a tidal wave, oppressive and threatening. To keep from screaming, she pressed her fist against her teeth and, shutting the painted wooden door, leaned her back against it and stared into the dim interior of the wagon. Closing her eyes, she inhaled deeply and tried to still the unremitting trembling of her body, but she couldn't stop the shaking.

She couldn't face what was before her.

She saw the truth with the sudden, stark clarity of gut-wrenching fear, and it shocked her. She'd been kidding herself all along.

Her stomach turned, and she felt as if she was going to lose the breakfast that she hadn't even eaten yet. Nausea ripped through her, doubled her over, and forced her to her knees on the rough wooden floor of the wagon. She caught at the side of the bunk, fighting with every fiber of her being for control over the sweating fear she felt.

She whimpered, and was disgusted by the sound of her own weakness. She was a coward. Had always been a coward. Why hadn't she recognized it before now? Why, when she needed every ounce of courage she possessed, did she have to discover that she possessed no courage at all? That she was a fake and a fraud? A charlatan?

"Susan!"

Vaguely, she heard the sound of her name, but she was so caught up in the tangled web of her fear that she could not answer. Did not want to answer. She only wanted to die before this horrible ordeal began.

"Susan!" Jared's voice was like thunder, demanding her attention.

She barely looked up as he burst through the door into the wagon. "I can't do this," she cried, sobbing. "I'm sorry. I just can't."

"Hush, love," he said, kneeling beside her and catching her into his arms, rocking her as if she was a baby. "You're feeling the fear? It's not you." She clutched at his shoulders, grasping at him as if he was the only steady object in her tormented world of fear. "It's not you," he murmured into her ear. "It's Collis sending those feelings. I'm getting them too."

Her hands transmitted the trembling of his body to her. "Collis? Collis is doing this? You feel it too," she said, as if saying it made it true.

He nodded and held her close. "Yes, I feel it too. Collis and Ruhl are—"

"Playing dirty pool," Susan said, her chin lifting

so her gaze could lock with his.

"Trying to frighten us. Trying to debilitate us before the battle," Jared said.

Another shudder wracked Susan's body. As long as Jared's arms were tight around her, the fear subsided.

"If the losers physically survive the Challenge, Clan law requires that they are put out into the desert with no food and no water."

"So the defeated die either way," Susan said, pulling back from the comfort of Jared's warmth for a moment.

"Regardless of this artificial fear we're both experiencing, if we are to lose, it would be far better to die honorably on the field of battle than to be sent into the desert in disgrace. At least this way, we have a chance to take Ruhl and Collis with us. They cannot be allowed to win, Susan," Jared said, his voice harsh.

Her fingertips feathered his smoothly shaven cheek, and she remembered that she had heard almost the same words from Mellissande. She had finally told Jared of the message in the crystal pyramid as he had driven the wagon onto the grounds of the Clan meeting place.

Earlier in the morning Jared had held the reins of the wagon while she had sat on the hard-plank seat beside him, giggling as he sang ribald limericks with his clear baritone voice. As the morning grew older, Jared's mood had softened. His songs had changed to songs of love and need and wanting and sadness. Ballads, he'd said, some of them hundreds of years old. Some of them even older. Susan had listened to his songs in contented silence, wondering at the similarities between the ballads of his time and the ballads of hers, her head resting on his shoulder, content.

At their midday break word had been brought
to him that Connor had regained consciousness
and was asking for him. With a heavy sigh of
responsibility, for it was obvious that he would be
the one to tell Connor of Lordana's death, he had
jumped down and walked slowly to where Connor
lay. When Jared emerged a long time later, his face
had been hard and he had withdrawn into himself.
Susan had respected his need for privacy, and she
had not pried into what had passed between her
husband and his friend. As they'd begun traveling
the road south again, she'd sat beside him in silence
until she told him about Mellissande's message.

Upon their arrival, the Widows had summoned
them, and Susan had gone into the soft darkness
of the Widows' tent with Jared, her hand clasped
tightly in his.

Drawing strength from Jared and feeling him
drawing the same from her, she had managed to
sit through the solemn meeting with the Widows
without giving offense, even though the only thing
she had wanted at that point was to be alone with
her husband. Once during the meeting Susan had
reached out to touch his mind, and she had felt an
overwhelming joy at the intensity of his own need
to be alone with her.

Immediately, Jared had risen to his feet, cutting the meeting with the Widows short. He had
offered no apologies other than to say that it was
time they both began to prepare for the morning.

Now, thinking back on all the intimate sharing
that had passed between them in the night and
looking at the strong lines of Jared's face as he
knelt on the floor in front of her, Susan felt an
incredible disbelief that these few moments might
be the last they would ever have alone together.

The Crystal Prophecy

He bent forward and touched his forehead to hers in a poignant gesture of pure devotion. She felt the love that was so newly recognized flow from him and cocoon her in its protective warmth. She experienced the helplessness he felt in not being able to spare her the experience of the dangerous ordeal to come. She closed her eyes and felt every nuance of fear that had pervaded her only moments ago recede. As long as she was at his side and in his heart, fear could not exist for her.

In that moment she realized she could never go back to her own time—her own world. Beside Jared was where she belonged.

Swiftly, she cloaked her realization from him, hiding the thought behind the mental walls she had so carefully built. If she and Jared survived the coming ordeal, then would be the time to tell him that she could never leave him.

The ability to retrace her steps into the past and undo and reweave the threads of her life had never been possible. She was not the same person who had followed Magda through the chasm between times, and she could never go back to being that person. That Susan was gone forever. In her place was a stronger woman, one who, after tasting both the delights and the horrors of this world, could not return to her own. Her world had marched on without her this past month, as she had marched on without it. If she returned, Susan knew she would march in counterpoint for the rest of her life, never quite meshing, never quite being in step.

Jared was here. She could not leave him to return to her old way of life, because life without him would not be life at all. It would be a living death. This time and this world in all its stark and strange beauty were hers now. She belonged here at Jared's side. She could no longer conceive of any other existence.

He cupped her face and looked down at her, his shining golden eyes gentle. "It's time. Are you ready?"

Leaning forward, balancing against his shoulders, she touched her lips to his in a chaste kiss, the softness of her lips lingering on the firmness of his. She nodded. "I'm ready."

Together in the soft morning light they walked the path that led past the tents of the Clan members who had come to witness the event, past the black silk of the Widows' tent, past the soft white stone of the Council building.

As Susan and Jared walked with hands clasped, the people of the Clans followed them, their footsteps muffled, their voices hushed. When at last Susan and Jared reached the plain behind the Council building where the Challenge was to be fought, the sky to the east was cast with the faint shell pink of dawn.

Susan looked out over the plain and her hand tightened on Jared's.

It was a stark place, a plain that glittered like a mirror in the morning light. Jared had told her that the black sand of the plain had been fused into a sheet of glass as a result of the Challenges that had taken place in the past.

The Widows, their black gowns and veils hanging heavy in the still, oppressive air, came forward in solemn silence to edge the plain in a single black line. Fedorra, supported on either side by a younger Widow, dispensed with their aid and stepped forward, alone, onto the roughly formed and uneven glassy surface of the plain, her arms raised up and out, as if in benediction. Her reflection was visible in hundreds of fractured mirrored facets beneath her feet.

"A Challenge has been issued and accepted." Her voice rusty and deep, her words rang out over the flat, unyielding mesa. "We are all witnesses to the outcome of the Challenge. May our witness be true." Dropping her hands to her sides, she took her place in the line of Widows.

Jared's hand clasped Susan's, true and strong, as they stepped together onto the shining, reflective surface of the plain of Challenge. Susan hesitated for a moment, surprised at the intensity of power that flared through her at the instant of contact with the ground beneath her feet. Far at the other end Susan saw two other figures appear, and she knew the figures were those of Ruhl and Collis.

There was a slight vibration beneath her feet, as if the glass beneath her was awake and aware of the import of what was to come. She glanced down, unnerved by the vibration, and smothered a gasp of astonishment. With every step she and Jared took, the glass directly beneath them and to either side of them turned a milky opaque white. Looking forward, Susan saw that as the figures of Ruhl and Collis advanced, the glass beneath their feet remained black as death.

The center of plain was marked by a series of smooth three-foot-high columns, some of a black marble substance, others of a milky white.

The opponents met on either side of the center of the plain, Ruhl and Collis on one side, Jared and Susan on the other.

"And so we meet, my brother," Ruhl said in his sibilant voice. "I warn you now that I do not intend that it be my life that is forfeit."

"Then we shall indeed do battle, Ruhl," Jared said, his tone steady. "Because I do not intend to allow either my life or the life of my crystal woman to be the price of your ambition and greed. Lives enough have already fed your desire for power. There shall be no more."

Ruhl grinned slyly. "Two more, I fear, brother. Then nothing shall stand in my way except that group of aimless old crows who call themselves Widows. I shall deal with them easily enough. I shall conquer this world, and then move on to the world of your crystal woman. The power offered here pales in the shadow of that available in hers."

Susan stiffened in protest. "The people who hold the power in my time would eat you alive, Ruhl, and spit you out."

His golden eyes that were so like Jared's, and yet so different, slitted with sudden, obvious rage. "Then perhaps I shall spare your life, crystal woman, and bring you with me. Perhaps I shall kill you only after you have seen the men of power in your world bow to me."

"The time for talk is past," Jared said.

Ruhl made an obscure gesture with his hand. "I agree with that at least, Jared."

Susan, alert to every nuance of the air around her, felt the building of power on the opposite side of the black marble cylinder. Her gaze for the first time shifted to Collis, who stood slightly behind Ruhl, her head bowed, her midnight black hair gleaming with a blue sheen under the morning sun.

The air thickened, acquiring a tingling quality and the taint of ozone, as if an electrical storm were approaching.

Instinctively, Susan threw up one of her golden shields, protecting both Jared and herself from the flash of crackling, searing light that strobed from the tips of Collis's suddenly out-thrust fingers and shattered into a glittering nova of white-hot burning sparks against the shield. Susan squinted against the after-image of light that imprinted itself on her retinas.

Jared instantly activated the mind link between them. *"Did you see, Susan? Can you do that?"*

She nodded and gathered her power, concentrating on condensing it into one bright light of energy.

"The shield, Susan! Drop the shield!" Jared yelled silently in her mind.

A fraction of a second before she flung twin lightning bolts at Ruhl and his crystal woman, she dropped the glittering golden shield from around them, knowing that if she didn't, the power would ricochet off the shield and fall back on them. If that happened, Susan didn't think there would be enough left of them to bother sweeping up.

One part of her mind concentrated on immediately reconstructing the shield around them while another part watched dispassionately as the twin bolts of light formed a nova on the shield of protection thrown up by Collis. At the same time, she noted that the brilliance of the glittering shields dimmed at the strike.

"You affected their shields!" Jared cried. *"Throw another."*

Susan frowned, suddenly aware of a feeling of wrongness and dissatisfaction about this trading of power bolts. But even as she identified her feeling as uneasiness, Collis was throwing another flash of light at them, and Susan was forced to focus her power on the shields. Even with the influx of power, Susan's shields weakened under Collis's onslaught.

"Ours weakened the same as theirs did, Jared," she said. *"I don't think this is the answer."*

It was then that she discovered that her attention to the battle had to be total, because in that moment of distraction, she had allowed the shields to slip. Ruhl saw and directed Collis to take advantage of the opening.

Twin snakes of lightning-like energy struck through the weakened shields.

The jolt of striking light nearly knocked Susan off her feet. Then the flickering agony hit her. Pain screamed through her every pore. She was consumed by fire, although there was no hint of a spark or the flicker of a flame. Her body was burning from within. For a brief moment, all the nerve paths were disrupted as pain took ascendance and she could barely think.

Then she understood how the physical battle would be fought.

Lightning bolt after lightning bolt of power would be traded until one of them faltered. She suddenly understood that she would absorb the power bolts until she reached her limit, and then she would turn incandescent and flame from within, burning herself to a cinder.

Susan twisted away from the pain and saw Jared do the same. They had lost the mind link for a moment. She couldn't let that happen again. Strengthening the protection that surrounded them, Susan reached out and reestablished contact with Jared.

"This is wrong, Jared," she cried silently. *"Surely there must be more to it than this."*

"This could kill us, Susan," he responded.

She glanced at him sharply, alerted by the strange fuzziness in his thoughts. His eyes were glazed, and she realized that he had been more strongly affected by the strike than she had been. Grimly she set her teeth. She couldn't allow him to be hurt. He was physically weak. He wouldn't be able to stand much of this at all.

What had Mellissande said? Something about using Jared as a magnifier of her power? A reflector?

"Jared, clear your mind and try to make it as reflective as you can. I'm going to focus my power on you. I want you to reflect it and channel it at Ruhl and Collis." She could feel his confusion, but he did as she asked. She saw him calm his thoughts, and she saw when his mind was as reflective as a clear mountain lake, the sunlight striking it and bouncing off.

He smiled at her faintly. *"I saw this lake in your time. Regardless of what happens, we shall take a part of your world with us."* She felt his concentration as she herself gathered as much of her power as she could.

When the moment came, she hesitated. If he couldn't handle it, he would die. Then she pushed her doubts to the back of her mind. He had to handle it. She linked firmly, immutably with his mind and then sent the blast of power along the thin, invisible silk of their linking, dropping their shields and keeping her eyes firmly fixed on Jared.

She saw his body jerk a fraction of a second after she let the power go, and then she saw the boiling energy explode from him and flash with stunning brilliance against the enemy.

Susan threw up her hand to block the blinding light as Collis's shields splintered and collapsed under the tremendous blow. A thin piercing scream of pain shrilled through the air, and Susan knew Jared's blow had struck true. But when she turned to him, she saw him stagger backwards. Before she could reach him, he had recovered, but they had lost several precious feet of the milky white glass beneath them. Where they had stood only moments ago had turned black.

"Strong!" Jared croaked.

Susan stared across at Collis, who had recovered but was pale, and at Ruhl, who was smiling oddly as he looked down at the glass of the plain beneath their feet. She watched Collis, who had closed her eyes again. The feeling of power crackled in the air around them, and yet Collis made no move to throw another of the brilliant spears of energy.

"Why did we lose ground, Jared? We struck at them and hit. Why did we lose ground?"

Jared frowned at the dividing mark, the sharply delineated outline of the contrast between white and black. "I don't know."

"This feels wrong," Susan said, feeling prickles of energy crawl across her skin. "The only thing that's going to happen is that we're all going to die."

Jared stared across at his brother. "That's what happened the last time, according to the legends. No one won the battle. They destroyed each other."

A hot, dry breeze blew across the plain, lifting Susan's hair from her shoulders and tossing it around her head. She saw the smile on Collis's lips before she spun on her heel and stared at the dark funnel cloud of a tornado as Collis formed it behind them. As she watched the dark, boiling clouds form into whirling death, Susan tried desperately to remember Mellissande's words.

In a brilliant flash of clarity, she saw the truth.

"Jared!" she screamed above the howling winds. "This is a Challenge of Power. The power that we possess is internalized. It's an extension of our essence, our soul. We're fighting this battle on the wrong plane of existence. How can good and evil battle each other in the physical world when their roots are in the spiritual one?"

"I don't understand," Jared said, grasping her close to him.

"Trust me, Jared," she cried. "I understand now what Mellissande meant. This isn't to be a physical battle at all. Mesh your mind with mine. Hold nothing back. Nothing at all. Open your heart, Jared, as I shall open mine. We must become one." She saw him frown, but he did as she asked.

He closed his eyes, grasping her hands tightly, even as she closed her eyes and returned the pressure of his hands. For another brief moment as she opened her mind and heart to Jared, she felt the fierce winds of the tornado whip at her. Jared's mind and heart opened to her and quickly, yet carefully, they not only linked, but meshed so completely that one was inseparable from the other.

And in that moment of becoming one, all awareness of the physical faded and they were in a place where the silence was unbroken and the weight of centuries were but dust motes in the darkness.

Susan opened her eyes and saw Jared in front of her. His skin glowed faintly with a phosphorescent light. She looked down at their clasped hands and saw that her flesh was alight with the same strange radiance.

Jared glanced around them in wonder. "Where is this place?" he asked, his voice barely more than a whisper.

"This is the true battleground, Jared," she answered, her gaze stabbing at the blackness surrounding them and failing to pierce it. "I think we are inside one of the black stones on the center of the plain."

"If this is the true battlefield, then where are Ruhl and Collis?" he asked.

Susan tilted her head and listened to the silence. There was no sound, but the darkness seemed heavier than it had a moment before. "The blackness around us grows more oppressive and weighted with every moment. Do you feel it?"

He nodded, and his brows pulled together, forming a dark slash across his forehead. "They are the darkness," he said, his voice deep and echoing in the stygian dark that pressed in on them. "To defeat them we must dispel it."

"How?" A shiver trembled through Susan as she pressed in closer to Jared's side. She thought for a moment she heard faint, mocking laughter drift on the murky gloom around them. "Did you hear that?"

Jared nodded. "It seems that for the moment at least my brother Ruhl is enjoying our dilemma." He raised his voice and, taking a step away from Susan, shouted into the tenebrous atmosphere that surrounded them. "You'll not defeat us, Ruhl."

"I will crush you into an unrecognizable pulp. This is all a part of my plan. After I defeat you, according to the terms of the Prophecy none will question my right to kingship." Ruhl's voice swirled with the force of the fringe winds of the tornado they had left behind in the real world. "It is too late for you to fight me. I have already won this battle," Ruhl taunted them.

Susan heard a whisper of sound, the sound of silk being drawn over velvet. She reached out to touch Jared, to reassure herself of his presence as, with a sudden jolt of horror, she felt the link between them weaken. Her hand struck a curving wall, an impassable, crystal-clear barrier that had dropped between them from nowhere. Her hands followed the wall, pressing against the curving surface until she had made a complete circle. She was enclosed, trapped in a sealed circle of clear crystal.

Jared pressed the palms of both hands against the wall, but could not move it, could not separate it, could not reach her. She saw his frustration, the anguish on his face when he pounded on the crystal barrier, his fists making no sound on the wall, his mouth forming her name silently.

The shadows around her pressed in closer, damping the phosphorescent glow of her skin, the air quickly growing thick and fetid. The awareness of evil grew even as her eyesight dimmed. She felt weak, drained of strength.

Feebly she called her power to her, only to realize that it was being sapped by the louring dusk. A tiny ball of brilliant blue witchlight was all she could manage as she sank to her knees, her palms pressing against the crystal wall, trying to maintain at least the semblance of touch with Jared.

The blue witchlight burned above her head, shedding its unearthly radiance around her. Through the crystal wall, its light touched on Jared's anguished face as his desperate hands formed into claws that gouged at the clear crystal wall that separated them and enclosed her.

Groping desperately with her mind, she found that the link between them had not been severed totally. It was weak, barely there, but it still existed.

Susan gasped against the darkness, fighting now for every breath she took, each lungful of dank, putrid air another moment of victory against the evil that closed in on her, and yet she knew it was over. A few more minutes and the battle would be over. And Ruhl would have won.

"Beloved," she whispered in her mind, using the same word he had used once—a long time ago, it seemed—sending the thought out along the thin, silken-like rope that was their link. She intended this as her farewell.

The sound of his voice came back to her. *"Don't give up. Fight them!"*

She shook her head. *"No. They'll take the power and turn it back on you. I can't risk that."* She sank closer to the floor of black marble. It was more difficult to breathe now.

His voice came to her in her mind more urgently as he followed her movements on the other side of the crystal wall and sank down to his knees, his face drawn and afraid, his golden eyes flashing at her. *"If you don't, then I'm dead anyway. We're both dead if you don't. Susan, they're making you feel this way. Remember how Collis made you feel afraid? She's doing the same thing now, but she's using hopelessness instead of fear. Fight it, Susan."* His voice in her mind faded to a whisper as if the link itself failed even as the blue witchlight above her faded and flickered. *"I love you, Susan. Don't let go. Dammit, don't let go. I love you."*

Something stirred in her heart at his whispered words, a faint, glittering spark of hope, and where nothing else had been able to rouse her from the lethargy that weighed her down, those words alone had the power to make her want to parry the blows that had been dealt by Ruhl and Collis.

To combat the inertia that held her, she looked inward to her essence, that hard kernel of truth and belief within herself. From that secret place, drawing upon the strongest emotion she found there, she pulled forth the strength she needed. From deep within herself she brought forth the love she held for Jared, her husband, her crystal mate, and it was like a torch. Burning bright and white against the blackness, the flame of her love pushed back the dark, leaving only the crystal purity of brilliant light wherever it touched.

Opening her eyes, she saw Jared on the other side of the crystal barrier. She met his gaze and saw triumph blaze from his eyes when he saw the life that burned in hers.

The blue witchlight above her head blazed suddenly into a ball of white light that sparkled and reflected off the crystal wall around her. The phosphorescent glow of her skin brightened.

A sudden sparkle from the crystal that hung between her breasts caused her to look down. Grasping the crystal that had once been Evie's and was now wholly hers, she saw that it no longer sparkled with the deep red of a married crystal woman. It glimmered with a white light of purity and innocence. Its facets caught and reflected the light, contributing to the aura of candent light that surrounded her and pulsed in time to the beat of her heart. The marriage ring on her finger also undulated with flaring white light.

She called the power, feeling it rush into her, pulled from the very air around her, air that was no longer foul and still, air that was pure and clean. It swirled gently until it lifted her hair from her shoulders and tossed it softly above her head, like a cloud of shimmering gold and rubies.

Smiling at Jared through the crystal wall, she reached out and touched her palms to the barrier, feeling the heat flow from her hands to the wall, and it began to melt until it was gone. With a sob of pure triumph she threw herself forward and into Jared's arms.

"I thought I'd lost you," he murmured, holding her tightly against him.

"Together, Jared, we can drive back the darkness," she whispered, realizing the meaning of Mellissande's message. "I know the secret now. Open your heart and your mind, as you did before. Become as reflective as you can." She touched her fingers to his lips and smiled up at him, ignoring the cold, dank wind on the fringes of her conjured light.

Standing at his side, her shoulder touching his arm, she cupped her hands and brought forth into the realm of the reality in which they existed at that moment the flame of her love for him. It flared in her hands, reaching higher and higher. She felt the heat, and yet it did not burn her.

Turning to Jared, she offered him the brilliance of the light in her hands and saw that he had found his own source of light. A bright fire burned brilliantly in his own cupped palms.

He smiled at her gently. "I have my own light, Susan. As yours is love for me, so is mine love for you."

Already the light from their twin torches had driven back the darkness from where they stood and the dark, cold wind had died.

"Then let us finish it, my love," she said, linking her mind firmly with Jared's until they were once again one inseparable being. They extended their arms. Susan concentrated all the power she possessed on brightening the radiant white flames that did not burn, and she felt Jared reflecting her power, magnifying it, until there was nothing left but pure, dazzling light that drove back the darkness and in the end consumed it completely.

As one, Susan and Jared heard a thin wailing, a roaring and a cracking, a rumble of thunder, a flash of light more lucent than all that had gone before, and then there was quiet and the feeling of a cool, soft mist on their skin. There was a split second of disorientation as their minds drew back from one another and became their own again. They once more stood on the glass-fused plain behind the Council building at the Clan gathering place.

Before them, waist high, stood a white marble column with no trace of darkness or shadow of corruption. Beyond the column Collis lay still on the rough glass. There was no trace of Ruhl.

Jared knelt by Collis, touching his hand to her throat. "She lives."

"But I thought she and Ruhl would die."

He shrugged. "She will die anyway. The Widows will turn her out into the desert." He rose and strode back to Susan's side.

Susan looked at him, joy and exhaustion warring for ascendancy in her gaze. "Then we did it," she whispered, and she felt his strong arms catch her as she began to fall, exhaustion overcoming her. Before the soft, unthreatening darkness of unconsciousness enfolded her, he whispered, his voice deep, his arms closing around her body comfortingly.

"Yes, my love, we did it together." Jared caught her up into his arms and touched his lips to the star on her forehead. The breath sighed out of his lungs as he held her close against his heart for a moment longer before walking over to where the Widows stood. His eyes met those of Fedorra and Magda before he knelt and gently laid Susan down onto the cold glass.

His fingers traced her lips, and then he stood and looked directly at his mother. "You are to return her to her time, Widow, as you promised."

"But Jared," Magda protested, her eyes widening at the implacability she heard in his voice.

"She belongs in her own time. You will take her back before she wakes. You promised me this," he said, his eyes blank, his voice distant.

Magda bent her head. "It shall be done as you ask, Lord Jared."

He hesitated for a moment, and then stepped off the edge of the glass plain, his boot heels rasping against the sand. The people of the Clans separated to let him through, and he strode away without a backward glance, having delivered his own death sentence.

Chapter Nineteen

Susan had a nightmare. She dreamed of jet planes passing by high in the air, leaving behind a long tail of white exhaust. Of skyscrapers and traffic and masses of people. She dreamed that after the battle with Ruhl and Collis, Jared brought her to the Widows and told them to take her back. She dreamed that the Widows carried her across the chasm of time, their voices hushed, their footsteps silent.

Thank God it was only a dream. She'd decided before the battle to stay with Jared. Now it only remained to tell him of her decision.

She turned on her side on the firm mattress. Her brain whispered to her that something was wrong, but she nudged the thought away and reached out for her husband, anxious for his reassurance, anxious for his love.

His side of the bed was empty.

She opened her eyes. Clenching her hands into

fists, she took a deep breath and tasted the taint of pollution on her tongue, the thickness of the air, the smell of green, growing things, the scent of newly mown grass. Her eyes roved the master bedroom of Drew's mountain home.

"Jared!" she screamed, and the sound of her voice, raw and full of pain, was enough to deafen her.

There was the sound of feet pounding up the staircase. The door flew open and Drew stood there.

Susan groaned her denial. "No! It can't be."

She reached into her mind and found the dark, empty, soulless place where Jared had once been. Where a part of him had once resided, her mind was a cavern of cruelly shorn nerve endings and raw, jagged, bleeding wounds. The link was gone, and the pain of loss was intolerable.

"Susan, love," Drew said, hurrying to her side, sitting on the bed, gathering her into his arms. "Oh, God! You're back. You're safe. I won't ever let anything happen to you again."

Tears of pain rolled down her face as she struck out, not wanting her brother to touch her. She wanted Jared. Only Jared. She wanted the world where the air was thin, where the sun was bright and hot, and it was a struggle to bring forth green life from the sandy, parched earth. She wanted the future. She wanted Jared.

Drew rocked her and crooned until she quieted once more into sleep, sobbing in her exhaustion and her despair.

The pattern was set.

Susan slept the sleep of exhaustion and pain, dreaming nightmares. Time and again upon awaking she denied the reality of the world that surrounded her, and Drew would come and soothe her back into sleep. It was only after a couple of days that she realized Drew was feeding her sleeping pills.

"I don't need pills to calm me into acceptance, Drew," she said. Her voice was groggy as she pushed away the tea that her brother had been doctoring.

"Then what do you need? For days you've been raving about this magical place where you claim you've been for the past month and a half. I've been searching for you. I've had the police looking for you. For Chrissake, I thought you were dead. I thought you'd be found raped and murdered in some ditch. I've been going crazy," Drew said, looking at her with frustration, running his hands through his curly hair.

"I need you to believe me, Drew," she said quietly.

He stood up and paced the length of the bedroom. Finally he turned and, running his hands through his hair again, smiled at her. "Okay, compromise. Let's say I want to believe you. What do you have to offer me as proof that you've really been to this future place? What proof do you have to show me that it really exists."

"My ring," Susan said, showing him her hand where her wedding ring sparkled blackly. She stared down at it for a moment, its ebony hue taking her by surprise although she'd already spent hours looking at it, not believing that it had turned black.

Drew shrugged. "It's a gold ring set with a black stone."

"Crystal," she corrected. "I have my necklace." Her hand clutched at the black crystal given her by the Widows.

"You had that before you disappeared. It's just another black crystal."

"What about the clothes I was wearing?"

"Green silk. Nothing unusual. No designer labels from another world or another time."

Susan didn't laugh at his joke. "And Pris? I left her there."

"Cats wander away all the time, Susan."

"The mark on my forehead. The mark of the star."

Drew paused. "Now that one does require a bit of explaining, but Marcy said that sometimes age spots show up early and in strange shapes."

"Cripes, Drew!" she cried, almost laughing at the ridiculous explanation. "Age spots?" Susan threw herself back on the pillows of the bed and shook her head. "What kind of proof would you accept?"

"I don't know. You keep talking about powers you developed there." He shrugged. "Show me something."

She shook her head. "Those powers belong in the future. I won't use them here. I don't even know if I can, and I won't try to find out. Besides, you've always insisted that I had special . . . abilities." She paused. "What about how I came back? You've never said too much about that. What happened?" She sat up straighter in the bed when she saw Drew half turn away from her. "Drew?"

"An older woman brought you back. She was outside on the deck. When I came into the house, you were here in the bed."

"What did she say, Drew?"

"She just said that she'd brought you back. I tried to ask her a couple of other questions, but she just walked away from me. And then she disappeared." He frowned and walked over to her, staring down at her, but his gaze was unfocused as if he were seeing something that was far away.

"Disappeared? As in 'poof' disappeared?"

Drew chuckled nervously at his sister's irrational question and shook his head. "No, as in disappeared into the woods."

"The woman had silvery hair that reached down to her waist, and she was dressed all in black with a veil, wasn't she?"

Drew nodded. "That *was* weird," he allowed with a murmur.

"That was Magda, my mother-in-law."

Drew shook his head. "This is crazy, Susan. I don't want to talk about it anymore. What do you want for dinner?"

"Someday you'll believe me," Susan said.

"What makes you think that?"

"Because—somehow—I'm going to find a way to get back."

Susan sat in the sunlight on the deck, staring out over the field in front of the house, her fingers idly swinging the black crystal on the chain around her neck, wondering for the hundredth time that day, as she did every day, why Jared had sent her back.

He'd said he loved her. She knew he loved her. So why had he sent her back?

Drew had been at her again this weekend to pull herself together and start living her life. He wanted her to go back to work.

She couldn't blame him for being annoyed. He'd had a difficult time while she'd been gone, and he'd had an even more difficult time since she'd returned. He'd been forced to explain to the police, and everyone he'd contacted when she'd disappeared, that she'd returned and that everything was all right—in a manner of speaking. She hadn't helped him at all.

She'd grown used to the looks of disbelief when

she told her story. People she'd once considered friends had figuratively run for the hills when she'd told them what had happened to her. The police were convinced she was a nut case, and were relieved when Drew had told them that she was seeing a psychiatrist—and she received a couple of visits from Marcy Lanier.

If it weren't for the wedding ring on her finger and the still raw and painful place in her mind, even she might doubt that anything out of the ordinary had ever happened to her.

She hunched down in the lawn chair, lifting the crystal on the end of the necklace up to her eyes and watching as it twirled, first in one direction and then the other. Theoretically, the inky color of the crystal around her neck and in the wedding ring meant that Jared was dead. As indeed he was—in this time. Jared had never existed here. He hadn't yet been born.

She wondered if the wedding ring that she had given him on the day of their joining had turned to jet. Her fingers tightened on the gold of the chain as she wondered how he was handling the loss of a second mind link.

If he had survived.

A sword stab of pain sliced through her at the thought. Jared couldn't be dead. She would never believe that. To believe that he was dead would be to give up her own life. There had to be a way that she could find out.

The Widows had come to her in her dreams so long ago. If the Widows had done that, then there must be a way for her to see into the future. Her mind grasped at that thought and followed it, her gaze finally focusing on the crystal that continued its hypnotic swing between her fingertips.

She had not used any of her powers since she'd

returned to this time. She didn't know if she still had them. Perhaps they only worked in the future, in Jared's world. But if they were available to her here, then maybe there was some way she could use them to help her.

The crystal necklace. She stared at it as if she had never seen it before. The black crystal had twice been a link to Jared, once through Evie and once through Susan herself. Perhaps it still retained something of his essence.

She stared at the necklace for a long time before she made her decision.

Firmly, she grasped the crystal between her thumb and forefinger and stared at it, looking to its heart. Slowly at first, she let her consciousness sink into the depths of the crystal, feeling its smooth, opaque facets rise up around her, the facets forming a maze that protected its secrets— the secrets that were also her secrets. She went deeper and with a sudden cry of joy and relief, she saw that the center of the crystal was not black at all, it was a deep, deep ruby.

And the very center of the crystal held a beam of golden light. She followed the light with her mind, knowing without doubt that she was tracing Jared's essence, that he still lived, and that the ray of light would bring him within her sight, if not within her touch.

She reached the end of the illuminated path suddenly with no warning, and she found herself in the bedroom chamber that she had shared for so many weeks with her husband.

He sat there in a chair by the window, his hands clasped together loosely, his thumb rubbing the black crystal of the wedding ring on his finger.

He did not see her. Could not see her. Soundlessly, she cried out to him. Love for him poured from her and she willed him to feel her presence, ethereal as it was.

"Beloved," she whispered, projecting the word to him. For a moment she thought she had failed, and then, slowly, reluctantly, he lifted his head and she saw his face.

Gaunt and thin, lines of pain furrowed on his forehead and on either side of his mouth, he was pale, as if the sun never kissed his skin any longer, as if he'd walled himself up in this room and never stepped outside it.

Her heart swelled with love for him and sadness for his suffering. *"Beloved, Jared,"* she whispered again, her heart crying out with the need and the wanting that swept through her.

She saw his eyes scan the room, his brows draw together in that familiar frown.

"Susan?" he asked, his voice halting and uncertain, and yet there was an indescribable look of hope in his dull gold eyes.

She nearly wept at the sound of his voice and at the look on his face. She reached out to him, to touch him, but something suddenly pulled her back. Her vision of him dwindled until the only thing she had left of him was the golden beam of light and then there was nothing but the black crystal before her eyes.

She was sitting in the lawn chair on the deck and Drew was bending over her, his voice angry.

"What are you doing? I've been standing here forever trying to get your attention."

"I've seen him," she said, a smile lighting up her face.

"What do you mean?" Drew asked, his voice suddenly cautious.

"I went into the crystal and found him. He's still alive," she said, and then she shook her head, realizing she was talking to Drew, who didn't or wouldn't believe. She dropped the crystal beneath her shirt. "It's nothing. I'm sorry I was ignoring you, Drew."

She changed the subject, knowing her brother simply couldn't handle the truth.

That night, deliberately using the crystal as an amplifier, Susan sent a call to Magda in the form of a dream. She knew it could be done, the question was only whether Magda would respond. In her mind, as a meeting place, she pictured the golden field in front of Drew's chalet. Finally, satisfied that she'd done all she could, Susan fell into a deep and dreamless sleep.

In the morning she sat on the deck, her eyes roving the golden meadow. She sat there all day, watching and waiting, and that night, she sent the message again. And the night after that, and the night after that. Every day she sat on the deck and waited, refusing to give up hope, refusing to believe that Magda would ignore her call.

Before she realized it, it was Saturday again, and Drew arrived from the city for the weekend. He found Susan sitting outside, her eyes combing the meadow in front of the chalet.

"Don't tell me," he said, joking. "You've been sitting here all week."

"As a matter of fact, I have," she said coolly, offering her cheek for him to kiss.

"Tell me you're kidding," Drew demanded in disbelief.

She shook her head. "No, I've been waiting." Her breath suddenly caught in her throat, and tears sprang into her eyes. She stood up, her eyes fixed on the meadow. "Thank God."

"What?" Drew asked, seeing the odd look of joy on her face, and turning to see a small woman dressed in black make her way across the meadow toward the chalet. "Oh, hell! It's her."

"Magda!" Susan cried, running down the steps from the deck and meeting Magda halfway across the meadow, catching the smaller woman into her arms and hugging her tightly. "You heard me! You came!"

"I have set myself against the other Widows once again for your sake," Magda said, her lips parting in a small smile. "But I could not resist your call. Your heart is in torment, my daughter."

"As is Jared's," Susan answered. "Take me to him, Magda."

"You are sure?" Magda asked. "Jared is near to death. He refuses food and water. He sits in his bedchamber and broods for your loss."

"Then why did he send me away?" Susan asked.

"He insisted. From the first night you came to us. It was a question of honor for him." Magda shook her head. "Other than knowing what he wanted for you, it is not for me to know what is in his mind and his heart. That is for him to tell you."

"And you? What do you believe, Magda? Do you believe it is right for me to return to him?"

"I believe that unless you return to him he will die," Magda said. "But he broods also for the loss of his world, a way of life that he sees passing away in front of him. He can do nothing about that and he suffers much."

"But he hasn't lost his world," Susan objected. "We won the battle against Ruhl and Collis. His world is safe now."

"But there are no crystal women left, Susan," Magda said gently. "There are only the Widows, and when we die there will be no one to replace us. Our world will change without crystal women.

Nothing will be the same in the future."

Susan stared at her in surprise. "But there are crystal women—or children anyway. Don't you know?" She gripped Magda's shoulders. "How could you not know?"

"I know only that Ruhl murdered them all," Magda muttered with a trace of shame in her voice.

"Ruhl couldn't murder those who had no crystals."

"What do you mean?" Magda asked. "There are no crystal women except those with crystals—other than you."

"But there are. Do you remember the five little girls? Garrett Lemaldin's nieces? They have the power. They helped me at Lemaldin Keep when Ruhl tried to take over my mind. They formed a matrix and drove him out. Their mother was a crystal woman at birth, but her crystal was deformed by illness. If five children exist with the powers of a crystal woman and no crystal, then surely there must be others."

Magda frowned. "How could we not know this?"

Shrugging, Susan said, "I guess maybe because you never had to know it. You always had women with crystals—with the visible signs of their powers. The future is far from being lost, Magda. We must tell him."

"If this is true, then the Widows will have much work to do in the future." There was hope in Magda's voice and she held out her hand to Susan. "Come back with me, my daughter, if this is truly what you desire."

"This is an hallucination, isn't it?" Drew asked from behind her, his voice harsh with disbelief. "Everything I've seen and heard in the last few minutes is an hallucination."

She turned to face her brother and shook her head, smiling at him gently. "This is real. I'm going back."

"You can't," he protested, running his hand through his hair. "You belong here."

"There is nothing here for me. The things you talk about are nothing compared to what waits for me across the chasm." She tilted her head and stared at him for a moment. "You did believe me all along then."

"I was afraid for you. You never lied—not to me. You're my sister. I love you. Stay here where you belong." Drew caught at her hand. "This place you keep talking about isn't real compared to what you have here."

She shook her head and gently but firmly disengaged her fingers from his grasp. "No, I never really belonged here. I've always belonged in Jared's world. The future is my reality." She gestured with the hand she wrested from his grasp. "This world was always the dream. Nothing was ever quite real to me, you know. I was always different. I existed here, nothing more. I could never make a difference here. I belong in Jared's world. It doesn't mean I don't love you. I do." Her eyes lit and suddenly she held out her hand to him. "Come with me, Drew. Come with me and see the future of mankind."

He stepped back from her, rejecting her plea.

"So be it," she murmured, echoing the words she had heard Jared say on many occasions, sorrowing at the fear she saw in her brother. "Remember me, and be happy for me. I'll be okay. I'll be happy." She lifted the black crystal from around her neck and pressed it into his palm, closing his fingers over it tightly. "Take this. If you ever need me, hold the crystal and call me. I'll hear you. I'll always hear you." She turned then to Magda. "I'm ready, Magda."

The Widow pulled back a curtain of air, revealing the black nothing of the chasm between times. Susan stepped through.

Magda closed the doorway, and with a sad smile of regret for the brother she was leaving behind, Susan looked ahead into the darkness that had so terrified her the first time she had passed through it. The black emptiness was still frightening, but it was a necessary journey if she were to reach Jared. To return to him, she would face any fear, any evil.

The trip through the dark seemed endless. But it finally came to an end when Magda opened the gateway to the same field that had originally greeted Susan.

Taking a deep breath of the thin air, Susan felt the burning strength of the late afternoon sun flicker on her flesh. As her feet touched the grass of the field, the mind link with Jared reestablished itself.

His sudden presence in her mind struck her to her knees with the strength of a dagger blow. She felt his equilibrium shift as he attempted to deal with her sudden presence in his mind, and she felt his disbelief, his refusal to accept the truth.

Scrambling to her feet, she ran like the wind across the field, heading for the Keep, holding back her thoughts from him until he could see her, until he could see that she was truly there. Entering the Keep, she crossed the courtyard, disregarding the cries of surprise and welcome that followed her as she headed for the stables.

At her direction, the stable boys saddled both Desert Moon and Gaeten, and she mounted her mare and led Gaeten out into the cobbled courtyard, halting beneath what she knew was Jared's window.

"Jared si'Dakbar!" she called.

"Susan?" he cried in disbelief. Barely a moment passed before he appeared in the window above her.

While trying to control the suddenly restive horses, she drank in the sight of him. He was thin, as if he hadn't eaten in weeks, his forehead had new lines, and the furrows on either side of his mouth had deepened. He looked older, but her heart leapt for joy when his eyes fell on her and she saw the smile that caused the creases around his mouth to intensify.

"The one and only," she said. "You're either a very lucky man or a very unlucky one."

"I sent you away," he whispered back.

"We're going to have to talk about that," she told him with mock grimness.

"I loved you too much to force you to stay here with me. I thought you wanted to go back to your time even though you loved me. I didn't think you would ever be truly happy here away from all that was familiar to you."

"Which doesn't make a hell of a lot of sense, you know," she said, fighting back the sudden spate of tears that threatened to fall to her cheeks when she realized that he loved her enough to suffer so that she would be happy. "You could have asked me what I wanted to do."

He looked thoughtful, although a smile kept pulling at the corners of his mouth. "But I'm a Clan Lord."

"Typical," she muttered, and then she laughed up at him, the happiness she felt inexpressible other than in laughter. "Like I said, we'll discuss all this in great and glorious detail later," she said with mocking severity, "but right now, Jared si'Dakbar, you have a promise to keep."

"A promise?" he asked, a puzzled expression crossing his face as he leaned on his folded arms on the deep windowsill of the stone wall, light coming back to life in his eyes. They sparkled down at her, as gold as the sun.

"A long time ago you told me you would ride the wind with me, Jared, my husband, my love." She projected to him an image of the day when she had been the one in the window and he the one on the horse. She recalled for him the memory of the desire that had flared between them then with the same explosiveness as now.

She felt the reckless joy, the erotic desire that washed through him.

He nodded. "I remember that promise." He ducked back into the room, disappearing from her sight.

She waited, content in the knowledge that he would join her.

It seemed like barely a moment later when he burst from the double doors of the Keep and strode down the stairs to meet her, his hand reaching up and closing over hers on Desert Moon's reins.

His hand trembled where it rested on hers. Shyly she probed at his mind, and she caught her breath at the intimate images that raced through his mind and spilled over into hers. Nothing was left out. He withheld none of his thoughts from her.

"Riding the wind with you is the first of many promises I intend to keep, my love," he said.

Looking into the molten heat of his golden eyes, Susan knew he spoke the truth.

Futuristic Romance

Love in another time, another place.

Anne Avery

"Ms. Avery opens wonderfully imaginative new
horizons!"   —*Romantic Times*

All's Fair. For five long years, Rhys Fairdane has roamed
the universe, trying to forget Calista York, who seared his
soul with white-hot longing, then cast him into space. Yet
by a twist of fate, he and Calista are both named trade
representatives of the planet Karta. It will take all his strength
to resist her voluptuous curves, all his cunning to subdue
her feminine wiles. But if in war, as in love, all truly is fair,
Calista has concealed weapons that will bring Rhys to his
knees before the battle has even begun.

_51937-2 $4.99 US/$5.99 CAN

A Distant Star. Jerrel is searching a distant world for his lost
brother when his life is saved by a courageous messenger.
Nareen's beauty and daring enchant him, but Jerrel cannot
permit anyone to turn him from his mission, not even the
proud and passionate woman who offers him a love capable
of bridging the stars.

_51905-4 $4.99 US/$5.99 CAN

Dorchester Publishing Co., Inc.
65 Commerce Road
Stamford, CT 06902

Please add $1.75 for shipping and handling for the first book and
$.50 for each book thereafter. NY, NYC, PA and CT residents,
please add appropriate sales tax. No cash, stamps, or C.O.D.s. All
orders shipped within 6 weeks via postal service book rate.
Canadian orders require $2.00 extra postage and must be paid in
U.S. dollars through a U.S. banking facility.

Name _____
Address _____
City _____ State _____ Zip _____
I have enclosed $_____ in payment for the checked book(s).
Payment <u>must</u> accompany all orders.☐ Please send a free catalog.

Unforgettable Romance By

KATHLEEN MORGAN

"Beautiful and moving...touches the soul!"
—*Affaire de Coeur*

Firestar. Sheltered and innocent, Meriel is loath to mate with the virile alien captive her mother has chosen. Yet as heir to the Tenuan throne, she is duty bound to perform the loveless act. Never does she expect Gage Bardwin's tender caresses to awaken her to passion. And when devious forces intervene to separate them, Meriel sets out on a quest that will take them across the universe and back to save their love.
_51908-9 $4.99 US/$5.99 CAN

Demon Prince. Untouched and untested, Breanne has heard the terrible legends about the Demon Prince, but the man who saves her from certain death is as gentle and kind as he is reckless and virile. Embarking on a perilous journey from which she may never return, Breanne vows to uncover Aidan's secrets, to release him from his enemies, then to quench the raging fires he has ignited in her innocent heart.
_51941-0 $4.99 US/$5.99 CAN

Dorchester Publishing Co., Inc.
65 Commerce Road
Stamford, CT 06902

Please add $1.75 for shipping and handling for the first book and $.50 for each book thereafter. NY, NYC, PA and CT residents, please add appropriate sales tax. No cash, stamps, or C.O.D.s. All orders shipped within 6 weeks via postal service book rate. Canadian orders require $2.00 extra postage and must be paid in U.S. dollars through a U.S. banking facility.

Name_____
Address_____
City _____ State_____Zip_____
I have enclosed $_____in payment for the checked book(s).
Payment <u>must</u> accompany all orders.☐ Please send a free catalog.

Don't Miss These Unforgettable Romances By

MADELINE BAKER

Winner Of The *Romantic Times* Reviewers' Choice Award!

Beneath A Midnight Moon. Kylene of Mouldour yearns for the valiant warrior that comes to her in dreams. And when Hardane of Argone appears in the flesh, Kylene is prepared to challenge an age-old prophecy and brave untold peril to find true happiness with her fantasy love.

_3649-5 $4.99 US/$5.99 CAN

Warrior's Lady. A creature of moonlight and quicksilver, Leyla rescues the mysterious man from unspeakable torture, then heals him body and soul. The radiant enchantress is all he wants in a woman, but his enemies will do everything in their power to keep her from him.

_3490-5 $4.99 US/$5.99 CAN

Dorchester Publishing Co., Inc.
65 Commerce Road
Stamford, CT 06902

Please add $1.75 for shipping and handling for the first book and $.50 for each book thereafter. NY, NYC, PA and CT residents, please add appropriate sales tax. No cash, stamps, or C.O.D.s. All orders shipped within 6 weeks via postal service book rate. Canadian orders require $2.00 extra postage and must be paid in U.S. dollars through a U.S. banking facility.

Name_____

Address_____

City _____ State_____ Zip_____

I have enclosed $_____in payment for the checked book(s).
Payment <u>must</u> accompany all orders.□ Please send a free catalog.

Three captivating stories of love in another time, another place.

MADELINE BAKER
"Heart of the Hunter"

A Lakota warrior must defy the boundaries of life itself to claim the spirited beauty he has sought through time.

ANNE AVERY
"Dream Seeker"

On faraway planets, a pilot and a dreamer learn that passion can bridge the heavens, no matter how vast the distance from one heart to another.

KATHLEEN MORGAN
"The Last Gatekeeper"

To save her world, a dazzling temptress must use her powers of enchantment to open a stellar portal—and the heart of a virile but reluctant warrior.

_51974-7 *Enchanted Crossings* (three unforgettable love stories in one volume) $4.99 US/
$5.99 CAN

LEISURE BOOKS
ATTN: Order Department
276 5th Avenue, New York, NY 10001

Please add $1.50 for shipping and handling for the first book and $.35 for each book thereafter. PA., N.Y.S. and N.Y.C. residents, please add appropriate sales tax. No cash, stamps, or C.O.D.s. All orders shipped within 6 weeks via postal service book rate. Canadian orders require $2.00 extra postage and must be paid in U.S. dollars through a U.S. banking facility.

Name_____
Address_____
City _____ State_____ Zip_____
I have enclosed $_____in payment for the checked book(s).
Payment <u>must</u> accompany all orders.☐ Please send a free catalog.

✦ Futuristic Romance

Nancy Cane

"Nancy Cane sparks your imagination and melts your heart!"
—**Marilyn Campbell, author of *Stardust Dreams***

Circle Of Light. When a daring stranger whisks attorney Sarina Bretton to worlds—and desires—she's never imagined possible, she is tempted to boldly explore new realms with Teir Reylock. Besieged by enemies, and bedeviled by her love for Teir, Sarina vows that before a vapor cannon puts her asunder she will surrender to the seasoned warrior and his promise of throbbing ecstasy.

_51949-6 $4.99 US/$5.99 CAN

Moonlight Rhapsody. Like the sirens of old, Ilyssa can cast a spell with her voice, but she will lose the powers forever if she succumbs to a lover's touch. Forced to use her gift for merciless enemies, she will do anything to be free. Yet does she dare trust Lord Rolf Cam'brii to help her when his mere presence arouses her beyond reason and threatens to leave her defenseless?

_51987-9 $4.99 US/$5.99 CAN

LOVE SPELL
ATTN: Order Department
276 5th Avenue, New York, NY 10001

Please add $1.50 for shipping and handling for the first book and $.35 for each book thereafter. PA., N.Y.S. and N.Y.C. residents, please add appropriate sales tax. No cash, stamps, or C.O.D.s. All orders shipped within 6 weeks via postal service book rate. Canadian orders require $2.00 extra postage and must be paid in U.S. dollars through a U.S. banking facility.

Name _____

Address _____

City _____ State _____ Zip _____

I have enclosed $_____ in payment for the checked book(s).
Payment <u>must</u> accompany all orders.☐ Please send a free catalog.

Futuristic Romance

Love in another time, another place

Topaz Dreams

Marilyn Campbell

"A story that grabs you from the beginning and won't let go!"

—*Johanna Lindsey*

Fierce and cunning, Falcon runs into an unexpected setback while searching for the ring that can destroy his futuristic world—a beauty who rouses his untested desire. Tough and independent, Stephanie Barbanell doesn't need any man to help her track down a missing scientist. But tempted by Falcon's powerful magnetism, she longs to give in to her burning ardor—until she discovers that her love for Falcon can never be unless one of them sacrifices everything for the other.

_3390-9 $4.50 US/$5.50 CAN

LEISURE BOOKS
ATTN: Order Department
276 5th Avenue, New York, NY 10001

Please add $1.50 for shipping and handling for the first book and $.35 for each book thereafter. PA., N.Y.S. and N.Y.C. residents, please add appropriate sales tax. No cash, stamps, or C.O.D.s. All orders shipped within 6 weeks via postal service book rate. Canadian orders require $2.00 extra postage and must be paid in U.S. dollars through a U.S. banking facility.

Name _____
Address _____
City _____ State _____ Zip _____
I have enclosed $_____ in payment for the checked book(s).
Payment <u>must</u> accompany all orders. ☐ Please send a free catalog.

Futuristic Romance

Love in another time, another place.

Saranne Dawson

"One of the brightest names in futuristic romance!"
—*Romantic Times*

Star-Crossed. Rowena is a master artisan, a weaver of enchanted tapestries that whisper of past glories. Yet not even magic can help her foresee that she will be sent to assasinate an enemy leader. Her duty is clear—until the seductive beauty falls under the spell of the man she has to kill.
_51982-8 $4.99 US/$5.99 CAN

Greenfire. As leader of her people, beautiful Nazleen must choose a mate from the warlike men who trouble her people. In her dreams, she sees the man who is destined to be her lover, and the thought of taking him to her bed fills Nazleen not with dread, but with delicious anticipation.
_51985-2 $4.99 US/$5.99 CAN

On Wings of Love. Jillian has the mind of a scientist, but the heart of a vulnerable woman. Wary of love, she has devoted herself to training the mysterious birds that serve her people as messengers. But her reunion with the only man she will ever desire opens her soul to a whole new field of hands-on research.
_51953-4 $4.99 US/$5.99 CAN

Dorchester Publishing Co., Inc.
65 Commerce Road
Stamford, CT 06902

Please add $1.75 for shipping and handling for the first book and $.50 for each book thereafter. NY, NYC, PA and CT residents, please add appropriate sales tax. No cash, stamps, or C.O.D.s. All orders shipped within 6 weeks via postal service book rate. Canadian orders require $2.00 extra postage and must be paid in U.S. dollars through a U.S. banking facility.

Name _____
Address _____
City _____ State _____ Zip _____
I have enclosed $_____in payment for the checked book(s).
Payment <u>must</u> accompany all orders.☐ Please send a free catalog.

Futuristic Romance

Love in another time, another place.

Don't miss these tempestuous futuristic romances set on faraway worlds where passion is the lifeblood of every man and woman.

Awakenings by Saranne Dawson. Fearless and bold, Justan rules his domain with an iron hand, but nothing short of magic will bring his warring people peace. He claims he needs Rozlynd for her sorcery alone, yet inside him stirs an unexpected yearning to sample her sweet innocence. And as her silken spell ensnares him, Justan battles to vanquish a power whose like he has never encountered—the power of Rozlynd's love.

_51921-6 $4.99 US/$5.99 CAN

Ascent to the Stars by Christine Michels. For Trace, the assignment is simple. All he has to do is take a helpless female to safety and he'll receive information about his cunning enemies. But no daring mission or reckless rescue has prepared him for the likes of Coventry Pearce. Even as he races across the galaxy to save his doomed world, Trace battles to deny a burning desire that will take him to the heavens and beyond.

_51933-X $4.99 US/$5.99 CAN

Dorchester Publishing Co., Inc.
65 Commerce Road
Stamford, CT 06902

Please add $1.75 for shipping and handling for the first book and $.50 for each book thereafter. NY, NYC, PA and CT residents, please add appropriate sales tax. No cash, stamps, or C.O.D.s. All orders shipped within 6 weeks via postal service book rate. Canadian orders require $2.00 extra postage and must be paid in U.S. dollars through a U.S. banking facility.

Name _____
Address _____
City _____ State _____ Zip _____
I have enclosed $_____ in payment for the checked book(s).
Payment <u>must</u> accompany all orders.☐ Please send a free catalog.

THE MAGIC OF ROMANCE
PAST, PRESENT, AND FUTURE....

Every month, Love Spell will publish one book in each of four categories:

1) *Timeswept Romance*—Modern-day heroines travel to the past to find the men who fulfill their hearts' desires.

2) *Futuristic Romance*—Love on distant worlds where passion is the lifeblood of every man and woman.

3) *Historical Romance*—Full of desire, adventure and intrigue, these stories will thrill readers everywhere.

4) *Contemporary Romance*—With novels by Lori Copeland, Heather Graham, and Jayne Ann Krentz, Love Spell's line of contemporary romance is first-rate.

Exploding with soaring passion and fiery sensuality, Love Spell romances are destined to take you to dazzling new heights of ecstasy.

SEND FOR A FREE CATALOGUE TODAY!

Love Spell
Attn: Order Department
276 5th Avenue, New York, NY 10001